AMERIKALAND

DANNY GOODMAN

LEFTOVER
Books

Library of Congress Control Number: 2023945610
ISBN 9798985107067 (paperback)
ISBN 9798985107074 (ebook)

First Printing, 2024

Cover design by Joanne O'Neill
Interior layout by David Wojciechowski

LEFTOVER Books
Rochester, New York
leftoverbooks.com

AMERIKA ALAND

Praise for
AMERIKALAND

"A contemplative, richly imagined, and…thrilling exploration of the near future."
—*Kirkus Reviews*

"With echoes of so many favorites, from DeLillo's *Underworld* to *Watchmen* to George Saunders and even Ralph Ellison, Danny Goodman has done something remarkable in this debut novel: crafted a voice and a world entirely his own. This is a wonderful novel, destined to become a cult classic."
—Daniel Torday, author of *BOOMER1* and
two-time winner of the National Jewish Book Award

"Utterly absorbing and gorgeously written, *Amerikaland* is the best kind of story, one I found lingering in my mind at the end of the day as if it were real. I know that Sabine and Sandy and their heartbreaking world will stay with me for a long time to come. I loved this haunting and unforgettable novel."
—Jillian Cantor, *USA Today* bestselling author of *The Fiction Writer*

"*Amerikaland* is a rare blend of unexpected elements: sports, adventure, terrorism, friendship. Its characters grapple with their own moral compasses even as they put their bodies on the line—as athletes and entertainers, but also as human beings trying to make the world a better place. A debut both thrilling and tender."
—Ilana Masad, author of *All My Mother's Lovers*

"*Amerikaland* swallows the past, clarifies the present, and projects a future that requires unbelievable courage to survive. An unforgettable, tightly plotted adventure, this novel is a glorious achievement, as epic as Donna Tartt's *The Goldfinch* and enchanting as Michael Chabon's *The Amazing Adventures of Kavalier and Clay*."
—Devin Murphy, national bestselling author of *The Boat Runner*

"With a page-turning plot, one that feels reminiscent of Philip Roth or Philip K. Dick, and a prescience and sensitivity that reflects the threat of today's culture, *Amerikaland* is an accomplishment indeed."
—Emily Nemens, author of *The Cactus League*

"An elegant, ambitious examination of our world with beautifully woven interiors that enable a rare intimacy between the reader and the novel's two protagonists."
—Simon Van Booy, author of *The Presence of Absence*

"Equal parts tragedy and triumph, *Amerikaland* is a sweeping, absorbing story for the ages. It's a feat to not only rebuild the world but also to reimagine it, and Danny Goodman does so with the heart of a poet and the eye of a sportscaster. Acutely felt and gorgeously crafted, *Amerikaland* soulfully explores the nuances of grief, hatred, humility, and love. You'll be cheering, even when it hurts—especially when it hurts."

—Jiordan Castle, author of *Disappearing Act*

"In *Amerikaland*, Danny Goodman subtly unfolds a world that seems much like our own—until it isn't. Lush and eerily prescient, *Amerikaland* is reminiscent of the works of Pynchon and DeLillo."

—Rebecca Renner, author of *Gator Country*

"*Amerikaland*, in its fidelity to beauty and daringness of invention in style, contributes something vital and lasting to the stories that help us make sense of our apocalyptic times."

—Chantal James, author of *None But the Righteous*

"Danny Goodman's wise and timely debut novel is as thrilling as a tie score final at-bat, with the future of humanity on the line. Yet for all its epic scope, this moving tale of family, friendship, and loyalty in the face of age-old hatreds resonates right from its parallel timeline into our equally troubled one."

—Sarah Seltzer, author of *The Singer Sisters*

"*Amerikaland* is a reverent, haunting, and heartbreaking story of love, hate, regret, and resilience. A masterful debut!"

—Catherine Adel West, author of *The Two Lives of Sara*

"*Amerikaland* delivers surprise after surprise—all in elegant, precise prose—and presents a rich and detailed reimagined present, more like our current-day world than we'd like to admit. Best of all, this book is a love story—the best kind—about close friends, ambition, vocation, and ethical passion in the face of true evil."

—Miciah Bay Gault, author of *Goodnight Stranger*

"Like Kafka's *Amerika*, Danny Goodman's powerful and compelling *Amerikaland* brilliantly depicts a contemporary United States that's both surreal and all too real. I'm not sure I've read another book that feels so timeless yet also torn from today's headlines. I couldn't put it down. It's a novel with a huge heart, and it reminds us of the power—and responsibility—we have to build the kind of world we want to live in."

—Andrew Ervin, author of *Burning Down George Orwell's House*

"In his major literary debut, Danny Goodman establishes himself as a modern day sportswriting superhero with this vital, ferocious story of love and hate, privilege and persecution, family and chosen family, the fight for justice and the violence of silence, cloaked as a tribute to America's beloved pastimes, in a cultural moment that could not feel more prescient or timely. *Amerikaland* is a gorgeous grand slam."
—Sara Lippmann, author of *Lech*

"In supremely confident, sure-footed prose, gorgeous, wise, and urgent, Goodman delivers a terrifyingly real vision of a possible near-future in which the unshakeable power of friendship edges up against its shocking limits. Tense and deftly plotted, *Amerikaland* shows the fears and lessons and presentiments swirling in our air, all made flesh here, breaking at the doorstep in this heart-stopping debut."
—Courtney Sender, author of *In Other Lifetimes All I've Lost Comes Back to Me*

"This marvel of a story offers a parallel reality that is all too familiar in its horrors and its violence, but also in the humble ways people find the strength to persist against hatred. With this novel, Danny Goodman shows us all what we might aspire to in sport, in love, in understanding, and in courage. What a beautiful, harrowing, and powerful book. *Amerikaland* is a story for our time and for the times to come."
—Nicholas Mainieri, author of *The Infinite*

"Danny Goodman's *Amerikaland*, with its pristine setting and brilliantly rendered characters, lulls you into a false sense of security. However, as you turn the pages, you start to understand you're knee-deep in a thriller, and you question everything. Each scene is more breathless than the next until you are spinning, unsure if you should lean into hope or despair. This is a gripping read that won't be easy to shake, nor should it be."
—Stephanie Austin, author of *Something I Might Say*

"Goodman artfully warns us that our uniqueness can be the precise fodder for dangerous groupthink. That a game can take a swing at everything and everyone in proximity. And that there is a difference between wanting to be noticed and wanting to be found."
—Claire Hopple, author of *Echo Chamber*

For Mom and Dad,
who live in everything I do;
and
For LB,
always.

And I always thought the very simplest words
Would be enough. If I say what is
Every heart will surely be lacerated.
That you will go under if you don't fight back
Surely you must see that?

—Bertolt Brecht, "And I always thought…"

WE WHO SEE

In the Brooklyn borough of New York City, a great baseball stadium rises. Across the way, beyond a glistening fairy-tale pond, stands a grand tennis center, home to the City Open. These theaters of sport are for those of us craving an escape from the everyday, an immersion in the very atmosphere that makes this the greatest metropolis in the world.

From the highest points, we can see everything—the island of Manhattan, aging but full of wonder; Coney Island, the beach and the ocean, the tall and colorful rides and roller coasters; along the waterfront in Queens and Brooklyn and spreading through the boroughs, a boom of buildings under construction and reaching skyward, an evolving megalopolis; and the Roebling Bridge, connecting Brooklyn and Manhattan, its spine broken and still in need of repair, even these years later. After its destruction, the people of this city turned to their sports heroes, to those willing to distract them, to fill the stage, to be the brightness drowning out the darkness.

As we celebrate this day, the world will look here as an example, a chance to start anew. This is where we will rise again. Our World Day.

And as the world watches, as the city and the country come together, New Ebbets Field—home to the Brooklyn Atlantics—and the tennis center will fill with people. The days, hot and heavy for the summer months, will grow cool. A weight will lift. On opening weekend, the gates will be unlocked, and Althea Williams Arena, the City Open's crown jewel, will be standing-room only. At the pond we will gather to watch, the aquamarine water like a mirror to another universe. By the afternoon, we will pack New Ebbets, too, cheering on our Atlantics, absorbed by the crack of a bat, the joy of a fastball carving up the Brooklyn air.

In between our breaths, the bombs will come. They will be unlike anything we have seen or imagined. Death beyond comprehension. *Light bombs*, they will be called. They will spread out in a giant flash, as if some monolithic lens holds us in its gaze. And when the shutter closes, when the bombs have done their duty, there will be almost nothing left. Piles of ash. A sunburn scorching every molecule, every millimeter of skin. Thousands of us reduced in a moment. The light will take us and never give us back.

I

FIRST THE BULLET

Sabine wants to forget. For a moment, looking out over the morning sky, every muscle in her body sheds its weight. Last night's storm gives way to a kind of purple and blue fire that burns everything. The clouds blanketing New Ebbets Field across the pond are an uncanny white and remind Sabine of Florida, her adopted home, of skies she thought only existed in photographs and memory. When she is here in Althea Williams Arena—as close to heaven as she can ever imagine being—it is easy to ignore the terrible things that have come before.

She stands at the top row of the arena, the center of the largest sports complex in the world, and she wonders if someone in the baseball stadium looks back at her. She wants to know what she looks like from far away, what they see. But she knows already that unmistakable gaze of embarrassment, of shame, she has felt for months. The ache in her shoulder a constant reminder, the way it speaks through her nerves, up and down her spine, until she cannot separate the feelings, the pain and being alive.

She remains up here, at peace, until she is told it is time to leave. *Too early*, a nosy security guard declares, and though it is not in her nature to break the rules, she cannot help this small indiscretion. Each year she has begun the City Open this way: nervous and excited looking out over the beauty of New York City, pretending for a few moments this palace is all hers. And not just in victory, not simply in winning every match for the next two weeks—no, this arena, this whole tournament, is part of her. She wants to feel ready once more. She wants to leave all of herself on this court.

Back at her hotel, after breakfast and a Prattlr Q&A with fans in Europe and Asia, she waits for her assistant, Alina, to return. Sabine is tense but tries not to show it. She rubs at the throb in her shoulder, which she has done her best to keep hidden. But her injury, her infinitely slow recovery, has been splashed across every digital sports page for months, and she spent the better part of the morning answering fan questions with misdirection and playfulness. She put on makeup and took a picture with her corgi, Roger, and watched as it spread across social media like a virus, comments written only in exclamations.

So cute!
Marry me Sabine Hellewege!
Er ist ein Glückspilz!
Okay we get it u love yur dog now play fuckin tennis!
Sabine N Roger 4EVER!
Aren't you over Budapest yet?!
You're a hero!
Your a joke!
Brilliant!
I wanna be that dog!
Damn ur hot!
Eat shite n go back to playin tennis u cunt!
Heil Hellewege!
Youre perfect I love you youre my favorite player of all time…ALL TIME!
Favorite. Reprattle. Share. Like. Hate. Unfollow. Ignore. Block. Report. Burn.

She wonders if it is worth it. Some players do not engage; they train and practice, they play their sport, do their job—they do not worry so much about pleasing the fans. They do not worry about being loved. They are simply tennis players, athletes at their peaks. She wonders if the men go through this, too, or if it is a burden gifted only to the women on tour: be the best, beat the best, and do not forget to smile.

Sabine cannot help herself, though. It is not enough to win, as she did for so long. Now, since her return, something has changed. When she double faults, the crowd cheers. When she mishits an easy overhead, when she yells out of frustration or pain after a point, the crowd cheers. They are against her. In their fickleness and their expectations, she fails them. She fights to be the player she was before—she will be, she tells herself like a mantra on the practice court—but she is not, not yet. She disappeared from their view for too long, perhaps, asked for privacy and understanding instead of entertaining. She is their champion still, in some twisted way, and they love to hate her.

When Alina knocks on her door and breezes in, Sabine wakes from her self-pity. Alina is stunning, Sabine has always thought, a combination of her parents' Nigerian and Swiss. A few years younger than Sabine—who herself feels aged far beyond her twenty-seven years—traveling the world has given Alina a seasoned bravado, something Sabine has always admired about her.

"You shouldn't post any more pictures of Roger," Alina says curtly. She straightens up the room as she speaks, and it makes Sabine uncomfortable, someone cleaning up her mess.

"So ridiculous," she says, more a reflex than anything else. When she is angry or bothered, Sabine's German accent drips. "Why should those people decide what is good for me?"

Alina plops down on the bed, her feet dangling over the edge. "They're your fans."

Sabine makes a noise like a bark, like she cracked a forehand just wide. "Bullshit."

"I'm just saying." Alina types on her phone, smiling, fingers banging away at the screen with a feverish glee. Roger whines at the foot of the bed, and when she pats the space next to her, Roger gladly jumps up, makes a circle or two, and lays down. He looks at Sabine, his big eyes begging her to join them.

"Look how cute he is!" She points at Roger and his ears raise. "Why the hell is having him with me an international incident?"

Alina pets Roger and he rolls over, offering his belly. "Everything you do is an international incident," she says, laughing at her own cleverness. She sits up, scoots to the edge of the bed. The movement riles Roger, who springs, ready to play. "Even if you don't send him back to your father, which you should," she says, her tone suddenly soft, "it's best if people think you've moved past all this."

Sabine leans against the window, behind which lies the city, skyscrapers outstretched, a world below filled with endless movement. "Is that what people think, that Roger is here because of what happened?"

Alina looks back at her, her eyes full of surprise and warmth and pity.

Sabine slaps her palm against the sill and storms from the room. She is being dramatic, she knows, but her anger, her frustration, are not affectations. They simmer below the surface, always just out of sight. Her father's daughter in ways she wishes were not true.

Alina calls after her, reminding her not to miss her appointment with the trainer, that tomorrow is Kid's Day and she needs to be ready. Before the elevator doors close, Sabine hears her say, "I know we shouldn't care!"

Out on the street, impatient people push by her. She rounds the corners of this labyrinth until someone stops her—a family of tourists from Luxembourg—asking if she is who they think she is. The youngest daughter, gangly and awkward, reaches out her hand. "You're my favorite," she says. Sabine thanks her and offers to take a picture with her. After they part, Sabine's phone chimes. The girl has posted the picture, both of their smiles wide, even though Sabine sees through her own façade, through the veil glossing her eyes. In the background, everything is blurred, a rush of the life swirling around her, and she focuses on that, on the blur, on the nothingness that carries her.

She tries not to think about Budapest. Even when asked, when some reporter has not heard enough about it, gone over it as Sabine has in excruciating detail, she manages to disconnect, to answer questions in a kind of autopilot, without the discomfort of lingering on those emotions for a moment too long. Social media, though, keeps things alive long after they should have died. Photographs—Sabine still sees them daily—reanimate every lost angle, every millisecond better left buried. Some capture the *just before*, and for Sabine those are the most painful. A glimpse into what she could not know, the seconds before her life would change, and though they flick across her screen with constant impunity, they bring her no understanding.

At Kid's Day, Sabine does her best to pretend. Cheers from the crowd, flashes of sunlight bouncing off the beams crisscrossing high above from the open roof, the raucous laughter of her fellow players, the microphones they wear exaggerating even the softest sound; every moment of it makes her anxious. Kids push down to the first row, their arms collectively outstretched. Every sudden or unexpected movement enough to race through her, fire her nerve endings.

She shares the court with three other players, all of them her friends since their junior days. They supported her after Budapest, visited her in the hospital, sent flowers and well wishes, both private and public. Yet their presence brings her no consolation. Beside her stands one of her oldest friends, Veljko Dragovic—Drago, as he is known—top-ranked resident clown, bouncing three balls off his racket, head, and foot, respectively. The crowd eats it up. Like a soccer header Drago knocks the ball high and his eyes grow wide, and at the same moment from the other side of the court a ball whizzes by, Stanislas Gutzwiller's face shaped in a devilish grin. He high-fives his partner, Lolo Samuels, a Harlem native and crowd favorite, one of Sabine's closest friends and confidants. Lolo and Stan hold their bellies as they howl, watching Drago lose his composure, his juggled balls smacked in all directions into the crowd.

There is meant to be a lightness to the day. Sabine cannot embrace it, though, despite what her broad smile, her infectious laugh belie. She did not attend Stan's wedding in the spring. She has yet to meet Drago's new baby boy. She has not seen or spoken to Lolo in months. The sight of her now across the net is enough to rip Sabine in half. She has missed her; she wants to run to her, wrap her arms around her. She wants to apologize for disappearing, for pushing her, everyone, away.

Sabine sees in Drago that smile unchanged since their youth. Lolo tries to lob a beach ball over Sabine, but it catches in the air, pushed like a feather against a tidal wave and remains hovering, a still life, as if the world for a moment has been paused. They stare up together, Drago's hand on Sabine's shoulder as he pretends to get dizzy watching it. And when he spins around and collapses to the ground, his breaths pumping his chest up and down, the crowd screams with joy. Lolo and Stan hop the net and come to his aid, and in their laughter, Lolo reaches out her arm for Sabine, who reciprocates, and the sheer act between them sends a signal through her body, a kind of fireworks. They raise their hands to the crowd and will their cheers to grow, to use the energy of their voices to lift Drago, all of them, up.

Late in the night, Sabine wakes to a series of messages from Alina. *You're not there?! Where are you?! Are you okay?! Wanna talk? Call me in the AM. No Roger pics Enjoy Get some sleep Kisses.* Her eyes bleary and seeing spots from the glow of the phone, she writes back *OK.*

She knows she made the right decision skipping the player party. The gazes of the press and the public are one thing, but she cannot handle the same from her fellow players. They are kind to her, yet it is exactly their pity she cannot stand. When she looks at them, when they look back at her, she knows they know, what she is only now beginning to grasp: she—her game—is mortally wounded. And like all great competitors, they watch her, and they circle, round and round their prey.

She makes herself a lavender tea and sits at the window, the city lit up around her. She thinks of the signs scattered throughout the tennis grounds announcing this year's theme, an agenda of a nation, of World Day: *Rebirth*. She has seen herself on one of the posters—face shaped in almost-victory, about to hit the backhand that would win her a second City Open title—and through the strings of her racket the word is animated, stretching, fading into the gut. It looks to Sabine like she is stealing it, or taking back what is hers. What this sport owes her. Her own private rebirth.

She presses her hand against the window and feels the coolness of the night. Her eyes are heavy but she does not want sleep. In the glass she sees her reflection. She is not the woman she was. This person, tentative and frightened, is who she trained not to be, who her coach—her father—and endless hours of practice taught her to be better than, to seek out, to destroy. She was strength. She was greater than. She was unshakeable. It took only one moment, one deranged person to change it all, to change her, to undo everything. A momentary lapse in security. One woman, a political radical. A crowd of protestors, screaming and chanting and meant only as distraction, and one woman, her print-at-home plastic gun, and a long, long second to take her shot.

The first question every reporter asked Sabine, disseminated to media outlets across the world, was the absurd one: *How did it feel?*

Sabine arrives at the complex early. She settles in the players' lounge, and as she waits for the trainer to arrive, she resists the urge to post another photo of Roger. She hears Alina's voice in her head. She does not know what they want from her, what more of herself she can give. She knows only how they see her—a broken champion—and how ugly the feeling when she sees herself the same.

When Lolo walks into the lounge, Sabine cannot help but wave her over. Several inches shorter than Sabine, Lolo's presence, her confidence, takes up the room. Sabine recognizes something of herself in Lolo's swagger, but it feels unreachable now. Lolo smiles and it is bright and for a moment pulls Sabine from her funk. They stretch out on couches opposite one another. Lolo sips at a coconut water, looking tired. But her skin, smooth and youthful, makes Sabine feel older than her years. She wants to tell Lolo she saw pictures from the party, how beautiful she looked, but all that comes out is, "Morning."

Lolo adjusts herself and sits up straight, like a careful yoga pose. "Is it though?" she says, as if it is the last bit of energy she can muster.

They laugh, carry on like it is the funniest thing either of them has ever heard. Sabine feels good, letting loose; it is something deep down, and it keeps going until her gut hurts and her temples throb, and Lolo begs her to stop.

"We missed you last night," she says. "I missed you. Those things aren't the same without you. You always bring the energy."

"I loved your dress," Sabine says, trying not to push back against Lolo's warmth. "So damn gorgeous." She remembers Lolo as a teenager, not so long ago, the few years between them enough to make Lolo a sort-of tag along. But the woman before her now impresses Sabine. She is hungry, having beaten Sabine in Australia for her first Grand Slam title, building a name for herself as a giant killer.

"Remember that dress I wore in Singapore?" Lolo says. She taps her fingernails against her lips, raises her eyebrows, waiting for Sabine.

"Oh god how could I forget! I get sweaty just thinking about it."

Lolo leans forward, playfully slaps Sabine's arm. "We had fun, didn't we?"

Sabine nods, and suddenly the weightlessness of that night comes back to her, the flash of a past life.

"That was right before Budapest," Lolo says, and what she means, Sabine knows, is *How are you?* The way Lolo looked at her during Kid's Day begged for confession. She slides closer, her hand outstretched.

Sabine fights not to break down. Maybe it is the very public nature of everything that has happened, or the fact that even in her darkest moments she finds she cannot escape this communal gaze.

"I didn't mean to dredge up old shit," Lolo says, her palm wiping at her friend's cheek. "You just deserve more of those nights, Sabby. Damn I've missed you."

Lolo's smile comforts her. She is grateful for her this morning, these unexpected moments, how necessary they can be. Before Lolo leaves, they exchange goodbyes, and she wraps her arms around Sabine, pulls her tight. "You've got two weeks here, baby," she says. "Give them something else to remember."

Sabine stirs in bed, her body aching from practice and treatment. She needs to sleep. She feels desperate for it. At three in the morning, she makes tea, and Roger ruffles at the waking, his sweet little growl.

"Easy love," she says, rubbing his belly. She returns to bed, mug in hand, and snuggles next to him. She lights up her phone. Roger turns on his side, using his front paws to cover his eyes, the screen an electronic moon in the room.

She sees quickly, without reading much at all, fans have already turned. On the eve of the tournament, they are out for blood, for answers, hoping to tear down what little privacy she has left. She flips through likes, comments and demands, angry adulations. Criticism masquerading as support. The death threats she can handle—they were coming long before Budapest—but the jabs, the needle-prick reminders of what happened, first the bullet but so much more the shame that followed, are more than she can bear.

She runs her fingers along her arm, up near the shoulder where her skin melted and slipped open and the sight of it, not the pain, had pushed her into unconsciousness. If the woman had been a better shot. These comments are a wound festering, one Sabine tongues, leaving it unable to heal.

Before she realizes what she has done, Sabine responds to the most recent one. *You are a sad miserable person*, she writes, and the barrage begins again. A litany of horrors with brief reprieves, a few hidden kindnesses. Photographs stream through her feed, a deluge of her worst moments, her failures and on-court frustrations, until their subject becomes Budapest—Sabine on the edge of defeat, battling back; flat on the court, bloodied, chaos blurred in the background; an empty stadium, save for the stain spread out and seeping into the court. Sabine pauses on a message, lets it sit large and emboldened on the screen: *The bullet should've ended you.*

She shuts off her phone, leaving her in darkness. Roger rolls over and, with a whimper, begs her to sleep. She whispers to him, tells him that in the morning everything will be fine. *Everything will be fine.* Tomorrow, the tournament begins. Tomorrow, she will win them back. Tomorrow, she will prove she is more than a misguided bullet.

*

The too-late night churns in her stomach. Sabine's is the first day match on Althea Williams, and she arrives early to get in a quick hitting session. She tears into groundstroke after groundstroke, forehand, backhand, down the line, inside out, and the rhythm of her mind does the same. Her shoulder steady. Topspin. Backspin. Never forget to follow through. Around her there are no spectators, and as if she has just completed the longest fiercest match of her life, she leans against the net, hands gripped along the tape, feeling its tautness. She tells her hitting partner she is okay, she just needs a moment; then, it comes. She feels its origin deep in her lungs, and the cries escape with an almost calming ferocity. It rips from her body and echoes beyond these practice courts, beyond this complex. She has been afraid of this release; she does not want to be weak. In her mind, she hears her father's voice. It is not a mantra but something like a migraine.

But this is not weakness. It is relief. It is strength.

Instead of heading to the locker room, Sabine wanders the grounds. She lets the morning soak into her skin. With the crowds not yet arrived, the complex is a quiet paradise. The ponds are crystal. Each green space like a tiny oasis. As she moves along the walkway—stopping at Court 17, where she played her first ever match at the Open more than a decade ago—she feels the sun bloom over her shoulders. Before her, the arena dominates the skyline; even when she tries to look beyond, it looms.

Once the floodgates open and the tennis center becomes a sea of people, Sabine, ready for her match to begin, bounces with anticipation. Her opponent, Jennifer Constanza, an American teenager who received a wildcard to play in this year's event, stands nearby, her face full of nerves. They walk the tunnel, listening to the announcer in the arena. The unranked American is called first, much to the delight of the day session crowd. She is already a favorite without hitting a professional groundstroke on this court. No matter, Sabine tells herself. No one else matters. And when she is announced, when they welcome her back, the cheers are loud, and the jeers, too, and so Sabine waves and smiles. She does her duty. As they warm up, she looks around at the people moving through the aisles, thousands of them appearing and disappearing from the exits.

Sides chosen, Sabine will serve first. She stands at the baseline and wishes, for a moment, she could hide, the way she used to at her uncle's house in the country when the family was together in Germany for the holidays. She would squirrel away somewhere, a closet or the attic or even a pantry, back when she was small enough to fit. She would curl up and cover her mouth and try to calm her breathing, keep quiet. Her heart would race. She loved the idea of people looking for her, of being sought out, of being wanted but just out of reach. She spent her childhood loving this feeling.

But she realizes now, these years later, what she truly loved, more than anything else, was being found.

She bounces the ball, her usual routine, three times with the racket, three times with her left hand. *Play*, the chair umpire orders; Sabine holds the ball in the air, and her opponent nods, signals she is ready. Sabine bounces again, her fingers tight. They feel as if they are not hers. She is hasty and sloppy with her toss, her shoulder drops, and she dumps her first serve into the bottom part of the net. The umpire quickly hushes the rumbles in the city crowd. Second serve. A new start. She sucks in the warming Brooklyn air. She raises her arm, slow and methodical, and tosses the ball again. It lifts and lifts and hangs, waiting for Sabine to come to it. Her legs are strong and full, a lifetime of training rippling through her muscles, and her calves propel her upwards. She is precise, she is balanced. Her racket meets the bright yellow, ball against gut, and she lets out a shriek; she feels the transaction, a simple vibration. In an instant, the ball is a hundred miles per hour and gaining speed. Her feet reach for that small bit of ground. The world around her silent. And then, the deafening slap of the tape. The ball falls in slow motion, back onto Sabine's side. *Love, fifteen*, the chair calls. Sabine struggles to take a breath. The crowd, the crowd rises, and roars.

DREAMLAND

Sandy remembers the day the leaflets rained down over New York City. From his apartment along the East River in the Two Bridges section of Manhattan, he thought he saw birds, or an early light snow, falling from the sky. He went outside and found his neighbors in the street snatching small sheets of paper out of the air. One fell, moist from brushing through a tree, and stuck to Sandy's head. The beige paper felt like petals between his fingers. At the top, bold black letters announced its purpose—A NEW AMERICA—and beneath that questions, varied between leaflets: *Is your family provided for? Is your money safe against Wall Street's thievery? What security do you have of your own existence? Who is the American Dream for?*

Sandy lingered on the questions, the words hanging off his tongue like a stray hair. He was about to grab another leaflet when a hand pressed on his shoulder. He turned to find a young woman, her eyes blooming.

"Holy shit," she said, and she craned her neck, keeping her hand and arm extended as if to hold Sandy in place, and yelled, "Hey Janet, you'll never believe it—look who it is!"

As he answered question after question—*Do you live in this neighborhood? Are you still on the Atlantics? Are you single?*—Sandy smiled, large and glamorous and pretend, the kind of smile he'd used to melt New York hearts since getting called up from the minors. He wasn't recognized often, and deep down he wanted to be, he wanted to be noticed.

Back in his apartment, which represented the entirety of his signing bonus, Sandy stared out the living room windows and tried to revel in the calm. But the drones overhead, their constant whir, and the words falling from the sky made it impossible. Even from here, this view, this life. How fucked things could be.

In the years since that day, Sandy has become a star.

Cozy in his apartment, Sandy flicks through the newspaper on his tablet, stopping on the sports section. His own smiling face beams center page. *Brooklyn Boy Helps City Prepare for World Day.* In certain moments, Sandy allows himself to believe that his ability to turn a double play or rope a liner into the gap actually makes a difference. People say he's amazing, but more and more Sandy realizes those people, the ones convincing him how important he is, just want something for themselves.

He picks up the phone and calls his mother, Esther, who lives in Brighton Beach, still in the same house where Sandy was raised.

"What's wrong?" she says.

"Very funny. Just wanted to say hi."

"How's the city?"

He laughs, happy to hear her voice. "Fantastic," he says, as if they're not separated by only a few miles.

"Your cousin Haim stopped by yesterday. He says hello. Also please visit me more so maybe I won't have to pretend to enjoy your cousin's visits, yeah?"

He realizes, on his end of the phone, he's anticipating his mother's words, as if this has happened before and will again. "I'm still coming next weekend," he says, remembering what he'd promised. "Any chance I'll get you out to the game this weekend, for World Day?"

After a silence, shuffling on the other end, she says, "So many people, dear. Too many for me."

"I have seats for you. And Uncle David and Bubbe, too. If you change your mind."

"We'll watch together, on TV. We'll make a party of it out here."

He hears her disappointment, how it stands in for his own. She doesn't like crowds, he knows, not since the bridge, since they lost his father. She says they make her feel buried alive.

"You and everyone else, right?" he says, deflecting. "The world will be watching!"

"I've seen the billboards, they're everywhere."

A message pops up on his screen, interrupting the call: *TIME TO GO*. The automated ping echoes through the apartment. He has to run, he says, and as soon as the phone clicks dead, he feels guilty, something his mother sends telepathically at the ends of their conversations. It sticks with him as he gets on the subway, headed to the stadium. When they hit the Wallabout Bridge, he looks up and down the East River. He takes it all in, and above, fluttering in the breeze, the American flag, stripes blood red, stretching end to end.

He puts on his headphones, turns up his playlist—classical music—and the depth of sound, the symphonic energy, enters Sandy's body and electrifies him. And as New Ebbets comes into view, he feels ready to take on the whole world, to match its gaze. If they will be watching, he will give them something to see.

Though his teammates are already outside practicing, Sandy stays inside, taking batting practice in one of the virtual training rooms. In between swings, he hears the footfalls above him on the field, the slap of a perfectly thrown strike, the crack of wood. He takes a hard swing and pokes a shot into the opposite field corner. Though the vibration on contact feels real, the size and scope of the field, he knows this is make believe. In a game, nothing is simple and everything is real. And that, Sandy knows deep down, is what he craves—the absolute immovable difficulty of catching up to a fastball before it leaves him behind, of making every person in the stadium believe in something greater than themselves.

He sends three consecutive pitches into the virtual stands, the last one smacking against the model replica of the Roebling Bridge just beyond the center field wall, and a raucous, exaggerated clapping fills the room. Sandy turns to find Nick Mattingly—the team's All-Star catcher and his best friend—smiling, arms raised in the air, as if the Atlantics have just won the pennant.

After Sandy's next swing, Nick says, "Hey Eighteen, you're dancing too much."

Sandy takes one more cut before bursting into laughter. He steps back and pats Nick on the cheek. Normally clean-shaven, Nick wears off-days of growth, wispy and golden against his fair Irish skin. Eyes an ocean of blue. His tall frame contrasted beside Sandy, the shortest member of the Atlantics.

"Come on," Nick says and lands his hand heavy on Sandy's back.

When they leave the clubhouse and step onto the field, the press swarm around Sandy with an anxious fever, and the words turn into a cascade of noise: *What's your strategy going up against Maddox? What's your process for staying hot this weekend? Any special plans for World Day?*

"I'm gonna swing hard," Sandy says, slipping on his glove and trotting out to shortstop. As always, he's careful to hop over the third base line. He turns to the mob, each holding up a screen, recording him, filming him, stealing away pieces of him. "That's all I got," he shouts, grinning.

As the grounders come fast and smooth over the Kentucky bluegrass, Sandy hears Nick talking to the press, his responses artfully crafted. "Being a ballplayer's a privilege," he says. "We work hard, and none of us take the responsibility lightly."

Such a goddamn statesman, Sandy thinks. He snags a liner out of the air and it stings his palm. He gets a holler—*Iron hands!*—from Ambrose Hussey, his manager, along with the silent snaps of dozens of digital cameras. Sandy repositions, bends his knees just so, shifting his weight on the fronts of his feet, and when the next grounder shoots up the middle, Sandy dives to his left, glove hand extended, and feels the disappointment of the ball missing the webbing, ticking off the edge, and sliding into center field. He gets up, dusts himself off and claps out his glove. He looks to Coach Hussey, whose eyes say it all.

By the time Sandy makes way for Danielle Garcia—one of the first women to play in the majors and the Atlantics' backup shortstop—he's bruised. He lingers in left field shagging fly balls before trotting off. As he shuffles through the dugout, a voice from the media scrum calls out to him, "Are you ready for World Day?"

Phones at the ready, and Sandy flashes that signature smile, he holds it as long as he can, and says, "I'm not sure World Day's ready for me."

In the morning, Sandy sits at his kitchen bar, light pouring through windows high above the river. Outside, a tugboat reports itself, asking for an unbroken path forward. A news alert flashes across the television, breaking his lack of concentration. Sandy shifts on the barstool, waiting for a video to begin. It's nothing Sandy, the world, hasn't seen before. These warnings started long before the Roebling Bridge attack. Terrorist threats and boiling anger—*Fuck America*, a familiar call to arms for like-minded revolu-tionaries. Social media carries their messages across cities and continents, from house to house. Photographs are shown on-screen, horrors one after another, the last of a child crawling from the rubble of a US airstrike in Iraq, and the voice behind the photos says, without even a tremor, the child was dead moments later. Sandy feels the reality in the backs of his eyes, a knifing at his nerves. In a bombed-out section of Baghdad, the video closes with a group of armed men holding a homemade sign for the camera, a broken misquoted piece of translated text: *There is no escape from the inferno of the living*. He wonders what this latest threat, if anything, will mean for World Day. He turns it off, trying to shake the image from his mind, any attempt to clear the noise. The sun on his face, the echoes of the city around him. All he's ever wanted and more.

He meets Nick for breakfast at their favorite spot, a diner tucked away in the Lower East Side. Sandy arrives first; he keeps his headphones on as he waits, hoping no one will bother him. A few people around him pull out their phones and snap conspicuously. Nick sneaks in behind Sandy, puts his arms around him and lifts him up. "Morning, Kitty," he says, and when Sandy's feet touch the ground again, they share a laugh.

The owner comes out and says hello, and Nick goes back and forth with him in Spanish before they sit.

"Goddamn showoff," Sandy says, the large menu open and shielding him completely.

"All the time we spent in Florida, I don't know how you didn't pick up at least a little."

Sandy pretends to ignore him. "Excuse me?" he says, smiling. "I wasn't listening."

"You're a delight this morning." Nick signals the server for coffees for them both.

"Just anxious," Sandy says. He doesn't mention his mother, that she's not coming to the game. He expected as much, though it disappoints him nonetheless.

"That's nothing new."

They order breakfast, and Sandy puts down his menu, takes in Nick's expression. He would slide across this table and kiss him if he could. The bitter coffee warm on their tongues.

"I've already had enough of this weekend. All this World Day shit."

"You love it," Nick says.

"It's a lot of eyes. And too many questions."

"You'd prefer they leave you alone?"

"It's just a lot."

When the food arrives, they tear into it.

"This day means something to people; they love you and they love this team. They're not the enemy."

"They take what they want and leave the bones."

The image, or Sandy's over-serious tone, makes Nick nearly spit out his eggs. "Jesus if you could hear yourself. If three-years-ago-Sandy could. They wouldn't give you the time of day. I remember. Some shrimpy Jew from Brighton. It drove you nuts."

"I just wanna play ball."

"Bullshit. You want them to eat you up and we both know it."

"They're distracting. How does it not get to you?"

"A distraction? You play the part pretty damn well."

"They wanna know who I'm fucking, what I'm doing every second of the day."

"So tell them."

"A, I'm not fucking anyone. B, it's none of their fucking business. C, sure."

"They don't care, Kitty, I promise you. I mean, they care, but not in the way you're afraid of."

"I'm a ballplayer. I wish we'd stick to that."

"You're more than that, and you know it." He scoops a mouthful of po-tatoes. "But fine. You're a shortstop and nothing more. Tell me how you're gonna keep that hot bat lit."

"Channel all this bitchiness into my swing."

"Gold," Nick says, clinking his mug against Sandy's. "You're unstop-pable."

After breakfast, Sandy walks to the esplanade along the river. He imagines leaning over the edge, diving in head first, letting the current pull him in. The water would boil with all that's inside of him. He closes his eyes against the weight of the wind coming across from Brooklyn. He wonders if Nick is right. He wants both sides—the fame, the talent that brings it on, and he wants his privacy, too, to be a ballplayer on his own terms. Maybe that's asking too much from one existence, but he feels incapable of compromise.

He follows the river north and back again, careful to feel each step, to absorb the energy around him. Every bridge he passes brings him closer to home. *A bridge is a work of art*, his father always said. In the distance, the Roebling tells that truth. Whatever artfulness it once held—along with those hundreds seared into its foundation, along with Lenny Katzmann, father and husband—burned away in an instant.

When he reaches his street, Sandy stands at its eastern end looking west. He thinks back to the day the leaflets came down, the way this very street was covered, and how little, how much, has changed. He still has one of them, frayed and wrinkled, tucked away in a drawer. He remembers the questions it asked—of him, of this country—and how almost nothing since has felt the same.

He's lost in thought as he approaches his building. He doesn't notice the people gathered. He nearly bumps into the crowd before someone turns, arm outstretched. Sandy recognizes him, one of the building's porters.

"Mr. Katzmann," he says, his voice flat and thin, "we've been looking for you."

The small crowd parts, and at the foot of the stairs lies the body of a boy, battered and bloodied. Sirens in the distance, their relentless scream, but from this boy Sandy can't look away. His prominent nose broken, shirt ripped from his body, skin bruised; his coat, heavy and black, hanging off his arm; the torn kippah beside his head; the word written in charcoal or ash across his back, the glyphs clear and bright as the afternoon: *traitor*, they translate, and their weight plumes like the smoke of everything else in this chimerical city. In its wake, this great cloud, Sandy finds it impossible to breathe.

THE ART OF PRETENDING

Sabine tries to catch her breath, calm the adrenaline surging through her like fire. The crowd trickles out, some jeering as they go, others clapping for Jennifer Costanza, the ousted American teen. They are off to other matches, to concessions, to the endless greens and shimmering ponds of the City Open complex. A few stragglers remain, though, scattered around the arena, cheering and chanting Sabine's name. A group of young women and men with their faces and arms and chests painted the colors of the German flag—*Helle's Angels*, they call themselves—scream their adoration, and the sound echoes through the promenade. She is still the champion of some.

"I gave it all I had today," Sabine says, sucking in the warm air. "First round matches are always full of nerves but this one even more so, I think for me and Jennifer. She played a wonderful match, really pushed me to my limits. She is going to be a player to watch here for a long time."

The on-court interviewer, herself an aging ex-player from New Zealand, leaves a quiet space for the crowd to fill. They do, and she claps along with them, a gesture without much meaning. "And speaking of a long time…how about these fans?" Her hands dance like a conductor's, orchestrating the masses. "Seems they've been waiting forever to see you back on this court."

"I could not do it without you guys!" Sabine raises her arms and waves to the crowd. "Seriously it means so much to come here and have you in my corner. You have all the energy. I love playing in New York!"

They are hollow, Sabine's words, though perhaps only to her. She knows some of these people are the ones who root for her failure, who take pleasure in her fall, who mock her on Prattlr, send death threats and compliments wrapped in discourtesies. She knows, but she smiles anyway. She stands and does not slouch and thanks everyone who remains. She has won something today, something greater than this match. She is ready for tomorrow and the next day, battles on and off the court. She will be brave, and like her father always demanded, she will do better. She will be better.

At the post-match press conference, Sabine squirms in her seat, all manner of camera and recording device fixed on her, and she tries not to crawl up inside her head. *Let it be natural*, she thinks. *You won, be happy. Remember how easy this all used to be.*

"Were you nervous out there, Sabine?"

She knows the question well and the reason for its asking. She will not give them the satisfaction.

"Always, I am always nervous. To be a champion, each match has to mean everything."

Voices trip over one another.

"There were a lot of folks booing you out there today—how do you cope with that?"

"I heard a lot of cheers," she says. She smiles wide, holds it the best she can.

A faceless figure in the back shouts, "How do you feel, Sabine?" A hush settles through the room.

"I am good, very good…how are you?" She is punchy, and laughter ripples through the group. This is not about bullet wounds anymore, nor shame. *Do not let it be.*

The reporter raises his hand this time, wagging to get Sabine's attention. "I meant physically, of course. How are you coping? It's been a while."

The raise of his eyebrows at the end is enough to make Sabine's skin burn. She nibbles at the inside of her lip. It is the kind of question only a man would ask. She slides forward, closer to the microphone she has been ignoring.

"Strong. Beyond ready, and strong. Thank you for asking." She feels the muscles in her arm pulsing, flexing as if she is still on court, and as she keeps her gaze locked on the reporter, she hopes he sees it, too, the power her body can wield. Like nothing he will ever know.

From behind the false wall serving as her background, which is covered in sponsor stickers and City Open banners and in the middle a gold seal embossed with *World Day*, Sabine sees Lolo poke her head around. She blows Sabine a kiss, enough to break up what these cameras are calcifying. It makes everything in the room lighter.

"How was it being back on Althea Williams?"

They want to hear something revelatory, something transparent. But she needs to keep something for herself, her joy and her unhappiness alike. Maybe that is what Alina has been trying to tell her, hoping she would hear. If everything is shared and dissected and torn apart, nothing can be hers anymore.

Sabine stands to leave, leans towards the microphone, and says, "Like coming home."

In the players' lounge, Sabine finds Lolo stretched out on a couch, her long muscular brown legs on display. She is talking to the acupuncturist, and when she catches sight of Sabine she smiles with her entire face.

Sabine totters to her and says, "You look like the Grinsekatze."

"That better be a good thing." Lolo curls up, pats the vacated space beside her.

To Sabine, Lolo is the platonic ideal of American beauty, an intimate perfection. And she must know this, Sabine thinks, because she carries it in her power and grace, displayed not as separate entities but as one united art form, making her impossible to look away from.

She thinks back to their youth, the courts around them full of other junior players, other hopefuls, an academy of students vying for brilliance. Though Sabine had only known Lolo for a few months then, they were already inseparable. *We'll never be stuck in one place*, Lolo had said. *The whole world is ours*. Sabine remembers the idea settling in her, the gift of this life, that she could be anywhere, everywhere. They practiced and they played, laughed and carried on. Some things were simple, shared. So much weight and responsibility on them, not only their own dreams but those of others, the hopes of the adults around them, and sometimes, this was all they needed to escape, to keep loving this sport—a friend across the net, and the luxurious art of pretending.

"If I sit," Sabine says, returning, "I might never leave." She lets her body collapse on the soft cushions. She feels it already, the pressure bleeding off her.

"You shouldn't do those anymore," Lolo says, her voice suddenly firm, "that stupid media shit. At least for a while, until things calm down."

"When will that be? I cannot afford the fines if I skip them." Sabine slips the corners of her mouth into a sly grin. "I have not won a match in so long."

Lolo absorbs Sabine's self-deprecation and sits up and takes her hand, grips it with a kind of victory. "Until today," she says, the electricity in her smile enough to energize this whole complex.

Sabine settles into the compliment, the generous support of her friend. With the heat of the match yet to fade, Sabine says she wants to get in a few more swings.

"Do you ever stop?" Lolo asks, sticking out her tongue. "Maybe I'll join you," she goes on, "even if I'd rather stay on this couch *forever*."

"You know it," Sabine says. "We stop, we die."

They leave through the back, avoiding any press on their way to the practice courts. On the far side, surrounded by fans pressed to the chainlink fence, are Elena Volkova and Alexei Volkov, the Russian wonder twins. They are perhaps the most internationally famous players, being the niece and nephew of the Russian prime minister, but the traveling circus of bodyguards and hangers-on do not seem to bother them or their game; each was a semifinalist last year in Brooklyn, and Elena's rank has rocketed from the high hundreds to mid-teens in less than two seasons; Alexei, though incredibly talented, seems incapable of focus, vacillating between tour victories and public breakdowns, benders, and missed tournaments. As a junior, he punched a linesperson in the face after a foot fault call. Only his family's power and financial influence saved his career, and though most players have forgotten or moved on, Sabine still holds it against him, the length and breadth he has been given.

Lolo waves as they pass the twins, smiling but unable to muster anything more. "What d'ya think it's like, being them?"

"I do not give it much thought," Sabine says, sure in the obviousness of her lie. "He is an asshole."

"I played doubles with Elena in Monte Carlo. Remember?"

At first Sabine does not respond—Monte Carlo was a few weeks after Budapest, a fact neither of them needs reminding of—then shakes her head.

"She's sweet, in her way."

They separate, taking opposing sides, and stay close to the net. Sabine feels the heft of the match cracking with each small volley. She is adrenalized; she will play another match, a possibility that even days ago felt foreign, almost entirely out of reach.

"Nervous?" Lolo asks, bending low and slicing the ball, too sharp for Sabine to return.

"Always," she says playfully.

Lolo pulls a ball from her pocket, and they begin again. "About World Day, I mean. All the people. The security, it makes me feel less safe. Does that make sense? I don't know." She takes a return early, swings hard and pulls the shot crosscourt, out of Sabine's long reach. "I just mean if it were me, I'd be nervous."

"If what were you?" Sabine asks, holding a ball in her hand and waiting for a reply.

Lolo tilts her head and smirks—*Come on, I'm on your side*, she is saying—and motions with her racket for Sabine to hit. "Someone shot you, Sabby. That's fucking terrifying. Do we have to pretend it's not?"

"If I cannot pretend," Sabine says, lofting an overhead into the air, "it is pretty damn hard to be out here."

"I guess so," Lolo says, taking the ball high. "Just don't turn into your dad. You wouldn't look good in stone."

"You know me," she says, her smile trying to lighten the mood. "I play, and everything else goes away. I may be a sexy statue, but I play."

She settles into a rhythm, her strokes a consistent mania. Lolo's coach arrives, announcing his presence with a joyous cry to the spectators. He is a well-known figure, Gerard Moreau, big and boisterous and round, which he hides well beneath his tricolor tracksuit. He has been Lolo's coach for as long as Sabine can remember, since he decided to leave his tennis academy in Nice to take her on.

Moreau yells something to Lolo that Sabine cannot hear. Lolo holds up her hand, stopping their rally, as he approaches. Sabine watches them, Moreau flamboyant and exaggerated, and even in his silliness or maybe especially in, Lolo seems grateful for his company. And though she has not felt so in some time, Sabine yearns for that, too. It has been years since her father stepped away from coaching her—or she pushed him, depending on the source—and the idea of a replacement, of a *new coach*, seems impossible now. She had one coach, and to Sabine he had been the best, the worst, the reason for her being on a tennis court. There is no possible second act. There are others without a coach, she reminds herself when this feeling creeps in. Yet in seeing what Lolo has, or perhaps more precisely what Sabine does not, she feels a great sense of emptiness, a vacancy on the other side of the net gone unfilled.

Moreau calls to Sabine, breaking her concentrated stare, and when she does not answer he repeats his question, "Ça va?"

Lolo motions for Sabine to keep hitting, to ignore him, and Sabine obliges, starting things up and taking big cuts with her forehand, hoping the focus on her face and grunt in her throat will be enough answer for Moreau. The song of ball and string fills the air, and Moreau leans against the net and says, "All healed?"

In the space between distraction and impropriety, Sabine takes a wild swing, pulls a backhand wide—*too early*, she hears her father chide—and turns to Moreau. "All that needs to heal has," she says. "La routine."

Moreau chews on Sabine's answer. "All that can," he says, his tone a correction. He winks at Sabine and pats the tape of the net like the shoulder of an old friend. As he strides away, the sway of his body lumbering against the breeze, Sabine is captured, carried off by memory.

It is the stillness of it all, even in her recollection, that strikes Sabine most. She wins the second set, leveling the match after a shaky and underwhelming first set, and she strides to her seat, certain of how the rest of the match will go. She is unapologetically confident; she looks around, sips her water and lets the sun fall heavy on her shoulders. She basks in the feeling. Almost as quickly, she shakes it off, tells herself to focus on the challenge at hand. The umpire muffles *Time* into the microphone, and Sabine readies. Up in the stands, a commotion begins. Protestors screaming at Sabine, at other members of the crowd. The crowd riles, a rage mounting. The umpire asks then demands the crowd calm down and let play begin. Sabine takes a step towards the court, her feet straddling the doubles line, when from behind her she hears the donnybrook lift and one voice clarifies.

Sabine turns and sees the woman, the gun, the faces in the crowd; everything is still. She knows the woman but cannot place her. An unsettling familiarity. She swears she hears beyond the stadium, the echoing waves of the shot to come. Time is a jumble—she feels the head of the bullet slipping through her skin; she stares at the woman and the gun trembling in her hand; she takes in the nameless faces of the heroes that stop a second shot from being fired; she is on the ground and her blood is on the court and she smells it, that metallic pong; she feels herself getting lighter but really she is already unconscious, aware and asleep.

"Hey!" Lolo says. When she finally catches Sabine's eye, she asks, "Where the hell are you?"

Sabine collects herself, shakes her head as if that will reset things. "They never found her, you know." She feels far away, her thoughts in the past.

"Who?" Lolo asks, spinning her racket head with her fingertips.

"The woman who shot me."

When Lolo looks at her, Sabine sees clearly the pity, the consolation. "Of course they did, Sabby. Didn't they?" She smiles, still full of an empathy Sabine does not want. She suggests they keep hitting, which stands in place of *I believe you.*

Sabine agrees, though for the time her mind is lost, scattered in the shapeless recesses of what she has allowed herself to remember and forget. And at the center is the grit of Moreau's words carving yet a new space: *All that can heal*, it says. All that can.

SANDY FUCKING KATZMANN

The summer Sandy turned twelve, he fell down a well. He'd been warned to stay away, but like most children, he took the warning as a challenge. It wasn't a deep well, but the walls were too jagged to climb, the location remote enough to cloister Sandy's calls for help. He spent the better part of a day down there, alternating between shouting his parents' names and sobbing. Eventually, he gave up, nestled his head against a rock, and watched an ant scurry along the damp ground, its small legs quick enough to be almost invisible. It moved back and forth, grabbing pieces of wood and grass before disappearing into a thin crack in the wall. On its last run, it tried to scoop up a piece of detritus nearly twice its own size. Sandy laughed at first, tickled by the absurdity of the proportion—he imagined it would be like trying to drag the family car along Surf Avenue—but the tiny creature persisted, lifting and tugging and stumbling until finally it slipped between that sliver of rock wall, its prize secured, and vanished. In the minutes afterwards, Sandy felt time stand still. He was more alone than he felt all day. He stayed fixed on that spot, the crack between worlds. He closed his eyes and pretended he could slip through, too. But when his father's voice finally echoed down, he looked up and, meeting his father's broad and relieved smile, Sandy wept.

He sits on the sidewalk outside his apartment building, remembering that well, as he stares at the body of this young boy. The intimacy of it, the feeling in the pit of his stomach, consumes him. The longer he looks, taking in the bruised and abraded skin, the boy becomes something absurd, not of this world or perhaps so primally of this world that Sandy can't recognize it. Around him, the city swirls. Everything kinetic except for him. Even this boy, this body, this unknowable thing—something inside still stirs, even without breath, without life. Sandy, though, remains at the bottom of that well, waiting for a way out, a way in, his mouth and his voice smothered as if by ash.

The ambulance arrives first, followed closely by police and a fire truck, which parks diagonally across the small street, its lights radiating off cars and windows. The police keep the crowd at bay, backing them up and Sandy, too, to a safe distance. He tells the paramedics as they shove their way through, *The boy is dead.* They ignore him and drop their bags, checking for signs of life. One shakes his head at the other, his fingers pressed hard to the boy's neck.

A hand lands on Sandy's shoulder. "Did you find the body?" the officer asks.

In the confusion of the moment, he says, "Yes," then almost immediately, "No."

The officer looks at him, his head and mouth tilted in disbelief, but before he continues, a wave of recognition passes over his eyes. "This is your place?" he asks, calling over another officer who, upon seeing Sandy, smiles in a way that feels unsuitable for a murder scene.

"I live here," Sandy says, pointing at the seventy-story building. "Near the top."

"Must be nice," the officer says, writing something in his notebook.

With the body covered, the crowd thins, and those who remain are questioned. Sandy's officer continues to chaperone. "You know this boy?"

"No," Sandy says, staring at the sheeted figure.

"Why here then?" the officer asks, his tone thick with accusation. "I mean, if you don't know him, right?"

Sandy, already tired, shrugs. "I don't know."

"Any idea what those symbols are?"

Sandy hears the question but his attention wanders again. His father's voice floods his mind, a mix of compassion and demand—*Watch me, son, and everything will be okay*—and the clarity with which he hears him, feels his intonations, gives Sandy gooseflesh.

"Katzmann?" The officer snaps his meaty fingers only a few inches from Sandy's nose.

"It's Yiddish," he says, coming back.

"Know what it means?" The officer chews on his lip, the way one might a toothpick.

"Traitor." Despite his efforts, Sandy's voice cracks.

"Excuse me?" He keeps his pen pressed to paper, though he has stopped writing.

"It's what's written, on his back. *Traitor*."

The officer takes in the information, and Sandy watches his eyebrows and cheeks dance. "That mean anything to you?"

Sandy's patience pulls apart like an overstretched muscle. "No," he says. "Of course not."

Once the body is taken away, Sandy asks if he can go. "Don't leave town," the officer says, and Sandy wonders if he's joking.

He declines to mention the team going on a ten-game road trip after World Day. He steps over the spot where the young boy had been, and before he goes in and up to his apartment, he hears the officer say to someone in the crowd, "Youknowwhothatis? That's Sandy Fucking Katzmann."

After a sleepless night of flipping channels and staring down at the East River, Sandy gets on the subway in the morning. The train crosses into Brooklyn, and he's certain of his destination without meaning to be. The walk from the station to his mother's house Sandy could make blind. Despite the time that has passed, these few otherwise forgettable streets are his own, his family's, no matter what else around them breaks away. Standing in the front yard, the house as it always was, small and unassuming like the Katzmanns, it's still the home he grew up in.

"You look like a maniac out there," Esther shouts, her head poking through the half-open front door. In seeing his mother, Sandy feels both a nostalgic calm and overwhelming anxiety, a phenomenon his father called *the Sthers*, an unmistakable collision of emotions that only Esther Katzmann could bring on.

"I'm looking at the house, Mama."

"It's the same," she yells, a universal truth rather than an opinion.

"We should paint it," Sandy says, finally taking those final few steps to greet her.

"We?" Sandy hears her finish the thought—*You mean* you, *baby boy*—though she doesn't say it. He hugs her, kisses her forehead, and before he can pull away, she puts her palms to his cheeks. "When was the last time you slept?"

"You look wonderful, too," he says, flashing her the same smile the press has come to love, his insecurities masked by teeth.

Esther slides her hand around her son's arm, guiding him into the house. "So touchy," she says. "I see it in your eyes."

"I'm sleeping," he says, biting back. "I just didn't sleep."

Esther mumbles an *uh huh* under her breath. She goes into the kitchen, and Sandy follows her like a puppy eager but shy for attention. She opens the percolator to make them coffee. "You and Nicky fighting again?"

"Nick's fine. We're all fine," he says.

"Good," she says, as if it's his duty to be happy, to make her happy. She somehow fills the percolator with water while speaking with her hands, fingers outstretched, arms pushing left and right in demonstration. "First you call and say I won't see you, then you're standing on the lawn. Who raised you?"

"Long day, long night, that's all."

Esther leans in close to him. "Tell me," she says.

He shares what he knows—the crowd, the shock, the boy and the bruises, the questions, the word—and Esther pours them each a cup of coffee and sits next to him, the steam from their mugs rising into the room. He sees in his mother's eyes a shaking. She is somewhere else, and when she breathes the sound is like a car dying. Sandy takes her hand, which vibrates in his own. "I'm sorry," he says, "I didn't mean to upset you."

Esther matches her son's gaze. "Don't be silly. I'm glad you told me."

Though he doesn't say it, perhaps has never said it, he's grateful for his mother; she's a haven, a beacon for him, whenever he's most lost.

"It's all so fucked up."

"Why didn't I read about this," she says, her voice regaining its usual bravado.

"The police are keeping my name out of it," he says. "Mel even called. *No need to drag our boy into this.*" Sandy mimics the Atlantics owner's voice, very unlike his own, deep and cartoonish. "And the cop, you know what he says? *Don't worry—you're one of us.*" Sandy's eyes grow wide and exaggerated. "What does that even mean?"

"It means you're not that kind of Jew, Schatz, at least not to him, not to the folks that watch your ballgames. Your face is a billboard over the tunnel for crying out loud. You're a Brooklyn boy, and especially after everything with your father, people just want to root for you. God knows we all deserve something to cheer for."

Her words sit between them, like the end of a powerful speech but in the seconds before anyone applauds, before the crowd, hanging on every word, thunders in unison. There's only silence, the kitchen a chamber holding them in a kind of stasis, an electric hum that fills them both.

"You should've seen him, Mama." Sandy takes a breath, preparing to say more, but in truth it's all he can do to keep from breaking down. "You should've seen him."

Esther pats her son's face, in a way that makes Sandy believe she understands, that she will always understand, even without explanation. She lifts their empty mugs, one in each hand, and places them gently into the sink. Sandy takes in his mother's kind expression. He's grateful for the sweetness suddenly there. Or maybe it has been there, unused in the background, stashed away like a box of old photos forgotten with time, hidden almost beyond discovery.

Halfway across the bridge back to Manhattan, the train comes to a slow unexpected stop. Sandy stares out the window, down to the small waves on the river. From this height, the sun reflecting off the water makes it impossible to look for too long. It reminds Sandy of summer days spent at the beach at Coney Island, most of which run together as one endless day, rocks and sand underfoot, sure that if he slipped into the cool water and swam and never looked back he would find a new world, where everything was his and there was no end in sight. Outside the train, police officers walk in a line along the path between the road and subway tracks. One points towards the train car behind Sandy's while another crouches down, using her hand to shield the intense brightness of the afternoon, and she shakes her head, disagreeing with whatever assessment has been made. Over the intercom, a man's voice, aged from smoking and too much yelling, booms through. "Sorry, folks. Held here due to police activity on the bridge. Please be patient." He repeats the information, and his tone tells them he's as annoyed as they are. It's little consolation, though. Sandy wants to be home.

"Whatdya think's going on over there?" An older woman sitting perpendicular to Sandy shifts closer to the window, closer to him. "We hit somebody?"

Sandy knows better than to engage, but he's feeling shaken still, unmoored, and the simplicity of another human being is comforting. "Nah. Traffic's stopped, too, see," he says, pointing to the line of cars. "And we would've stopped fast if we hit something, right?"

The policewoman whirls her finger in the air and shouts to someone. Traffic begins moving and the train kicks to life, the mechanisms below crying out against the metal track. Sandy feels his phone vibrate but he ignores it, taking in one more view of the river, of the boroughs along both shores, like a final gulp of breath before they leave this freedom and disappear beneath the city.

"I bet it's another bomb threat," says the woman, who Sandy forgot was still beside him.

He shuffles over, making more space between them. "It was nothing," he says. He wonders if she can hear it, the *Don't worry* buried between his words, kept there to sate himself.

"Huh," the woman says, half-smiling and nodding. She collects her grocery tote bags. "Do I know you?"

He wants to say yes, the way she looks at him like they're old friends. But he smirks, shakes his head. "I don't think so."

The woman stands as the next stop approaches, a few before Sandy's, and says, "I doubt that very much." She steps off the train, and Sandy watches her shuffle across the station, the bottoms of her bags bouncing slightly off the tile floor.

The rest of the ride feels like hours. Outside, he cuts over to the esplanade and weaves up and down streets. He avoids going back to his apartment. The scene will be clear by now, but he can't deal with a reporter waiting for him or neighbors congregated around the phantom shape. When he finally turns the corner of his block, his steps light and hesitant, he sees someone, and for a moment he almost doubles back. But it's Nick sitting on the steps, his arms resting across his knees. Even seated, Sandy thinks, he looms.

"Where you been, Kitty?" Nick shouts, Sandy still half a block away. "I've been messaging."

He slows, anxious to reach Nick but relishing, from this distance, seeing him. It surprises Sandy, Nick's unannounced presence, though it shouldn't. Nick has always been that friend, and Sandy hopes he has been the same in return, even when they lived states apart, when Nick's family left Brooklyn and Sandy wrote emails and sent kitschy vintage Coney Island postcards to the middle of the country, somewhere vast and unknown to him. For years Sandy worried about losing his best friend to some other kid, somebody new, someone who could run faster and chase down his fly balls and who didn't, even if he wanted to, complain that Nick was always the star, always the beautiful one, always the one people idolized, the one everyone wanted to be or be near, the one, like a ball lost beyond the fence, always uncatchable.

"So you heard?" Sandy's voice is more stilted than he means it to be.

From the ground between his legs, Nick slides out a pack of beers. He holds one up, and Sandy takes it. "Nothing CJ knows stays secret for long," he says, and they laugh at the thought.

"He's really the worst PR guy," Sandy says.

"Or the best?" Nick pouts his lip, shrugs his shoulders. "Maybe the best," he says.

They walk towards the river and find a bench along the esplanade, where they can drink and talk surrounded by the city, entirely invisible.

"Don't ask me about it," Sandy says before Nick can begin. "You already know, so don't ask."

"Okay," he says, acquiescing. "You're okay then?"

"That's asking. Something else."

"So no, got it." Nick leans down and picks up a small rock. Without standing he rears back and lets it fly from his grasp, over the railing and diving down unseen into the waiting water below.

"Don't bait. I'm fine. Distract me, asshole, please."

"I finally fucked Francesca last night," he says, his smile the same roguish one from when he was a kid.

Sandy's head jerks towards him, mouth open, though he shouldn't be surprised. "Is she the influencer-slash-philosopher-slash-poet-slash-supermodel I always thought she was?"

"Listen, state-school, she speaks four languages and runs an empire." Nick raises his eyebrows, the way a cat's tail bushes out when it's energized, and says, "Yeah."

"Did you just call me state-school?"

"If you're gonna be a prick."

Sandy kicks at the pebbles underfoot, scattering them. "What's she like?"

"Hell if I know," Nick says.

Sandy finishes his beer and is carried off. He's happiest in these moments with Nick, has been so for the entirety of their lives together. Nick's a playboy, a womanizer, but Sandy knows the vulnerability behind the show, the person underneath the catcher's padding, exposed only when the cameras are no longer filming. And this is what he wants, Sandy feels it now more than he ever has—something comfortable and familiar and passionate. A partner this beautiful, who knows him, can read him, call him out and lift him up. Sandy wants a love like that. A love like this.

"Whatdya say, after World Day, we sneak off somewhere and just have a day?" Nick scoops up another rock, this one larger, and he stands, puts the weight of his legs back, and throws. It arches high into the air, almost out of sight until it begins its descent, a meteor cutting through the sky.

They follow the esplanade downriver and pop into a pizza place near Sandy's apartment, and Sandy realizes only then he hasn't eaten all day. The grease on his lips like a rebellion.

Before they part ways, Sandy tells Nick about the boy, how the whole thing shook his mother. Nick says he should visit her, that he misses her. "Your dad, too," he goes on. "Good ol' Lenny." And when they hug, Sandy knows there's a strength in what they have, in what they have built over their shared lifetime. He watches Nick walk to the end of the street, disappear into a car. He will see Nick at the ballpark, both wearing their uniforms, their armor, their insecurities hidden beneath.

Later, beyond exhausted and his stomach knotted, Sandy teeters in the space between waking and dreaming. He races. He sees the boy, hears him crying out. His purple skin melts into the night sky. *Why can't I help him.* He sees the boy, dirty and weeping. He tries to listen but he can't understand. He's angry and he's scared and he's dying. He sees the boy; he is the boy. Everything is dark, so far down. No one will find him. He's lost. And the secret Sandy holds, will forever keep for himself, sits with him at the bottom of that well. *Don't find me*, he begs. *Please, don't ever find me*. He looks up, out of the well, this room, into the world. All around him, the lights, the city, they are constellations.

BEYOND THE SEA

ornings when Sabine ran along A1A, she sometimes saw manatees gliding slowly across the surface of the Florida Intracoastal Waterway. She would stop her run and watch, mesmerized by their quiet, graceful movements. They reminded her of cows, or giant water sloths, and when she was young she dreamed of becoming famous and rich if for no other reason than to have an aquarium in her house large enough for at least two manatees, even a family of them. Her father always laughed, strong and full from his belly; he encouraged her, told her she could have whatever she wanted if she worked hard enough—she could make the world hers. A manatee's paradise, he joked, to her delight. *When I am great, I will change the world. And the manatees*, she would say, *I will keep them all safe.*

She wakes thinking of this, her hotel alarm clock buzzing. Roger pressed to her side, stretched out and snoring. On her phone, she finds messages lighting up the screen. Save for one, they are all from Alina.

Don't forget the trainer today

Don't post about Rog pp

Are you up I have questions

Interview req womens mag young writer are we interested (think we are)

Sabine reads them as they are written, breathless, the words and thoughts blending together in much the same way Alina speaks. Sabine always wonders if it's an affectation or if Alina's mouth and brain really run at so high a speed.

The last message, from a number Sabine has not seen in some time, reads *Gorgeous stuff out there. So glad you're back. Keep. It. Up. Miss you like crazy.* Guilt and happiness wash over her, stick to her through Roger's morning walk and her shower; she debates writing him back. She wonders how even to begin.

On television, they talk about her opening match. "Do I want to know?" she asks Roger. She turns up the sound—*battling back from a terrifying ordeal*—and mutes it again. The room is otherwise quiet, save for the white noise of the city outside, cars honking, the carrying voices of construction workers on nearby buildings. "Much better," she says, and with that Roger is up. He shuffles his stubby legs over to Sabine, whines with his mouth wide open like a yawn, and plops his head against Sabine's open palm.

She messages Alina, tells her she is leaving for the complex to visit the trainer. She has ignored the swelling in her shoulder—she knows she should not have practiced so long with Lolo—but she will have to get it down before her next match. She was lucky against Jennifer, whose greenness was enough to offset Sabine's sluggish start, her hesitation after each serve, feeling that tweak, a chink in her armor, like the whole thing might at any moment come crashing down.

Alina responds with a single heart, and Sabine follows with two messages—*No more interviews during the tournament*, and a picture of Roger she took on their walk holding a stick twice his size—and tucks her phone away. It is a hard thing to avoid, to ignore, the constant stream of breaking news and attention, all and none of which is truly urgent. The world is an ugly place, but she used to be able to block it out, seal her mind and keep focused on her game. She has let it in, though, not all at once but slowly, like a cancer gone untreated, and what she wants desperately now is to be rid of it, to rediscover that space in her thoughts where only she and her tennis exist.

Though she moves around the complex largely unnoticed, Sabine stops to sign autographs for a few fans, all children, because it is their admiration alone—unencumbered and wholly genuine—she can tolerate these days. The adults tend to yell things to get her attention, and she is careful to remember what they call her. She catches Lolo on the practice courts, slicing away at Moreau's obtuse forehands, and she waves to her friend, unseen. She resists the urge to join them, ducking instead into the lounge to find the trainer.

"You've been avoiding me," Imani says, her Southern accent thick.

Sabine slides onto the massage table. "The shoulder feels fine, for the most part," she says, hesitant in her lie. "I feel fine."

Imani laughs, nudging Sabine over with her arm. "You're just like everyone else here, ignoring anything that might keep you off court." She leans down and whispers, "Except for Milner—that guy is never *really* hurt." She winks and keeps on laughing, and it is an infectious sound, one Sabine cannot fight.

"You are good at this," she says.

"You're great at your job, I'm great at mine."

Sabine winces as she works from neck to shoulder.

"Deep breaths," Imani says, and it reminds Sabine of being young, the strains in her body new, foreign, and how quickly they became a part of her.

"Where are you from?" Sabine asks, a distraction more than anything.

"Tennessee. Chattanooga born and raised." She presses harder into Sabine's back, using her other hand to brace, to keep her from shifting away. "How 'bout you?"

Sabine turns her head, grimaces. "I think you know."

"Tell me anyway." Her tone, more maternal than medicinal, puts Sabine at ease.

"I grew up in Bonn," she says, "in Germany. We moved to the States when I was a teenager, to Florida."

The way she says it makes Imani chuckle, and she slides her fingers up Sabine's spine, nerves ignited along the way. "Not a fan, I take it?"

"Florida has its moments," she says and pauses, letting the physical discomfort pass. "My father still lives there, our home is there, so I cannot abandon it completely. Training there is not so bad, I guess. It has a beautiful sun."

"Do you miss home?" She moves down to Sabine's lower body, and Sabine releases a breath she had been keeping inside.

"Sometimes. Not as often as you might think."

"It's good you're so damn awesome out there," she says, and gently slaps Sabine's leg, letting her know she is finished.

"I feel like a new woman," she says, trading her kindness for a smile, something wide and full and real.

"Same time tomorrow," Imani says, and her accent sings to Sabine like a lullaby.

Sabine wanders the complex after, sticking to the private, players-only areas. She is happy to be back here, finally, where she belongs. She finds a perch on the northern side overlooking the practice courts and high enough, too, to see the baseball stadium beyond. Out on the pond, crowds brim. The water shimmers, like a cavern of crystals unearthed. A few children jump in and splash around, breaking the rules though no one seems to mind. Beyond the pond, the stadium shines. She has come to love it over the years—its sisterhood with the Open, partners in something truly unique, bound by the battles raged within. But more than anything, it is Sandy's stadium. He could be there right now, she knows he will be. She feels the shape of missing him, the way it hollows her.

Messages come through on her phone without her realizing, mostly Alina agreeing about the interviews. The last is not a message at all, rather a missed call. The name, its bold white letters across her phone, catches her from somewhere buried in her lungs. Her father has never, not once, called her during a tournament. She wonders if he is dying and immediately hates that it is her first thought. Even then, she is sure he would rather risk not telling her than interrupt a major. The tennis court is no place for sentiment, he always preached. It is one of the things they fought about constantly, Sabine begging him to see it from her side, hoping to chisel away at even a piece of his stoniness, get him to see the paradox for which he was asking—to be great, you must love the game like nothing else, it must be your passion, your reason and your life—and for Sabine there was no ability to suppress, no vessel within which to cork these emotions. They are on her sleeve and her face and her racket and her body. They make her the player she is, the one she has always wanted to be. But not, she still struggles to accept, the one her father had hoped for.

She puts her finger to his name, as if she will feel the bristle of his rough beard, which has long since turned silver, and the screen lights up, the ring of the call being sent, and the way it goes on and on without answer sounds to Sabine like the horn of a ship, distant at first but louder and louder, shaking the very air as it approaches shore. She will not try again; she can only wait, hope he will surprise her once more.

*

When she arrives back at her hotel, she turns off her phone. A sense of calm washes over her as she watches the screen fade to black, and she leaves it on the dresser. So much clambering to get in. How else to keep it out.

In the quiet that follows, she is transported. She is a child again, waiting for her father on the practice court. Her first junior tournament. Rifling through her tennis bag, she discovers a note, tucked into the side pocket. Her mother, Petra, likely meant for her to find it after her match, not before, but Sabine cannot wait. She tears open the envelope, runs her finger over the hand-drawn letters, their intricate curves. She reads through her tears, though she does not understand why she is crying.

> *If there is one thing I impart to you, my darling, one thing to carry through life, it is this: see everything. Your father and I have agreed on little over the years—it is why we love each other so fully—but we agree on this. There is much for you to see, each city and every continent a new adventure to explore. And oh the people you will meet! The majesty of the world around you. Everything so special. Like you, a treasure. You are something mighty, unique and irreplaceable. You will be great. It begins today. But only if you are looking, my sweet Sabine. Only if you are seeing.*

Sabine remembers most clearly this lebensfreude, which her mother hoped desperately to pass on to her daughter, to everyone she met. She was a brilliant woman, educated and beautiful, her days as a model given way to university and marriage and, eventually, motherhood. And though Sabine knows facts, has heard stories of her mother's life before her, she thinks of her now only as she knew her, as her mother. And this letter, one she revisits every so often, a reminder of what is often invisible or unknown to a child, to anyone—the depths to which they are loved.

Roger's whine brings her back to the present, and she straps on his harness and leads him for a walk. In the elevator, a white man, around Sabine's age and handsome in a way she finds boring and predictable, stares at her, and when she looks back at him, hoping he will disengage, his gaze remains. He smiles, presumptuous, and for a moment Sabine thinks about leveling him, the satisfaction that would come from sinking her fist into his oily smarm. She tugs on Roger's leash and he growls. They have practiced this, and Sabine is grateful he is here, perhaps only to save her from herself.

In the lobby, she slows and lets the man go ahead of her; he does not give her another glance. Scared little men, she thinks.

Out of the corner of her eye, Sabine catches something on the television above the bar. Sports highlights, and thankfully not of her; no, it is baseball—she recognizes the skyline, the careful brick and bright greens of New Ebbets Field. And suddenly, there he is. A home run beyond the sea. That round helmet and blue pinstripe uniform. It has been too long since she has seen him in person. His sweet face.

"I miss you," she says to no one, to the television on the wall, to the space across this giant city, "my dear Sandy."

At her feet, Roger, having grown impatient, makes a sound like a grin, a kind of giggle-howl calling out to Sabine, reminding her of his presence, her little manatee desperate for adventure. "Okay, okay," she tells him, and he pulls her to the door. The evening swirls in her mind. The city envelops her. Tomorrow, the world will be watching.

NIGHTSWINGING

The stadium is a silhouette etched out of the night sky. Beyond it, on the other side of the pond, the brightness of Althea Williams Arena is enough to light up the borough. Sandy saw the late match on the scoreboard coming in—top-ranked Dragovic versus Quincy, an American journeyman—and, by instinct, he wonders about Sabine. When she'll play again; if she got his message; and, though it may be too much to hope, if he'll see her. Even in passing, simply time enough to wave, to share a smile, to let her see how he has missed her.

In the humming artificial glow of the virtual batting cages below the field, Sandy pretends it's not the middle of the night. An electrical storm rushes from his brain to his arms, hips, legs, and back again. He's a conduit; he sends pitch after pitch into the outfield, beyond the short porch in right—redesigned specifically, some say, with Sandy in mind—and opposite field over the taller wall in left, called The Sea both for its expanse and ultramarine façade. If he's sweating or tiring, he doesn't notice. He feels the vibrations in his hands, his fingertips, a mix of euphoria and pain; he swings, again and again he swings, chopping away at something invisible, intangible maybe, but real.

How long will it take for word to reach the press, he wonders. Even with the team's efforts to keep it quiet, a Jewish child murdered and left at his doorstep might be too much to resist. He takes another cut, a line drive sneaking over the center field wall and landing in Player Park, a line of plaques and busts honoring former Atlantics, including the owner's wife, who perished, like Sandy's father, when the Roebling burned.

The next three pitches elude him—slider, curveball, split-finger—and he holds up his hand, stopping the next, and sucks in the circulated air. It's enough to make him sick. His mouth fills with spit. He closes his eyes, tries to steady his breathing. His head feels light enough to break away and drift out of the stadium. He fouls off the next pitch, then another and another until he drives the bat head down into the turf, which leaves an imprint but only for a moment, reshaped back to normal like nothing happened. The pitches come and he doesn't stop them, their velocity leaving a phantom trail in the cage. He watches them pass—strike one, two, three—and in his mind the tally begins: the pitches missed, never challenged, out after out, an inning and a game and a lifetime. At least with a swing there's an attempt at greatness. A want. Bat on shoulder, though, is defeat, hoping for something without controlling it.

L'chaim.

He steps into the batter's box, his body's small sways, bat setting the rhythm, and when the next pitch comes—ninety-five miles per hour, grazing the inside corner—Sandy turns on it; he hears the crowd leap to their feet in unison like waves crashing against a jetty, and the ball lifts and curls and, beyond even the digitized horizon, disappears.

In moments like these, real or otherwise constructed, Sandy wonders how anyone can do, can be, anything else.

Manhattan lights guide the train ride home, the river a dark and glassy reflection of the bridges and buildings above. Sandy finds himself wishing, maybe not for more, but wishing nonetheless. Apologies, reconciliations, goodbyes—things left unsaid. The Roebling comes into view, and the memory of what its destruction wrought becomes impossible to ignore. He hears his father's words, something from childhood that feels now to stretch the very length of his life: *The world is a narrow bridge, and the essential thing is not to fear at all.*

He remembers obsessing over a video of the attack, one released later as part of a trailer for an upcoming documentary. Sandy spent days watching it, focused on one moment in particular when his father, the expression on his face, was clearly visible. A second explosion, everyone rushing to escape the damage, and a drone flying along the Brooklyn shoreline zoomed in, changed its focus, and in the midst of the chaos there was Lenny Katzmann. For the briefest moment he looked out at the river, out into the distance—wishing maybe to be there, on another bridge or in another borough or another life—but just as quickly he turned around and tried to help, organize the havoc, calm the uncalmable. His hands and arms outstretched to a woman carrying her two sons, offering up his own body to lessen her load, when the third bomb detonated. The screen filled with black smoke and heat-induced static. The bridge burned, and he knew his father did, too. Sandy was lost. He couldn't shake from his mind that look, his father's long stare out into nothing. How badly he wanted to ask what he saw.

In the empty subway car, the solitude and memory overwhelm Sandy. As if a dam has been opened he's crying, fast and short of breath, and like the certainty of his swings he leans into this, lets himself lose control. Through fogged eyes, beyond the bridge and towers of Lower Manhattan, he steals a glance of Lady Liberty, her unwavering presence, her bright flag lit from below, thumping in the night like the city's heartbeat.

Whatever pours out of him now, Sandy feels lightened by its escape. When they are underground, these haunted tunnels hold at bay the weight of the secrets above them. People board the train but Sandy takes no notice, and he doesn't stop. Through the blackness between stations he sees himself in the windows, his eyes and his face red, though the reflection, for the first time in a long time, looks to him like something true. He takes comfort in this, in the possibility that one day—not now, and maybe not soon—he might see the man he wants to be staring back. A Brooklyn boy. A shining symbol. His father's son, his mother's. Proof that although so much of this city, this country, has been broken, it can be mended. Proof that what you are and who you want to be can't die on a bridge or a plane or a battlefield, can't be reduced or scorched or drowned. There are swings to be taken. There is hope enough yet still.

WE ARE WORLD DAY

The day does not begin like any other. The air electric, the city vibes, each of us and our energy a part of its central nervous system. We know today is different. It's ethereal perhaps, but impossible to ignore: everything today is meant to be extraordinary.

The subway carries us to the tennis center early in the morning; the first crowds arrive by nine, and though the lines to get inside are long and slow, we're excited for all that's to come. At the gates, the majesty of this city encircles us—Brooklyn and its shimmering towers, its canals dark and hopeful, and beyond the depths of the East River the mightiness of Manhattan, its tenacity and its grandeur, begging us to wonder how we could ever be worthy of such a place—and we snap our pictures and videos, sending the images off into the interstices between our thoughts, where the virtual world hums.

We fight for position around the practice courts, the high chain-link fence providing small diamond porthole views of the players. We each have our favorite—American queen Lolo Samuels, volatile sex symbol Stanislas Gutzwiller, fallen champion Sabine Hellewege, clown prince of tennis Veljko Dragovic, elder statesman Florian Frei—and though we want to see them rip into forehands and pull their perfect backhands crosscourt and, with their hands out in front to guide their bodies, line up a perfect overhead, we call out their names anyway. We distract them as they distract us, as they peel away our fears and our preoccupations; we lose ourselves in them, in these stars, in the care they take with every swing, every purposeful step across the bright green court.

To our delight, three-time Open winner Juan Álvaro Moyà goes through his series of obsessive ticks as he awaits serves from his hitting partner. When he completes his routine and the serve drops in, he rears back that strong left-handed forehand and tears his return up the line. His body, we can see even from this distance, sculpted with strength. We cheer and he turns to us and his smile is garish and golden.

We watch Florian Frei—passing around rumors of retirement, of tabloid marriage troubles, of his wife's frustrations with his declining performance—transfixed by his glorious backhand. *Like an angel's swing*, someone says. *This is his last Open*, says another, and we recognize it as an old refrain. *He'll be forty-five before he retires*, and we choose to believe that, because we can't imagine this tournament, this sport, without him.

Across the net from Frei, returning those perfect slicing backhands with quick volleys, stands Sabine Hellewege. The Happy Champion, as she was nicknamed early in her career. She's tall and muscular, a superhero amongst mortals. She and Frei speak in German to one another, and we pretend to know what they might be saying. She barely survived her first-round match, but we would scarcely believe it watching her practice. She floats around the court, laughing but chiding herself for missed shots, and Frei plays along, commenting impishly. He has been a mentor for her in many ways, taking her under his wing when she first broke out on tour, and for those of us watching closely enough, it's clear all these years later what good friends these two champions are.

Eventually we disperse, choosing to find our seats in Althea Williams Arena or one of the other small courts spread around the grounds. We secretly hope the match we choose is *the* match of the day, the one everyone will be buzzing about. Though the City Open has always been a widely-televised and celebrated event, this year it's heightened, and we feel it, like the rush before a dive or a fall, the brief moment when we're no longer of this earth. There are cameras everywhere, lines of them in the plaza and people walking around with phones and even a helicopter making slow passes over the complex. Every movement tracked, filmed, recorded. The first matches about to begin, and we are, all of us, watching.

We are World Day.

*

Across the pond, where the cheers of tennis fans can still be heard, we storm through the open gates of New Ebbets Field. The trains to Brooklyn seemed capable of hemorrhage but we braved the discomfort, and now, climbing the stairs and riding the escalators up to our seats—boxes and suites and field level and mezzanine and upper deck—it feels like Opening Day. The season will be over before we know it, but for now, for today, everything is brand new.

The Atlantics come onto the field early to meet the crowds, and we fill the stadium with our applause. Nick Mattingly is the first to greet fans, posing for pictures and signing autographs, and we tell him with each shutter click and pen scribble that he's the heart of the team, the one that will carry us to a title. He's humble to a fault and shrugs off the compliments. *We're a team*, he says, *and all twenty-five of us'll get us there*. He trots back out to the field, where he meets shortstop Sandy Katzmann, and the two share a laugh before jogging through the wide outfield. We talk about last night's game, about deJong's lights-out performance and Katzmann's clutch hitting, and though we're *sure* this is the Atlantics' year, we remain skeptical of the universe, that it could possibly bring us so large a gift.

The loudspeakers around the stadium crackle, and we stop what we're doing, giving the anticipation our undivided attention.

"Ladies and Gentlemen," the PA announcer's voice booms, "on behalf of the Brooklyn Atlantics...Welcome to World Day!"

A massive screen emerges behind center field, and on it we watch scenes from around the globe, sporting events sharing in this international display of peace and unity. On the field the Atlantics and the Seals stand along the first and third base lines, respectively, each woman and man a statuesque representation of what this day is all about. Tears well up in our eyes. We hear music in the distance, a kind of symphonic swell. The players clap and Nick Mattingly bends down and lifts a flag high into the air, its stripes swaying in the breeze. There's a swell in the crowd; we're overcome and we cannot be otherwise. The fireworks that follow boom, they shake our seats, and we feel them on our skin.

The ceremonial first pitch is an emotional one—a first responder from the Roebling Bridge disaster, balancing his weight between a natural leg and a bionic one. He tosses a high strike to Mattingly, who trots out to the mound, shakes his hand, and the two pose for the cameras. We remain on our feet for the national anthem, both here and carried across the pond to the tennis center. When the Atlantics take the field, spreading out from the dugout each to their position, their uniforms are an opaque white against the grass. Second baseman Oswald Jones does a flip at the edge of the infield dirt, and we cheer for more. More of everything, we mean, more of this entertainment, this celebration. In the bottom of the first inning, Sandy Katzmann pulls a long home run down the line and over the short deck in right field. It splashes into the pond, and throughout the complex we hear a massive roar, like tens of thousands of us here join our voices together. Katzmann runs the bases quickly but looks up, points at us, and we choose to believe he's giving us the credit, he's thanking us: *None of this is possible without you.*

In the afternoon, when the sun is at its apex and the day is warm and impossibly vivid, the festivities pause. The Atlantics lead by three runs, and Florian Frei is set to start his match in Althea Williams Arena. A moment of reflection, one we take in unison. This is World Day, after all, and even though we can see the shattered skeleton of the Roebling from here, still look to the sky when we hear the engine boom of a jet overhead, stand by as citizens of this country are deported and others simply denied entry; even though we hear reports of riots in Turkey, car bombings in France, war crimes from Russia, we choose to believe something better begins today. We've never been one entity, one cause, but today we must be. We must set aside our differences and come together. We must be greater than what we've been given. We must not be hate. If we can be one voice, we must be, and they will hear us now.

Baseball begins again. Our spirits raised, we float along the rhythm of the games. The ping of tennis ball against racket echoes through the courts. We jump to our feet as the Seals try a double steal—sending a runner home and to second base—but Mattingly doesn't see it and he throws wildly, pulling Katzmann off the bag and into the air. The runner's legs catch him and he tumbles over, their bodies tangled in the infield. We scream for the runner to be thrown out, for Katzmann to get up. One run scores. Katzmann remains down, writhing, and Mattingly keeps his hands on his head as the trainers go to the shortstop and, once he gets to his feet, walk him off the field. Katzmann and Mattingly share a few words, a pat on the shoulder, before Katzmann disappears through the long tunnel beyond the dugout.

The inning continues, and at its end, as we hear the call of the chair umpire in Althea Williams Arena in the background, a new American flag is raised beyond the scoreboard. It waves in the afternoon, its colors thick and vibrant against the sky. We watch it move. We're sure it's alive.

Something happens then, like nothing that can be explained. No warning. It's not a sound but we feel it in the backs of our eyes, in our spines, in the tips of our fingers and toes. Some of us move our mouths, we try to speak, but we hear nothing. The lights suddenly all around us, the absence of sound, are everything. There are many; they are fast and blinding. We do not move. The concrete and earth beneath us give way. We are reduced. And when there is nothing left of our bodies, we become the air on this beautiful day. The very substance of World Day. We are together in this.

II

SPRINGTIME IN PALM BEACH

In this darkness, the emptiness here, Sandy hears words from his past, spoken long ago—the beginning of a mixed bag of advice from a grizzled veteran—but not lost.

You never forget your first spring.

Sandy was barely twenty-one when he arrived in Florida, and he couldn't know then that soon everything would be different, that he would move quickly up the ranks of the Atlantics' farm system, that even by the following spring he would be on the cusp of the majors. Yet, he sensed the largeness of the moment, knew the coaches were watching his every move; he was desperate to impress them, to win over the Palm Beach crowd, to convince everyone that he, little Sandy Katzmann, was the future of the Brooklyn Atlantics. It was his first spring, and as Coach Hussey later recounted, he was full of piss and fire.

Sandy ran onto the field for this opening game, the perfectly manicured Bermuda grass crunching underfoot, shuffled over the third base line, and when he reached second base he jumped onto it with both feet, a wispy cloud of infield dirt kicking into the air.

"Welcome to the show," the second baseman said—Oswald "Oz"

Jones, whose All-Star career was easy for Sandy to admire. They'd never spoken before and, for Sandy, this was a dream come true; he spent years in little league and through high school imagining himself Oz's double-play partner. He had an Oswald Jones rookie card in his locker, hoping to get it signed, but now, standing next to the legend, Sandy knew he could never ask such a thing.

Sandy was tested early, his nerves barely able to keep up. In the first inning, a hot-shot back up the middle—Sandy went hard to his left, which he preferred to ranging to his right, but the ball ticked off his glove and into center field. Two batters later, a line drive just over his outstretched arm. He watched the coaches in the dugout shake their heads, the scouts in the stands scribbling in their notebooks. To complete his trifecta of failure, on the next play Sandy scooped up a grounder but double-clutched, and the runner beat his throw. One run in, on his shoulders. Eventually, mercifully, the inning ended, and as they jogged off the field, Oz sidled up beside him, slapped him on the arm and said, "Don't forget to have fun, baby."

Sandy didn't get pulled right then and there, as he expected to be, and so when his spot in the lineup came, he was still sitting on the bench. Coach Hussey stood in front of him, mouth full of gum, his thick arms triangles at his side. "Well?" he said. Sandy's eyes were wide, like he'd just been dropped into an ice bath. He grabbed a helmet and bat and ran out into the batter's box. The pitches, the swings and misses, were swift and painless. The crowd was subdued, but as he slinked back to the dugout, Sandy looked up, he caught those sun-kissed faces, and somehow, despite all the embarrassment of only one full inning, he felt full, and alive, and, for maybe the first time in his life, exactly where he was supposed to be.

He didn't last three innings. Sandy Katzmann—the number six prospect in baseball—seemed incapable of fielding a ground ball, something he had been doing for as long as he could walk, or connecting his bat to that motherfucking ball. It was a furious kind of sorcery.

He sulked in the dugout, gnawing on sunflower seeds, sucking at their salted shells. During the seventh inning stretch, Oz roused him, and Sandy followed him atop the dugout, where they led the crowd in *Take Me Out to the Ballgame*. It was the best Sandy felt in hours. A few rows away, a young woman caught his attention, her singing and enthusiastic clapping both dangerously out of rhythm. Her smile like a firestarter. He recognized her, though from where he couldn't place. After the game, before retreating into the clubhouse with the rest of the team, Sandy called out to her as she stood to leave.

"Do I know you?" he said. He felt stupid, adolescent, but curious.

She laughed, as did her friend beside her.

"You look so familiar."

"Is that a line," she said, her voice and accent a kind of sing-song. Her friend leaned over, whispered something in her ear. Her face shifted slightly with surprise, eyebrows curling upwards, and when she looked back at Sandy, it struck him.

"The Olympics, right?"

"Warmer," she said.

"Basketball? No," he shook his head, "tennis."

"You're a damn magician," her friend said, her sarcasm playful.

Her friend was American, that much he knew—he'd watched her win silver last summer. "Lolo Samuels!" He pointed at her without meaning to, but the exaggeration of the act made her, all of them, laugh.

"One for two."

He thought of it then, and he was embarrassed it hadn't come sooner. "Sabine, right?" He worried he'd pronounced it wrong, but it was too late now.

"Sabby."

"Sandy."

"We know," Lolo said, pointing at the scoreboard.

"Yeah," he said. He felt too earnest, meeting new people in this new place. He couldn't figure out how to simply act normal.

"Lolo wanted to show me baseball," Sabine said. "She thought I would like it."

"And?"

"Not bad," she said. "A little slow, but fun."

"Good," he said, smiling from the corner of his mouth. "You all training nearby, or?"

"I live pretty close," she said.

"This is your first time here?"

"My father does not like baseball. It bores him."

"Lame," Sandy said, trying not to try so hard. "Well I'm glad you came out!" He looked to Lolo. "You a fan?"

"Go Highlanders," she said, a sneaky grin widening.

"Damn," he said, "right in my face and everything."

"Can't mess around," Lolo said, and he tipped his cap to her.

From the dugout tunnel, Coleman, the team's center fielder, popped out his head. "Christ son," he said, "you ain't wasting no time!" Sandy felt his face redden, but when he looked up, they barely noticed. "Coach's on the hunt," Coleman said before disappearing back the way he came.

"I gotta run," he said, his attention back on Sabine and Lolo. "But if you ever want to hang. I don't know anyone besides these guys. Anyway, I'm easy to find. I'm always here."

He waited for them to go. It was nice, he thought. He was always around men, professionally or romantically or otherwise, and it was hard to meet new people. His life was baseball, and although he wouldn't admit it to anyone, he liked that it was all-consuming. Every now and then, though, he needed something else. *Other people can be a comfort*, his mother reminded him more than once growing up, in moments when he chose to shut himself away. He was on his own now, and he began to understand. He didn't know why, but he felt a connection to Sabine. Like without effort they could be close. He wondered if anything important could be so easy. He hoped anyway. He hoped he would see her again.

Instead of sleep, Sandy spent the night marinating on each botched play, each disconnected swing. How did something so natural, so familiar, suddenly abandon him? He felt sick. He vacillated between thoughts of running away, hiding from his coach and his team and this sport, or going to the field at dawn, throwing the ball against an empty wall like he did so many mornings back in Brooklyn, trying to remember how beautiful and simple this game could be. It had been, hadn't it, once upon a time? So fucking simple.

Early he went, the stadium quiet in the already humid morning, the infield grass still slippery. It was a small place, nothing like New Ebbets but with a charm nonetheless. So many careers born here, and Sandy wanted desperately to join that list. All that pressure and nonsense needed to fade away, though. He just wanted to play ball.

To his surprise, as he walked out onto the field, dragging the pitch machine behind him, he realized he wasn't alone. A young man in the outfield, whipping a ball against the wall, the sound of which was like a gunshot hanging in the air. He turned, his face brilliant, as if he'd been waiting for Sandy. He was lean, his blond hair newly cut. He kept on throwing the ball, each smack now a clap, calling Sandy forward. The sight of Nick, even at a distance, caught Sandy's breath, and he sucked in until his lungs were full and he was floating.

"Kitty!" Nick shouted as Sandy crossed center field, not in full sprint but something close, and when he reached him Sandy threw his arms around him. He could feel their muscles, the strength shared between them fused together.

"You're here," Sandy said, almost a question. He knew he would be, after the team's split squad game yesterday, but forgot in the excitement of the day.

"No," Nick said, his palm patting Sandy's cheek, "*you're* here. Finally. Welcome to the rest of your life."

How did he do that, Sandy wanted to shout. How was he always there. How did he know what to say, what Sandy needed to hear. Their whole lives. How.

"Fucking cheese, my god," Sandy said.

Nick laughed and gloved his last throw. "So what are we doing?"

Sandy tilted his head, shielded his eyes from the growing sun.

"Let's start with some wood," Nick said. He scampered through the outfield, and Sandy followed close. "Your swing looked like shit yesterday."

"I hate you!" Sandy shouted. He hated the calmness he felt now, the way his body bounced in the batter's box, the way the ball carried, cut after cut. When his shoulder dropped, Nick was there. When he opened his hips too soon, when he was impatient, too patient, Nick was there.

Though this wouldn't be their last spring together, Sandy would re-member it clearly. His first, their first together. And when it came to an end, they would go their separate ways—Sandy to Double-A, Nick with a promotion to the majors—and Sandy's jealousy would get the best of him. He couldn't know how soon it would happen for him, too. He felt ready and not at once. He needed to bulk up. Find his consistency. Mature. He'd heard it, he knew it was right. But he wanted to take the next step, leap there if necessary. *There are heroes*, his father used to say, Sandy stretched out in bed in his pajamas, body sore from a summer's day spent on the diamond, *and there are unforgettables*. That was everything he wanted. To be an unforgettable. To make his father proud, his mother. Nick. To return to Brooklyn, show them what he had become.

Together, they remained on the field practicing until the rest of the team arrived. By afternoon, the sun high above the Palm Beach stadium, it was nearly game time. Sandy would start again at shortstop. "Show 'em what you got, baby," Oz would tell him as they sprinted onto the field. And that was it, really; every time Sandy looked back, it was to that moment, those words. He would do it. He would show them, and they would never forget.

DER SONNENSCHEIN STAAT

The fire burned through the night, leaving only a pile of blackness at the center between them. Even Sabine's carefully chosen stick, tip carved to a point with her father's pocketknife, was eaten up. In the morning, she felt hot, as if the air around them had somehow absorbed the heat, a blanket of unceasing warmth. The weight made it hard to take a breath.

"Looks like you need a new magic staff to roast those marshmallows," her father said in English, poking the remains of the fire with his sneaker.

He was making an effort to speak less frequently in German, to make her—or himself—more comfortable with the language living around them. It did not matter, though, what he did to make it seem as if they belonged. Sabine was not thankful, not for being brought here, her world upended at the whim of her father, who assured her that her life, her burgeoning tennis career, could only flourish if they moved to Florida. She missed her mother, and Germany, and feeling completely at home somewhere. She wondered if this place could ever be that—home. She did not know the word could mean so many things, or, as would often be the case for her, nothing at all.

Sabine looked up at him from the tucked papoose of her sleeping bag.

It had been his idea to go camping, to take this *adventure*. She hoped her expression told him exactly how she felt about being out here.

"You are a clown," he said, hoping to coax a smile from his daughter.

"Like you, silly Jürgen," she said. It made her feel grown up, she decided, to call her father by his name. She felt already so much older than her years. Her father reminded her often how young she was, that children did not know everything. But she did know everything, of that she was sure.

He scooped up a few small dry branches and pages of the local newspaper and lit them. When Sabine complained about the heat, he told her in German to get out of bed and put her face in the stream. His first good idea since they arrived, she thought, and she popped up and sat on the soft ground beside the stream, sliding in up to her ankles and splashing the freshwater onto her cheeks. It was chilled and perfectly refreshing. When the fire was strong enough, her father took eggs from the cooler and cracked them into an old heavy pan. He hung it over the flames, and Sabine could hear the eggs sizzling. The sound made her even warmer, and she shifted onto her knees and leaned down and slowly let the cool water cover her face. She stayed there, holding her breath.

"Achten Sie auf das Monster!" her father shouted. He laughed a deep, jolly kind of laugh, and when Sabine's head shot up, water splashing over herself, his laughter cascaded. She wanted to throw a rock or splash him, but she was struck by how nice it was to see her father's teeth when he smiled, and hear that roar come from down inside his belly.

"King of clowns," Sabine said, enunciating her imperfect words.

Before Sabine's mother died, Jürgen was happy; Sabine remembered this clearly. He was a bold man. He loved Petra. She had her passions and he had his, but they were a team. A volatile mix of two personalities who somehow came together. Sabine longed for that again. Now, they lived in a house too big for two people, in a town called Wellington. Jürgen ate clementines like candy, and his skin browned in the Florida sun. Everything smelled like swamp, and the give of earth beneath her feet made her feel the whole place might be swallowed up, disappeared into whatever lied beneath. The tennis court in the backyard, though, was hers, theirs, and secretly she loved it. There was that, at least.

She slapped at her bare, pale arm, where a mosquito sat calmly feeding. Her father had covered her in bug spray but it did nothing to keep the tiny vampires away.

"We will be very happy here," her father said, as if making a wish. "It is not Bonn, I know. It is not Hamburg. But it is our home now."

Sabine sucked in the air. She spoke without a breath, perhaps too without thought. "It is where we live, Papa. It is not our home. They are not the same."

Though their conversations were brief and reserved, she hoped for some greater tenderness from her father, some compassion, but she offered so little herself, at least since her mother died, which felt like so long a time.

On the plane from Germany to Florida, Sabine had asked about her brother, Tobias. Before that, somehow, her father had never spoken of him. Sabine had only ever asked her mother, and she—normally an exaggerated storyteller—was reserved. But she gave Sabine a few pointed details: he was named after their grandfather, Jürgen's father; he was a large baby, even by Hellewege standards; he liked when she read to him and the sound of his father's laugh; he was a surprise, unplanned, a part of their life unexpectedly and, after he drowned on a trip to Lake Constance, gone just the same. Her father did not repeat any of this, though. He fought her at first, asked why she wanted to know, and after she persisted he emptied one of those tiny bottles of vodka into his plastic cup, drank it in two quick gulps and turned to her in the window seat, her round face silhouetted by clouds somewhere over the ocean, and said, "He looked just like you, your brother. Or you him, I suppose. You look just like him." With the exception of a few hidden away photographs, Sabine had never seen her brother's face. He was an apparition, one she was happy to reanimate, give shape to, if for no other reason than to have something of him to hold on to.

After breakfast, Sabine asked to take a walk. Though she meant alone, the idea brought a smile to her father's face, such that when he leapt up and asked where to, she could not bear to correct him. They hiked along the river, her father insisting on teaching Sabine the river's name, even though he could barely pronounce it himself: Locks-ah-hatch-eee. His accent emphasized all the wrong parts, but he kept saying it, slower then faster, trying to get her to follow suit, until the word was nothing but nonsense.

Along the ground, lizards scurried about. She remembered a story her cousin told her after a trip to Disney World about catching these little green things and holding them and letting them bite her earlobes, where they would hang like crazy earrings, their tiny tails swinging like a tick-tock. Seeing them all around her now, Sabine was afraid she might catch one underfoot, but they were faster than her steps, and it made her doubt her cousin's story, the possibility that such creatures could be snatched up so easily.

They watched birds gliding overhead and others standing like statues in the tall marsh. With the toe of her shoe, Sabine made a divot in the grass. A long thin earthworm crawled from the spot, its pink flesh slick and spasming, and Sabine kept watch on the small creature as it struggled to find its way back underground, back to where it belonged. The sight of it made Sabine's heart beat faster and faster, as if she were the one digging, the one desperate to return to the cool, earthen darkness.

Ahead of them, a sign read *NO SWIMMING*, its red letters melting in the heat. Waves lapped against the bank of the river, and around them a deep throating roar, maybe from a frog or alligator her father guessed, and it sounded to Sabine like a rooster's crow, waking this swampy fairyland from the dead. It was startling, foreign, but Sabine found comfort in it.

"You know what would really be wonderful?"

Sabine glared at her father as he pointed at a school of fish close to shore feasting on a dead crab.

"If we caught our lunch," he said.

She doubted her father had ever fished in his life. She remembered her grandfather talking about fishing during one of his many *back in Poland* storytellings, but her father was never a part of those. Her mother had been the adventurer, the explorer, preferring family vacations in Africa or India, riding an elephant or conversing with chimpanzees to her father's quaint cabins, his quiet family time. Sabine loved them both in different ways, but she admired her mother, wanted to be her, and she knew her father knew this, too. He knelt down beside the river, slid his hands into the water and registered surprise at its coolness, and asked her to join him. He was trying so hard.

"The water is gross," she said. "It is dark. There are no fish."

Sabine saw the glow in her father's face change, as if some part of him was slipping away from his body and into the river, lost amongst the mangroves. Before she could say another word, or think about the cruelness she kept aimed at him, his shirt was off and he was in the water. The splash was playful, and the water flying every direction caught against the sunlight of the day and made tiny rainbows along the riverbed. Sabine's eyes were kaleidoscopes, trying to take them all in at once.

For the first time in what felt like the longest stretch of her young life, Sabine did not think. She slipped off her shoes and ran to the edge and leapt, sinking into the murky depths. Nothing felt this good, not since her mother had gone, not since her father took her from her home and dropped her into the strangeness of this land. Florida. Even the name sounded like something to escape from. But she was not running away now; she was here and letting the river lap over her, her father's smile lighting them both. She buried her head underwater, and when she came back up she pretended she could see the whole world below.

"They are everywhere, Papa," she said, sucking in her cheeks and puckering out her lips and using her hands as fins.

They remained still, trying to catch a glimpse of the graceful movements beneath the surface. Sabine's eyes darted back and forth. She was already imagining the two of them huddled by the campfire, dinner bubbling in the pan. She could almost pretend her mother would be there, too.

Then, a crunching in the tall grass along the bank. Tiny insects bounced off the water like they were walking on glass. Sabine took it all in, the center of the menagerie.

From the corner of her eye, Sabine saw a gap in the marsh where something made a path. The still surface broke. The swish back and forth, small opal eyes peeking. The calm hurried rush. Her father reached out his hand and Sabine took it. He pulled her close, his arms around her meant as the surest protection, his hand gripped on her torso where, once she was old enough, Sabine would have the words of a German poet tattooed on her skin, words to acknowledge the loss she carried.

Jürgen saw its body then, the alienness of its skin, almost indistinguishable from the river. They were too far from shore. He was frozen; he said as an exhale, "Nicht bewegen." It would not hurt them; he had to believe this. It moved with purpose. There was nowhere to go. He felt Sabine shaking. Sabine felt her father shaking. In the water their bodies were heat and electricity and without meaning or wanting to, they were calling out. *We are here*, they were saying.

Sabine held her father tighter, and he said, "Close your eyes." She wanted to but she looked straight ahead. Ripples spreading out. What. Are. You. Its gliding a terrible music. Her nails lanced her father's arms. She did not think of her mother, nothing so wonderful. It was almost to them. When it arrived, she knew she would not see it. Below her waist, her body was hidden in the darkness. She could not escape the thought. What could happen down there.

It disappeared, under. She felt in his chest her father screaming, but he made no sound. The monster parted the water; everything was warm and pressure.

From above then, filling the sky, came an explosion, a kind of crying out from the horizon. The earth moved around them. The monster's tail twisted and turned underwater and slapped Sabine's leg. She felt its retreat, swimming fast then up to the surface and out onto land. It was back in the tall grass, taking shelter, before Sabine and her father could even look up.

But eventually they would, and they would see: the plane, the flames pouring from its body, the smoke and the breaking, wings and tail and nose falling in pieces to the swamp below, crashing, the waves of which reached Sabine and her father but only in the smallest ways, enough to know something had happened, something had joined them in the Loxahatchee. They could feel the heat even from here, could smell the dry marshes ablaze. They listened for things they dared not acknowledge. There were no human sounds in this place, save for the two of them, their fast breaths, pushing the waves away from their bodies. They stayed there in the river gripped to one another, until there was nothing left to be afraid of, until all the terrible things had burned away.

WE THE BURIED

Beneath the rubble, we dream. We remember, somewhere beyond waking.

Not all of us are buried. No, some are gone, disintegrated in an instant; some of us are alive but barely, pieces of our bodies vanished as if to another universe. But us lucky ones, we are the buried. We are alive, in ways that take on new meaning.

Alive.

We dream. We are dreamers now. We relive our pasts, our failures and successes, our victories and losses. Our simple quiet pleasures. Our gut-scooping sadnesses. The things we know and the things we don't. We create it, one way or another. Everything is real because we make it so, because we continue to breathe, don't we. We hear the voices of our memories, clear like the waters of a secret lake, and we feel their reach. We're grateful for what we have, for our bodies and our voices, long before we awaken. We the buried are asleep, but soon, and with violent clarity, we will stir, and we will shake, and we will rise.

III

ASH

All Sabine can think about now is answering the phone. Her father waiting on the other end of that endless ringing. The last thing she said to him silence.

The world in front of her is too harsh to see. The smell, the kindling, overwhelming. The quiet, the possibility she is dead, that the thin line of brightness she sees is the end.

And then, the light parts. A ringing in her head, a return to this plane of existence. The ash covering her body not dust or dirt but people. All that remains. She touches her side, her skin. She feels the raised letters. *You will go under if you don't fight back*. She is still here. Not in pieces or particles but as one. Whole. She wraps her arms around herself and opens her eyes to the sky, to the burning sun, and from the deepest parts of her, she screams.

—

They tear at Sandy, these faceless hands. He should move, lift himself up, but the pain in his head and the weight of this wall are too much. The hands have voices, and they reach for him. *We see you*, they say, which feels like the most unbelievable thing.

—

Around her, Sabine sees what is left. People hold her upright, strangers with arms wrapped around hers, and she thanks them even though she does not need their weight. She stands on her own while these stadiums cannot. With pieces of Althea Williams Arena crumbling, and in the distance New Ebbets, too, she sees all the way to Manhattan, to the horizon gleaming against the destruction. *Who would do this*, she wonders, and when a woman in front of her turns, gives a placating sort of sigh, Sabine realizes she has asked the question out loud. The ringing in her head subsides, replaced by the unmistakable cry of human suffering, of confusion, of voices united, demanding to know why.

There is little blood, Sabine notices right away. Whatever this is, it has vaporized, eaten away at people with precision. Those bleeding are trapped under rubble or hurt rescuing others; the rest of the wounded, along with those no longer seen, make up this ash blanketing the air. Sabine feels it with every breath. She is taking someone in. Her body now not only her own but housing the disparate particles of those gone. Their bodies, their minds, their hopes and their fears, lost in the afternoon, finding refuge inside the comfort of her lungs.

The very idea, the responsibility of it all, overwhelms Sabine. She scoops up a child and takes the hands of the girl's brother and their father, who says something to her though she cannot hear it. She leads them through a clearing of shattered concrete and out along the still shimmering pond. Her legs, redwoods of stability, wobble. She is unsteady. She lays the girl in the grass, and though around her the cries grow, she hears less and less. Her mind escaping from her body. She turns to go back in, to bring more people out, but at last her body refuses. She slides to her knees, hands down in the cool grass. Beside her, she sees a bird, twitching, dying slowly. Missing a wing. A thin trail of blood trickling from its beak. She should help it, end its misery, but she is not strong enough. She reaches down, runs her hand along the slick feathers. There is still a heartbeat. Each pulse breaking her. She lets herself crash to earth. She watches the bird, counting its breaths, matching them to her own. That sliver of blood, for which she is grateful, a reminder from this perfect creature of something familiar, something human.

—

"What are you doing?" Sandy asks. They don't answer but keep carrying him. His body weightless, helpless, in their arms. He repeats his question, and one of the women looks down at him and says, "Stop fidgeting. We're almost there."

Sandy recognizes her, first her voice then her face—his teammate, Danielle Garcia. He stretches his fingers to touch her elbow. He says her name, once then twice. He wants to thank her.

"Basta," she says firmly, her grip on him tightening. "You're not making any sense."

He wonders what she means. When they stop moving, Sandy's in the middle of the field, which feels like make believe. His eyes dart, the sun overhead like a torch struck in the dark, and he tries to sit up.

"No!" Garcia yells and points at him. "Your head's bleeding, Kat. Don't move."

And then she's gone, running back towards the rubble. He hears footsteps, the crunching of grass underfoot like bone. As he drifts in and out, others appear around him, some laying or sitting or curled into themselves. Some are bleeding, missing pieces of their bodies. Others, like him, are mostly whole, save for the shock of what they're taking in. Sandy shifts forward, sits up slowly, his head sore and heavy. They're in the outfield, hundreds of them, maybe more. A section of the stadium has fallen. There are more bodies underneath. He thinks of the voices he heard. He feels again that terrible weight. He watches as people are pulled from the rubble; they join him in this elysian field, and when his head becomes more than he can hold up, he collapses back onto the ground of New Ebbets. Beside him there's a boy and his father, side by side and embracing, weeping together as if the world's ending. And Sandy, unable to comprehend anything beyond these two people, joins them, the lift of his cries released like starlings through the afternoon sky.

—

When she comes to, Sabine hears herself ask the question, over and over like a terrible song. *What happened?* She does not know where she is—a tent maybe, because the walls bounce in and out. She asks again, hoping to interrupt the chaos. She sits up, her head swirling, and looks around for her phone. She pats the empty pockets of her shorts. *Where is it*, she says out loud to no one. She wants to focus, ask questions. What happened. What is this. Where is she. Lolo. Alina. Where is everyone. Where is her phone. She says it loud enough to feel it this time.

A teenage boy sitting near Sabine pulls out his phone and hands it to her. "Here, Ms. Hellewege," he says, voice shaking. "You can keep it if you want."

She feels the boy's nervousness. Her own panic grows, a fear she has not experienced in years, not since she was a little girl gripping her father in the warm waters of the Everglades, a monster creeping towards them.

"Just one call," she says, curt, her eyes wide. She dials her father's number, the deepest kind of muscle memory. The subsequent rings ping against her eardrums, trace the pathways of her brain. She debates whether or not to leave a message, but when the time comes all she can say is, "Papa. I am okay. I am alive." She hears in her own voice how hard she tries not to break down. Not to scream. Not to tear at the thin sheets holding the room together.

She returns the phone to the boy and thanks him. Around them, everyone is quiet. She pushes her tongue against her lips, feels the deep scratch of her throat. Her eyes swollen with irritation and tears. She looks at their faces, and she understands. They are afraid.

———

On his own, Sandy stands and, finally upright, sees the scope of the damage. Through the back of the stadium ambulances pour in. Small fires run amok. Entire sections of the stands collapsed. Maybe half of New Ebbets remains. In the distance, the ruins of the tennis center are aflame. And around him, as far as he can see, bodies. Bodies and smoke and ash.

He tries to steady himself, and when a paramedic runs by, Sandy puts out his hands to stop her.

"Are you okay?" she yells, startled.

"Where's everyone?" he asks, trying to find the right words. "The team. Where are they?"

The paramedic turns, distracted by a shouting behind her, then back to Sandy. "I've seen Ms. Garcia. And now you."

"And?" He wants to let her know it's Nick he's worried for, but he eats it, chokes slightly on the withholding. He tries to step towards her, but his body tilts off-balance.

She braces him with both hands. "I don't know," she says. She helps Sandy to the ground. "I'm sorry I don't know. Stay here. Stay awake. You're gonna be okay."

—

Sabine gets up and leans on the bed. The swaying of the tent walls dizzies her. Though the medical staff begs otherwise, with her forehead gauzed and taped, her arms and legs cut and bloodied, bruises along her thighs forming like galaxies, Sabine shuffles out.

Around her are dozens of tents. She moves from one to another searching for anyone familiar, for someone to explain what has happened, any sense that this may still be the world she knows. Each looks the same, such that Sabine can no longer tell which ones she has already visited. But as she steps into the next tent, she is greeted by a sea of faces—fellow players, coaches, and teams—and at their center, laid out, eyes closed but wet, is Lolo. Gorgeous, wonderful Lolo. Sabine nudges people out of her way, the pressure against her muscles mounting but not stopping her. Though an air cast covers her leg, Lolo's tibia is visible, ripped clean through her skin, and the sight of it, its deep contrast, nearly knocks Sabine to the floor. She says her friend's name. The look in Lolo's eyes, the distance and the pain, are enough to wrench her insides.

"My girl," Sabine says, and, as if this was all the permission she needed, Lolo grabs her hand, takes it in her own; she releases a sound, a kind of wailing Sabine has never heard before, something like the end of everything.

As she runs her bandaged fingers over Lolo's, Sabine feels without seeing that Lolo has lost her pinky. Clean, and disappeared, the empty place where it should be chalky and vacant.

"My Sabby," she says, her voice grizzled and rough.

"We are a mess," Sabine says.

"Still sexy as hell though," Lolo says, fighting through her tears. And as it turns to laughter, which comes simply because they need it to, Sabine sees in her friend what they both leave unsaid. Who is left. Who is not. We are a mess because we are here.

Their hands, their fingers, remain interlocked.

"Have you been out there?"

Sabine tightens her grip. She tries to stand up straight. It is something her father taught her, or maybe her mother, she cannot remember, to always deliver bad news standing tall. She can almost feel her mother's hand on the small of her back, pushing, making her grow.

"None of it makes sense," she says.

"It's gotta be okay. It does."

Sabine brings Lolo's hand to her lips, kisses it. She lets her, lets them both, believe it is true—everything will be okay—and though she knows Lolo is tired and full of painkillers, Sabine takes solace in her optimism. It keeps her from collapsing, from tearing at her heart, from screaming what must certainly be the truth, that all is lost.

—

At the edge of New Ebbets, Sandy waits. He's fogged, but the familiarity of this place—his stadium and his town—even crumbling as it is, anchors him. The shriek of sirens disconnects his thoughts. Nick. Sabine. Are they okay. Mama. Where is she. Alone. Dead. Find her. Safe. Strong. It's a sudden burden he feels, the realization they're all that's left of each other.

"What's happening?" Sandy, laid out on a stretcher, asks one of the medics, a small but wide man.

"We gotta move you," he says.

"I don't understand what's going on. The stadium, the people. What is—"

"We don't know, Mr. Katzmann. Bombs, something. Fucking pandemonium. We don't know. I just gotta move you."

"Where are you taking me?"

"Where do you wanna go?" the man asks, a smile in the corner of his mouth.

"The diner," Sandy says, and he hears the choppiness of his words, the fracture in his speech.

The man shuffles close to Sandy and says, "You're not dying, you know."

When the sun's nearly setting or Sandy's concussion makes it seem so, everything glows. He feels the breeze, the coolness of the IV in his vein, the pulsing behind his eyes. He's going to be okay, someone tells him. He stares ahead, or up, he can't tell which. A banner flies, singed at its edges, framed by this blood sky and flowing in the ashen air, its words fading. *World Day*, they read. The World Will Be Watching.

—

We're scattered amongst the remains of World Day. Spectators, players, journalists, first responders, passersby, residents. Tennis star beside school teacher, ballplayer arm-in-arm with mother of three. There are no hierarchies in rescue. Everyone's life is one worth saving.

We dig through broken concrete and warped metal until we find our cousins, our sisters, our neighbors, our heroes. Danielle Garcia, pulling her teammate to safety. Sabine Hellewege, dazed and bloodied, screaming. Juan Álvaro Moyà, unconscious, or so we tell ourselves. Oswald Jones, arm crushed and face seared but smiling, asking how *we* are. Lolo Samuels, bone spearing from her leg but somehow trying, on her own, to walk to safety. Florian Frei, eyes wide open, body missing below the waist.

We collapse in the green grass. We run, and we knock people out of our way. We don't look back, and we look back. We laugh together. We weep. We close our eyes. We see beyond the horizon. We stop. We spin. We feel the earth, the city, beneath our feet. We feel the ash, the people it used to be, how it becomes our skins.

GOLEM

In the car from the hospital to her hotel, her body bandaged and her shoulder pounding in time with her heartbeat, Sabine wonders how she will find Alina. But she is there in the lobby, on a call, her face wrinkled with worry. Sabine goes to her, and their embrace, in a room full of people hoping for their own reunions, could go on forever. They are both bursting. "Come," Alina says after. "Someone's waiting for you."

Into the evening, the three of them—Sabine, Alina, and Roger—lay curled in bed, comforter pulled to their necks, and it reminds Sabine of being young, sleepovers at friends' houses, and the coziness of her own bedroom in Bonn. The beautiful, necessary art of doing nothing. She feels the day finally shedding. She has never been so tired. She tries not to think about what she has seen. They still do not know what happened, not in any substantial way. *Light bombs*, the news says, but they wonder what that means. Fifty thousand already lost, and the number grows. The immensity of it all is too much. She hears the screams—her own and those around her—each time she closes her eyes. She remembers when she was shot, the dissonance first then an absence of sound so impossibly loud. But this is nothing like that. She feels invisible waves move through her, reading her, taking her apart, rearranging what she is made of and, in an instant, putting her back together.

Finally as they drift to sleep, Roger pressed between them, all Sabine hears is a question rattling in her mind: *Who is left now?*

Sabine dreams she is back on center court. Not in New York, instead some imaginary place, a grand slam cathedral, the stadium filled with friends and family. Her father, watching from her box. *Komm' jetzt*, he shouts. Her mother sitting courtside, demure in her celebrations. The cheers, the cries for victory, are ceaseless.

Across the net, Sabine's opponent takes shape. Its face remains in shadow, but it looms even from the baseline. Sabine readies, the muscles in her legs tightening, winding up, anxious for release. Her serve, her *weapon*, tears from her racket. The crowd hushes, breaths echo. Sabine pours everything into each shot, forehands inside out and down the line, backhand blasted crosscourt; they are her strongest groundstrokes in ages. And each, somehow, returns to her with equal force and precision. The electricity in her strokes could light the stadium. But on the other side of the net, the golem stands firm. Capable of absorbing everything Sabine has, everything she has worked so hard for. Taking that strength for itself, using it against her to fight, to break.

When she wakes, Sabine's body feels inflamed. Beside her, Roger snores. At the window, Alina stares out at the smoke trails still threading up and across the horizon. Sabine thinks it would be easy to stay right here, ignore everything outside this room. Her bones crack, hiss, as she gets out of bed. She is older than her years. She moves to Alina, this woman who has been like a sister, and slides her arms around her thin torso. "What do you see?" she asks, resting her chin on her shoulder.

Alina's eyes are wide, bloodshot. "I don't know," she says.

The throb in Sabine's shoulder becomes too much, and she lets go, sits on the edge of the bed. "We are alive, Al," she says.

Alina points across the river, her face cold and certain. "Look out there. They're saying sixty thousand now."

The number, its incomprehensible size and anonymity, drubs Sabine. She stands, kisses Alina on her forehead. When she is alone in the shower, she comes apart. Steam fills the room and for the briefest time becomes a cocoon. All she can do to feel human. Snuggle with Roger. Be strong with Alina. Shower. Cry. Feel the pain in her body. Like this is any other day.

*

But later, too soon, she is called to answer questions. What she has seen. She must speak, and she must listen. Learn who she has lost. Try to understand why she is still here, and they are not.

She takes a car to a building downtown. The office they sit her in is unbearably cold. Right away, Sabine asks, demands, and a bald man with a freckled scalp at the end of a long table, eyes glued to his tablet, says, "Are you sure."

"Tell me," she demands.

Drago.

Elena.

Alexei.

Jennifer.

Florian.

Each name slices at her flesh. Drago, her oldest friend, her first childhood boyfriend. Alexei, Elena. Jen. All so young. She thinks of hugging Jen at the end of their match, the belief she had everything ahead of her.

And Florian. *My god how does any of this exist without him.* He is what she hoped to be, the very embodiment of their sport.

She is grateful, and feels selfish for thinking so, not to hear Lolo's name.

"Shall I keep going?" the freckled man asks.

Her face, raw, pulses in time with her heartbeat. So fast. Out of control. "Who did this? Why?"

The freckled man sits calmly, his expression vacant. "We're working on it," he says, and Sabine wonders what the hell that means.

"What now?" she asks instead of beating her fists on the table between them.

"We have more questions, when you're ready." People shuffle in and out of the room, men in suits, information passed in whispers, everyone stoic but rushed, measured but limping under the responsibility.

"I will never be ready," she says, "but I am here. So go on."

He asks for details of—as he calls it—the *Event*, where she was and what she remembers. Sabine recounts what she can. She has more questions than answers, she tells the freckled man. "Don't we all," he says. It is meant to lighten the mood, put them on equal footing, but instead it sits as a statement of fact, a state of their collective being, their utter inability to make sense of what has happened.

"What were you doing," he asks, "when the Event occurred?"

She cracks her neck, as if to dislodge the immediate discomfort the question brings. She cannot remember, and she says so, only that she can see the people around her—trainer, Lolo's coach, a few fellow players—right before the flash. "Normal things," she says.

"Was your father with you?" The freckled man pushes up his glasses, which have slid down the bridge of his nose.

"My father?"

"Isn't he your coach?"

Sabine considers explaining, the intricacies of the player-coach-father-daughter relationship, but she keeps it simple. "No," she says. "He is in Florida."

"And…" the freckled man asks, pausing, "…your mother?"

Sabine shakes her head. "She passed away, years ago."

"Petra Hellewege." He looks at her quickly then back down to his tablet. "Yes?"

She nods, annoyed but trying her best to mask it. The freckled man writes something down.

When she is done, when she can—to use the freckled man's words—*piece together* no more, she leans back in her chair, folds her arms across her chest. "Why am I still here," she says.

"You're free to go," he responds, and though she shifts forward in her seat, grips her fingers to the table, Sabine does not tell him that is not what she meant.

"I was there," she says and stands. She steadies herself, fighting back what threatens to wash over her. "I was there and I do not understand anything. I have no answers. I was there and I want to know. I want things to make sense."

The freckled man walks her to the door and thanks her for coming in. He reassures her, or tries to, that they will solve this. That it does make sense. That he is sorry she was there.

In the years, decades, to come, Sabine will say—when asked about what happened, about all that followed, the changing of the country and world, about all that was lost—*I was there. I am still here.*

When she arrives at the hotel, her bags have already been packed. She is not sure how she will make it without Alina, without Lolo. She has not been back to Florida in months. She looks around the room, struck by its emptiness, almost as if they had never been there at all. She has taken so much comfort, she realizes, in these places, these invisible hideaways.

"You'll need this," Alina says, and hands her a new phone, nearly identical to her old one. "It's all set up, I think."

Sabine takes it and thanks her, hoping Alina does not hear how difficult it is to keep all this at bay.

Alina swipes Sabine's itinerary onto the screen. "I have you in first class," she says, "and I've already contacted the airline, informed them you won't be speaking to the press. Roger, too."

She has thought of everything, Sabine thinks. She marvels at Alina's focus, her ability to do what needs to be done. "Roger hates the press," Sabine says. She laughs, trips over the words, and it is enough to bring Alina with her. "What about you?"

"Going to my parents in Basel," she says. "They're freaking out."

"You should be with them."

"They asked about you. My mother cried; she's so glad you're okay."

"I wish I was going with you."

"Your father will be beside himself," Alina says.

"He does not even know I am coming," Sabine says, mimicking a smile.

Alina's phone pings and, in her distraction, she shrugs. "He'll know soon enough."

Sabine laughs, the certainty of the statement. She tells Alina she will pay her expenses home and—she leaves this open-ended—anything else she needs. Her fingers brush over Alina's cheek, where she feels the remnants of her crying, thin drought-dried rivers.

"I hate this," Alina says. "I hate that I'm glad. I'm glad it was them and not you." She stops, holds herself back. "Is that terrible?"

They are sisters, Sabine tells her, out loud as much for herself. She loves her and she is grateful, too. She is grateful they are both alive. That they have survived. She knows she will come undone later, on the plane when she is alone, but for now she bites the inside of her lip, lets the sting numb her.

They share a car to the airport, and although there is a quarantine around the tennis center, they can see the scope of the devastation. Embers still aglow. Brooklyn burning. Her eye catches on New Ebbets, its gaping wound, and she thinks immediately of Sandy. If she had not pushed him away, she knows, they would be closer now. She would know he is safe. She would see him. She watches until the stadium fades from view, and she hopes he is okay, that she will see him again, that the closeness they had for so long can somehow return.

Before the plane takes off bound for West Palm Beach, she calls her father. *I am coming home*, she says on the voicemail. She smiles, nervous, but her father will not see that. He will only hear her curtness, the purposeful shape of each word. Sabine looks down at Roger, rubs his head, the softness of his fur a comfort that has become necessary. "Almost there," she says.

She cannot comprehend the totality of it yet, what it means for her life and her sport and everything, the world beyond. Her phone vibrates—Alina saying goodbye once more—and before tucking the phone away, Sabine sends her a kiss. She messages Lolo, begs her to stay in touch. And as the plane's wheels leave the ground and she is no longer bound to this earth, her stomach pitching as if at the apex of a roller coaster, she messages Sandy, with the only words she can muster: *I hope. I hope, I hope, I hope.*

BRIGHTON

Once he wakes in the hospital, stir crazy and begging for answers, the first thing they tell Sandy is his teammate, his best friend, Nick Mattingly is dead.

Back in his apartment—the cut on his forehead clean and sutured but the rest of his head, the insides, still unmoored—Sandy tucks himself onto the couch. He turns on the television and flicks through the news. One station has a drone circling above the stadium grounds around the clock, as if the smoldering heaps will somehow reconstitute and become the people they were and rise up and walk home to their families. The death toll appears and disappears in the corner of the screen.

On SportsDesk, a montage of those already found, already lost. He's not ready but he can't bear to change the channel.

Hussey.

Alvarez.

Parker.

DeLucchi.

Mattingly.

Sandy wonders who's left of the Atlantics. He wants to scream their names, claw at his skin. His friends gone. His love, his game. Everything gone.

He received calls from his agent, the team, friends, family on both coasts. He made one call from his hospital bed, to his mother. They spoke with a sense of urgency, brought on by the immediate possibility that the conversation might never have happened. He cried, though if his mother did Sandy couldn't hear it. She wanted to come see him, but he steadied himself, made her promise to wait. He would be there soon. She agreed, finally, and before she hung up, she said, *You're a good boy, Sandy Beach.*

What Sandy didn't say, couldn't commit to words, was why he needed time. Why he needed to be alone. *Nicky is gone*, he practiced saying. Things they said about his father, words that still stung when repeated. He never imagined a life without Nick, and it's too soon, too sudden, to start now.

A message, its robotic chirp, interrupts the room. It's simple but enough to open him. He reads, and whatever restraint he held on to dissolves away. He mouths the words. *I hope*, he reads, over and over. And in response, his face wet and sore, he writes simply, *I'm here.*

In the car on the way to Brighton, Sandy's careful not to look east beyond the river. They pass beneath the Wallabout Bridge, and he watches the train cross overhead. He knows the view well, *his* view of Brooklyn. Today, they take the tunnel. Its cloistered suffocation feels fitting. Slight flicker of lights. Checkpoints on either end slow traffic, but Sandy doesn't mind, and he tells the driver as much, which he seems grateful for. He smiles at Sandy in the rearview as they are waved through.

"I think that cop wanted your autograph," he says.

Sandy smirks, all the human decency he can muster.

"Everyone thought you were dead," the driver says, his crooked grin caught by the mirror.

"I was," Sandy says. His hand rests on the crown of his head.

"You look good then," the driver says, his caustic laugh equal parts unsettling and ignorant enough to comfort.

On the other side of the tunnel, with the Brooklyn sky bright blue and unstirred, the car zips along the expressway with barely a sound. Sandy's eyes remain locked on the clouds and, though the source of the impulse eludes him, he says, "Mattingly is dead."

He finds something remarkable in sharing this with a complete stranger.

"Damn shame." This time, the driver keeps his stare locked on the road ahead. "Hussey, too, right?"

Sandy doesn't answer, not out of malice but of speechlessness. He's lost again.

"Damn shame," the driver says.

They're silent the rest of the way to Brighton. The thump of the car against road reminds Sandy of a ball bouncing through the infield, its speed and destination a product of careful hours spent practicing, swing after swing after swing. Or, as is so often the case, luck. He sees that trajectory as if he's still standing at shortstop, feet digging in, glove open and fingers flexed wide, toes dancing. The ball off the bat. Quick to his left. The feeling of security in the leather webbing. Maybe the only thing he can truly control. In his mind, it happens again and again, each time it's like he's there, he feels the sting of impact against his open palm.

The sharp tone of the driver's voice brings Sandy back to the present. "We're here," he says.

"Yeah we are," Sandy says. "Thank fucking god."

Esther stands in the doorway, and Sandy knows from the way her knuckles have gone white she's bracing against the frame, allowing it to hold her up and hold her back. When he's close enough she releases, and their embrace is strong and goes on, until the force of her arms around him is more than he can bear.

He steps inside, and he's a child again. Scared and uncertain and happy for the familiarity of this house, this woman. His father's absence towers. Esther adjusts the pillows on the couch, making space for Sandy, and when he sits, she takes the throw from the recliner and drapes it across his legs. It's his father's blanket, one of Sandy's favorite keepsakes. It still smells like him, too, that unmistakable mix of sweat and patchouli. His mother moves around him as if he's an unexploded bomb that she alone, with each careful touch, must diffuse.

In the kitchen, the percolator bubbles. It brings them back in time, to mornings around the breakfast table—his father reading the newspaper, ink smudging onto his long fingers, sharing the occasional story, his chance to show off his position as the Katzmann family keeper of knowledge, their sayer, the man who knew more about nothing than anyone. And yet, as they sit together in the living room without him, they find themselves desperate for more.

"So," Esther says, tired of the silence. "Tell me."

"I don't know," he says. "It all just happened. That stupid collision at second base." The choke in his voice, an involuntary response, stops him. Nick's name on the rough edge of his tongue. "I was down in the locker room. The doc was icing my head. And everything went dark." He sips his coffee, its simple singe the perfect distraction. "And then, they were pulling me out. It was Garcia, I think. It felt like the whole stadium came down on me."

Esther drinks her black coffee and listens. She saw him injured, saw Nick pat him on the shoulder before he left the field. The crowd on their feet, all for her little boy. She saw the flash, the light, before the feed went dead. And after, she waited. Hours before she heard anything. The first call came from a reporter. She hung up. A litany of calls followed from friends and relatives. Didn't they know she was waiting, too? By the time she heard her son's voice on the other end, she'd convinced herself he was gone. Days had passed, weeks, but only hours. And now, as he tells her what he can't remember, she knows she won't tell him any of this. She'll keep it to herself, as she has so many things before, and when she comforts him, when she calls him *Sandy Beach*, it's only this he'll know, the love of his mother. They're partners in this loss, inseparable, because they, for better or worse, are the ones who remain.

As night falls after dinner, Sandy grows tired. Being in this house, its proximity to both his parents, is enough to ease him. He tries to leave, but his mother demands he stay; she's worried, and he's a good son. She tells him this while making up his bed, an old twin not long enough to hold him now. She shouts to him, insistent, from upstairs, "Make some decaf."

He leans on the kitchen island and feels his father standing beside him. He's taking a trip to the West Coast, he says. Then Germany, and Greece. *You know how your mother worries.* As a child he thought his father was a secret agent, and when he brought Sandy books from foreign places, it only seemed more real. He never told kids at school about the books. His father's secret to keep. He hasn't thought of them in years, but as he pours his mother a cup of late-night decaf, the kitchen filling with the dark roast scent, he hears his father's confident voice so clearly. *You know how your mother worries.*

They sit on the deck as the night inks the sky. Esther reaches across the small table between them, takes his hand in her own. He feels the strength there.

"He knew," she says. "Nicky knew you loved him. And how much."

She squeezes, leaving him unable to hold back any longer. His release could drown even this grand city.

Later, as Sandy drifts asleep, Esther tiptoes into his bedroom, guided in the dark by muscle memory, and kisses her son goodnight. He won't sleep well, and so she stays up as long as she can, watching reruns of old shows and trying to remember when she first saw them. It's hard to recall a life before Lenny, before this family. She had been a girl, a student, a historian before she was a wife, a mother. Before she was alone. But not alone, not now, not yet. She still has him. The walls, they have bound this family. They hold everything up. And she still believes, despite all that has happened, all that will, that these walls can keep them safe. Her. Her memories. Her little Sandy Beach.

In the middle of the night, when he's sure his mother has fallen asleep, Sandy slides out of bed. Hidden in the back of his closet he finds a box of books. He tears at the cardboard, small cuts forming on the softs of his fingers. Near the bottom of the box he sees it, the tattered hardcover, gold letters embossed and still shining. He brings the book back to bed, turning each page as if he's reading, though he knows these stories by heart. The weight of the paper, the small hush of its movement, is enough. He can't see the tiny smears of blood he leaves on the corners of the pages. The book, its presence in his hands, will calm his mind. He will eventually sleep. But for now, he's content to be awake, to be breathing, tethered to these fairy tales in the dark.

WELCOME HOME

The perfection of Florida for Sabine lies in its ability to change and never change at once. The Everglades, while birthing new life, continue to recede, to vanish. The beaches, though beautiful beyond measure, erode. And Jürgen Hellewege, her dear father—he, too, is an enigma, a land mass stretching for every mile of her life, his terrain unpredictable and bound always by the confines of their shared madness.

He is not at the airport to receive her. She feels foolish for expecting otherwise. She hires a car, and soon they are driving west to a house and a man that have become strangers. As the Everglades come into view, Sabine thinks of the monster. She still feels the way it moved in the water around her, like a shadow given shape and weight. Its dinosaur skin imprinted on her own, along her hamstrings to the backs of her knees. A year passed before Sabine went back in the water. Her father—more focused on the plane's tumble to earth, its crash so close to them and the blaze that continued for hours—was nervous to fly after, making travel for tournaments difficult. Eventually, he preferred not to go at all. They fought about it constantly. How could he be her coach if he was not with her? She was strong enough, he argued, to get through matches without him there, without the crutch so many others relied on. She would be a better player for it, he demanded. She would make herself a champion. But what Sabine never grasped, not even these years later, was her father's unwillingness to recognize the reality of the experience, that the plane's destruction, its impact, had chased the creature away. The bodies lost to the swamp and the water and all the unseen monsters—they had, every precious body, saved them.

Even from the end of the long driveway, the house still looks too big to Sabine. The thick humidity hangs over her skin and shoulders like a shawl. The earth underfoot, pliant beneath a sharp layer of St. Augustine grass, feels most familiar. It cradles her.

She sees her father at the window. His gaze, its passivity, and the space between them, makes Sabine feel small, in a way even the largest arenas have not. She waves, as if her father is a television camera at the end of a match. He returns the gesture, letting the curtains fall back into place. She knows, hidden there for a fleeting moment, he is raw. Roger nudges at her legs, and she grabs her bags, walks toward the house; she knows by the time she enters and feels the artificial smack of air conditioning, the rise of gooseflesh along her arms and up her neck, he will have composed himself. He will be sitting on the family room couch reading the news, and her arrival will pull him only momentarily away; he will smile, polite and purposeful, and in German he will welcome his daughter home. His mood, his cadence, as measured as a perfect drop shot, artful and full of deceit.

She does not knock, though she considers it. Her father stands at the door. His shoulders as broad as ever but his body hunched, his eyes plump and red. His thick arms are around Sabine before she can drop her bags. She feels the depth of his breaths. She grips him back, and the longer they hold up one another, the clearer she hears her father's quiet words. *You're alive, my girl. You're alive.*

She sleeps through the afternoon, the last of the energy in her muscles giving way. Through the thin walls of the house she hears the cry of wilderness around her—the incessant whir of insect wings, the baritone yodel of alligators in the nearby marsh, and birds in constant conversation—and it serves as a kind of lullaby. She wakes in the early evening to a stillness in the room that unsettles her. She stretches her neck, pulled tight like fishing line. She turns on the television and, as the news flashes across the screen, immediately regrets it. Every station, it is incessant. Talking heads and destruction. Who is responsible. Why. Questions without answers, answers full of nonsense. The crawl shows the names of those already identified. The sheer volume turns her stomach. On the left, static in bold white letters, sits the current tally. Nearly a hundred thousand now. Sabine puts her finger to it, as if for a moment the reality of that loss can be transmitted through her touch. In the shower after she weeps until she is hollow.

During dinner, she stares across the table at her father. Jürgen has reset, his emotions in check. He cooked—schnitzel, a Hellewege family recipe—which she did not expect.

"You like?" He takes a bite but does not look up from his plate.

"Very good," she says, wanting to go on.

"Dein Lieblingsessen," he says, with no hint of question.

"Is it?" She watches him take slow careful bites, as if he is deconstructing a masterpiece. He must know it is not *her* favorite, but rather was her mother's. Maybe for a moment he has confused them, she thinks, these women he has lost.

"How long are you staying?"

She says, "A few days," though if she is being honest she is not sure. Her body, her nerves, will heal, but her sport, what it has suffered, she is not so certain. What will it look like for those still here.

"Good," he says, looking up at her.

She smiles at him. "Yes, good," she says, and as they return to their meal, Sabine is brought back in time. The empty chair filled, the banter between her mother and father like an orchestra, a mix of language only the three of them could understand. She is young but she is bright; she is not an audience to this symphony but a player—*the background is no place for you*, her mother told her after she lost her first tournament. *You belong up front, all eyes on you. You hold them.*

She knows she and Jürgen will not speak about what has happened. They will chew through their discomfort. Sabine remains at the table after she has finished. In the crevices between their silences, she listens for that music, the ghosts of what this family once was.

She eases into life back in Florida. Outside, it is light for too long, and the days pass almost unnoticed. She hears a constant tapping in the background, tiny explosions whose origin she cannot discern, and she wonders if she imagines them.

Her father goes about his life as if nothing has changed. He cooks for them. They share light conversation over meals, but he otherwise exists in his own normality. Twice a day, though, after breakfast and after dinner, he wraps her shoulder in ice.

One morning, Sabine finds a note on the kitchen table:

1. *Dropping your elbow on serve.*
2. *Rushing your backhand. Pushing.*
3. *Wait. Stop reaching. Feet.*

She drinks her coffee and a smoothie on the patio. She reads through the list. She takes her father's usual seat, with a perfect view of their court. He has kept it up; it is pristine, raked and smoothed. She remembers herself on this court over the years, and it sends a charge through her tired muscles. She races upstairs to change, pulls her hair in a tight ponytail. Roger joins her outside on the dewy grass as she stretches. The sun, the heat, are already upon her, their weight familiar. She sets up the ball machine, sweat lining her brow. The whine of the machine kicking on. She trots to the other side of the net, takes a few half-swings at the air. The thwack of release, the ball gunning towards her. She reaches back, a forehand nice and easy. Her shoulder hums. Another. Again. Within this constancy, she begins to well. She is here, on a tennis court still. She can swing. She feels the vibration in her fingers, her hands, up her arms and down her spine and through her legs. The motion. This racket, her body, these small yellow worlds. It overwhelms her. Consumes her. And she knows now her father's first words to her are true—what she has not known, not truly, since World Day, that she is alive.

Sabine ignores not only the news but the world outside this house. Messages and missed calls pile up. Lolo, Alina, the head of the Tennis Federation, the president of German tennis—a distant cousin of her mother—reporters, old acquaintances, and forgotten friends. Empty voicemails. Unknown numbers and vaguely familiar ones. Sabine rejects them all.

In the morning, she runs. She lets herself enjoy it. The strength and beauty of her own body. She keeps her headphones loud; the music takes over. She stays along the edge of the swamp, and in the marshy wetlands she sees life, turtles and fish, the slick black bodies of cormorants slicing through the surface. Overhead, an osprey, wings spread and gliding in the still morning, shadows her. They keep pace with one another, two halves split between land and air. Sabine, with each footfall, each flap of wing, feels weightless. And when the great bird turns, she stops to watch as it dips lower along the treetops, its beauty both prehistoric and futuristic at once, and it vanishes into the Everglades beyond.

She returns the back way to the house, through the trees surrounding the western side of the property. In the distance, those same strange tapping sounds. She finds her father in the corner of the yard, talking on the phone. His voice carries, his angry words inseparable from the humidity. He speaks in German, and she slows trying to make out what he is saying. He sees her inching closer, and he ends the call. His face, seconds before creased with rage, regains its stoic normalcy. Back to ready position. No hint of his next play.

"Papa!" she yells, continuing her run through the yard, as if she stopped not at the sight of him but rather to catch her breath. He waves halfheartedly before disappearing into the house. Sabine rounds to the front door. Between the half-walls in the foyer she can smell herself, a sort of herbal ting, sweat and ointment coalescing and leaking from her skin. She is out of match shape, she knows, but she feels good.

She leans against the marble kitchen countertop, drinks water too quickly. As if he has entered through a secret door, her father appears beside her, the expression on his face entirely unreadable.

"Hallo," she says and takes another pull of water.

"You ran." His voice is flat but not without surprise.

"I needed it," she says.

"Good," he nods. His attention turns to the window, to the court and the land beyond them.

"You seemed upset on the phone before," Sabine says. "Everything okay?"

He tilts his head, an attempt to pretend he does not understand the question. "Everything is fine," he says.

"Nothing is fine," Sabine says, cracking a smile, the laugh caught in her throat.

"No," he says, the solidity of his voice absent.

"It's nice for you here, hidden away. The trees keep out the rest of the world."

"Do not be foolish," he says, stern once more. "The world is here."

The mystery, the implication, hangs in the room.

"So tell me."

He ignores her, staring off into the backyard. He says, "You have been hitting?"

It catches her off guard. "Ja," she says.

"That machine used to be your boyfriend," he says, and Sabine hears a hint of his playfulness.

"I still love him," she jokes back.

"Let me see," Jürgen says.

It has been a long time, she wants to say, since she practiced under his watch. But she does not answer. She does not say she is tired, that she would rather climb into a bath upstairs or drive to the beach and collapse in the surf. She walks past him, out the sliding doors in the living room and into the yard. The ball machine is already full and in place. She removes her racket from her bag. She kicks her legs up and back as she steps on court, the Har-Tru sticking to her wet calves. After a few practice swings, she starts the machine. Her old boyfriend. Forehand, forehand, forehand, each pointed to a different line. She bends, her legs foundations. She feels the power they hold.

"Your shoulder!" Her father's voice vibrates off the net. "You are dropping it!"

She ignores him as she would a heckler at a match, letting him become part of the ambiance of her strokes.

"Too fast!" he shouts after a crosscourt backhand. Two more, she swings brutishly through each. He claps, the sting echoing across the yard. "Where is your patience?"

She takes her cuts behind the baseline. It is an amazing feeling, doing this, loving this after so many years.

"Close your shoulder!"

"Head up!"

"Finish! Do not push!"

Her forearms ignite. The impact of each ball, each criticism, radiates through her fingers. She swings without thought, spraying her shots. Her father calls out again but she cannot hear him. He is on the court with her, across the net, his cherry red racket gripped in his large hand. She swats a forehand and he volleys it back. Another. A backhand; she tries to sneak around him but back it comes. "Why are you staying back!" Her forehand immediately returned. "Charge!" And again. Again. She cannot outswing him. Forehand, backhand; he is a machine. She changes pace, slicing a return. He mishits his volley and it pops up, hangs in the air above the service line. Sabine charges. She readies. Swinging volley. A winner, finally, if she lands it. Her feet leave the ground. She grunts, exhales, as she connects. Her follow-through is barely finished when she touches down, watches the ball explode against her father's thick nose, his body and his blood mixing on the Har-Tru. The surprise in his eyes catalyzes her. She is stronger now than he imagined. She is electricity. She feels herself rise in this heat, the weight of this Florida day, wings spread, reborn.

CARTOGRAPHY

The thump of tennis ball against the side of the house echoes down the street. Sandy whips his throws sidearm—a habit his coaches tried for years to rid him of—and shifts left and right, scooping the ball on one hop. Countless summer afternoons and hours after school lost to this wall. That quick bounce honing his reactions. Even at New Ebbets, he and Nick would do the same behind center field. Something satisfying in the simplicity of the drill, its familiarity. But now, it's like there's a weight, a batting doughnut wrapped around his head. The ball quicker than he is, the bounce smarter. A step in either direction, planting his feet, sounds an alarm between his ears. After only a few minutes, he can barely stand.

The phone rings and his mother answers. She pokes her head into the living room and calls Sandy's name. He feels her voice in the back of his skull. When his eyes meet hers, expectant and unsteady, he realizes he's back inside the house. He still hears the thrumming of his throws, their reverberations, as if they exist in the very walls. "It's the team," she says.

He takes the phone and listens to the person on the other end. They ask how he is, and he barely answers. Two weeks, they tell him. They repeat it. They ask if he understands. His mind drifts. He feels his eyes might roll out of his head, his entire body deconstructing.

"Two weeks what?" he says, interrupting. In the silence afterwards, Sandy hears his mother breathing in the other room.

Our first game back, they say.

This reality, absurd and inevitable. "I'll be there," he says. The details—team meeting in a week, home games at their city rival's stadium in Hudson Heights, long road trip, international games still on—pass through Sandy like vapor. He hands his mother the phone and collapses on the sofa. From the front window, the sun tears into the house. It's sharp enough that he can't see beyond it, this veil of gold and fire.

"What did they say?" Esther asks.

"We start again in two weeks," he says, closing his eyes against the light, the way his head still screams.

She slaps her hand against the back of the sofa, like she used to when Sandy was a teenager and ignoring her, captured by something Lenny was doing. "Well you should stay until then," she says, not missing a beat. "You've got time—it's a gift—you should be here."

Sandy shifts off the sofa and bounds up the stairs. In his old room, he's replaced by the thin frightened boy who once lived there. The fears, the insecurities, haven't changed. The walls turn to paper; the foundation spins. He feels delicate and heavy at once and drops onto his bed, the weightlessness not like a roller coaster but something closer to a dream, one where he's falling from a high-up place, impact and earth waiting at the bottom, but the dream, his own subconscious, won't let it come. Just that feeling, the way it stretches out, and wishing, hoping, for its end.

The fairytale book remains on his nightstand. In the middle of the night, before the sun and his mother have risen, he opens it, runs his fingers over the imprint of the illustrations. Creatures in the woods, creeping closer to the villagers' houses, ready to upset their small quiet lives. These stories are tattoos to the past, to his father. If he tries to focus beyond that, on anything below the surface, his head pounds. It starts at his temples and wraps around until his eyes and his skull are pinched. He has been injured before—broken fingers, toes, nose, knee, wrist, some from baseball others from the recklessness of youth—but nothing like this. The voices in his mind, first responders and doctors and his mother, they ask: *Do you know what you've just been through?* The truth is he doesn't. Nothing makes any sense. His father's death. A dead Jewish boy. Nick. One hundred and twenty thousand people—the toll still climbing—murdered in an instant. The question is not what he, they, have been through, but rather *what is happening* still. How can he care about baseball, about playing a fucking game, when no matter how this city is doused, it continues to burn.

He tiptoes down the hallway, the old hardwood giving slightly, and into the guest bathroom, what used to be his. He rummages through drawers and under the sink. He doesn't know what he's looking for. But in the back of the medicine cabinet, he spots it. He reads the label and remembers picking up the pills for his mother after her foot surgery. The way he would sneak a few here and there. Either to forget or remember, he can't be sure now. To grasp or numb whatever he was incapable of feeling. Nick had stopped him then, angry and compassionate when he found out how Sandy had been coping. Had he called Sabby, too? Maybe. It's a tangle of memories he can no longer sort.

He takes two, sucks at the faucet to wash them down. He wanders the house after. In the living room, lit only by the moon and the rainbow trails of streetlight, he sees his father. Legs crossed reading the newspaper, glasses slipping ever so slowly down his strong nose. His long fingers curled, dancing. Cartographer's hands, his mother always said. Sandy looks at his own, callused, cut, and bruised. Ballplayer's hands. He wonders if they could become something else.

"What are you doing here?" he asks his father. *Lenny*. When he was a kid, he hated how similar their names were, how his mother could say them in the exact same way, as if they were interchangeable. But sitting across from this apparition, Sandy takes comfort in the similarities.

His father doesn't answer. He winks, and smiles softly. He returns to his reading.

"Dad," Sandy says, firm and demanding, as if to assure himself that it's real. He stretches out on the couch, rests his head beside his father's chair, where he hears the words his father reads; where he can smell his father's familiar scent; where he pretends none of this is fantasy; where he will, for tonight and the next night and next, find sleep.

The days slip away. Sandy's head chews at him, takes him apart from the inside. Pills like candy. How they are familiar. And once the ache becomes manageable, his return to the game creeping closer, Sandy knows it's time to go. As he packs his duffle bag, his mother waits in the kitchen. She offers him a cup of coffee.

"It's a short car ride home," he says. Though almost imperceptible, he sees the change in her face at the word—*home*—used to name some other place.

"I don't understand," she says. "You sick of me already?" In Sandy's silence, she sucks the backs of her teeth. "I think you should stay."

"I want my bed, Mama. My things. My place." He tries to keep his manner delicate.

"You have that here," she says, "but do what you need to."

"It's not the same, you know that."

She steps towards him, her hand extended, before shifting back into the kitchen. She fusses with the percolator. "Make sure you call me. I don't want to worry."

He leans forward, kisses her on the top of her head. "Like anything I do'll stop that. But of course I will."

She looks up at him, her face awash with disappointment. He sees her nibbling on the inside of her cheek. "I didn't want to bring it up, with everything that's happened, but since you're leaving." She waits, as if giving Sandy the chance to stop her. "The boy… have you heard anything?"

He shakes his head, scrunches the sides of his mouth. She accepts this, his ignorance, but he knows, like any good Jewish son, what he's offered isn't quite enough.

When his car pulls up, Sandy hugs her, squeezes until he feels her skin resist. She kisses his cheek. "Call," she says, her eyes spreading. "No excuses."

He watches her out the window as they drive away, and he rubs his temples, grateful for the temporary medicinal calm. He hates that she's sad, but if he doesn't leave, he might never. It's all he can do to keep from bursting apart.

In the weeks to come, though he doesn't know it yet, he won't see his mother, but he'll wish for her presence often. He'll forget so much but somehow not enough. And he'll think of this moment—her wave, the bittersweet curl of her smile, the feeling, the knowing, that he should've stayed.

RISE

On her last morning in Florida, Sabine runs. She heads away from the water, where the landscape grows thick with forest, in the direction of the strange sounds she has heard for days on end. She has not gone this way in years—a subdivision once existed here before the swamp swallowed it up—and now the land seems to go on forever. She cuts between a row of trees and out into an open field, acres and acres surrounded on three sides by trees. The grass is shiny and well-manicured. Bales of hay are grouped and stacked, though she sees no animals. Around the stacks, the ground underfoot changes, as if a layer of stones sits below the grass, making her footfalls uneven. She bends down, scoops one up. It is not a stone. Its golden skin is hot from the sun. A bullet, long and sleek, blistering against her palm.

In the distance, there is movement. Sabine tucks the bullet into her pocket and runs back the way she came. She hides behind the hulk of a tree, watching. A group of men approach, several with long black guns slung over their shoulders. She has seen guns like this before but never here. Never so close.

The men joke and laugh, like little boys at summer camp. One steps out in front of the group and calls for attention. Sabine recognizes the symbol on the band around his arm, the shock of which pulls bile into her throat. He lines up the other men, and they take turns firing their rifles and their handguns into the haystacks. It is overwhelming, this mechanical otherworldly shrieking. The sound, its intensity, unsettles her whole self, vibrates away any sense of comfort she held. Each crack pushes Sabine further back into the woods until, eventually, the men are disappeared and the gunshots are far enough away to let her breathe, though her muscles do not calm, the thunderclap of this storm's approach still too close on the horizon.

Jürgen sits at the kitchen table, spooning grapefruit into his mouth.

"Do you know those men?" Sabine asks, accusing without meaning to. "Your neighbors."

He shakes his head. "They are noisy," he says.

She does not believe him. How could he not know? "They have guns," she says, and when this produces in her father no reaction, she slides out the chair opposite him and sits. His nose, swollen and discolored, distracts her. He wheezes as if his nostrils are pinched, but he pretends nothing is out of the ordinary. She wants to reach across the table and touch it, feel its swell, the way the skin pulls but is still his, leathered and thin, knowing she is the cause. "There is something else," she says.

He gets up, places his bowl in the sink. The sound startles Roger, who barks in the other room. Jürgen stands in the kitchen and looks out the small window.

"They are wearing a symbol. Like a bird—a Phönix—black lines against red." She stops herself, looking for a reaction from her father. An acknowledgement to match the churning in the pit of her stomach. She has seen it before, this symbol, and he has, too. The inside cover of her mother's favorite notebook. Drawn in a moment of boredom, Sabine always thought, nothing more than a doodle. Runes connected to form something greater than its parts. But it is exactly the same; her memory is clear. She searches her father's face for some sign of recollection, something to explain the existence of both this memory and its sudden, violent rebirth.

The way his shoulders hang perfectly translates his apathy. She stares, and she waits for him to put her mind at rest, curb her confusion with anything other than his dispassion. A single idea, inescapable now and maybe for Sabine, for them, forever. She speaks it—*Mama*—and when still her father does not crack, does not flinch, she stands from the table, the chair's legs scraping along the tile floor before it flips on its side, crashes down, the sting of which echoes through the house. She steps towards him, her frame broad and powerful, and she feels this in her fingertips. For a moment she believes in letting what boils inside her brim over, but she simply gets close enough to see the way the sunlight pours through the kitchen window as she towers, casts a shadow over this man who is now, suddenly, small.

"What are you hiding," she says. She wishes she could keep her curiosity at bay, that her swelling anger and fear and uncertainty could be spoken, reciprocated, understood. She leans forward and kisses him on the top of his head. She will go upstairs after and shower, pack Roger and her things, returning the room to its former state, and she will leave. The kitchen chair still knocked on its side. The air conditioner refrigerating the damp air. And, in the distance, the *pop pop pop*, the echoes of which move closer and closer as if they are surrounded, coming from all sides, waves carried through an endless ocean, inching slowly up an eroded shore.

But, for now, in this kitchen with these two giants, there is only the quiet rhythm of their breaths. The burden of what they have left, will leave, unspoken.

She hears gunfire, imprinted in her eardrums, on the drive to the airport. She sometimes feels she lives in airports, in train stations, and wishes this house in Florida was still her home. It is hard now to imagine it ever was. No place without her mother, without the version of her father that existed with her, has been capable. Only the court—its constancy, its manicured grass and swept clay, its painted lines, its tight fair net, its exposure and its spotlight—has truly felt like home. The pressure of winning, every time she steps on court. It is not enough just to play. Just to be. She steadies her body, her tendons and ligaments tight but stretching against that reality. She knows it is time. To return. To win once more. She is ready.

FEATHER

The ball off the bat, its guttural crack, and Sandy's reaction is immediate. The moment stretches like a note held, Sandy its conductor. He leaps, his toes the last to leave the infield, and he lifts and lifts until, finally, he's floating, arm outstretched, the webbing of his glove open wide. He watches the ball inside, housed and safe, and he's six inches off the ground or six feet; he's in a pocket universe where the laws of time and space don't exist, where the burdens keeping him bound to earth are negotiable and compassionate, where he can, for a few passing milliseconds, control the very shape of his existence.

Nick always said it was inevitable that one day Sandy would go up for a line drive and suddenly slip between universes, disappear into nothingness. Or, as Nick put it, *everythingness*. And now, looking out over his teammates, Sandy knows this is exactly where he should be. A chance to reshape, brief as it may be. A chance to grieve, if such a thing still exists.

He missed them; he knows as soon as he sees them running sprints on the field at Rock Creek, the bright green grass contrasting against their crisp warmup uniforms. Their familiar faces. The way they move like old dance partners. The sun is relentless and Sandy welcomes it. The air on Long Island lighter, a moment to step out of the madness.

After stretches and a slow jog around the stadium—a college park, a fraction of New Ebbets but still with its charms, a faux brick fence and views from the stands high enough to see the Long Island Sound—Sandy picks up his glove, slides his cleats along the infield dirt, back and forth until he has readied his space at shortstop. He settles in, trying to ignore the tremble in the backs of his legs. His hamstrings have butterflies. But once the grounders start, instinct and muscle memory take over. Quick reaction, seeing the ball into the leather, laser throw to first base. Again and again and again. If only he could do this every hour of every day, perhaps things would be all right.

Sandy reads the next tricky hop, moves into the hole and spears it with a backhand. He turns and throws to second without looking at who'll receive it. He knows it won't be Oz. His hero, though still alive, will never play again. Sandy can't remember a game without Oz beside him, his silent and sometimes not-so-silent mentor. The reality of playing without him is too much to process.

"Kat!" The voice shakes him awake, brings him back. His eyes focus, and he sees Garcia, her glove pointing at him, strands of her jet black hair creeping out from under her cap. "Nice stab," she says, smiling.

He hasn't seen her since World Day, since she pulled him from the rubble. *You saved my life*, he wants to say. *Holy shit you saved my life.* He imagines breaking down on the infield, thanking her over and over. *I'm alive because of you.* It will never be enough.

"Nice turn," he says. It's the most human he has felt in weeks.

Later, as fly balls lift to the outfield, Sandy stands on second base. Beside him, Garcia asks if he's okay, and though he registers the question, he has no answer. He looks around, takes in the faces. A kid from Triple-A at first base. *Hell of a time for your first call up.* Garcia. Sandy. Robinson, the veteran, at third, thrust back into a starting role with Alvarez gone. Behind them, pitchers playing catch, goofing off as distraction. A hodgepodge of outfielders, their usual starting three now lost. Minor leaguers and rookies and old-timers aswirl with activity. Amongst them, wrangling and cracking jokes, is Rob Ferguson, former bench coach now manager, left with the insurmountable task of replacing a legend. They look alike, Hussey and Ferguson, in the way salty, leathered old men often do, and Sandy wonders if they'll still call him Skip, as they always have, a nickname Coach Hussey never would've tolerated.

"Second base!" Behind home plate, a catcher removes his mask, points out to Garcia and Sandy. It's not Nick, a fact Sandy felt certain he could ignore, compartmentalize, but there it is, flesh and blood. The Atlantics have a new starting catcher, and his best friend is dead.

Sandy steps off the base, and, without looking back at Garcia, walks across the infield and into the dugout. He throws his glove into the water cooler, disrupting a stack of neatly arranged cups. On the other end of the bench, a young boy sits, a teenager Sandy recognizes as Robinson's son, Hendrick, his eyes wide with surprise.

"Sorry," Sandy says, and he makes a face, a kind of playful horror face, and the boy laughs.

"It's okay," Hendrick says. "Dad did the same thing earlier after bootin' a few grounders. I can restack 'em."

"I'm an asshole," Sandy says, this simple exchange a relief, like he can breathe without wanting to scream. "Thank you."

"Any time, Mr. Katzmann," he says, his voice cracking on the vowels.

"Please, call me Kat."

"Dad calls you Feather," the boy says, laughing. "He's always saying you're gonna fly away."

In the locker room, the quiet chills Sandy. These are the easy things in life, practice and teammates and playing ball. The right things. There's baseball, and there's everything else.

Nick's locker is empty but Sandy still smells him, that mix of almond and body odor which hadn't changed since they were teenagers. They had known each other most of Sandy's life, all of his baseball life. How did people do this, lose fathers and friends and soulmates and still carry on. Maybe not how by why. Eyes closed, deep breath, and there he is again, his Nick. *Why you and not me.* He says it out loud but no one's there to hear. *Why you and not me.* It's not a question for which there will ever be an answer, though he will never stop asking.

On the ride into the city, Sandy thinks about tomorrow, their first game back. There's going to be a ceremony, a moment of silence, flags at half-mast, special hats for not just the Atlantics but every team in the league. The spectacle of it all. Everyone will cry during the national anthem. The Atlantics and the Seals players, most of whom haven't seen one another since their game on World Day, will both be inconsolable. The cameras might not see it, the players—these *remainders*, as some have called them—tucking away their heartbreak, but it'll be there. They'll watch the flags waving in the wind, mouth the words being sung. For some, those words will mean everything. For others, for Sandy, they'll be empty. Then, their caps placed back on their heads and the lumps in their throats choked down and their eyes caught by the lights and the humidity of the night, they will play ball.

Though Sandy has woken up nervous before games, today's something new. With the shades drawn, his apartment is a cocoon. It's dark enough that he doesn't know what time it is. He turns on the news. They talk about tonight. What will people be feeling, is playing the right thing to do. They splice together shots of World Day and its aftermath with highlights of recent games. Sandy sees the narrative spread out before him. When a story scrolls along the bottom, as inconspicuous as the weather—*Man arrested in condo arson on Staten Island, says he was trying to "kill all the f—ing Jews"*— Sandy wonders if he's read it wrong. He thinks of the boy. From his nightstand he takes a container of pills, nearly empty. They're dry in his mouth. The world's softer then, even pressed against the images on the screen.

His phone rings, interrupting the news. "Mama," he says, filling the room, "Was just thinking about you."

"How sweet," she says. "You know what normal people do when they're thinking about someone? They call them." Her voice, its consistency and its reliability, reassures Sandy.

"I know, I know. I've been a little busy."

"You're still asleep. I can hear it."

"I'm tired, it's early."

"Not so early," she says.

Sandy throws the covers off like a spoiled brat and opens the shades. The morning is hungover, a silver blue-gray, cloudy enough to veil the sun, but even in this state the river looks like rippled glass, cut by ferries and tugboats, the Wallabout alive with movement, the Roebling quiet and restful. His two bridges.

"You watching tonight?" He wants to ask her to come to the game, to be there with him.

"So you're going through with it?" Before Sandy answers, his mother sighs. "I don't like it." She sounds as if she's reading from a script, like she's anticipated his answers and practiced her disapprovals.

Sandy hasn't rehearsed, though, and when he says, "This is my life, Mama," he knows it's the wrong thing.

"It's bullshit is what it is. You're not being courageous going out there. It's not heroic to invite getting yourself blown up."

"That's not what this is." He goes into the kitchen, pours a cup of iced coffee, and takes breathless gulps. "I'm not trying to be a hero. I'm doing my job."

"Hitting a few baseballs isn't going to fix anything."

"It will for me," he says, and even as the words pass through the phone, he doesn't believe them.

"It's a game, Schatz; it's not worth your life."

"It was worth Nicky's," he says, not sure what it means, or why he said it.

"No, you stupid boy," she says, fast and full of her brand of motherly love. "No, no, no."

Sandy hurries back to the nightstand and swallows another pill. His mind, everything outside, presses down. "Well I hope you watch. I'll pretend you are."

Before hanging up, they both say *I love you*, something his father always insisted on, no matter how angry they got, how ugly the fight. You always love one another. Otherwise, there's no point to any of this.

Sandy enjoys the final moments of solitude on the drive up to Hudson Heights. The view along the FDR—the gleam of the East River; the green of Minnehanonck and its trams passing overhead; the cricket fields of Tenkenas Island and the Hell Gate in the distance; the beauty of Harlem curving along its river—is everything he wants, enough to sate his mind for a moment.

Highlander Stadium stands like a mighty castle, flanked on either side by the Hudson and Harlem Rivers. Home to the New York Highlanders, it's one of the oldest and most revered baseball cathedrals in the country. From its upper deck, fans are treated to a view of the Washington Bridge and the river and New Jersey beyond. Though the Atlantics and Highlanders share a crosstown rivalry, it has, necessarily, been put aside, the Atlantics given refuge. The Highlanders, on a West Coast road trip, are set to appear briefly on the outfield jumbotron during tonight's ceremonies, wishing unity to their town.

Team meeting, infield practice, press conference, extended batting practice, and it's almost game time. The sun sets, the lights kick on, and this place is a celestial body, the city and country satellites in orbit around it. Reporters collect behind the dugout, waiting for the players—the club-house is off limits tonight, both before and after the game, an extra layer of privacy and security—and when Sandy emerges, medicated and his body welcoming the night, questions fly at him, at Garcia and Robinson and deJong.

"What are you thinking about going into tonight's game?" Minka Albanese—one of the team's beat reporters and Sandy's favorite, an old friend—asks. She's shaky, Sandy can tell. He's glad to see her, alive and well. He can't imagine what she has gone through in the weeks since World Day, what anyone has gone through. He feels selfish that way.

"A friend of mine once told me you've gotta be good and lucky to even get here. Most people don't know how true that is. And since I already know how lucky I am, I guess I have to be good. Maybe better." She hears the crack in his voice, he's sure, the reality behind how lucky he is, how lucky they all are to be standing there when so many are not.

"That's a lot of pressure to put on yourself." She raises her eyebrows, curls the side of her mouth. The familiarity puts Sandy at ease.

"Being good, or being alive?"

They laugh, as do those listening around them, a collective muffled, uncomfortable sound.

"Are you ready for tonight?"

"So ready," he says, and the dishonesty feels almost good, as if there's hope in the deceit. It's exactly what Nick would want him to say. "It's all I've been thinking about. All of us have. We're back. We need this."

When Sandy and his Atlantics take the field, the atmosphere is elec-tric. The players and fans sing their anthems, shed their tears, and the sta-dium opens up for them. There's grass and dirt beneath Sandy's feet, and of all the details of the evening he'll remember these most clearly. Like for those few hours, in a way that feels to him inevitable, he's part of the very bedrock of this city.

Once the oddity of the night settles, it becomes, as Skip had insisted it would, just a game. Snag ground balls, turn double plays, pick your pitch-es, shorten your swing with two strikes—everything simple, everything learned. The perfect weight of the bat in his gloved hands. After the initial excitement, everyone's adrenaline red-lined, the bats go quiet. The Atlan-tics down two in the bottom of the ninth. A walk then a strikeout, and in the on-deck circle, Sandy hopes Garcia will bounce into a double play. End it here, let everyone go home. He knows that's not what he should feel—he can hear Hussey shouting at him, *Winners want the bat in their hands*—but maybe easy is better than winning right now.

Despite the nerves of the moment, Garcia knocks a single off the end of her bat. Runners at first and third. Sandy spits on his hands and claps. His grip too tight around the bat. The first pitch, a fastball down and away, is by him before he realizes. He steps out of the box. His heart feels as if it might rip right through his rib cage. For a second he closes his eyes. He's not here, not in this stadium. He's somewhere far away, somewhere full of sun, the sound of water, of waves cresting nearby. He's not alone. Nick's breath on his neck, the way it raises his flesh. Their bodies pressed together and unbreakable. Sandy opens his eyes, steps back into the batter's box. His bat hovering above his back shoulder. Nick still with him. The next pitch comes the same as the first, down and away and tough to handle, but he reaches out. The contact shakes him. The pitcher doesn't look up. The crowd lets him know what happens. They're on their feet. Sandy's legs barely there, but they carry him around the bases. His teammates meet him at home plate, an ecstatic mob. For some, it will be their greatest moment. This celebration. The collected voices in the crowd. How high they're lifted. A girl in the stands will keep the ball as a souvenir. She will pass it on to her daughter one day, who will return it to her mother on her deathbed, cremate her with it so that they're always together, her mother and this memory. It will be like that for so many.

In the morning, Sandy reads the newspaper and, at first, it makes him smile. The things he said before the game repeated but with something Minka added, something he hadn't imagined. *And in that moment, those few seconds, Katzmann showed us humanity at its best, heroes on a different kind of battlefield, giving us all something finally to cheer for.* The words give him release. They give him permission to break apart completely. Make way for everything he has felt in the weeks since World Day. The terror and the shame. The heartbreak. It spills out of him, and after, when there's nothing left to feel, he is empty.

WEAPON OF CHOICE

Before they ask about her recovery, before they mention the burden, the responsibility of being back on tour, of carrying on when so much has been lost, they ask her why she loves tennis. Why do you still play. What does it mean to you.

Tennis is life, she says. She knows they want something short and sweet, a headline, something simple to post on Prattlr. But what she wants to say is tennis is her blood and her anguish and her savior; she loves the game, the strategy and the power, the way a match can turn on a single point, a botched call, a persistent swarm of flying ants, a passing rainstorm, shaded lines from a half-open roof, a bullet and sweat, a breath not caught. Everything matters, every decision, every movement. Risk and reward and consequence and defeat. Victory, but only sometimes, enough to savor, enough to treasure and, for the next second and the next and the next, begin again.

The weather in England is cooler than she expected. Her shoulder stiffens in the morning crispness, and she takes a walk to try and loosen up. She posts a picture of the tangerine horizon and her morning tea. It is pretend. Alina has long tried to convince her she is the author of her own story. But what that looks like now, she has no idea. All she knows is it cannot be what is real, what she truly feels—she is overwhelmed by the idea of *being back*, nervous to step onto a professional tennis court again. It is different than before; then, it was only about her, her recovery, her return. This, this is so much more.

On a television screen outside the media area, Sabine watches Lolo, a boot visible around her leg, settling into her new role as an analyst.

"Sometimes you just gotta get your butt kicked," Lolo says. The camera loves her smile. Sabine wants to tell her she is shining. "You either win or you learn, but you never lose. That's the difference between champions and everybody else."

Sabine knows Lolo is talking to her, has heard her say those words in encouragement countless times before. She carries them onto the practice court, repeats them in her head: win or learn. She hits with Ionia Williams, a young American player and daughter of the tennis legend whose namesake arena was destroyed. Ionia was not in New York for World Day, and though Sabine sees in her eyes the desire to ask, they do not talk about it. Sabine wants simply to practice. To find her form.

They trade groundstrokes and volleys and light conversation, quick chuckles and polite smiles. Sabine envies Ionia's youth, her agility and her strength. Her naiveté. Wonders if she was ever so young. Sabine holds her racket tighter than she should. She feels the exchange happen inside her, emotion converted to energy, to focus, a current through her arms and fingers. She watches the ball leave her strings, cross the net, and return. She does not look around at who is missing.

"First tournament back!" says Sam Stone, though the tilt in her Kiwi accent makes it sound more like a question.

Sabine smiles awkwardly, hands on her hips and leaning away from the microphone. Her first match over. Her first victory.

"Great shotmaking today," Stone says, filling the void, "but a lot of errors too. A little reckless tennis, some might say. Maybe going for a bit more than usual." Again, her tone frames it as a question.

"The demons are always there," Sabine says, "but you cannot measure success if you have not failed. My father never let me forget that. If I play aggressive and my shots land, I win. If they fail, I am reckless. I will take that chance every time. I cannot focus on winning or losing. Only getting better." The words, in all their fullness, have lived inside of her without her knowing.

"Wise words from a champion!" Stone pauses for cheers. "And how is ol' Jürgen? We miss his fireworks on the tour!" The crowd erupts in laughter, though Sabine suspects they do not know why.

She takes a breath, a small laugh. "Yes, he is good. He is very much the same," she says and though she means to stop, continues, "I miss him, too."

The night before their final, Sabine finds Lolo on television interviewing Ionia. During the first set break of the men's semifinal, Lolo sits on a couch with Jim O'Brien beside her, Ionia across from them. The fit looks natural on Lolo, her presence already enough to hold an audience. But below the surface, Sabine sees the heartbreak. Lolo will never again play professional tennis. Only Lolo's team and Sabine know, and suddenly the weight of that understanding, the kindness and excitement on her friend's face, is overwhelming.

"We watched you practice with Sabine at the start of this tournament, and now you two will meet in the final." Lolo pauses, the space filled by Ionia's excitement. "What're your expectations for this match?"

Ionia is subdued, as if the question is unexpected. "Sabine is one of the best. And this is my first Elite final. I'm just thrilled to be here. I'm gonna give it my all."

Well coached, Sabine thinks. Young, and strong, and she already knows the right things to say.

"You understand each other's games well—" Lolo says, but before Ionia can respond, O'Brien cuts in. "I think Hellewege's game is pretty well known: power power power." He chuckles hard, though no one joins him.

"There's a lot more nuance to her game," Lolo responds, and Sabine knows she is biting the inside of her lip. O'Brien mutters *of course*, barely audible enough for the microphone to pick up. The whispered concession of a man.

"I think something people don't realize about Sabine is how fast she is," Ionia says. "She's powerful and she's fast—I think that's why I like hitting with her so much. She makes you raise your game."

O'Brien, over the breath of Ionia's last word, chimes in. "Her fitness will be key. We've seen her play a few matches since returning from her horrific injury in Budapest, and a few more still since the tragedy in New York. She's strong as hell, and she's overcome a ton, don't get me wrong. So damn happy she's still on tour. But to me, she hasn't looked herself yet."

Every time he speaks, Sabine's blood boils. One of the all-time great players, sure, but as a television analyst, as a source of tennis knowledge for the public, O'Brien is sexist and opinionated and a reason to switch the channel. He is the least objective observer in history, she and Lolo have joked. And as she thinks it, through the televised distance, Lolo receives it.

"Was it four or five years ago, you and Sabine played one another in an exhibition match—"

"Aces for Autism," he interrupts, a shit-eating grin on his face, as if he knew already what Lolo would say.

"Sabine made a lot of money for that cause against you, didn't she?" When O'Brien chuckles and shifts in his seat, Lolo continues, "Is that the Sabine you're looking for?"

"I may have gone a little easy on her then but yes, that's exactly the player I want to see out there. She's a hellcat by nature, but maybe she's lost some of that fire."

Immediately, and with a grace beyond her years, Ionia leans forward and gives O'Brien a stern eyebrow-raised smile. "As someone who's practiced with her," she says, "someone who's about to play her for the championship, I can tell you the fire's there. Practice court, center court, it doesn't matter. She lights it up."

Sabine turns off the television, and the room fades to black. Tomorrow is the final. She tries to put the thought out of her mind. But it remains there even as she drifts to sleep, or what her sleep has become, a riotous tossing, a search for calm that will not come.

She wakes not because it is morning but because she can no longer lay in bed. Roger sighs beside her. Though the physio suggested rest, Sabine wants to practice before the match. She would get up and smack forehands against the walls of her hotel if she could.

Roger begs to go outside. After their walk, even though the sky's grayness hints at rain, she leaves him in the room and runs along the river. *It is no Rhine*, her mother used to say, but Sabine finds its charm, as if its banks can take her back in time.

When she was young and just starting out, they had been all over the world together, Sabine and her mother and father. Jürgen enjoyed coaching her, the competition, seeing the fruits of his tireless labor pay off with junior titles one after another. They were a reflection on him, she knew, though he never said this out loud. Her mother, though, while always openly proud of her daughter, had her own life, her own aspirations and intentions, things separate from Sabine. She had friends in almost every city they visited, people Sabine had never met. When they entered a restaurant, whether in Milan or Melbourne or Miami, someone inevitably stood up across the room and said, *Petra is that you?* She was that kind of person. A model in her youth, a socialite of sorts, she carried that air with her into adulthood, into motherhood, for better or worse. The center of the storm. Always the star. And in the years since her mother left them, Sabine has thought about this often—the kind of person her mother was, the kind everybody knew or wanted to know, connected with instantly—and wonders if her mother shaped her in ways she never understood.

Her body alight after the run, she peels back the curtains in the room. She feels the day opening itself to her. Roger darts around before settling on the bed. He wriggles. Sabine believes he can hear her thoughts. She unzips her bag and takes out a racket. She rolls a tennis ball across her knuckles, cradles it in her palm. She drops it, and Roger's backside arches. She swings through, and when it smacks against the wall, reverberates through the bones of the old hotel, Roger flies from his ready position, leaps from the bed, and takes the ball midair. He drops it at Sabine's feet, his mouth curled in a smile, his body eager with anticipation.

By midday, the sun breaks free of the clouds. The crowd favors Ionia, even though most of them, trained by generations of British tennis ceremony, are too polite to admit it. At the edge of the stadium Sabine reads a sign draped across empty seats—*Herz Statt Hetze*—and though she cannot place the words they are familiar, like a lullaby from her childhood hidden away and suddenly unlocked. Ionia's mother, the ever-famous-face-of-women's-tennis Althea, sits in her box amidst a swarm of celebrities. Three actors, two musicians, Ionia's aunt and coach, herself a top-ten player for over a decade. Everything the tournament could have hoped for, a center court packed with champions of past and present. And though the surroundings are modest compared to other events around the world—Edinburgh, Paris, Sydney, Stuttgart—Sabine feels dwarfed by the entirety of it, as if she has been invited to someone else's party.

The first set opens with quick holds, both players serving with confidence. Feeling each other out. In the sixth game, Sabine falters. Two double faults, and Ionia jumps on a tentative second serve at fifteen-forty to grab the first break. On the walk back to her chair, Sabine seethes. She tosses her racket, and it crashes into her water bottles. The chair umpire covers her microphone and mumbles a warning to Sabine. Her mouth is heavy and thick. Sabine closes her eyes, and she hears Lolo's voice. *Win or learn.* Her pulse steadies.

Time.

When she opens her eyes, the green of the grass is piercing. The banner in the corner now draped over the top of the arena, flapping in the light breeze. The crowd at standing room. A swell of exuberance underfoot. She wonders if everyone else can feel it.

Her groundstrokes, her serve, her rush to net: everything is grace and power. She is dialed in. Though the first set was competitive, Ionia is caught off guard. She peals when her heavy forehand skids off the line, her first point in three games. But in a blink, the second set is over. Sabine pumps her fist, focused on the ground beneath her.

Final set, and the momentum swings again. Ionia holds serve—*finally*, she shouts on the changeover—and follows it with a break. Sabine looks up at the scoreboard, her zero as if in bold. The crowd roars for Ionia. Sabine paces the baseline, hand clenched in a fist. *Come on*, she says through gritted teeth. She takes her time. She waits until the clock ticks down before tossing the ball in the air, her legs and hips exploding, the racket her weapon of choice. Ace. Service winner. Ace. On game point, Ionia catches a piece of the serve down the tee, floats it back. Sabine charges in behind it. She recognizes the panic in her opponent and moves forward, takes the volley out of the air. With Ionia nimble at net but out of position, Sabine sends the shot back at her body. Ionia uses her racket like a shield but twists awkwardly to avoid the ball, and she goes down. Sabine, adrenaline like whitewater through her veins, leans on the net, chest heaving, watching Ionia cry out in pain. She holds her leg, writhes. Quickly, the trainer is beside her. The way she grabs her ankle gives Sabine chills.

During the medical timeout, Ionia off court receiving treatment, Sabine wonders if she will continue. Overhead the clouds shift and slide, casting unpredictable shadows across the court. She replays points in her mind. Minutes pass like days. She stares off, lost in concentration. From deep within the crowd, she sees a woman, watching her with the same intensity. Sabine can almost make out the cracks in her skin, the familiarness in their ravines. As suddenly as she appeared she disappears, enveloped by the swelling, impatient crowd.

Sabine jogs out beyond the baseline and stretches, kicks her legs, flips a ball off her strings like a party trick. Cheers erupt when Ionia emerges from the tunnel, calf and ankle heavily wrapped. She waves at her fans. She walks gingerly. She bounces, testing, and Sabine waits. As she prepares to serve, Ionia pauses to once again let the stadium encourage her. Her first serve sails quite long, and Sabine understands all too well—she cannot put her weight down. She steps inside the baseline, and off Ionia's weak second serve, she tees off. She rips an inside-out forehand winner. Ionia does not move. The crowd is a low rumble of discontent. In an instant the set is back even, Sabine holds, and again Ionia struggles for movement, looking to her box for answers. *What am I supposed to do?*

Sabine tries to ignore it, focus on her own shots. Trailing fifteen-forty, Ionia hangs her head. Her broad shoulders limp. Finally, though, she lands a first serve, and Sabine barely gets a piece of it. They rally, flat forehands and slice backhands, the longest exchange by far since the first set. Sabine wants to move Ionia all over the court, but her powerful strokes keep Sabine locked up, aiming for the lowest part of the net. Finally, she skids a deep backhand off the baseline, and it pushes Ionia back, produces a mishit, and, masterfully disguised, Sabine carves a drop shot. Ionia charges, or attempts to but she cannot plant, and she howls. The ball lands, spins with a kick along the grass.

Game, Miss Hellewege.

Jeers rain down from the crowd, loud and consuming like thunder. Sabine, her eyes wide at them, fawns confusion. If they wish it, she will be their villain.

Up a break, she does not look back. She makes Ionia run, boos growing stronger. Ionia struggles after every point, her limp more and more pronounced. In this way, Sabine drags Ionia to the finish. The final line does not do the match justice. They will focus on this after, Sabine knows already. *What if,* *Would she have,* *Not a true test.* But she won. *No matter what happens on the other side of the net*—they say this, too—*you gotta play your game.* Close the door. That's what champions do.

At match's end, the two meet at net. They embrace, Ionia barely able to hold back her tears. Sabine tells her it was a great battle, that she hopes Ionia is okay, and, to both of their surprise, that she is proud of her. "You are the future of this game," she says, and Ionia mouths *Thank you* before they shake the chair's hand and part ways. Inside, Sabine is ecstatic, and she wonders if she is smiling. She wonders what they see.

When Sam Stone calls her back onto court, Sabine jogs out, waves to the crowd. Immediately, and without respite, the chorus of boos comes.

She laughs, playful, because what else can she do. Stone gives them a moment, leaving Sabine to fidget.

"Heck of a match," Stone says, loud enough to interrupt. "It's good to have you back in the finals!"

Sabine keeps it light. "It means a lot to me to be back here, playing good tennis."

"You're looking fit out there, which I know you've worked hard at. What goes through your mind when you see your opponent struggle physically?"

Sabine nods, biting her lip. "First, I want to congratulate Ionia on an amazing tournament." She turns to her opponent, still seated with an ice pack wrapped around her leg. Ionia acknowledges the crowd, whose cheers sound to Sabine like waves crashing. "She is a hell of a fighter, and I know she is going to be a champion, just like her mother." Ionia, overwhelmed by the moment, gives a thumbs-up to Sabine. "I know what it is like to be in pain, to play in pain, and I wish you a speedy recovery, Ionia. Thank you for an amazing final."

"Wise words from a champion," Stone says, met immediately with booming discontent. She adjusts the microphone in Sabine's face. "I think this crowd has painted you the villain today, haven't they?"

Sabine waits a moment, smirks in frustration. "I know you all wanted to see Ionia win. I kind of did, too"—she laughs, trying to diffuse—"but I am grateful for the chance to be here, to play and show what I can still do. It has been a long road back."

From behind her, Sabine senses something happening. The jeers turning to whistles and *we love you*s, and there is a hand on her back, which makes her flinch. Ionia leans on her for support. Stone shifts the microphone to her. Sabine sees the wet lines dried along her cheeks.

"Y'all," Ionia says, "thank you for having my back this week, for being so wonderful today." Pause, for exuberance. "But stop this right now. This woman is a warrior. She's out here killing herself. Don't you boo her for me. You cheer us both. We deserve it."

Sabine embraces Ionia, and she enjoys for those few seconds some semblance of peace, some contentment in the sport she has loved her entire life. After, when the current in the air has dissipated, Sam Stone looks to Sabine a final time and asks, "It's been a wild ride, Sabine… are you still having fun out there?" Her accent, like a cartoon twang, is the perfect exclamation point.

Sabine stares out at the crowd. She wants to understand them, why they hate her and why they love her, why she works so hard to be in front of them. "We have to have fun on court—the joy to play the matches, the big points. I think this is the challenge. Without the passion and without that fun, you cannot play your best, because this is what we love. Being here, playing in front of all of you. This is something really special." And though what follows—the applause and the fans on their feet—is not for her, Sabine hears it anyway, and pretends.

Later, they ask her what this title means to her, what it means to be a champion once again after all she has gone through. She wants to ask them how one stops being a champion, how one loses something they have already earned many times over. She wants to ask if they know what it feels like to be the villain, rather than the hero, of your own story. But instead she says simply that it means everything. That tennis is her life, a new chapter being written, and she can finally turn the page.

IN LIGHT OF
RECENT EVENTS

Sandy searches the sea of faces, the airport teeming.

"Isn't that her?" Garcia's voice rises and sputters, like she's tried too late to stop herself from asking the question.

The terminal buzzes with activity. "Who?" he asks, though he just wants to hear Garcia say it.

"Sabine Hellewege," she says. "You two are friends, yeah?"

Sandy stays locked on the crowd. He hasn't heard from Sabine in too long, only that single message since World Day. It's not her, though, and it's wishful thinking, he knows, imagining she would wander by, her golden hair caught in the florescence and lighting up this colorless place. That it could be so easy.

In Sandy's silence, Garcia shuffles on the balls of her feet and says, "She mentioned you back in the day when we did that photo shoot together. We hung out a couple times after that. But it's been a while. Hope she's okay."

"She is," he says, also hoping. It's all he can do for now.

Garcia smiles, pulls up the handle of her suitcase and walks in the direction of the gate. Sandy shuffles behind. They wait together, moving as a group outside to the tarmac and onto the plane. Robinson stretches across a row and before takeoff falls asleep. Sandy envies him, the peace visible in the sleeping lines along his cheeks. Years ago he would've been called an old-timer, but now he's their anchor, something to tether them to a calm that only comes from experience, from having seen it all. Robinson's son, Hendrick, traveling with the team—*in light of recent events*—sits in the aisle across from his father, eyes covered by VR goggles, playing a game. Jimmy deJong leans his head against the window overlooking the wing, oversized headphones leaving him oblivious to the movements around him. Everyone seems to have found their place. How, Sandy wonders. He sits by himself and downs two pills. In the thin space between his skin and muscle, something crawls, relentless.

Separating them and the Atlantic is a wall of cloud, as if they're traveling in their own universe. They'll land in England soon enough, the second installment of the league's new international tour, but for now the distance—from everything—is a gift. *Kismet*, Skip called it, though none of them had heard him use a word like that before. *It's the best thing for us*, he said, *going away*. Sandy thinks about this as he drifts in and out of consciousness, the sky around them changing from light to dark to flame, and when he opens his eyes again, groggy and unsure where he is, it's because someone shakes him awake, repeating his name. When he focuses, he sees Garcia, her face in a panic. "Have you seen this?" she says. She points her phone almost close enough to touch his nose. "Look!"

It takes Sandy a moment to understand what he's looking at, for his mind to wheel back in time. The sports section, front page. *Brooklyn's Katzmann.* His building, the dead Jewish boy. He doesn't remember anyone taking pictures outside his apartment, but of course they did. They were supposed to keep this quiet. They assured him. He should've known better. He tries to read beyond the photographs. The words jumble. He hands Garcia back the phone. He'll explain later, he promises, though he knows he won't. He curls against the window. They haven't landed yet; he can't tell where they are. He takes another pill, rough against his dry throat. He closes his eyes. His heart and his head pound. They are unbearable.

Once he settles in London, Sandy messages Sabine. He wants to see her, he says, and that it's been too long. She's already gone, but he tells her he'll be in Berlin next. The London games will be a whirlwind, a circus for which he's not prepared. Berlin will be a vacation, a word that has lost nearly all meaning. No baseball, no practice, no press, no responsibilities. He struggles to imagine even the shape of such a thing. His time his own. He only hopes Sabine will join him. He has missed her more than he's ready to admit. He gets along with his teammates; they're his friends, a closeness specific to sport, to the days and weeks and months and years spent together. Sweating together, losing together. So much of this life is performance, though, especially without Nick. Garcia tries, and he's grateful to play beside her, to have her friendship. But she's not Nick. She's not Sabine. How they've made him feel whole, in a way he no longer does. Everything just out of reach.

He disappears into himself. His pills. The game, too. The field, the swings and misses. Throughout the three-game series against the London Kings, Sandy is fire and ice—four strikeouts in game one; a single short of the cycle in game two; a home run from each side of the plate to go with two strikeouts and a game-ending double play to close out the finale. The British fans eat up the drama. Near the close of the trip, reporters ask about World Day, how he's recovering, how the team's managing. He says all the right things, about unity and resilience. The strength of his country. And when their questions shift to the incident making headlines—the Jewish boy left dead at his doorstep—Sandy does as instructed, muttering *No comment* into the microphone, his expression changed, numb and unfazed. A reporter mentions the home run at Highlander Stadium, the history it made, the way it lifted a city in need. Sandy is grateful, in his way, for the recognition.

"And what about New York," they ask. "How is it?"

"Broken," Sandy says, too candid. "Healing. It'll never be the same, but it'll never change. It's New York."

SCHWARZWALD

She is on a plane bound for Stuttgart when she receives his message. *Are you still here.* She asks where, and when Sandy replies, *England,* she is surprised. She had ages ago forgotten he would be coming to Europe, that their timing could sync. She turns up the music on her headphones. She lifts her phone and snaps a photograph out the window, the clouds a sea beneath her, everything beyond a purple infinity. *Just missed me,* she writes. She waits for his response, the anticipation of knowing he is typing. *Always the way.* The saccharine sadness of the thought warms her. *Where to now,* he asks. *Stuttgart,* she tells him, and later, as they prepare to land, her phone vibrates again. *Viel Glück,* he writes, and, with no further explanation: *I'll be in Berlin next week.* She smiles, knowing it is an invitation, that the time spent apart—what seems now like decades—will soon disappear. She hopes he can forgive her for how far away she pushed him, that the gulf can be bridged. She hopes he will know how much, in ways she can barely comprehend, she has missed him.

As has long been the arrangement, Sabine stays at the apartment of an old family friend. Her mother's roommate from her university days, she thinks, though she has not seen the Mitford family in years. Her mother then her father always made the plans, and when he stopped traveling with her, Sabine began just showing up. The key with the doorman, the apartment ready for her, she only had to say her name. *Willkommen in Stuttgart, Frau Hellewege.*

Roger settles in quickly, nestled in the corner of the couch and facing the window overlooking the Neckar. Sabine snaps a photo and posts it. *Flying always tuckers him out.* She laughs at the idea, his little corgi ears like propellers. She changes clothes and, as is her way, she runs along the river. Her legs are heavy; she still hears the crowd, the jeers like rainclouds over the stadium. *Herz Statt Hetze*, singed into her memory. That woman's face, seen only for an instant yet familiar. Ionia did her best during the post-match interviews not to blame the injury for her loss, even though it is what everyone wanted to hear. *Felt like I had it, but that's why tennis is a three-set victory. You gotta play every point like it's your last, and Sabine did that.* Sabine tried humility, too, knowing it could last only so long. Her father would be furious. He hated when she made herself small, when, as he used to say, the whole damn stadium should be on their feet for her.

Distracted, she makes her way past the Unterer Schlossgarten and the zoo. The river at her feet flows northward, carried from Schwarzwald and on to the Rhine, and in its surface she sees the buildings around her reflected, a glassy distorted reality.

The doorman at the apartment, smiling and awaiting her entrance, tells her she has a visitor, that he has let them upstairs. Someone on the approved list, he says, which is not something she knew existed. Her mind ticks through the possibilities, few as they are, and is delighted to find Lolo stretched out on her couch, Roger standing upright on her thighs demanding attention.

"I'm sorry I didn't get to see you after you won," Lolo says, Sabine pouring them both a glass of white wine.

"It is fine," Sabine says, "really. It was all such a whirlwind. I was anxious to get here, honestly."

"It was fucked up," Lolo takes a long pull, "the booing and shit. I can't believe Ionia had to tell them to shut up. Like what the hell." She readjusts herself, her boot sticking to the couch. Roger jumps to the floor and watches something out the window.

Sabine finishes her glass, the sweetness coating her tongue. "Tell me something, anything," she says.

Lolo grins at the request. Around them, the city turns to night, a veil Sabine is happy to slip beneath. "I met a boy," Lolo says, almost spilling her wine. "In England. He's a soccer player."

"A footballer," Sabine jokingly corrects.

Lolo scoots closer, holds up her phone. A picture of Lolo and her new beau, laughing on the roof of a hotel. Lolo looks wild and happy.

"Hey, that is Marcus!" Sabine says, pointing with her wine glass.

Lolo's eyes dance with surprise.

Sabine, hesitant, says, "It is, no?" Marcus, a few years younger than Lolo, is tall and lithe and fit. Sabine remembers him—a night out with Alina and Florian and Nicole Ahn and a host of nameless faces—and how he spent the evening hanging off Alina, and that boyish grin when she caught him sneaking out of Alina's room before breakfast.

"Do you know Marcus?" In Lolo's voice, Sabine hears a hint of accusation.

"Only because I am a fan!" She giggles, trying to defuse. "I met him once, after a tournament in Nottingham, I think. We were at the same club."

"Like, you met him, or you *met* him?" Lolo slides onto the floor beside Roger. He rolls over, bares his belly to her. She raises her eyebrows at Sabine, motions for more wine.

"Not my type," Sabine says, winks. She opens a bottle of red, and when she fills Lolo's glass, the moonlight swirls inside.

"He's a damn snack."

"You two are adorable."

Lolo looks back at the photo and beams, and they share a drunken laugh. When it is late and Lolo is ready to go, they hug, kiss each other on the cheek. It feels like a goodbye, though Sabine does not understand why.

"I'll see you at the tourney, yes?" Lolo asks.

Sabine nods, tilts her head. "You are sad," she says.

"It's just the wine." Lolo shakes it off. Her black hair has grown long in the past few months, down to the middle of her back now, and Sabine reaches out and runs her fingertips across its edges.

"Well I miss you. It is not the same out there without you."

"It's not the same, in so many ways." She looks at Sabine, her eyes bloodshot and her shoulders tired. "But that's okay, isn't it?" Before Sabine can speak, before Lolo kisses her once more and disappears into the Stuttgart night, she says what Sabine, too, is thinking: "It has to be."

Sabine mistakes the alert that wakes her for her alarm. She presses it and flicks open the news, the light from her phone irritating her eyes. A row of talking heads bandies back and forth, arguing while saying nothing of substance: groups taking responsibility for World Day, blame shifting, fingers pointing. Accusations abound. Now the focus shifts to outliers from a group of refugees making their way through southern Europe. There are others, they say, in Hungary and Croatia, Slovakia and Poland, all headed for Denmark and the Netherlands. Splintered-off sects of revolutionaries have already been detained in Moldova as well as the US. Footage rolls in the background, anonymous bodies, women and children and men. Her thoughts brim over. *These families. Look at them. How could they possibly be responsible.* But none of the talking heads entertain this. They go on and on until everyone—all these faces—are guilty.

Security at the tournament is unprecedented. Broad men with guns, disappearing into dark corners. People take pictures beside the guards, pointing and laughing like they are at Buckingham Palace. Their presence and their weapons—*Mord Maschinen*, her mother called them—unnerve her. They do not make her feel safe or protected; they give the massacre at World Day a constant audience. They are tools not of order but of fear.

After her match—which she wins in straight sets, three and two—Sabine hurries off court and back to the apartment. She will return early to practice, but today she cannot linger in this atmosphere. She feels the way these men and their guns tighten around her. To calm her nerves, Sabine indulges in a glass of wine with dinner. Her father never allowed her to drink during a tournament, and she is preoccupied with this thought, the constrictions of her youth, as she settles into bed, her head light. Roger nestles beside her. She hears his little heartbeats as she drifts asleep.

During the night, moonlight prisming through the windows, Sabine wakes to Roger barking, a rhythmic, furious sort of noise. She senses what he already knows: there is someone in the apartment with them. She reaches for Roger, to calm him, but her touch spooks him. He growls. His restlessness shoots through Sabine and she is up, her muscles and defenses engaged; she grabs her Babolat resting against the chaise. Her grip is tight. She moves through the rooms of the apartment and, finding each empty, the weight on her chest grows. She holds her breath without realizing, the way she did as a kid before ripping a forehand. Her knuckles are white against the navy overwrap. She stands outside the final door, head heavy and lacking oxygen. She bursts screaming into the study and finds herself alone. The silence rings between her ears. Around her, the walls are lined with books. The room smells like old paper and sherry. Sabine remains in ready position, her back straight and knees bent, arms pulsing and ready to fire. Behind her, Roger shuffles in, stopping between her legs, and he looks up, ears bent in confusion, and Sabine stares back at him, her little familiar, just the same.

In the morning, already late for practice, she feels acid beneath her skin as she moves around the apartment. She takes inventory, though what was here before she arrived, she cannot be sure. Roger stands by the front door, tail sliding slightly back and forth, staring up at nothing, and to Sabine it is the most discomforting element of it all. What was there, what remains that she cannot see.

The practice courts are quiet. Overhead, the sun cracks open a shell of clouds, its bright heat spreading through the day. She remembers mornings like this from her childhood, the way the air could be thick and crisp at once. Her hitting partner, Carolina, a young up-and-coming German player, does not keep her waiting long, and the two exchange a formal embrace and pleasantries before beginning mini-tennis. For a while, they are the only two on court, and Sabine is grateful for the momentary privacy. Carolina does not challenge her, is not capable really, and for Sabine this is just right. She is tired and her shots sluggish. For years her father demanded she practice with players who would push her—Florian and Drago and Althea—but she tries now to enjoy the lightness of this act, the simple pleasure of swing, of back and forth, burned into her muscles.

Across the net, Carolina asks about Julie, their countrywoman, and whether or not she is coming back. "I have not heard," Sabine says. She has not played with her country during the International Cup since before her assault, and it occurs to her in that time she has lost touch with many who she once thought of as dear friends. She thinks about them, their absence from her life, and what wells up inside her is a terrible mix of sadness and nostalgia.

Along the perimeter of the courts, watched closely by the armed sentries, crowds form, early tournamentgoers shouting out names and snapping photographs. A few yell to Carolina, who turns and waves. "My friends," she says, coupled with a carefree smile that Sabine returns, and marvels at Carolina's youth. Sabine is not old herself, she knows this, but she feels it, women of her generation retiring and moving on to the next phase of their lives as the courts and tournaments fill with players a decade younger, faces in which Sabine sees what she has lost. She motions to the crowd as well, though she does not know anyone.

She and Carolina trade groundstrokes and volleys. Carolina asks for overheads, and with each reach back and follow-through, she makes a kind of cartoon sound. Sabine cannot keep from laughing. When Carolina, confused, opens her palms in a shrug, Sabine composes herself and imitates her, loud and exaggerated. The impression sends them both into a frenzy, doubled over and lost. Sabine lays down on the court and spreads her legs and arms wide. She presses her body into the ground. Carolina grabs her phone and snaps a picture. She asks if she can post it. *Sweat angel, Real angel*, she captions it, and she tags Sabine, such that her name appears in the center of the imagined wings.

They ignore the guards' admonishments when they walk together off court, greeted by Carolina's friends and fans alike. Amongst them, a young woman catches Sabine's eye. They both smile, and Sabine finds herself held by her gaze. She cannot place her. Her light brown skin, strong dimples, dirty blonde hair curled above her shoulders, perfectly messed. The patch of freckles on either cheek. All of it familiar. Sabine and Carolina make their way along the pebbled path to the players' area, posing for selfies and signing oversized tennis balls. Sabine and the young woman exchange glances, lips curved, conspicuous. But as the crowd swells, they lose one another. Inside, she and Carolina part, and the remainder of the afternoon dissolves in a haze of massage and acupuncture and aromatherapy. Healing, the trainer calls it, but for Sabine it feels like tape over the leaking hull of a ship. Still, she cannot ignore the reality—that she needs these sessions maybe more than practice, that the ache in her shoulder and legs and back increases with every match, every hitting session, and will not simply heal on its own. That perhaps her days playing on these courts are numbered.

Later, she walks along the river. She is loose, finally, though the lack of rest has settled in the wrinkled space between her brows. She listens for the sound of water, its current barely audible. Back at the apartment, she turns to the front door and stumbles into someone, nearly tumbling over in the process. Two arms reach out and steady her. When Sabine looks up, those familiar patches of freckles greet her.

"You," she says, unable to hide her surprise.

"It's me," the woman says, "and it's you. All figured out now."

Sabine reddens, embarrassed. "Do I know you? I mean, I do, right?"

Before she can respond, the doorman peeks out and says, "Ach! Ms. Mitford, I didn't know you were coming."

"I didn't either! It was all very last minute."

"Victoria," Sabine says, a bit too loud and full of ah-ha.

She takes an exaggerated bow. "It's good to see you, Sabby. Been a long time." Her English accent sits light in the air.

Sabine ticks through memories, flashes of childhood, afternoons spent picnicking and playing tag in the park, Victoria and her brother, David, giving chase. Their parents collected on blankets, laughing, caught up in their own world. *Intrigieren*, her mother used to joke. It has been years. They were children last time they saw one another—Sabine a few years older than Victoria and maybe the same age as David—but she feels instantly at ease with her, this woman whose family's apartment she has been staying in, whose occasional bed she has slept in, whose simple presence transports her back to a time when attractions, their lack of repercussions, were anything but complicated.

"You look the same," Sabine says.

"Only a foot taller," Victoria says as the two walk upstairs.

"But the same," Sabine says, her grin sharp. "How is your brother? And your parents? What are you doing here?" The questions come out at once, the path from Sabine's thoughts wide open.

Inside, Roger runs around like a mad man. Victoria opens a small refrigerator in the corner of the kitchen, one Sabine had not noticed before. She removes a bottle of wine, and almost in one motion opens it and pours herself a glass. "You?" she asks, holding up the bottle. Sabine does not answer, considering her match tomorrow, but in her silence, a full glass appears at her fingertips. "Prost," they say.

She is here, Victoria, to get away from things, though she shares nothing more specific. *To get away*, she repeats. Her brother at school in America, her parents on an endless parade of cruises around the world, and she left alone, her job running the family travel business unfulfilling, no relationship to speak of.

"I could disappear," she says later, "and not a soul would notice."

Between them, there is a familiarity, one that seems unbothered by the passage of time. So few are left, Sabine thinks, who ease her as such.

"Is that why you are here really?" Sabine feels her nerve endings warming. The stress of the day, the tournament and its armed battalion, melting off her. "So someone will notice?"

Victoria slides closer on the couch to Sabine. She kisses her, slow and timid, their lips parted just so. Testing. Sabine reciprocates, her fingertips grazing those freckles. She takes quick hot breaths.

In bed, Sabine awake and watching the moon, she wonders when the day turned to night. Victoria, naked and arm draped across Sabine's bare chest, exhales soft and heavy, its tang and melon reminding Sabine how long it has been since she shared a bed with someone. Besides Roger, she thinks, which makes her chuckle, her eyes locked on the natural nightlight illuminating the room.

"Are you laughing at me?" Victoria asks, kissing Sabine quick and wet on the chin.

"Definitely."

"What time is it?" Victoria stretches, her body long and thick and muscular. "It's dark out."

"Night," Sabine says. "Not too late."

"I thought it was morning." She yawns, exaggerated like her head might crack open. "I hate jet lag."

Sabine adjusts the pillows behind her and sits up. She resists the urge to pull tight the blanket and cover herself. Victoria repositions, rests her head on Sabine. "Where are you coming from?"

"America," she says with a tinge of annoyance Sabine hopes is not directed at her. "New York City. Hadn't seen David since all the terribleness." She stops and looks at Sabine, her eyes caught. "Oh god, you were there. I remember on the news. I remember them looking for you."

The idea strikes Sabine, nearly knocks the wind from her. It is a part of her own story that belongs also to everyone else. "I think I was asleep for that part," she says, trying to dissolve both of their uneasiness.

Victoria smiles, and she kisses Sabine. "I'm glad," she says.

By the middle of the night, they have barely slept. They make love in fits. They take turns going to the bathroom and getting water for the other, fruit and chocolates, too. Victoria returns to bed with a small glass of Madeira. Sabine smells its sticky sweetness even against the sweat in the room.

"Do you like New York?" she asks, uncertain of where the question has come from. Maybe it is the annoyance she sensed earlier, which has lingered in the front of her mind. "Before everything happened, I mean."

"I almost like it better now. Is that horrible to say?" She does not look at Sabine, who imagines Victoria's expression is unapologetic despite her words. "The city has this energy to it now. I don't know how to describe it—like it's still on fire but in a good way." She waits, and in the pause, Sabine feels she might drown. "Does that make any sense?"

Sabine remembers the stories told to her by friends and fellow players about their cities after war. The flames that never stopped burning. The smoke a permanent part of the air, of each breath. The bombs, their echoes, etched into every skull. How practicing became a respite, tournaments a perverted sort of getaway. And yet, going home always felt like a return to something necessary, a comfort, no matter how completely it had broken.

"It does," Sabine says, though she knows Victoria does not believe her.

"I saw it destroy David, even before all this." She finishes her drink, clanks the glass onto the side table. She sits up, propped against pillows, and for the first time in hours Sabine can see her straight on, the way the lines around her eyes reach out every time she smiles. "I don't know what to make of it now. I always believed if you were a good person and put good vibes out into the universe they would return to you. But New York breaks you of that. Like if you're a good person, a train will come when you need it, a taxi in the pouring rain, the elevator door held for you. When you need a miracle it will be delivered. But New York doesn't work that way."

Sabine fights her first instinct, to tell Victoria she is spoiled, that she is foolish. *My god can you hear yourself.* Instead, she leans forward, she kisses Victoria hard. She bites her lip, runs her nails over her warm skin. She leaves marks, trails that show where she has been. She does not say what she is thinking. She lets her body want and demands of it no apologies. This strength and this desire, when nothing more is needed.

They wake to Roger's incessant barking. It is still early, Sabine feels it in her temples. Everything cloudy. The room stings of sex. Something, though, even in Sabine's fogged state, feels off. She hears it in the way Roger whines. And as if that animal sound has conjured him, Jürgen stands in the living room—framed by the open bedroom door, arms at his side, shoulders like a statue's—peering at his daughter. For a moment, Sabine cannot remember where she is.

Sabine, get up, she hears him say, though his mouth remains shut. She is out of bed and standing before him. He looks past her, over her shoulder. "A friend?" he asks in English, which surprises her.

She turns, as if wanting to see for herself what her father sees. "Victoria." She waits, gauging his reaction. "You remember her," she says.

He cocks his head. "All grown up," he says, eyes directed downward, out of respect or disgust Sabine cannot tell.

"What are you doing here?" she asks, moving him by the arm away from the bedroom into the kitchen.

"I'm here to watch you play."

"Bullshit," she snaps without thinking, taken aback by her own forwardness, as is Jürgen. "When was the last time you were at a tournament? The last time you were in *Germany*?" Her voice grows, and she sees Victoria stir beneath the covers.

"Too long a time," he says, drifting to the window, and the way he stands there almost motionless reminds Sabine of how he looked after her mother died and neither of them spoke for days.

In the silence between them now, Victoria shuffles from the bedroom. She wears a long t-shirt down to her thighs, thin and revealing.

"Mr. Hellewege?" She rubs her eyes. "Were you expected?"

His eyebrows curl downward, his forehead an aging tapestry of worry. "For my daughter, I would think I'm always expected."

Sabine feels the heat rise through her, a rage born of years of passive, repressed aggression. Before she can erupt, though, Victoria says, "Well I'm not sure that's true today."

Jürgen looks to his daughter, expressionless, for response. "I have been welcome in this house many times before."

"*Mom* was welcome," Sabine says, her front teeth clicking together, grinding down.

"You're not unwelcome, Mr. Hellewege, don't misunderstand. Simply not expected. Had you been, I'd have dressed for the occasion." Victoria smirks at him, at Sabine, something devilish and playful. As she moves past them and begins making coffee, she kisses Sabine gently on the cheek.

Jürgen steps away, settles back at windows in the living room. He cannot hide his disfavor, Sabine thinks. Roger sniffs, ignored, at his feet.

Sabine scans for luggage, for any sense of her father's purpose here. "I have a match today," she declares.

"Yes, I know," he says, gaze locked on the city outside these walls.

"I have to get ready." Sabine, lips crumpled, closes the bedroom doors behind her. She knows, as soon as she is out of sight, he will leave. In the shower, Sabine is grateful for these last few moments of solitude—interviews before her match, a meet-and-greet with students from a local tennis academy, warm-ups, post-match press conference, treatment, and a Prattlr Q & A before returning to the apartment—enjoying this calm. Hot water, her muscles, her nerves, a moment at rest.

The apartment is still, save for Roger's snores. Victoria and Jürgen both gone. Sabine laughs at the thought of them leaving together, the awkwardness of slipping out one after the other. She walks Roger around the block, her mind still pinched from lack of sleep. She moves through the motions. The image of her father standing in the living room, the look on his face, haunts her. Why is he here, she cannot stop asking. If it were anyone else, she would imagine he missed her and was here now to make amends, to shake hands across the net. But not Jürgen. She knows him better than anyone. He is here for himself. Her mother's words rattle in her mind even now: *He is selfish, your father, not by choice, but because he cannot be anything else.*

In the bedlam of the past day, she has neglected her match. A quarterfinal meeting with an old rival, Zhang Qiang, one Sabine should be preparing for, but instead, as she warms up with Carolina, she is adrift. The physicality is there—the imprint of a perfect swing—but she cannot focus. She sees her father moving around the practice court. She sees him but he is not there. She finds it is often the case now, since World Day and maybe before; she is certain of nothing that is, only of what is not, of what is missing.

The match starts in the high heat of the afternoon. The stands are filled with German flags, with the cheers and energy of the face-painted Helle's Angels. In Sabine's box sits Jürgen. His arms crossed, sunglasses shielding his expression. She stuffs down her impulse to shout to him, to demand he leave. She stares back at him and hopes he understands. Sabine remembers a time when his presence was a comfort to her, an inextricable part of this game, this career. But now, he is wholly out of place.

Things move quickly, and in her distraction, she drops the first set without notice. During the changeover, she bakes in the heavy sun. She feels the texture of her skin changing. She glares at her father, who gulps from a large water bottle. Behind him, in the corner of the stadium, a group of fans catch her eye. Demure and polite, but vocal. Careful clapping. Well dressed, hair manicured. Their whiteness exceptional only in its unbrokenness. And pinned to their chests, which Sabine sees in a flash on the large overhead screen, a small broach, a phoenix—made to look like something older, something evocative—drawn with straight lines, black runes against red.

She continues watching them between points. The match evaporates. Jürgen leaves after her loss without a gesture. She skips her post-match press conference, her Q & A, and in the car back to the apartment she replays the faces in that crowd, their measured smiles, the distant, confusing familiarity of it all. Roger greets her at the door, bouncing. She calls out for Victoria. She searches each room, repeating her name. There is no sign of her, no sign she was ever there. The apartment is empty and her voice echoes. Roger cries out, as if to say *here I am, I am here!* She looks down at him and understands his impatience. There is nothing here. She is certain only of this.

GATES

On the train to Brussels, Sandy floats. He dozes off under the Channel and is surprised at how soon they arrive in Belgium. Later, he sees out the window signs for Bonn and Düsseldorf. He sleeps through Dortmund and Bielefeld and Hanover, waking in a haze at Berlin Hauptbahnhof, the pills he got courtesy of a teammate's cousin's friend on Tottenham Court Road keeping his anxiety at bay.

Eyes fuzzed, he takes a taxi to his hotel, an old Bauhaus building home to a members' club he'd joined back in New York, a gift to himself after signing his long-term contract. It's the sort of extravagance he would never tell his mother about and, therefore, feels like an ugly secret. A staff member shows Sandy around the house and to his room, regaling him with the history of the building, the neighborhood, the well-known celebrities who have frequented the establishment. Sabine is included, amongst a party several years earlier getting out of hand. "There was blood in the streets," they say, accent a continental kind of English and a smile to let Sandy know the story's end is cheeky rather than tragic. "Nothing this place hasn't seen," they continue. "Communists were here, before the Wall came down. And before that, Hitler stole the building from Jews and made it the Nazi Youth headquarters."

"So, actual blood in the street," Sandy says, channeling his father.

They grin back at him, mascara-curled eyelashes like butterfly wings. "So long ago," they say. "Now, *glamorous*." They spread their arms wide, making sure Sandy takes in the modern, careful architecture.

He's ready, for at least these few days, to disappear into this city, where no one knows or cares who he is. Except Sabine. He sends her a message, tells her where he's staying, and another message—*Waiting for you as always. Come say hi.* He knows they'll find each other again, even so far from home and after so long a time.

Outside, Sandy hears the train running along the street, a hum over the clink of metal. On the brick wall surrounding the park across the way, someone has graffitied *Mad World* in English, the letters bold and white like cartoons against neon pink and green and black. The day is alive. Sandy follows Torstrasse through Rosenthaler Platz and into the heart of Mitte. On his walk to the river, he stops at a restored synagogue, now a museum, its gilded dome a sun over the city. He remains there for his parents, the purpose of this place one of remembrance, a warning, a reminder of how easily things can turn. A celebration, too, of the ability to build something new. He wishes his mother, his father, could see this, her spirituality and his antiquity. They would lift him, in all the ways he needs.

After picking up lunch, Sandy wanders through Monbijou Park and settles along the Spree. He wants to bottle the breeze off the cool water. In the days that follow, he swaps the synagogue for the zoo and Museumsinsel. He shops and eats and gets lost. He befriends a polar bear and he drinks wine. Everywhere, though, he's reminded of his Jewishness. Brandenburg Gate, Potsdamer Platz, Checkpoint Charlie. *What are these*—he can hear his father's cynical, unapologetic voice—*if not monuments to our erasure.*

Back at his hotel, he downs two pills, numbers etched into small shapes. He waits for the lightsomeness they will bring. Well past midnight, he heads downstairs, a quick drink at the bar. Outside, the night is cooler than he expected. He ambles, pretends he knows where he's headed, though he has an address written on a napkin and his phone to guide him. A few wrong turns later, he arrives. The music inside the bar is loud and blanketing, the sign above the rows of liquor bottles flashing in twinkle lights. The people around him, their arms bare and sweaty, shoulders against shoulders, heat the air. Sandy takes a shot to wash down another pill. Soon he's dancing and singing and his skin is wet and everyone looks happier than any person he has ever seen. A pale white man in a Suedehead t-shirt smiles at him and pulls him close, fingers curled through

Sandy's belt loops. They dance until Sandy needs another drink. He's at the bar and whatever's in the glass burns going down, and someone has their hand around his and they're in the bathroom and they know Sandy's name. On the countertop rough like stone, there's powder and Sandy takes it in without a thought, his sinuses ablaze. He feels his teeth as if they're aliens in his mouth. He looks up and they're kissing and their lips are like sugar and he's on the dance floor again. His head is a rush of blood and his tongue swells, the flavor fades, gives way to an overwhelming numb. Sandy is raw and alight. Conversations mix inextricably with the music. He doesn't know what anyone is saying, and he's sure it doesn't matter. Somebody hands him another shot and he drinks it, head snapping back then forward too quickly, and everything spins, and someone grips his hands and he's walking, bouncing off a sea of bodies until suddenly it's quiet and he's in a corner he's never been in or maybe he's outside and Suedehead shirt is there, too, hair red flames and shining, and he unbuckles Sandy's belt. Sandy tries to look at him, see him, but he's on his knees and Sandy can't stop from crying out and afterwards, he vibrates. They switch, Sandy tearing at the t-shirt, and when he finishes he grips Sandy by the hair. He pulls him close and their swollen lips catch fire. He's dancing once more, the drugs and the music and the taste of this stranger combine inside of him and in the middle of this place he is a conduit, he is the conductor, this electricity coursing through him not only his but everyone's, and he, at the center, controls it all.

Later, hours or days, it's morning, and Sandy's back in his hotel room. He's in bed, warm and alone. How this came to be, he doesn't know.

⌇

Outside the door of Sandy's room, Sabine finds one shoe, a t-shirt, and Sandy's wallet, empty of its euros. She knocks and, to her surprise, the door is slightly ajar. She tiptoes in. The sun pours through the windows on the far side, overlooking the park. The bed empty, but she hears Sandy, curled on the floor, wedged between the bed frame and the wall. He looks comfortable, peaceful. She considers leaving, letting him sleep. He will wake to a litany of messages from her, sent with increasing worry over the past few days, but he is fine, he is here—that is all that matters.

An odor, though, stale and acidic, pulls her further into the room; she finds its source in the bathroom, pooled in the tub and shower and over the floor. An attempt has been made to cover it, resulting in a pile of sick-soaked towels. She struggles to keep Roger away, shooing him with her foot. The smell overwhelms her, and she hurries back to Sandy, shaking him, shouting his name, her hand hovering outside his mouth, feeling for proof of life. His skin is hot and the corners of his mouth are caked a dark yellow. He is breathing but he does not wake. She grasps him by the torso and lifts him onto the bed. His eyelids, when they slit open, nearly bring Sabine to tears.

"Sabby," he asks, his voice chalky and worn.

She is not sure he can even see her. "You bastard," she says.

"Yeah." His cracked lips smack.

"Are you alive?" She slides her arms under him and shifts him to the middle of the bed. His stomach makes a sound like a ghost howling.

"I don't know," he says.

She grabs a bottle of water from the table and opens it and puts it in Sandy's hand. "Drink," she says.

Most of it dribbles down his chin, but anything is better than nothing, she thinks. The space beneath his eyes, dark and sunken, makes him look like someone else, someone Sabine does not recognize. She runs her fingers through his hair, feels the heat radiating off of him. She asks if they can get him into a shower, and he says no. He asks if she has seen the bathroom. She assures him someone can come and clean it. He shakes his head. "No one can see me like this."

For only a moment she enjoys the unsaid intimacy in his words, that she is not anyone, not *no one*. "Okay," she says. She pulls one of his t-shirts from a drawer, wets it and wraps it around Sandy's forehead. "Stay," she demands. "I will be right back."

Downstairs, she asks for a room of her own. She is not a member, but she is Sabine Hellewege, German sports heroine.

"Frau Hellewege," they say at the front desk, "whatever we can do for you."

She finds their accent, their slight lisp, endearing. "Danke," she says, a smile to match, the kind they will photograph and post on Prattlr and share with the world. Not yet, though, she knows. Privacy and caution first in a place such as this, both of which she will demand in abundance.

Sandy is barely awake when she returns, moisture from the t-shirt running down his face. She helps him from the bed—only after a firm promise he will not be sick—and walks him to her room. It is a short corridor, one she has been assured will be entirely theirs for the moment. Sandy moves slowly, his steps measured yet wobbly like a child's. Roger is ecstatic for the company. In her bathroom, Sabine strips off Sandy's clothes, steadies him in the shower. There is a smooth marble bench on one side, and she sits him there.

"Clean yourself," she says. "I am right outside."

She feels the stress of the week in every muscle. Her father, Victoria, the crowd, all of it. She is unsatisfied with a quarterfinal finish, but she wants to put it out of her mind, focus on Sandy. She has no idea what has happened, how he came to be like this. He messaged her only days ago—a photo of the Spree, his picnic for one; then again in the middle of the night, and her panic began—*where are you*—with no response from him after, no apology for a drunken late-night message. She hurried here, all too happy to leave Stuttgart, visions of her father and his eternal disapproval looming still.

She collapses onto the bed, Roger nestled beside her. She calls out to Sandy, checking in. Roger barks in response. Steam leaks from the bathroom and trails through the room. She feels the stress dripping off her like condensation. Knowing, finally, her Sandy is safe. When she hears the shower turn off, she waits a moment, asks if she should come in. "I'm okay," he says and opens the door, towel wrapped around his waist. His chest is strong, covered in a light layer of black hair, his shoulders broad. He is fitter than when they last saw each other, still small but muscular, toned. He takes deep, purposeful breaths. She steps to him, kisses him lightly on the forehead. She takes in his features, details she has missed, feared she may never see again. She presses her palm against his unshaven cheek, and, with a crack in her throat, she says, "There you are."

———

It's been too long. Years, *fuck*, Sandy almost says. But it doesn't matter now. She's here, thank god she's here. He throws his arms around her. He squeezes her until his fingertips tingle.

"What have you done to yourself?" Her voice, her sing-song English, fills him with an overwhelming comfort.

He's crying, they're side by side on the bed, and Sandy pets Roger's exposed belly and feels this release might go on forever.

When he has calmed, the three of them, Sandy still towel-clad, scamper quickly to his room. Sabine had asked for his bathroom to be cleaned—*You're a goddamn angel*, he says—and the previous ungodly scent has been replaced by bleach and citrus. Sandy remembers very little of the past few days. He tells her what he can. There are faces, neon flashes, but nothing of substance. Everything like a dying star. This *supernova*. He says the word out loud to Sabine.

"Are you going to explode?" she asks, her tone soft, lighthearted.

"I already have," he says, and she reaches for him.

"You are alive, my dear," she says. "We are alive."

Sandy lays down. The room is a kaleidoscope. He searches for moments from the last few nights. He feels it in his temples, his cock, in the bones behind his eyes. His nose burns. He's happy to see Sabine—he needed her more than he realized—but he wishes it wasn't like this.

"I miss him," Sandy says, and it's as if the words are not his own, like he's watching someone else come apart on this bed. He sobs, his stomach tight and retching. Roger cranes his head and licks at Sandy's salty skin, and Sandy can't help but carry on.

"I know," Sabine says. "I know, but this is not you." She's being kind, yet Sandy can hear the impatience in her voice, the desire to shake him violently out of this.

"I think it's the most me I've ever felt," he says, wallowing.

"No." She slaps her hand down on a pillow. "You are hiding here. This—you are a ghost."

"It's too fucking much, Sabby. The dying and the playing and so much fucking pretending. I don't know how you do it. I can't anymore. It's worn right through me." He sits up quickly, lets his chest inflate, lets the vessels in his head sting. When he exhales, he imagines something more has been released.

"You are not a coward," Sabine says.

The way she looks at him, Sandy's afraid of what she sees.

"I'm not you," he says, more cutting, accusatory, than he means.

"No one is asking you to be."

"I can't keep it all tucked away."

"And this is the only alternative?"

He stands, his body acclimating to the movement. "Maybe," he says. In the bathroom, he searches for his pills. In his suitcase, his bag, on the table and in the kitchenette. His head pounds.

"What do you need?" Sabine asks, then, as Sandy continues rummaging without response, "Can I help?"

"Just something for my head." He bites the inside of his lip, his teeth grinding.

"I have," she says and pulls a bottle of over-the-counter medicine from her bag.

He thanks her, sucks at the bathroom faucet to wash it down. He knows it won't help. He stands in the middle of the room, the pressure swallowing his head. He hears music imprinted on his membranes. He'll need to find his own pills, or something stronger, soon.

Sabine waves her hand, snapping him back. "Still with me?" He nods, smiles. He knows she can see right through it. That she's afraid for him. "Put on some clothes and we go for a walk."

"Now? I don't know if I'm up—"

"Take me to the river," she interrupts. "I want a picnic."

"Picnic for two," he says. "That sounds nice."

Sabine goes back to her room before they leave—fetching Roger's leash, she tells Sandy—and flushes his pills. She will search again later when an opportunity arises, make sure there are no more. It is hard for her to look at him like this, the exoskeleton of a person she has known and loved for so long. She knows this is about Nick. She knows what he meant to Sandy, how deep it ran. She sees what World Day has done to him, how it has picked him apart. She thought she understood what that devastation would look like. But not this.

When she was shot, when her life unraveled, Sandy wanted to be there for her. He tried to support her, offered over and over to spend quiet hours with her watching movies, drinking wine, cooking dinner, being as close or as far as she wanted. But instead of asking, instead of opening herself up even a little, she pushed him away. She did this with purpose. She pretended she was doing it for him, keeping him at bay, becoming a ghost, a phantom on the other end of his messages. She could not bear the weight of his friendship, the belief that she did not deserve it, did not deserve him in her life. She had heard her father through the thin walls of their house say that to her mother many times—*I do not deserve you*—and only now does she understand the depths to which that belief settled in her. But even in her worst moments, Sabine did not allow herself the luxury of coming apart. *Supernova.* No, she had to be stronger, and she wants the same for Sandy. She knows now she made a mistake when she pushed him away, cut him from her life. They need each other. This is the proof; they are both here. They remain. That must mean something. She believes it when she watches him slide a shirt over his shoulders, strong but overburdened by the weight of survival. The restless nights settling beneath his eyes. The constant crack in his voice. She recognizes what he must have in her—not someone in need of saving or too damaged for fixing, but her dearest friend in need of love, asking for it without words, arms outstretched, hoping they will take this journey together.

The river moves differently today, Sandy notices. It steals away the melancholy of the past few days. Weeks, months. He rests his head on Sabine's shoulder. It's her, he knows. His Sabby. How he has missed this. The smell of her skin is a perfect mix of coconut and sand and sweet. He hasn't felt so calm since losing Nick, maybe before. He remembers once saying to Sabine, half-joking, that she was the love of his life, which still feels true, in ways he never imagined the word to mean.

"I like it here," he says. For a moment, Sandy wonders if he isn't still passed out in his hotel room, dreaming, slipping away.

"I thought we lost this," Sabine says.

Sandy settles his head against her abdomen, drapes his leg over hers. "Tell me something," he says, "something real."

"Like what?" she asks, running her fingers through his hair.

"Tell me about this place," he demands, his voice like chamomile.

She looks around, squinting against the sunshine. She points at the river. "It is gorgeous, yeah?"

Sandy nods, heavy against her body. He almost drifts, not out of tiredness but calm.

"Well not below the surface. When the wall was up, people were shot trying to get across. Children drowned. And the law said they could not be rescued—the GDR would shoot you for entering the water, even to save a child. Both East and West watched them die. Can you imagine what this river looked like to those people trying to cross? Look over there. The same city, the same people, and yet not. Spree. Die Mauer. Can you imagine?"

Sandy sits up, unable to hide his shock. "Jesus, Sabby." He pulls his knees in tight, cracks a smile. "What the hell?"

"It is important to remember, I think. To see beauty but also know where it came from. We are not like Americans; we do not pretend these terrible things never happened. We recognize them, we live with them, we use them to make us stronger."

He hears her, what she's trying to do for him, but he can't leave it there. "Something else happened here and, believe me, I feel it. Maybe you want to pretend it's a thing for museums and plaques, a history everyone has grown from, but it's very much alive to me."

"It is for all of us. That is what I mean. It has to be, or we have learned nothing."

"It's not the same," he says, his tone sharp, "and you know it."

"To be a Jew in this city is to know exactly of what I speak." She reaches down, takes cheese and dates from their picnic bag. She watches Sandy in a way that makes him feel protected.

"In this world," he says, stealing a date from her pile. "And it's not history if it's still present."

"Exactly." She smacks him lightly, and her hand feels cool against his warm skin.

He would keep going if he had the strength—the wall his own country built to keep people out; the tensions growing even in his hometown; the boy, not in a river but on his doorstep.

"Stay just like that," he says, using his own hand to press Sabine's harder against his face.

"You have a fever," she says.

"It's the hangover, don't worry. This is helping. You're so damn cold."

"Ice queen," she says, and he collapses back onto her, the two of them laughing. And for some reason they keep on going, like a kind of scream but of laughter, and it fills the air around them, swept by the cool breeze across the river, and safely onto the other side.

"We should do something tonight," Sabine says. She curls along the blanket, resting her head on Sandy's chest. He takes deep breaths, hoping the noise in his mind will quiet. This is the longest he's gone without taking something in weeks, a thought he tries not to focus on. He opens himself to the sun, the steady movement of clouds, and feels Sabine's heartbeat melt into his own. Everything measured, serene, so very unlike him.

—

When she gets out of the shower, Sabine finds Roger laying atop her phone as it vibrates.

"Abzischen!" she shouts, chuckling at his silliness. Expecting Sandy, she is surprised to see her father's name flash across the screen. She ends the call without answering, tosses the phone back onto the bed. It goes again, a voicemail, before Roger envelopes it with his fluffy body once more. "Braver Hund," she says.

At dinner, Sandy fidgets. He looks ill, pallid. He is quiet. He needs to rest, she thinks, begin to recover some sense of himself. But she cannot force healing on him. She knows this all too well.

"How is your mother?" she asks between bites.

His face changes immediately. He wipes his lips. "She's okay, I think. On edge, but what else is new."

"Does she know where you are?"

He shakes his head, uses the careful slicing of his salmon to delay. "It's been a bit," he says. "Since just after everything."

"I am sure she would like to know you are okay." She catches herself.

"She knows," he says, smiling from the corners of his mouth, his most sarcastic smile. "It's a sixth sense Jewish mothers have—they know everything about their sons, it's like a super power. I could call her right now, and she'd say *what's wrong you sound like you have a headache*. It's endlessly frustrating." He laughs, his silverware clanging against the plate.

His self-deprecating humor, its sharpness, never leaves him, she thinks. It is refreshing to see. She envies what Sandy and his mother have. She cannot remember the last time she and her father shared something sweet. She used to blame him for her mother's death, but that excuse long since faded. They had their chances, Sabine and her father, and perhaps it is better if what they have now, this inescapable cycle of aggression and dispassion, is laid to rest, replaced by a total and complete nothing.

Yet his showing up in Stuttgart plagues her. It had been years, as far as she knew, since he traveled across the Atlantic, content to fade away in that Florida swamp. His calling, too, highly out of character for Jürgen Hellewege, and she struggles to grasp its purpose, to find a space inside of her still willing to make room for him.

A sea of faces—her father, Lolo, Alina—tick through her mind. Drago, her first childhood love. Victoria. Those that have been closest to her, in one way or another. She looks at Sandy, the brightest face perhaps, and he is saying something, his lips move and when they stop, he watches Sabine, waiting, and it brings her back.

"What?" she says and takes a cheekful of wine.

"Bitch, have I been talking to myself this whole time?"

She dips her fingertips into her water glass, flicks them at Sandy. "You hush," she says. "You like the sound of your voice too much anyway."

"I said we should finish and take a walk. I've been loving the nights here."

"It is a wonderful city. We used to visit when I was young. My uncle lived here. There was a junior tournament and on my off days, my mother and uncle would steal me away from my father, and we would eat in some smoky restaurant or bar, somewhere that felt like a secret. They would talk to strangers like they were old friends. Then, off to the zoo or a museum or a cruise on the river. The zoo was always my favorite. I loved the pandas."

"Let's sneak in," Sandy says, and Sabine can tell by the devil in his eyes that he means it.

"I did not come back here to get arrested, good sir."

"You're the worst," he says, and after, when they leave the restaurant arm in arm, she tells him what she sees—that he is lighter than before, that whatever cloud hovers above him might be clearing. He laughs, and she loves the sound of it, the way it echoes throughout the Tiergarten. But she hears its stretch, too—not disingenuous, not fully meant, but somewhere in between.

They pretend they hear animal sounds as they move through the park. Sandy imitates a rhinoceros by making elephant noises. He is a little drunk, and Sabine enjoys it. He is still the sturdy, stubborn boy she met those springs ago, though that skin is covered now by one worn down, aged more by circumstance than time. She sees it in the cracks around his eyes, spread out like a star. In his voice, which sounds always tired. She hears the tremble and feels the tremble, like something happening in the world runs through him and his body, his vocal cords and his fingers and his mind, shaken to the point of near destruction.

Sandy guides them, though to where Sabine has no clue; their conversation pauses, replaced instead by the rhythm of their steps. Dim streetlamps and passing headlights illuminate their path forward. They turn down a street lined with bars, English and German music leaking out. There are people around them but they are alone. Sabine slides her arm around his, and they continue on, quiet, until Sandy looks up and stops and says, "We're here."

———

He leaves her sitting at the bar nursing her second drink, and he follows the dimly lit corridor leading to a single bathroom. There's no line yet and once inside, the smell an overwhelming blend of smoke and piss, Sandy waits. He sits on the porcelain, pretending it's anything but what it is. When a knock comes, Sandy's hesitant and opens the door. A young man, eighteen maybe twenty, stands before him, shoulders hunched, his cheeks pockmarked. He hands Sandy a tiny plastic bag of pills, which Sandy palms and exchanges for a folded mess of euros. The young man pockets the money and disappears without a word down the corridor. Sandy swallows one of the pills dry. It's nothing strong, just enough to take the edge off. He repeats the thought: *It's nothing*.

Sabine moved to a high top in his absence, making way for the crowd thronging the bar. He takes her in—long muscular legs, shoulders thick, white skin tan from years spent on sun-drenched courts, her smile wide and bright and slightly crooked—and he imagines she must look to everyone like a god amongst mortals. She is tall and uncanny, the strongest person he has ever known.

They were kids when they met, he reminds her later, an exaggeration she seems to understand. They dance, the music swelling beyond the capacity for conversation. They dance and they sing, their bodies sweating and glistening under the lights. Sandy feels weightless. Sabine smiles as she moves, and he wonders what she sees when she looks at him, how it could possibly be good. She spins around him, her fingers tickling across his back. The music swallows them. He's sure of only one thing in this moment: if he lets go, if he's falling, Sabine will catch him.

He reaches out, and she takes his hand. She pulls him close, wraps her arms around him. She kisses him, slight but tender, their lips touching then not.

"I love you," she says, quiet enough that it blends into the rhythm around them. "You know that?" He nods, his face warm like it might explode. "This is the last of it, yes?" He crinkles his eyebrows, and her eyes lock onto his. "Whatever you took tonight, and before. It is done, yes?"

He feels the color drain from him. He nods once more. He's grateful for how close she is, that they're together again. The tempo of the music quickens, volume rises, and they are limbs and torsos and bodies capable of great things.

On the walk back to the hotel, Sandy tosses the bag of pills into a bin in the park. He and Sabine aren't quiet, too tipsy to listen for animal sounds. Sabine asks him what he'll do now, when he'll return to the States and his team. He shakes his head, which feels heavy in its coming down.

"Soon?" she says, grinning.

He laughs at her playfulness. "I've got a long career ahead of me. Maybe I don't need to rush."

"Silly boy," she says, tightening the loops of their arms, "we are getting old. The world is dropping buildings in our path. Take nothing for granted."

Sandy's expression contorts, cartoonish and inquisitive. "Who *are* you, Sabine Hellewege? Who's this wise oracle before me?"

"Hush," she says, bumping her hip into his. "Besides, my career will long outlast yours."

"Will it now?" He raises his voice, such that the question echoes beyond them.

"I have lost time to make up for."

Sandy's mind drifts, caught up in the realization that, at some point sooner rather than much later as he always imagined, he'll no longer be a ballplayer. He has heard veterans and coaches and broadcasters on the eve of retirement say things like *once a ballplayer always a ballplayer*, and *the game never leaves you*, but that's not true. Eventually, it'll go; it'll be gone, and he'll no longer play this game. He remembers the times his mother said he was more than just baseball, how he hated her for saying it, how it made him feel the game wasn't worth a life, his life, but he wanted it to be. He wanted, still wants, to be the best, to be remembered, to leave the kind of legacy that would make his father proud. *An unforgettable.*

He remembers sharing this with Nick during their first spring training together, before Nick got called up and left Sandy behind in the humid impossibility of Florida. He met Sabine then, too, a series of events he never considered until this very moment. The connectivity of their three lives, of countless others, the things they shared, would still share, or never would again.

"Hey!" Sabine's voice snaps him back to the present. "Do you know where we are?" She's drunk, for the first time he hears it, and it lightens him. "We have been walking. I have no idea where."

"Come." Sandy grips her hand, spreading out his fingers between hers. "Muscle memory," he says, knowing he got home all the nights before, completely out of his head.

He asks about Lolo and Alina, both of whom bring a smile to Sabine. She asks if he'll walk Roger when they reach the hotel. He says he will, that perhaps he'll kidnap him and they'll run off together, a boy and his stolen dog. She assures him Roger can't survive without her.

The night is brisker than before. Sandy taps on the metal gate along the edge of the park. "Here," he says, pointing at the building on the corner, the streetlights creating shadows like storm clouds on the horizon.

As they walk upstairs to his room, Sandy fumbles for his key. "Wouldn't it be wonderful," he says, "to pass out together."

In the quiet that follows, he glances up at her. She stares at his door, her expression a kind of empty terror. He follows her gaze, and when he sees it there, that small pink triangle affixed just below the knocker, he can't breathe, and at some point soon he'll have to relearn how, to take in air, let it fill his lungs, and release again. But for now, for this millisecond and the next and the next, he must be content to live, if ever briefly, without it.

—

She watches him pack his bags. He has not said a word, not since last night, side by side in bed, Sabine listening to his cadences. He did not understand why or how it was happening, only that the symbol was meant as a threat, regardless of its reclamation.

"Who are these people?" he asked before finally falling asleep, before Sabine could think of how to respond. She wrapped her arms around his torso. It was an impossible question.

In her blood and her muscles, she feels everything she drank, as if a tighter, dried out version of her exists beneath her skin, something petrified, like lava exposed to air.

"I wish you would stay," she says, hearing in her own voice the heartbreak, the contradiction, knowing as she does how she has encouraged him to waste no time. "For a little while longer, at least."

"I have to go," he says, clearing his throat after. Sabine wants to reassure him, but she knows she cannot. In America, she has seen this sort of hate growing, felt it melting into her flesh. Xenophobia, bigotry, like bullets. But here—she wants to believe they do not happen here. The thought is so noisy in her mind she is unsure if she has said it aloud.

"It's time anyway," Sandy says, and they both hear how uncertain he is.

"It has been good, being here with you. Being close again."

"It has," he says. He shoves down his clothes and zips his bag shut. He pushes it onto the floor, and Roger quickly hops up on the bed and rolls over, tongue hanging to the side. "But it's time."

Even if she will not say it, Sabine understands. She misses the court, the practice, and the training. She misses the simplicity they bring to her life. The comfort of knowing what is to come. "I used to know everywhere I would be. Feels like a lifetime since that was true."

The way Sandy looks at her, Sabine knows he is barely holding himself together. "Yeah," he says. "I can't even remember the last game I played. They all mash together."

"You hit a home run," Sabine says, trying to lighten them both.

He laughs, collapses on the bed beside Roger, squeezes him like a stuffed animal. "Something like that," he says.

Sabine joins them, Roger sandwiched in the middle. She does not want this to be the last time they are together like this. She is scared for herself and for Sandy. If he leaves, she cannot keep him close. If he leaves, he goes back to being a text message, a distant voice on the end of a sporadic call, a phantom baseball star on the nightly highlights. If he leaves, they will have to find each other once more.

"I saw something," she says, her thoughts brimming over. When they both sit up and adjust on the bed, Roger, given the space, stretches out, such that a front and back paw presses against each of them. "In Florida, when I visited my father after World Day. There were men there." She does not know why she is telling him now, maybe as a warning, or an unburdening, the selfishness of knowing something evil yet keeping silent.

She goes over every detail, the men and what they look like, the guns, the terrifying familiarity in their insignia. Sandy pushes her to say more. She shakes her head while she explains, as if to convey the unease of it all. She knows what she saw—something she thought private, a symbol belonging to her mother—and despite her father's claim to the contrary, she holds that recognition strong against her chest. She still hears the violence in their machinery. Across from her, Sandy's eyes water, and it is only in his tears she realizes she, too, is crying. How can you go back to that, she wants to say, but she sees clearly the lie, the fantasy that here, that anywhere, is safe. Europe is not safe, not Asia, not America. There is nowhere to run from this hate.

The next day, after Sandy leaves for the airport, Sabine walks to get lunch. The city is calm, and she takes her time, absorbing its energy, bikes filling the streets, conversations blending like a grand meal, footfalls on every corner. Back at the hotel, a letter has been slipped under her door, an explanation of what has occurred. *We apologize*, she reads, and *reported to the police*; she crumples the paper, tosses it across the room. Roger gives chase, confusing it for a ball. He tears at it until it is nothing but strips of indistinguishable language.

She packs slowly, makes calls and sends messages to Lolo and Alina and her agent, but she relishes these last remaining hours of complete solitude. She will travel to Gstaad next. She is anxious for those grass courts. Where her pace and her power and her touch—that holy trinity of tennis, Jim O'Brien once called it—go on full display. As perfect a next thing as she can imagine.

Caught up in the sounds of Berlin outside, Sabine drifts. She is back in Florida, in the past but her present self. She stands alone in the mangroves, the thick swampy saltiness enveloping her. The ground underfoot gives way, and her bare feet sink, her toes covered in muck. Around her, all manner of fish and plant life move. A gray egret along the shore, cormorants diving down. The water has been cooked by the summer heat. The Florida sun unforgiving. Sabine swings her arms just below the surface, the brownish swirl cut by the whiteness of her open palms. She dances, she flies, she is weightless. She kicks herself up, her breasts and torso exposed in the afternoon air. And there, in the distance approaching with careful ease, a manatee. Sabine wades towards it, her feet stirring up tiny jellyfish and tangled, broken mangrove branches. She breathes in deep, takes in water, too; around her she smells smoke, faint at first but growing. Along the banks and for miles in every direction, the Everglades burns. She cools her face, and when she surfaces, the manatee is close. Sabine thinks it will rescue her, whisk her off to safety. She stops swimming and waits. Deliberate, slow movements. It is only too late, when Sabine notices the eyes of the creature, the reptile armor it wears, that she understands why she is here, why she cannot move. She remains this way, still and resolved and unbroken, as the great creature, its yellow eyes flicking for an instant, disappears into the darkness. Soon, and completely, she feels it everywhere.

*

The day is nearly gone when she wakes, an orange and blue-violet fire out her window as the sun sets. She cannot shake the dream. She collects her things, though she takes little care in their organization, a pile of underwear and sports bras and t-shirts and a separate bag of shoes and Roger's toys and bowls and his little raincoat. Sabine arranges them by the door. Someone will collect them when the time comes, and she will fly to Bern, where Florian Frei was born and raised, where his tennis and his humanity made him the proverbial King of Switzerland, where a memorial to him has already been erected, and where Sabine will stop on her way to Gstaad to pay her respects, though the thought of it now, of the memorial's very existence, makes her want to scream. Everything these days makes her want to scream.

When Roger barks and nudges her leg, telling her it is past time for a walk, she wonders how long her hand has been balled in a fist. "Ja ja okay," she says. "Let's go!"

The evening is humid. Roger leads her around the block, down a street she has never been where she stops for gelato. They walk until Roger tires, his tiny legs sluggish, and Sabine tosses the melted remains of her dessert. Outside the hotel, a black SUV idles, with two suited men spanning the sidewalk. As they approach the front door, Sabine steps between the men, a half-hearted *Pardon* spoken under her breath.

"Frau Hellewege," the larger of the two says, dark-skinned, maybe Greek she thinks, his voice warmer than she expects. "Wir brauchen dich, um mit uns zu kommen."

Her body tightens. She is no stranger to violence. She wishes suddenly for a racket. "No thank you," she says and turns, reaching for the hotel door.

"Don't do that," the other says, his voice thick, chunky, Irish or Scottish, she cannot tell. "Don't make a scene. Just get in the car. You and the dog'll be safe."

"Will we now?" She wonders why she is not running, or shouting, anything. She is unable to move. "And if not?"

The men smile at one another. "He's a cute dog," the Greek one says.

If she could, she would send Roger down the street rather than pressed against her leg. Her fist balls and lands flush on the cheek of the Irishman. She feels the way his teeth dig into his lips. She is strong, but he is a sturdy man, a brick wall, and four arms are around her in an instant. She kicks and writhes, but once she is inside the car, the windows tinted to blackness, there is no more fight. The Greek man looks at her, trying to calm her she thinks, and she spits at him. Her saliva runs down the side of his face before he wipes it away.

"You're not in any danger," he says, quiet and measured.

"Fuck you," she says. Roger barks, growls at the men. It is almost enough to make Sabine laugh, if she was not already terrified. "What is this?" she asks. "Wo bringst du mich hin?"

"Like he said," the Irishman shouts from the driver's seat, tilting the rearview mirror to look Sabine in the eyes, "you're not in danger. Just sit back, pet your dog. We'll be there soon."

She feels for her phone in her pocket. She is certain she could get off an emergency call, but then what? She does not want to make this worse. They drive for what seems like hours, though she can tell from the street sounds they have not left the city. She closes her eyes and hopes when she opens them, this will be just another nightmare.

They stop finally, and the Irishman exits and walks around the car and opens the door. He spits on the ground, rubs his jaw with his meaty fingers. The Greek man says he will hold on to Roger. When Sabine refuses, still unwilling to leave the car, he leans forward and whispers, "I'm not asking." Sabine lets Roger jump down, and the Greek man takes his leash. "We'll be outside when you're done."

As she steps from the car, Sabine takes in her surroundings. Small street, quiet street. Voices in the distance. The Irishman has a hand on her shoulder but she could run, she knows she could outrun both these fuckers. But not without Roger, no.

They are in front of a restaurant—*Constance*, the sign reads—and the lights inside are dim. The Irishman opens the door. She steps through, and he does not follow. With the door shut, the restaurant is even darker. But there is movement, the clinking of a glass. "Hello," she asks. She tries to steady her voice. She is scared, but she does not want whoever is here to know. "What am I doing here?"

A figure, a silhouette at a table, waves her over. Sabine takes barely a step. Her legs are iron gates.

"Komm, komm setz dich."

A chill, a flood of chills, they cascade over Sabine. The voice, how familiar it is, ices her blood. She steps closer, until the silhouette is shadowed no more. Every cell in Sabine's body thrums.

"My sweet, come. There is so much to say."

Sabine sucks in as if she is drowning. The woman across from her does not move. She looks back at Sabine, smiling, like today is a day she has waited for. Her hair is shorter but the same. Her face, her eyes. It has been years, but she is the same. Her mother is just the same.

IV

WE THE PEOPLE

What happens, happens around us.

We exist and we hurt, we shake our heads and our fists in disgust. We condemn. We march in the streets. We raise funds. We prattle. We meme. We vote, and under our breaths we are resigned. We are loud because we know the truth, because we must be heard. We boycott and we burn.

We are lawyers and doctors and schoolteachers and taxi drivers and train conductors and servers and managers and successes and failures. We are politicians. We join hands and we disagree. Lines are drawn, whims that will ripple through time, tear apart towns and cities and families and generations and countries. We are thrown into camps, thrown from restaurants, thrown from schools and hospitals and pulled from our very streets, cars, houses. We listen to those who say it is right; we punch and we protest. We see the hate, the way it grows, evolves, spreads, when left unchecked. When fertilized. We know there is no longer a place for peace.

Our parks empty, some too afraid to go outside, our soccer pitches and baseball diamonds and tennis courts barren, and on our streets men with guns demand papers of proof, and people are disappeared or attacked in daylight because of who they are or where they are from or who they love or who they have always been inside. These things are real and not the fodder of history or fiction. Right now is nothing like we imagined it could be.

What happens, happens inside us.

GHOSTS

The first thing he's going to do is get pizza. He has craved a slice since England. As he takes in the last views of the Atlantic, the clouds like cotton, he knows he's homesick. He hears Sabine's voice, urging him to calm, to center, to keep himself upright.

They're curving around Jamaica Bay before he realizes he has given the driver his mother's address. He sits back and absorbs the rolling dark blue out the window. His whole life, though he has never lived away from it, he has taken the water for granted; but at this moment, he feels grateful, lucky, to have something so simple be a part of him.

The driver clicks his tongue against his teeth, pointing at Sandy in the rearview. "Hey, you're him," he says, his bratwurst finger nearly covering the mirror.

"I'm nobody," Sandy says, avoiding direct eye contact, wishing his beard had grown long enough to disguise him. He's tired, and the idea of a long back and forth with this stranger about the Atlantics lack of bullpen depth, his own erratic hitting, the spirits of the team after losing so many— no, he prefers silence, even one brought on by coldness.

Once they arrive in Brighton, though, and the familiarity of his neighborhood, these streets of his youth, he's relieved. He poses for a picture with the driver and signs his tattered Atlantics cap before they part. "For my little girl," he says to Sandy, who knows it's not true but smiles anyway.

The house has been repainted, almost teal with the sunshine reflecting off the grass. It unnerves Sandy, this subtle change. He goes in without knocking. He calls out for his mother. He leaves his bags by the front door as he explores each room. It's like a movie set, dressed to give the appearance of a full family home. It makes him sad to think of his mother here all alone. "It's too much space for one person," he says out loud as he leaves the master bedroom, and the sound gives him chills. His father's voice, coming from his own mouth—when did that happen?

His old room, unchanged since his last visit, is bright and cozy. On the nightstand sits the book of fairy tales. He scoops it up and settles outside in a chair on the deck, sipping a beer and waiting for his mother to return home. He doesn't message her; he doesn't want her to worry. He'll just be here, held by his father's tales and these magic walls, and like all good Jewish mothers, she'll know. She'll know without him saying a word.

When Sandy wakes, the old book open across his chest, hours have gone, the sun set. He goes into the house. "Mama," he shouts, and the word reverberates through empty rooms. Sandy decides on tea over another beer and sits at the dining room table. Around him, the room fills with his parents' voices.

Pass the zucchini bread, Tess, his father demands. *Are you eating enough?* his mother asks, a question followed by a pat to his abdomen. She slides a second helping onto his plate without asking, maybe pot roast or kugel or both. Gefilte fish had been off the menu since Sandy was a child, since Bubbe forced it on him and he, in return, sprayed it back over the table, to the horror and delight of his grandparents' visiting friends. *How was practice?* his mother asks, a loose noodle dangling from her fork. *Let the boy eat*, his father says, which Sandy hears as *breathe*. Their silverware clanking against their plates takes on its own kind of rhythm, fast then slow with quick interludes, and he can see his mother's pleasure in this, the music of their tradition. His father tears at a piece of challah. *Practice was good*, Sandy says, his head and his eyes down, to keep hidden that he and Nick snuck away after practice and ate pizza, their bodies hot and their stomachs craving something forbidden; to keep hidden that he's full, from the oil and cheese and conversation; to keep hidden that he wanted to stay with Nick and would've except for Nick's insistence that Sandy not miss

Friday night dinner, that it's important to honor the sorts of things that make us who we are, that it's important even if we don't understand why. Sandy feels the place on his shoulder blades where Nick's hands pressed as they parted. This, too, he keeps hidden, though perhaps only from himself. His parents discuss a new mapping project his father's working on for the university. Sandy doesn't focus on their words, only their expressions, the way his mother reaches over and squeezes his father's hand, the way she says *Lenny* as if she couldn't be prouder, the way his father's arms move like a conductor with his baton, more and more animated until, at the story's climax, they're outstretched and wide and inviting them all in, into this symphony that is their simple extraordinary lives.

By the time the tea cools, the voices have faded. Sandy sits alone again, the book open on the table. He wishes to live in one of these tales, one where nobody dies, or, if they do, they're brought back to life because when someone is loved, needed badly enough, they can't possibly stay gone forever. Why can't that be real? His father believed in things so brilliant. Nick, too. Sandy misses them both, now more than ever—though he knows that scale will always slide, appreciate, such that any moment of any day will be more than ever—and on this last night before his return to the sport of his life, Sandy decides to stay in these feelings, let them swell and fill the rooms around him, knowing they'll fade and they'll never fade, that he'll carry these two men with him, that they'll never die, that they'll always, forever, be dead.

He sleeps in his childhood bed until sunrise. He sips coffee on the deck, flipping through the news on his phone. He didn't miss this constant barrage. Pictures of children—faces caked with dirt, canals of saline-clear skin down their cheeks—caught at the southern border and wrangled into camps. Similar photographs pepper the international section, as the imaginary lines separating countries turn continually to concrete. As world leaders, their smugness and their propaganda and their fear mongering, see the futures they want for this world taking shape.

When he can read no more, he flicks to the sports section. The season has gone on in his absence post-England. He'll return from the injured list—a fabrication, if injured can mean only the physical—for the start of tomorrow's series with the Browns, according to the article. "Good to know," he says out loud. His hamstrings, his calves, stiffen at the thought. He needs to go back to his apartment, he knows. In this house he's soft, comfortable, impossible. The longer he's here, he can ignore his agent, his lawyer, the police. Everyone wants him back for some reason, and despite himself he knows it's time. Nick's voice, Sabine's, they tell him so—*Time to be the Sandy we know you are*—even if he struggles to hear them.

He sends a message to his mother, asking how she's doing. *Great*, she replies later, as he packs his duffel. *Visiting Aunt Marie in Camden. The weather here is perfect. How are you? Hope Europe isn't making you fat.* He doesn't mention being at the house, or missing her. He says that all is well, that he loves her, and he's glad the weather's everything she hoped for. He tucks the book of fairy tales into his bag, sure his mother won't notice. He sneaks a few more comforts from home, hoping they'll sustain him once he's gone. In his nightstand, beside an old diary, he finds a key he's never seen before, one he's certain doesn't belong to him. He takes it, tries it in every door in the house, his mother's small safe in her bedroom, the file cabinet in her study, what used to be his father's at-home office. Nothing. He drops his bags at the front door, gives the house one last look. He's stalling, but he doesn't care. The attic, he remembers. He rushes upstairs, pulls down the creaky wooden stairs. Everything smells of mothballs and old sweaters. He steps gingerly along the beams, crouching to avoid hitting his head. In the corner, covered in dust, sits his father's drafting desk. Only days after the bridge bombing, his mother demanded Sandy clear out his father's office, move the desk up here. *I can't*, she kept saying, *I can't look at it a minute longer*. It was the last time, until this moment, Sandy had seen many of his father's things. The large, thin drawer running the length of the desk has a lock on it, and he wipes the metal mechanism with his forefinger. The key slides in, and turns. Inside, stacks of white paper turned almost tawny. His father's personal maps, hand drawn, some fictional landscapes, others artifacts of their lives. Family vacations, genealogies, stadiums where Sandy has played and Lenny visited. An atlas of his father's life, their lives.

One, still in-progress, spans the entire country. Peppered throughout the map, in place of dots or some other iconography, are tiny, perfectly drawn swastikas. Beside each of them, the name of a city. *New York. Chicago. Boston.* And smaller places, too—*Carson City, Cottage Grove, Wood River.* In Florida, a name jumps out, *Wellington,* and he recalls the story Sabine told him of the men with guns living on the land next to her father. He holds up the map, the paper rough against his fingertips. Slivers of sunlight illuminate each Hakenkreuz. A vision of the country Sandy doesn't understand. In the bottom corner of the map, written in pencil in his father's recognizable script, a single word: *Lebensraum.*

He rolls the map, slides it into one of the empty cardboard tubes scattered around the attic. He puts the rest back, locks the drawer. In the kitchen, he leaves the key on the counter atop a note: *Sorry I missed you, Mama. See you soon. Love you—S.* He wonders if she'll recognize the key, if she left it for him to find.

When he leaves the house, bags heavy in tow, he worries. As he walks to the subway, too impatient to wait for a car, he can't shake the uncanny feeling. Not that he has done this before, but that he'll never do it again. A sort of reverse déjà vu. He turns to the house. It looks small and inconsequential from here. It's anything but. The strap of his duffel digs into his flesh, and he continues on. He rides the train through Brooklyn, aboveground then under and out again and over the bridge. The river roars, white crests churning. From here he pretends, as he always has, to see Brighton. The sun reflects off the buildings and stings his eyes. And the stadium, New Ebbets, half-broken and surrounded by cranes, metal and brick spread everywhere, like something ancient destroyed and left for the future. In Manhattan, they slide underground once more. The movements of the train, the recycled air, the conversations and the kinetic energy of bodies. Soon, he'll be back in his apartment. He'll watch from his window as the sky changes. He'll tell Sabine he's safe. He'll settle into the solitude, the calm before his return. He'll be ready for what comes next, now that he's home at last.

REVELATIONS

The grass in Gstaad is a luxury Sabine does not just need but craves. She feels light, almost like she can defy gravity while on court. Her strokes are precise, her shots heavy. Her backhand slice barely skips off the ground. She stays low, her hamstrings barking though she does not show it. Across the net, her opponent appears hapless. Sabine runs her until she is empty. An ace down the tee, two hundred ten kilometers on the radar, and the match ends. Sabine exchanges a kiss on each cheek, shakes the chair umpire's hand, waves to the cheering crowd. They jump to their feet, call out her name—they are hers, moved by her smile and her mirth and other pretend things. They do not know she has not slept. They do not know she has played in a kind of trance, focused only on the tennis, her movements, the weight of the racket in her hand. They do not know how two days have changed her. She slings her bag onto her shoulder, sore, one last wave before disappearing from their view. The semifinals, over. Another Sabine Hellewege victory.

She is mistaken. The woman, this thin, languid creature perched behind a table—she is not her mother. She cannot be. She still hears her father's voice, the way he tried to mask his sadness when he said her mother had died. He never used the word, never *died*, always *gone*. Her mother was gone. She remembers repeating this to friends, teachers, fellow players, the media. *Petra is gone*. In looking at the woman before her now, Sabine finds no other words. "No," she says, shaking her head, the woman wearing a stoic smile, unmoved. "You are gone." And once more, as her legs, her chest, her mind give way, "You are gone."

After treatment, her body pliable, back in her hotel room Sabine finds American sports news on the television. She does not look for herself—this tournament is too small to reach a mainstream audience in the States—and as she waits, she stretches across the bed, sun pouring in, bathing her tennis-tanned skin. Her mind, though, races as if she is on court. She feels her heartbeat in her toes. Roger curls beside her, watching her, such that she is sure he can see all the new and terrible thoughts digging their way in. She closes her eyes and remembers she has not slept. She sinks into the comforter. Then, his name, his team's, and she sits up, sees Sandy at bat, the words on-screen—*Activated from Injured List Today*—and his swing, smooth and effortless, launching the ball over the model cityscape in center field. The camera follows him around the bases, and Sabine sees clearly on his face something close to happiness. Then he is in the clubhouse, hair tousled and wet, phones and microphones pointed at him. "Yes," he says, "it's great to be back. I love playing in Europe—the fans there are fantastic—but it's nice to be home."

Off-screen, a reporter asks, "Even with everything going on here?" Sandy nods, a seriousness to his face, and the reporter continues, "You seem to be in the crosshairs, so to speak."

The word, the very idea, it sucks the air from Sabine, like her chest might cave into itself. But not Sandy. In her dear friend's voice, she hears a confidence she has missed. "Things here have been tough, I won't lie," he says. "But I love this game and I love this city. As a Jewish man, as a Brooklyn boy, I'm so damn proud to represent it. And there's not an asshole alive who's gonna change that." The cut away from him is quick, surgical, and they are on to another game, someone else's story.

She is proud of him, mixed inside her with protectiveness and terror. The combination churns until she is only acid. She runs to the bathroom, and the little she has eaten is gone. Behind her, Roger watches, a kind of broken whine trickling out. She stares at him, the darkness of his eyes, and lets the sound fill the empty space she has become.

*

"Sitzen, mein Kind." She stretches out her arm, uses her open palm to offer Sabine a place beside her.

"What *is* this?" Sabine asks. The lump moving up her throat is a boulder. Her voice is loud. "Who are you?"

The woman shakes her head, tsking.

"What is this? What do you want?"

"Still asking so many questions. Please, sit. Let us find some answers."

The dining room of this restaurant has tables shoved to the sides, chairs flipped upside down, seats on tabletops. The floor is freezing, the lights dim. Through the front windows, moonlight leaks in like a quiet storm. Sabine, the walls, spin. Her eyes thrum. "You cannot be here."

The woman, her grin, disarms Sabine. "I am, dear one." She points to the seat across from her. "I don't want to ask again. Please."

Sabine acquiesces, her body a near perfect ninety degrees, hands gripping her thighs, fingertips turned white. She stares at the woman across from her. "Why?" she asks. *Why are you here. Why am I. Why are you dead. Why are you alive.*

"It was time," she says.

"Does he know?" Sabine asks, sure of the answer. She only wants to hear this stranger say it. The possibilities, the iterations of a life unlived, run rampant through her mind. The uncertainty of it all, of the very ground beneath her opening, swallowing her whole.

"Stubborn, your father. Slow to change. Slower still to understand." The coolness of her voice, the steadiness, chills Sabine.

"Who would possibly understand this?" The muscles in her back pull tauter with every word, the insanity of this.

"You, I think. You will. You are strong enough now to." Her fingers, long and veined, stretch out atop the table.

Sabine is afraid to ask, afraid whatever is happening, if not carefully considered, will spin out of control. Or, more out of control. How could she understand. She wants to run, outrun this woman and her large men, keep running until she is out of Berlin and out of Germany and somewhere far enough away to finally breathe.

But there, too, sits this woman. An apparition covered in flesh. Her voice familiar, like the icicles returning to their family home each winter, beautiful and sharp. This woman, a stranger, dangerous by her mere existence, by the lies that make it so. Her eyes, as Sabine remembers, almost black, speckled with flecks of silver. A constellation, they used to say. Sabine is sure she has not blinked, not as long as she has been looking at her, studying her. This woman. Her mother.

"What," Sabine asks, unsteady. "What do you want to tell me?"

Petra leans across the table, her open palm waiting for Sabine's. "Everything," she says.

"Zéro quinze," the chair announces. Sabine, certain her backhand skimmed the line, does not challenge. Sweat in her eyes, she double faults, followed by a slice dumped into the net. "Zéro quarante." In the echo of the call, she mutters under her breath. She takes her time getting back to the service line. Her toss, slightly too high, gets enveloped by the sun. "Let, premier service." She breathes, her pounding heart racing, and she rips an ace. Then another, kicked out wide. A body serve, a surprise rush to the net, and she puts away an easy volley. "Quarante A." Two points to victory. She tries to steady her mind. Be here now. They trade shots, points back and forth to each. The afternoon is cooler than previous days, but Sabine burns. She is saturated, dripping. A mishit forehand, a big backhand down the line. She grabs her towel. She swaps one ball for another. Two points to victory. "Égalité," the chair calls once more. The word, in its repetition becomes a kind of nonsense, meaning only she is close, closer, yet the ending impossibly out of reach.

Sabine readies herself, her back strong, her hands on the table to match Petra. "You are dead. Start there."

"My death was at your father's behest." Petra pulls back and slides her interlocked fingers in front of her chest, moving them up and down like wings. "Much of what transpired was your father's doing. Some misguided notion of protecting you."

"Protecting me," Sabine says, shaking her head, her neck a knot of tension. Each movement, each word, steeped in disbelief. "From you?"

"From a life he didn't understand."

"That is not an answer."

"He was protecting you, yes, but also himself. Jürgen is a family man, but selfish. He likes things his way."

"The way I remember, it was you. Your rules. Your decisions. Always you."

Petra's mouth curves, lips elegant. "He has done well reshaping your memories."

"He barely spoke of you. I tried to remember all I could. He never wanted to talk about you."

"It wounded him, my leaving."

"Wounded," Sabine repeats, a mix of laughter and rage. "It destroyed us. It colored every day after. Even now."

Petra stares at Sabine, who can see how hard she tries to give away nothing. That much, Sabine thinks, has not changed.

"He—" Petra begins.

Sabine jumps from her seat, pacing across the empty dining room. "Enough," she says. "This is about *you*, not him."

Petra leans back, crosses her legs under the table. "Then ask," she says.

"Are you Petra Hellewege?"

"Yes." She elongates the end of the word into something like a hiss.

"Did you die?"

"Nein."

"Are you dead?"

"Nein."

"Where have you been?"

"Everywhere."

"That is not an answer."

"It's an absurd question."

She is amazed, though she knows she should not be, to see Petra so composed, unemotional in the face of this moment. "Why have I not seen you?"

"I already explained why."

"Have you seen me?"

"Many times."

"Have you been hiding?"

"From?"

"Me, us. Everyone."

"You and your father are not everyone."

"Why have you been hiding?"

"I have, at times, hidden, when necessary. But not hiding. I've made many discreet choices."

"Discreet choices," Sabine says, chewing on the words, their bitter taste lingering on the back of her tongue.

"I'm not invisible."

Sabine, her frenetic steps slowing, takes stock of her mother, as if to confirm the validity of her statement.

"Is Tobias dead?"

This—*finally*, Sabine thinks—shakes the façade. Petra's eyes, they give her away, even if her posture, her composure, do not. She gnaws at the inside of her cheek, a habit Sabine remembers from childhood, a sign of her frustration.

"How dare you."

"Oh, I see. Good to know you have limits."

"Whatever you think of me, I'm not a monster."

"No, just a dead woman masquerading as one."

Behind them, the door opens, and one of the men who took her, the ugly one, stands in the doorway, his hair and shoulders dripping. The rain comes down in sheets, and he looks at Petra, awaiting permission or confirmation, but she shakes her head, shoos him out. "Not yet," she says, and without hesitation he steps back into the downpour, the weight of the door banging shut shaking the foundation beneath her feet.

From under the table, Petra pulls a thick brown folder. On the tabletop, she spreads out papers and photographs. "I know you have more questions, and we will get to those. But first, I want to help you make sense of all this." She holds up a photograph, the empty back of it facing Sabine. "If you're ready."

Sabine crosses her arms, locks the muscles in her quadriceps. "Show me," she says.

Petra smiles as she turns it around, figures taking shape in the dim light of the restaurant, Sabine and Victoria, their hands joined, walking along the Neckar with Roger in tow.

"Where did you get this?" Sabine asks, or screams, she cannot tell. "How do you have this?"

"Victoria gave it to me."

"Victoria," she says, her throat, her skin, cracking.

Petra nods, slides the photograph along the table. Sabine inches closer, her tendons pulled almost to breaking.

"Are you ready now, my dear?" Petra asks. "Are you ready to listen?"

When the match finally ends, Sabine's body locks up. Her legs, her back cramp and spasm. She struggles to get to net, to kiss her opponent's cheek, shake the chair umpire's hand. Wave to the crowd, who are excited, expectant. They are here for her. Another victory. Another Sabine Hellewege championship.

"Gave you a bit of a scare at the end there, didn't she," the stadium commentator says, met with glee from the crowd.

"She played so well this tournament. We both definitely gave it our all out there." Sabine's voice—she hears it amplified through the main court—is sterile, monotone. She hopes the crowd is deaf to it.

"You've been in the zone this week. Didn't drop a set! What's helped you get through this tough field and win your third title here in Gstaad?"

She nods, trying to smile. "I am here to fight, always. I never lose faith in myself. And, of course, I could not do it without you," she says, pointing to the stands. "Your support means everything."

Later, as she holds the sharp, abstract trophy she fought to earn, poses for photographers in front of the surrounding mountains, Sabine feels she will explode. She wants to tell anyone who will listen what she knows, the secrets now burdening her, what is expected of her, the things she cannot fathom. The trophy, the weight of it, is almost too much. She squeezes it like a stuffed animal, so tight it will cut marks into her skin, as if she could push it into her chest, absorb it into her, to keep it close, to keep from turning around, hurling the wood and metal off this mountain, listening for the sound of its shatter at the bottom.

In the photograph, Victoria is smiling. She was laughing at something Sabine said, she remembers, and Sabine could not help but watch her, relish her joy, her energy for life. She was jealous of her, how beautiful she was without trying, without a care. Like the world was hers. And, for a moment, Sabine felt the same, that such a thing was possible.

"You know Victoria?" she asks, and the look on her mother's face reminds her of their history, the friendship of their two families.

"Not as well as you," Petra says.

"I mean now." She is flustered, reeling, trying to make sense of one confusion after another. "How did you get this picture?"

"I asked Victoria to visit you, to watch over you."

"Watch over me?"

"You two—" and when she stops herself, Sabine sees something new in her, distress maybe. Something, perhaps, she did not know about her daughter. "She was supposed to reacquaint herself."

Sabine feels immediately the bile churning. How she allowed herself to open up. The ease with which she lowered her defenses. "We fucked—is that what you wanted?"

"So vulgar."

"I do not understand," she says and notices, beneath the table, Petra's leg tapping furiously. "Why would she do this?"

"I asked her to."

"Why? Why spy on me?" The impatience, the panic in her voice, drips.

"Keeping you close," Petra says, "not spying."

Her mother's tone sends a chill through her bones. "Have you done this before?" she asks, already knowing the answer.

"You're my daughter. You're important. We've done what is necessary."

Sabine shouts each word like a reflex. "We? What else? What else have you done?"

Petra shifts, uses her foot to push out the chair opposite her. "I wish you would sit, mein Liebes."

"Sabine. My name is Sabine. I do not know you."

Petra accedes. Sabine, too, taking the empty seat.

"Your life,"—Petra reaches for Sabine but retracts—"at times, you needed a push. You needed a path."

"And you put me on this path? You are a fucking ghost. You do not know me. But *you* have given me a path?"

"I'm happy to explain."

"Did this path include getting blown up? Getting shot? My life has been a disaster. What I have, I built, I fought for. I nearly lost everything. I have scraped back."

"You're right, of course. You're a fighter. So much adversity, you've faced it head on. It has made you stronger."

"So, what then? Where else have you taken pictures? Who else have you had watching me?" Immediately, she thinks of Lolo. Alina. Sandy. She cannot suspect any of them; she cannot survive suspecting them. Her eyes wander the room, waiting for Petra to respond.

"When I said *path*, I may have misspoken. We helped you find direction. You always had final say, the choices you made. Please don't misunderstand. You're here because you chose to be."

"I am here because you kidnapped me."

Petra laughs, and the way her cheek dimples, her mouth curls wide, Sabine is frightened to see herself reflected.

"Do you remember where you were before the incident in Budapest?"

"Before…what? No, it was a long time ago. Maybe Spain? No."

"Not where physically. I mean, where were you—how was your career? Your life? Where were you headed?"

Sabine stares ahead, confused and thinking back to that time, trying to understand what Petra is asking. Things were good before Budapest. She was struggling without her father on tour but settling into that new normal. She was content for a while to not have a coach, to fight these battles, for the first time in her life, alone. She was quietly seeing someone, an actress, who she met in Cannes. She signed a new endorsement deal and was premiering a new kit in France. Only a month before, she was celebrating with Lolo, who had won her first grand slam in Australia. Life was good; she was sure of it.

Petra waits with no hint of impatience.

"Everything was fine," Sabine says finally.

"Freefall," Petra announces. "I believe Jim O'Brien used that word. You failed to win a tournament for almost two years. Your friend, objectively your lesser, beat you in the Australian final. Your ranking its lowest in years. Without your father, you were left to your own devices. And always with that Jewish boy. You were distracted. You were in danger of losing everything you had built."

Sabine shakes in angry disagreement. "And then I got shot, so."

There it is again, that smile. Outside, the storm pitches around them.

"And then you got shot. And all of that, your failures and your distractions, they were washed clean."

"I could have died!"

"You were hurt and scared, but you were alive and once again ready to overcome adversity."

She remembers laying on the court, blood pumping from her body, the screams in the crowd, the wind swirling, coating her face in clay. She remembers feeling detached, unsure of the physical space she took up in the universe. She does not remember, then or now, being washed clean. "I do not understand," she says and wants to keep saying, because it is the only thing that can possibly be true.

"Small corrections were no longer enough. Something large, of consequence, needed to happen. We took the necessary steps."

"What the hell does that mean?"

Petra taps her fingertips in a rhythm that sounds like a folk song. "Are we ready to be candid with one another, put this dance aside?"

Sabine is up, her seat kicked over from the force. She slams her hands onto the tabletop, feels the legs almost give way. The rage in her body limitless. Who in god's name is this woman.

"Did you have me shot?" She keeps her voice resolute, trying to gauge Petra's reaction. But there is none. She sits opposite Sabine still and calm, as if she is not back from the dead speaking to her daughter for the first time in years, as if she has not just been accused of something so awful. It is too much for Sabine, and her body trembles as the words rise up in her dry throat once more, screaming, "Did you have me shot?"

And without hesitation, as natural as can be, Petra says, "Yes, my dear. Of course, yes."

Her press conference over, Sabine makes her escape. On the vanity sits her trophy, the Alps carved from metal. The symbol of her success. Tennis champion. What she wanted. All she is.

She tries calling Sandy. *Just want to hear your voice*, she messages and throws her phone into her bag. She cannot help her worry. Petra's words—*that Jewish boy*—impossible to ignore. Sabine strips off her clothes, nearly tearing her warm-up jacket in the process, and throws them in a ball on the floor. The coolness of the room gives her gooseflesh. She steps into the shower, turns the water to its hottest until she can barely stand it, until the sinews of muscle underneath feel as if they will burst through, until she knows, entirely, she can never wash it all away.

As she packs her bags, Sabine becomes absorbed by the beauty outside the hotel window. The mountains, the way they blanket the Palace, the village below, something out of a fairy tale. She could stay here, hidden. She could become a character in this universe, someone new and invisible. She would not have to return to places she is now afraid to go. She puts her hands against the window, pushes as if the world might move. She cries out, something animal and cathartic. Day turns to night. Her fingers, the longer she holds them to the glass, grow cold enough to break.

In her hands, the chair is light. She rears back, brings it forward with a mighty force, her release a perfect follow-through. The front window shatters like a small explosion. Stormwater runs off the awning, pools in the shards and on the floor. Occasional streaks of lightning brighten the room. The thunder, it fills the walls between them, but it is not enough. She hears her own gasps, chasmic and erratic. She takes them as a sign she is still alive.

"That temper," Petra says, the sound of rainwater and disappointment invading the room, but she otherwise ignores the violence. "You were never in danger. Please don't mistake our intentions."

"In shooting me…those intentions?" Her voice, fractured and guttural, has gone wild.

"You became a symbol because of it. A survivor, a warrior overcoming the terrors of this world. You already had the stage—it was yours, and you were losing it—everyone knew your face, your power, your success. But it was slipping, you were slipping. You needed a nudge, a guiding hand. As I said, we tried more discreet methods, and when those failed, something grander was necessary."

Sabine ingests every bit of what her mother is saying. The piercing in her mind, though, is almost unbearable, the way ears ring in the presence of invisible waves. When noise and silence become the same sound.

"The woman," she says, "the one who shot me. I knew her? I told Lolo." In the space between, waiting for some sign from Petra, confirmation or otherwise, Sabine raises her voice again. "Did I know her?"

Petra, her eyebrows raised in surprise, grins at Sabine, something almost tender. "I cannot believe you remember. You were a child. I never imagined you would recognize her."

The memory hits Sabine, the woman's eyes full of rage, her face as she called out in the crowd, and that same face framed in laughter, Jürgen's hand on her shoulder, Petra sipping something red and dark, such that it stained the ridges of her lips. Friends around a table in a nondescript restaurant, and Sabine, who should otherwise be asleep in bed, a small perfect wallflower.

"Why? Why her?"

"I needed someone I trusted, someone close. Not the sort of thing one leaves to chance."

Though her mother's sense of humor had always been macabre, Sabine is still struck by Petra's chuckle at her own thought, that her daughter's staged assassination could not be left to chance.

"Your friend—what is her name?" Sensing Petra's reluctance, she goes on, "She was never found, I know. The person they blamed, I knew it was not her. I told them. They said I was *confused*."

"They know what we needed them to know. What was easy for them to understand."

"Are you still close?"

Petra shakes her head, breaks eye contact with Sabine. "She was a loyal friend, an asset always."

Sabine opens her mouth to speak and the words nearly choke her. "How can you be my mother?"

"I suspect we're more alike than you know."

"In what universe could that be true? You are a monster."

"So dramatic. We're both willing to do whatever it takes. We do *not* settle. You get that from me. Hellewege women, we win."

Sabine feels in her lungs that she is crying. "How is it things were better when you were dead?"

"See," Petra says, that wide condescending smile spread across her tight face, "your mother's daughter after all."

"What do you want from me?" The sharpness of her own voice catches her. "Why have you brought me here?"

For the first time since Sabine's arrival, Petra stands from the table. Her legs are ravines of scarred flesh. She moves around the room like a heron inching through marshland. Every step she takes seems purposeful, full of calculation.

"It's time. So many years waiting. So much planned, so much in motion. The world is finally changing. But now it's time. We believe you're ready."

"You keep saying *we*—who is that? What *we*?"

"Oh my dear. I will explain. I will tell you everything. Show you what's real. This is about so much more than you and me."

Sabine Hellewege is back! The tagged headline on Prattlr, along with thousands of comments below, argues for and against. She returns to the top five; *her rightful place*, the article proclaims. Other words—*elite, aging, fierce*—become chum in the frenzy. She thinks immediately of Petra, of her *assets*; are any of them commenting now? Are they likes, hates, both? She imagines two people virtually fighting, unaware they are cogs of the same conspiracy. She reads through, suspicious of everyone. The *narrative* must be exactly right. *Control. Important in ways unrealized. The excitement of what comes next.*

She finds Sandy's profile. The last thing he posted, from the night of his return, is a repost of his game-winning home run. He added a tag, #JewsWhoRake, and although she is happy to see him embracing his Jewishness, wearing it like a badge of honor, what that means now worries her beyond her comprehension. She replies only to Sandy, a fire emoji between two hearts. Frivolous, vapid maybe, but she is there, reacting, like the brush of a fingertip against skin after too long an absence. *I am here and I love you*, she wants to say. No matter what happens. She wants to reach across the world and shake him, make him see the splintering in her eyes, the fault lines tearing her body apart. *It is me*, she would say, *do not forget. It is me.*

Petra speaks slowly. She enunciates each word, as if by doing so they will be imprinted on Sabine's mind. Sabine finds she is unable to move, barely blink. She sinks. Petra and the We, they followed her for years. Stalked her, manipulated her social media. Protected her. Exposed her. Shot her. The way Petra explains, it almost sounds logical. What had to be done. *We. Keep you safe. Lift you up. Prepare you. The world will know, will trust, will follow. It has to be you.*

"Would you like something to drink?" she says, and it snaps Sabine like out of a trance. She shakes her head; she wants Petra to keep going. She feels suddenly insatiable, that she will not be able to function until she has heard everything. "Well, I would," Petra continues, and she goes behind the bar, pulls down a bottle of red wine. She carefully cuts the foil, removes it with a single pull. She twists the corkscrew down, but she looks at Sabine. Watches her watching her. She fills a glass, the wine a bold purple. Petra hesitates, her nose drinking before her mouth. Sabine hates herself for being anxious, for wanting Petra to go on.

"You said this was not about me."

Petra, her lips arched and crimson, says, "You, but not only you. This world—what do you make of it, of what it has become?"

"The world is fucked," she says, "but it is always fucked."

"You understand, I know you do. You travel, you see. This world is torching itself. Do you never question why?"

"There is always war," Sabine declares, like it is the truest thing she knows.

"Can you honestly say nothing has changed? Nothing has gotten worse?"

Sabine laughs, a reaction she does not expect. She imagines walking to Petra, stealing a drink from her wine. Their stained mouths matching. "I choose to hope rather than dwell on the ugliness." The lie, it sticks to the back of her tongue.

"You're a minority then. Where you see hope, most see fear. The outsider, the terror next door. Horror of the unknown. Do you not see this everywhere you go? Do people in your beloved adopted homeland not look at you this way?"

"My otherness comes with protections," she says, and when Petra's eyebrow raises, razor sharp, she continues, "Fame and whiteness are like fortresses."

Petra, struck by Sabine's candor perhaps, catches herself mid-sip. "Neither are impenetrable, but yes, that's exactly right. A protection for those deserving."

"Deserving," she repeats, the word bitter.

"And what of those who see you, your whiteness, and wish harm upon you? Blowing up cars and streets and bridges."

"Stadiums," Sabine says, a knee-jerk reaction. "People."

"Where's your hope then? When you're buried beneath the rubble."

"In the strangers who reached out their hands, risked their lives, saved me and so many others."

"America, Europe—they are overrun. Countries like ours, here, guilt-ridden by past sins, opening their borders to any and all. Your home, my home, they're unrecognizable. My neighbors, they're from everywhere but here. They may pull you from the rubble, but aren't they the reason you're buried?"

"I cannot believe that. I *do not*."

"Then you're pretending. You're not truly seeing. If you were, the truth would be clear."

"People are afraid, I admit. I have seen it firsthand." She thinks of saying goodbye to Alina, the fear in her voice, anxious to get out of New York and be with her family, be somewhere she felt safe. "Things are past breaking; they are broken, yes, but they are not beyond saving."

Petra carries her glass by the stem, swirling her wine as she returns to the table and sits opposite Sabine. "That, my daughter, is where *we* come in, where we finally agree."

"You are saviors? Shooting people and taking blackmail photos?"

"You—you've been *my* project. My block of marble to sculpt. What I've done for you is something between a mother and her daughter." She stops, leaving space for Sabine's skepticism, then goes on. "But we, we will save the world from itself. We're the fire and the phoenix. What burns, what we burn, will be reborn, and we will rise from the ashes. We will retake what is ours, what we allowed for too long to slip away. We will, as you said, save. Europe, America, the oceans in between—they will be razed, cleansed, purified. They will be ours. Our fatherland, our motherland. As they're meant to be."

The air stabs through Sabine, as if at the end of a long match when everything inside her has been used up. "You must know what that sounds like." She does not hide her shock, her disgust.

"Give people a monster to hunt, vast and intangible, and eventually, they turn on one another. They will suspect everyone—even their neighbors, even the hands pulling them from the rubble."

"What have you done, Petra?" The name in her mouth like rust.

"We set events in motion. We acted where others only talk."

Sabine shakes, confused, and leans closer to Petra. "Are you a part of this, these groups? I do not understand. What they do, you cannot be a part of it. These terrorists, the people they say are responsible for World Day… why help them?"

Outside, the storm calms. Sabine has lost track of time, the darkness somewhere between midnight and early morning. In the absence of rain, the restaurant, its quiet, unmoors her.

"The answer's there, on the tip of your tongue. I hear it." Petra taps her foot against the base of her chair. The wine glass between them catches the dim overhead light and flickers like a star.

"Did you have something to do with World Day? Please tell me no. I cannot believe—I mean look what they did."

The expression then on Petra's face, Sabine will never forget.

"There is no *they*, mein Schatz. No *them*."

"What does that mean."

"They are the monster. They are what we made them, what we needed people to believe they were."

"That is insane," Sabine says, springing to her feet, unsure if, given the chance, she should run from this place and never look back. "What they have done, the death—"

"We gave people what they wanted. Brown faces to blame, to battle, to revenge. And in return, we got what we needed—a hate strong enough to divide, to make space for something new to grow. For us to bring order. For us to save the world from itself."

Sabine finds herself backing away, inching toward the door. She hears the wind moving outside and pretends it is what her dreams sound like.

"But New York. All those people. It is too much."

"World Day. And Paris. Istanbul and London. The Roebling. Cairo, and Warsaw before that. The opera in Vienna. Flight 592, one of our first."

Sabine, her entire being, quakes. The tremors running up her spine are paralyzing. Minutes or hours or seconds pass, her chest heaving, her head heavy and spinning. "Why," she says, once or maybe over and over until it sounds like one thing, one endless cry. She is to the door, using the frame to hold herself up.

"The world was close once, my dear. Close to a kind of perfection we see only in stories of the past. But they can be alive, they can be this life. We can remake the world as it was intended. It can be perfect once more. We're almost there. You will see."

When she leaves Gstaad, en route to Charleston, South Carolina and the American hardcourt swing, Sabine allows herself a moment of relaxation: a tiny bottle of vodka and an old romantic comedy. Seven miles up, she stretches out in her suite, a luxury she has rarely indulged. But the idea of looking at another human being on this flight is more than she can bear. She tucks away, clouds like apparitions brushing against her window then vanishing, dissolved into the transatlantic air.

In the end, Petra simply let her leave. *We will be in touch*, she said, which Sabine heard as a threat. Sabine demanded never to see her again, a request Petra refused to acknowledge. In a panic, she asked questions about her friends, what this new world order would mean for them, if they would be protected. *Give me your word*, she said, and Petra, like everything else that came from her mouth that night, used her forked tongue to say nothing. And now, as Sabine sits anxiously waiting to hear from Sandy, she replays Petra's callous dismissal, how easily she could reject the pleas of her own daughter.

On her way to the airport, she received a message from Lolo, a heart and a flexed arm. She asked if Sabine would be in Charleston, and when she said yes, a string of smiles and kisses followed. *See you soon, love*, Lolo wrote, and Sabine looks at it again, to remind herself. Lolo is safe. Alina, tucked away with her parents, is safe. And when Sandy finally responds, when she tells him she will be in Florida after Charleston, while he is there for a series against the Mantas and she will see him in the flesh again, she will know he is safe.

A serenity comes, white noise filling the cabin. Sabine finishes her vodka and asks for another, though it sits unopened beside her as she watches the movie. She is exhausted. She tries to ignore the sound of Petra's voice echoing through her tired mind. She knew where to find Sabine; she knew Sandy was there, too. *Why did you not leave me a triangle, too?* Sabine had asked, hoping to press Petra, force her to reveal something more, anything. Was it a warning not just to Sandy but her as well? Petra must know how important he is to Sabine, given all she knows, has seen from the shadows. Sabine tries to convince herself it will be enough, their closeness, enough to protect him. But she worries now the opposite may happen. What if their friendship, their love for one another, makes him a target. *Crosshairs.* What if she cannot keep him, or herself, from harm.

Before she fades, the movie nearing its end, Sabine sends another message to Sandy. *Almost home*, she writes, and after, she closes her eyes, lets the sounds carry her away. When she wakes, she will be back in America, the place, Jürgen always told her, where anything is possible.

BROOKLYN BOY

In the morning, Sandy walks to the bodega and buys a newspaper. A photograph of him fills the sports section front page, his arms wrapped around a teammate in celebration. And at the top, the headline bold: *Brooklyn Boy Is Out!*

For a moment, Sandy feels a swell of pride, one he didn't expect but embraces. He has come out in small ways every day to himself for as long as he can remember. This, though, the *world* knowing, feels like an unexpected, terrifying victory. It won't be long before his mother sees, before one of her friends from the neighborhood calls and demands an explanation. *But the girls love him,* he can hear them saying. *All those years in locker rooms, whadya expect.* He hears because he has heard it before, and each time he remained silent, let the comment pass into truth, he felt himself disappear a little bit more. And though his mother knows, has known for perhaps longer than Sandy, she'll let her friends and cousins go on about her son, the shock of it all, before scolding them. But mostly she'll be disappointed at Sandy for not warning her first, not giving her time to prepare, even though, she'll say, this isn't about her. *It would've been nice,* she'll say, and leave it at that, the tone of her voice enough to translate the perfect amount of guilt.

Before turning off his phone—an absolute necessity at the moment—

he confirms with the team he'll be at the stadium early for the pregame press conference. Though it wasn't a secret from them, problems had emerged in the clubhouse when Sandy came out to them, a few loud voices trying to drown out the rest. Now, with the news going *wide*, the team needed to *get out in front of this*, they said. Sandy's first reaction—frustration—led him to ask for clarification. *I hope no one's expecting an apology*, he said, and they replied quickly, *Of course not*. Reassurances made, and a compromise set: statement by the team in support of both Sandy and more players coming out, and a Q & A before the game, where Sandy can clear up any *uncertainties*. Not perfect, but a means to the proper end for all parties, or something like that.

With the apartment finally silent of notifications and news alerts, Sandy takes his coffee onto the balcony. The river shimmers, waves chopping in the morning wind. He remembers when this building, and others like it along the water, didn't exist. This view, impossible a decade ago. He doesn't deserve it, or, maybe more precisely, he wants to believe he does. The insanity, he thinks, of someone earning this by playing a game. By following their childhood passion, their impossible wish, and ending up here, able to see, to do, what others only dream of. He knows he must find a way to be the kind of person that deserves something like this, a life so well imagined. He has hidden, pretended, tried to become the person he believed the world wanted him to be. And now, with everything out there, he's a frightened and beautiful kind of naked: *Jewish. Ballplayer. Brooklyn Boy. Gay. All-Star. Sandy Fucking Katzmann.*

The press conference goes on for too long. Nearly every reporter asks the same questions; they're most interested to know if Sandy has ever dated another player. Even if he had, he says, he wouldn't tell them, because it's not his place to out anyone else. The murmurs tumbling through the room bring about a kind of tribal agreement.

"Why now," Minka Albanese asks, and without her saying, Sandy hears *with the team in a pennant race, with everything still so chaotic in the league.*

"It's time," he says, nodding as if nothing else could be true. "My teammates, my family, they've known. They know who I am. Today, this,"—he spreads his arms, pointing them at the reporters gathered in the small room—"no one should have to hide who they are. There are people out there who think they can scare us into hiding. Well, no more. We fuck who we want, we love who we want, and at the end of the day, we're all the goddamn same. Except I come to work and win pennants." Sandy grins, catches his breath. His legs shake, though they're hidden by the table. He should tell them about Berlin, about the symbol left on his door, but with Sabine there, too, it feels more complicated now, too nuanced an explanation for this group. No, he said his piece. This performance, it has done its job.

When the other reporters have gone, Minka stays back and walks with Sandy out of the media room. Alone in the hallway, she says, "Off the record?" Sandy raises an eyebrow. "Nick would be proud." Even though Sandy hopes it's true, to hear someone else say it aloud fills him up. "Were you two…?" she asks, keeping her voice low.

Sandy can see the curiosity in her expression. Always the reporter. He shakes his head but keeps his eyes raised, focused. "I loved Nick Mattingly, I will always love Nick Mattingly." The answer satisfies them both, and once they part, Sandy listens to her footsteps tapping against the floor. He turns and down the empty hallway shouts, "On the record. All of it." And though he knows she won't share it, it feels good to say it, to be—in this, in everything—unafraid.

The homophobic chants and fan-made signs displayed during the game, expected but their ugliness nonetheless real, do little to affect the overall energy in the stadium. The crowd's desire to cheer for Sandy and the Atlantics is hardly swayed; they do the wave and leap to their feet and they sing; they raise their hands and lose their voices in celebrating victory; they ride the subway home with smiles on their faces, invigorated and inspired. For tonight, Sandy remains their hero.

He takes a car back to his apartment. On the drive, he wonders what he'll find when he arrives. Something new affixed to his door. Another innocent body. Flyers, propaganda, blanketing the neighborhood like autumn leaves. But as they pull up his street is quiet, lights overhead dim and flickering. *Everything as it should be*, he hears his father say. Sandy wonders how long he'd been repeating that line, knowing it wasn't true. His parents were never people who put on brave faces or sheltered him from the realities of their life, of life as they knew it. Or so he thought. At some point, they stopped, his father especially; they began keeping things to themselves, things they felt too dark, too *something*, for their only child to shoulder.

The new night doorman greets him with a "Great game tonight!" and a smirk Sandy immediately understands. He imagines the conversation that'll happen later at the bar, the doorman and his friends laughing, making fun of Sandy, jokes and vulgarities; someone, though, will interrupt and remind them their fandom takes precedent, that Katzmann still rakes and who cares what he is as long as they win the pennant. And when they agree, the doorman and his friends high-fiving, they do so with the understanding that the way they see the world—simple and straight, entirely in black and white—is the only possible reality.

"Thanks," Sandy says before getting into the elevator, riding it nearly to the top, scanning the door for anything left for him and locking it once inside his apartment. "We're almost there."

On the late sports news, there's a story about Sabine. She's at Florian Frei's memorial in Switzerland. She wins a tournament in Gstaad. She looks as if she hasn't slept in weeks, the space around her eyes dark, almost bruised, her voice clipped and robotic. She's back at the memorial; she's crying, her cheeks sunken in. "An impossible loss," she says, a swarm of media unaffected by her tears. "The world will never be the same." She barely gets out the words. She's in Gstaad again, lifting the trophy. She smiles, which Sandy see right through. Whatever's weighing on her, Sandy knows it's something beyond the court. The story comes to a close with a slow motion shot of Sabine's tournament-clinching forehand, her subdued celebration, the hint of her body on the verge of collapse. He'll ask when he sees her in Florida, direct and unfiltered because he can, because she's his Sabby: *Who was that person? Where did you go?*

With the curtains open and the city lights enough to keep him awake, Sandy's mind moves. He reads, television off and on and off again, as hours tick by. The glow from his phone cumbersome. He stares from the balcony out into the river, the flecking of lights like stars dotting both shores. The bridge a brilliant path through the darkness. And the other, unlit still these years, a phantom.

He remembers then his bag from Brighton, tossed beside the couch and still unpacked. Inside, the book of fairy tales, its golden embossing announcing a secret treasure. And rolled up, tucked away still, his father's map. He unfurls it atop the breakfast bar, marble cool even through the thick paper. He uses the book to hold down one end, his knife block the other. In the hue of his apartment, the map looks older. His father's hand, though, was careful. Even with something private, his father took pride in his abilities, his particularities. Sandy wonders where the research for the map came from, if it still exists. He imagines his father pouring over spreadsheets, interpreting anomalies, tracking news stories, and collecting it somewhere in a cloud, somewhere protected. Only here, on this rough paper, does his father reveal the breadth of his explorations. Sandy opens a search window on his phone. He finds a pencil to scratch down notes of his own. He begins with the smaller cities, looking for anything to explain its place on the map: in Carson City, an attack nearly a decade ago, three heav-ily-armed extremists gunning down concertgoers, over a hundred dead, thousands injured; in Wood River, a series of antisemitic vandalisms and attacks and—*unrelated?*, he writes—a suicide bomb at the nearby Chain of Rocks Bridge, which he remembers from his days in A-ball, attributed by multiple news sources to anti-Russian revolutionaries; Cottage Grove, a small town in Oregon, makes for a complex search, a place with deep bigoted roots, lynchings well into the seventies, a local militia hell-bent on *protecting against outside forces*, though random mass shootings in consec-utive years at the town supercenter raise concerns—*whose?*, Sandy writes, underlines—about just how safe the townspeople are; other cities, scattered across the country, reveal more shootings, car bombings, attacks and graf-fitis, most blamed on newly-arrived migrant populations, gang members from across the border, Islamic radicals and Salafist jihadists. Apart from a few prominent incidents—Pittsburgh, Boston, San Francisco, New York—Sandy can't match the remaining runes on the map to any specific event. He wishes he had access to his father's work; perhaps these links would make sense. Maybe back in Brooklyn, in the attic, he thinks. He clicks off his phone. He's alone, a reality painfully present, one normally not both-ersome but tonight, after Berlin and everything else, one he can't shake.

He would message Nick, ask him to take a walk, get lost along the esplanade or ride out to the stadium, sneak into the batting cages or run sprints in the outfield. When he was with Nick, Sandy could make sense of the world. He closes his eyes, imagines they're together, Nick across the breakfast bar, those blue eyes and that devastating smile.

Talk to me, Kitty, they demand, and so he does.

"I don't understand," Sandy says. "It's all here. But I don't understand."

You've never been afraid to take those swings. Sandy still hears Nick's voice clearly, even though he fears, as each day passes, forgetting.

"What am I supposed to see?"

The question lingers in the room until a tap on the window, like tiny pebbles tickling the glass, breaks his concentration. Sandy jumps, fright-ened by the unexpected visitor—a drone, hovering on the other side like a fat bird covered in lights. It seems to be looking at him. They're not uncommon, the skies over New York City often littered with them. He remembers when they moved like a flock of starlings overhead, dropping leaflets down onto not only his street but, as the news later reported, streets all across the country. Our *dreamland*. He stares back now, mechanisms twitching, LCDs twinkling, trying to communicate.

"What do you want?" Sandy yells. "A picture? What?" And when it stares back at him, little expressionless machine, Sandy smacks the window and says, "Get the fuck out of here!"

He turns and faces the bar, the map upside down before him. The shapes spread out, his notes filling in the white spaces. Maybe the flashing lights kaleidoscoping through his apartment have revealed something, something his mind had otherwise been unable to piece together. But there it is. His father laid it out for him, for anyone willing or able to see. He'd been charting, chronicling. How long had Lenny known what was happening? He pictures his father adding city after city, a pattern emerging. Not suddenly, no, but slowly, then all at once. The pieces fitting. The extremists and the radicals, migrants and immigrants, the gang members and their overnight border crossings—they're smoke. They exist, of course, and but they're not the ones terrorizing this country. He sees it clearly now in the careful runes of his father's map. A narrative, one not invented but certainly perpetuated by the ever-degenerating administration, the ugliness of white America brewing below the surface. Taking back what they believe they've lost. His father knew, he saw, long before anyone else. His mother, too, which Sandy spent his childhood laughing off, being embarrassed by. But the signs were there, waiting to be discovered. The Nazis aren't simply coming; they're here. These invisible monsters, no longer in hiding, everywhere.

That sound again, sand misting the glass, snaps Sandy from the map. The drone still there, and Sandy swears it's smiling at him. An opening, and something sprays out, a dark liquid. Paint, Sandy realizes, and the fat robot bird slides slowly left and right, letters forming on the window. Sandy leans against the counter, his fingers gripped underneath. *We See You.* And when it stops, shifts back slightly, the noise of its quiet motor is loud enough to cover the music of the city. Sandy's fingers release, his knuckles regaining color, and he moves closer until he's at the window, his view of the drone, of everything beyond, skewed by the words. Something new is happening, a light, a panel opening. A puff, the glass cracking. A pressure against his rib cage. No more air. And then, only darkness.

FLORIDA

In Charleston, Sabine is one-and-done. She cannot concentrate on court, her shots erratic, her movements undisciplined. On changeovers, she searches the crowd for Petra, for her compatriots—*We're everyone, we're no one*, Petra told her, words impossible to hear as anything but a warning. Even in loss, the fans demand of Sabine, line the exit with oversized tennis balls and selfies at the ready. She waves, her smile composed entirely of disappointment, and she walks by them, she does not stop. Their excitement and their shouting, their hands reaching towards her, the accidental touches—it is all too much. She hears her opponent's voice channeled through the speakers as she thanks Sabine for the match, for the chance to play one of her idols. She is a teenager, brawny and thick, a Romanian living in Canada, full of confidence and youthful arrogance. Sabine envies her this. She sees the titles in her future; she played Sabine with no fear, no possibility of defeat. She wins or she implodes, nothing in between. Sabine envies her this, too.

Lolo finds Sabine after a shower and quick treatment on her ankle. She is glad to see Lolo, know that she is okay, but this moment, so immediately after a defeat like that, is one Sabine prefers in solitude.

An embrace, Sabine's skin hot.

"So what was *that*?" Lolo asks, playful but insistent.

"Please," Sabine says, shaking her head. "No."

"Can I quote you on that?" Lolo smirks as if she is still on camera, an audience enjoying her gibing.

For Sabine, the last remnants of performance strip away. "If that is why you came in here, you can go."

She turns her back to Lolo, who steps around immediately to face her. "Excuse me?" They lock eyes, and when Sabine distracts herself with packing her bag, Lolo goes on. "What's up with you?"

"Just lay off," she says, listless but firm.

Lolo steps closer, commands Sabine's attention. "You don't answer my texts. You don't call when you're here. I don't see you out at practice. You barely fucking show up for the match. And I should just *lay off*."

Sabine releases a deep breath, looks at her friend, who is trying. "I am tired, Lo. Exhausted. I cannot deal with this shit right now."

"And what shit is that, your worried-ass friend bothering to make sure you're alive? What the hell, Sabby? Tell me something."

"You should go," Sabine says. "Talking is not going to help."

Lolo puts her hand against Sabine's cheek, sturdy enough for them both to feel its weight. "I don't know what's going on with you, but I'm here."

Sabine reaches up and takes Lolo's hand in hers. She cannot help running her finger over the vacant space where Lolo's pinky should be. She squeezes before letting go. "I know," she says. And though she knows there is more, that Lolo is waiting to hear it, she grabs her bag. "I am sorry. I wish I could explain. I wish I understood where to start." Before Lolo can ask anything else, supportive or prying, Sabine walks past her to the door. "Florida. I will see you in Florida." She knows it is not enough, but, for now, it will have to be.

After declining to talk to the media, which she knows will bring a fine, Sabine stops briefly back at her hotel—her bags, barely unpacked, and Roger, eager as always—before heading to the airport. She flies private to Fort Lauderdale, barely ninety minutes. What she said to Lolo is true, maybe the most honest she has been with herself since leaving Berlin. She does not want to talk. She pretends she will sleep, though she can do nothing but stare out the window. In the purple-gray haze of the horizon, Sabine becomes lost. Petra's words, her revelations, like rolling thunder. She is tired. She watches the clouds and the world and the heavens move away from her.

A sudden tremor in the seat jars her, an isolated turbulence. In her lap, her phone lights up. A voicemail, the message reads, from *Papa*. She scoops up the phone, throws it the length of the cabin. She wants to scream, empty herself in this vacuum, but she knows it will not help. She knows eventually she will land, and once she does, this rage will find her anew.

After they touch down, Sabine stretching her pressure-sore muscles and slow to disembark, she finds him waiting on the runway. His shoulders are a mountain range. She has almost forgotten what he looks like, the image of him in her mind one from childhood, when his presence, his proximity, could still be a comfort. She is not sure what to say, what he will say. She hears Petra's voice in her head—*My death was at your father's behest*—and, to her surprise, she feels not anger for him but pity. What he must have gone through then, his wife leaving him, their family, to join some deranged rebirth of the Third Reich. Every time he said she was gone, what thoughts must have run through his mind. The weight of knowing something terrible and, out of his own sense of responsibility, keeping silent.

"Hello, Papa," she says as she approaches, the air on the tarmac warm but breezy, raising gooseflesh across her skin.

His face does not change, his arms crossed across his chest. Roger runs to him, stands at his feet awaiting recognition, his little body kinetic. If she did not know Jürgen so well, she would think him upset. But his being here, voluntary and unannounced, shows her far more than his demeanor ever could. When she reaches him, Sabine puts down her bags. Though he has lost weight in recent years, he remains a broader version of her. In his face, she sees herself. A tiredness matched now in their eyes. He opens his arms, steps forward without a word, and suddenly he has embraced her. His strength, his sturdiness, surrounds her. She reciprocates, but only slightly. She lets him hold her. She feels the heave of his breaths. He releases, and she is shocked to see the red around his eyes, hear the sandpaper in his throat when he says, "Welcome home."

She thanks him for coming, she did not expect him to, and together with Roger they walk, on each of his shoulders his daughter's tennis bags. She is struck by the sight, a scene years-old come to life again. They make it to Jürgen's SUV before she asks, "What are you doing here?"

He opens the back and piles the bags. He walks to the driver side and gets in, Roger following suit, immediately laid out on the backseat. On Sabine's side, the window comes down, and she bends in to meet her father's look. "Picking you up," he says.

She does not understand him, this man who is her father. They drive north. The sun setting turns the sky to fire. They keep the windows down, ocean salt coating their lungs. Sabine remembers, when they had first moved to Florida, she would get sunburned on one arm, one side of her body, as they drove to and from tournaments or the academy in Orlando. The other kids laughed, told her it was called a trucker's tan. Secretly, she loved it, the sun marking her travels on her body. She wonders now if those burns still live in the layers beneath her skin, chronicling her time here.

"Where are we going?" she asks, still watching out the window.

"To your hotel," he says.

He does not ask which hotel, he is simply driving, and she thinks better of picking this fight.

His eyes locked on the interstate ahead, Jürgen says, "I am sorry, Sabine."

The words, the way he says her name like no one else in the world, reverberate through her. She has not heard him apologize, not to her, not to anyone, in so many years.

"What does that mean?"

"I should have told you." He flicks on his blinker and changes lanes. The light, its low tick, keep on.

"Tell me now." She leans forward and grips her knees on the seat, aims her expression, the need in her eyes, at her father.

"It has been a long time. I thought, I hoped, it was all over."

"Stop," Sabine says, slapping the side of the door from the outside. "No more bullshit. Just say it."

"She called me. She told me you have seen her."

"She kidnapped me."

He shakes his head like he has tasted something sour, the only sign that this is difficult. "You are okay?"

"No. I am absolutely not."

"What did she tell you?"

"Everything," she says. "Every fucking thing."

"More than I know," he says.

"I hope so. Because if you know half of what she has done—"

"She has been dead for a long time."

"Not long enough, evidently." A gust rips through the car. Sabine feels the humidity sucking at her. "She said it was your idea, that she be dead."

"She was, she is."

"That was her on the phone, when I visited you." He nods, barely perceptible. "How long has that been going on?"

"I was as surprised as you."

"No," she says, leaning closer to him, "I doubt that."

"I had not seen or heard from her. A month before you arrived, she called. After those men showed up."

It catches Sabine, the reminder of what she saw, how close it was to her father. "They are hers, those men."

He looks at her, perhaps in shock, or simply weary. "How do you know," he says, but it is clear to Sabine he knows, knew the moment he spoke to Petra, knew when Sabine came back to their house and told him of the symbol she had seen on the men.

"She is not with them, Papa. They are with *her*."

She watches her father process the statement, its implications, the gravity of its meaning.

"She had ideas," he says. "She was passionate."

"She is a fucking Nazi. That is not passion, that is insanity."

The color drains from his face. She has never believed denial could exist so deeply in a person.

"She wanted to take you," he says. "I would not let her."

"You had to know. What she is." Sabine recognizes the exits they pass, almost to Boca Raton.

"How could I?"

"She has killed people, Papa. She had me shot!"

"Nein," he says, flat but full of all the emotion she knows him capable of. "I sent her away. She was dead, she was gone. She promised."

The more he says, the clearer she sees how wholly in the dark he lives. Petra was right—he was protecting her, sacrificing his marriage and his family to keep his daughter safe. With Tobias already gone, it must have been an impossible choice. But he made it; he thought he made it completely. Only to find out now, all these years later, how many lies are buried within the lie.

His hands grip tight to the steering wheel. He drives with singular focus. They pass exits for Deerfield Beach, Boca Raton. She does not stop him. She lets him drive, his muscle memory most certainly taking him to Wellington, to their home. The glare from southbound traffic makes it hard for Sabine to see the road ahead.

Her father's ignorance, once born of necessity, has remained, but now it has swelled, it is plump, into something in need of remedy. The walls this family has built she must tear down.

"I am happy to see you," she says. "After all that has happened, it means a lot that you are here."

They barrel on, a heaviness slowing everything. She cannot imagine playing tennis in two days. Gstaad feels like an eternity ago. Berlin another lifetime. Sandy will be here soon, she has almost forgotten. She wants to throw her arms around him, hold him without letting go, but how? How can she possibly see him now?

Her concentration, focused out the window as these familiar towns zoom by, is broken by a weight suddenly gripping her hand. Her father looks straight ahead, but he squeezes. If he is crying, Sabine cannot see.

"That woman, she is not your mother."

She knows what he means. She wishes she did not, or that the words meant exactly what they sounded like. In the silence that follows, Jürgen notices the blinker is still on. He clicks it off, and after there is nothing. Only the road, the wind through them, and, somewhere out of sight, waves crashing against the shore.

In the morning, they are both awake early. Sabine, for her part, has not slept. Jürgen makes coffee and they sit in silence, the steam coating their faces, watching the sun rise.

"Do you remember the plane crash?"

The question, its presence in the room, surprises them both. Sabine has been thinking about it, about all the events in her life touched by Petra. It feels like a long string connects everything, right up to this moment. How can she ever cut it loose.

Jürgen looks up from his mug and stares into the backyard, as if the answer lives out there. "I remember the alligator more than the crash."

"Yes," she says, seeing the creature and the flames in her mind once again. "It was so hot. I still feel it sometimes."

"You had a rash from the heat for days."

"Did I?" She searches for the memory but finds only that old sensation, her skin on the verge of melting.

"Your first day at the academy after that, the sun drove you mad. We coated you in lotion."

Sabine thinks back to New York, to the crowd and its jeers, the unbearable brightness upon her.

"So long ago," Jürgen says.

"Just remembering," Sabine says, not ready to reveal to her father how far his dead wife has gone, how terrifying she has become.

"It is hard to think about life before Florida."

"Sometimes," she says, "it feels like the crash is my first memory, like there is nothing before."

"You came out of those Everglades different. Suddenly grown up."

She knows he is wrong, knows she was a child in so many ways long after, but he is right, too; she emerged from that marshland changed, cauterized. And yet there is nothing nostalgic anymore, no growth, no girl becoming a woman, no immigrant settling into her new homeland—now, there is only Petra, her ugliness and her plans, her marionette strings, her chisel and hammer, shaping Sabine into something, someone, she no longer recognizes.

"Will you come to my match?" she says without hesitation.

"If you would have me."

She means here, this tournament, but she cannot help entertain the fantasy that someday he might coach her once more. The way he bunches his lips reminds Sabine of when he had a mustache, how it would dance.

"You must do better than Charleston."

She nods, tries to take a sip of coffee but pauses, unable to keep her laughter at bay. It did not take much, she thinks, just the tiniest opening, to get him through the door. "I was barely in Charleston. I was still in Berlin, with her. It was impossible." It is impossible, she wants to say.

"This is your hometown tournament. It is yours. It is only right. Florian in Bern, Juan in Barcelona, Sabine in Boca Raton. You are their champion."

It overwhelms her at once, hearing her father's words. His praise, a rare gemstone suddenly, even if only for a moment, unearthed.

"The last time I saw you," she says, unsure if she wants an answer, "why were you in Stuttgart?"

"I think you know," he says, putting down his mug, folding his arms.

"It was a shock for me," she says. She was furious then, he a foreign body in her life, but now how it pales.

"She called." He clears his throat. "Said you were being reckless. That you were in danger. I had to go."

Sabine flicks her tongue against the back of her teeth. "You could have called."

"She assured me it was dire."

"Of course she did."

He shuffles in his seat, like his entire body is tapping. "You and the young lady—it was a misunderstanding. I should not have gone."

"Petra set you up, you know that?" Sabine stares at her father, tries to catch his gaze, what lives behind his stoic eyes. "She sent Victoria there to watch me."

Jürgen spreads his palms wide on the tabletop, curling his fingers in and out as if scratching the surface.

"She played us both," Sabine says.

At the back door, Roger cries to go outside. Jürgen opens the screen. Roger follows him into the yard, squatting briefly and zooming around like a madman. He rolls in the St. Augustine grass, pieces of earth kicking into the air. Jürgen watches, and, behind him, Sabine watches them both. The sun is high now but still forgiving. A crack in the distance, far away at first then inching closer like thunder announcing an unseen storm. Sabine steps out and joins her father. Roger lays barking in the center of the yard, ears pinned back. Sabine flinches with each report. A rhythm emerges mimicked by her heartbeat, as if the two sounds cannot be separated. Her father stands beside her, unmoving. They do not speak, but they understand what they are hearing. The sounds fill the air and sneak inside the open door, piercing the walls, burrowing.

HUMMINGBIRD

The echo of cars honking and trains rattling across the bridge fill Sandy's apartment. He looks around without moving, a breeze on his face. He doesn't know where he is, not at first. Everything is upside down, backwards. The pressure on his chest. Shards of glass spread around him. Behind him something crackles, and he cranes his neck to see. A large paper on his tiled kitchen floor, dancing with each small rush of wind. His stares, blinking furiously, until he understands: his father's map. He sits up slowly, the back of his head throbbing, and rests on his arms, curves his legs at the knee. Across the window, still mostly intact, he sees the writing. The hole in the glass, spidering out in thin cracks. The smells of the city leaking in. He remembers now. He lifts his shirt, sees the welt swollen along his rib cage, feels the sting of whatever lies beneath. As if he might cave into himself. The brightness of the day stings his eyes. He's alive.

Rubber buckshot, the detective tells him, or something like it. "Fired point blank like that, it coulda done a lot of damage."

Sandy doesn't say it felt like air bursting through him. "What the hell was this?"

"A warning, perhaps? Using a drone, that's new," the detective says with, to Sandy's mind, too much excitement. He looks more like a disheveled professor than a cop.

"What do I do with that?" Sandy says. "I'm supposed to leave today." He stretches his torso, gauze and tape pulling at his skin. He feels hungover, dazed. For a moment, he wishes he could take something strong, something to wipe away both the pain and the image in his mind: that robotic bird hovering outside his window, its illogical blinking, its message like metal through bone.

"We've spoken to your people," he says, his attention on the splintered glass, the cityscape beyond. "They'll have someone traveling with the team, to and from the airport, at the hotel. Extra security in Palm Beach. You'll be in good hands."

The detective says this without looking at Sandy. The whole thing unnerves him. He wants to ask if maybe he shouldn't go, if he isn't better off staying put, going out to his mother's house. At least then he would be somewhere familiar. But he doesn't want that either. He doesn't want to put her in danger. He doesn't want to hide. The words still black against the window, they are meant to terrify him. Make him disappear.

The detective turns and smiles, a courtesy Sandy can tell he doesn't often give. "So tell me about this," he says, pointing at the map spread on the breakfast bar.

"I think it's pretty self-explanatory," Sandy says.

"Is it yours?"

Sandy hears the accusation in the detective's voice. It's a fair question, given what has happened, but invasive nonetheless. "It was my father's."

"It's, eh, provocative to say the least."

"He was a mapmaker. He had his obsessions."

"We should speak with him, given what's happened."

"You're a few years too late." He almost mentions the Roebling, but he can't stomach any more pity.

"I'm sorry to hear that. This was research he'd been doing?"

"Honestly I don't know. I just found it." The newness, the intimacy, of finding his father's work, hidden away but desperate to be discovered, leaves him raw, unable to share anything beyond the obvious.

The detective leans over the map and makes noises under his breath. He runs his gloved finger along the surface. Sandy wants to tell him not to touch it.

"Could we take this? It might be helpful to give it a closer look."

"I'd rather you didn't," Sandy says, hoping the sharpness in his voice is understood.

"We'll take photos for now and go from there." He again flashes Sandy that knowing grin. "It's been a lot, everything that's happened, but we're working on it. We'll figure it out."

When he leaves the detective and his crew to finish their business, Sandy notices a man, a police officer, following him. Funny how he already feels less safe, more in danger, being watched. He walks to the river, north along the esplanade. He sits on a bench, *their* bench. He remembers their last night together here, after the boy was killed—another warning, he recognizes now, maybe the first—the comfort he found in Nick, his compassion and his steadiness. He's overwhelmed by the memory, the tenderness he felt, still feels, from Nick, from Sabby, the way you can love someone so deeply, romantically or otherwise, that even after they're gone you trace their impact on you like the raised lines of a tattoo, scars inked with artistry and emotion, leaving you to revisit them over and over, lifetimes lived not in chronology but in these clearest moments looped forever, creating and destroying you at once.

Sandy tries to stand—he needs to go back to his apartment, pack for Florida—but his legs are concrete. His head swims. He's certain something is changing, the walls of this island and those beyond closing in on him. What has always been a second skin, an inextricable part of himself, is becoming foreign, intangible. This city is becoming a stranger.

From the freefall in his mind Sandy is cut loose, his phone trembling the bench. "Mama," he says, a relief washing over him, mimicking the sound of the river flowing.

"So you only visit when I'm away, huh?" Levity coats the bite in her tone.

Sandy laughs, and the expulsion of what has been inside frees him. "How was your trip?"

"Your aunt's a treasure as always," she says. "Your cousins say hello."

His mother's presence on the line fills him in a way he has not experienced before, grateful and guiltless and complete. Maybe it was being in the house alone, finding his father's map, hoping his mother left the trail for him to follow. Maybe it's that he's scared, truly terrified for the first time in his life, or that he isn't, not nearly what he should be. Maybe it's everything.

"Get to the beach at all?" he asks, a group of joggers stampeding by.

"Nonstop," she says, her voice echoing. "You know me."

He musters the strength and at last stands from the bench, but the ache in his ribs is too great, the swirl in his head too dislocating, and he inches closer to the water, resting his battered body against the metal railing and watching the slow current churn.

"Glad to be back?" she asks. He hears her bang the kettle against the wall of the sink, shuffle to the stove and the click-click-click before the burner ignites. For a moment he wishes he could skip this road trip and head out to Brighton.

"Yes and no," he says. "England has its charms."

"You sound terrible," she says.

"Just tired."

"And hurt? Your name's been all over that injured list."

"You saw," he says, unable to hide his embarrassment.

"I see all," she says, chuckling to herself.

"It was fatigue more than anything else. Traveling, you know. I just needed some rest."

"Shmei drei."

He touches his chest, recoils.

"The headaches stuck around longer than I would've liked."

"And?"

Sandy hears her fingers tapping the countertop of the kitchen island.

"I don't want to keep you," he says, and he knows on the other end she rolls her eyes, pretense and insinuation her greatest annoyances.

"Tell me," she says, a demand he can't ignore.

As if it was ready to explode out of him, he tells her about Berlin. That he was there with Sabine, resting. He tells her about their walks in the city, the picnic on the Spree. He tells her they mimicked the sounds of animals in the park. He almost stops there. But he hears her anticipation, her expectation of what he's avoiding. The words come out choppy: late, lightheaded, silly, door, pink triangle.

Her breaths in the receiver are grave. "Never in my life did I imagine," she says, her voice like stitches ripped from their seams. "Rosa Winkel."

"I came home right after. Sabby wanted me to stay, I think she was worried about me, but I needed to come back."

Sandy hears the squeak of the living room recliner, his father's favorite spot, as she collapses into it. He imagines she's staring out the front window of the house, finding some small comfort in the familiar view.

"I'm so sorry this is happening," she says.

"Even before World Day," he says, "everything feels different."

"It's been a long time coming," she says. The certainty in her voice stirs him.

"Did Dad know, you think?" He doesn't want to talk about the map, it'll overwhelm him, but he's desperate to understand what he has seen.

"Of course he did. He knew more than he ever said to me. He spoke to people, important people, and they ignored him."

"He never wanted me to be afraid."

"He wanted to protect you, we both did. Protect our family."

"He still does, I think."

In his mother's silence, Sandy worries the line has gone dead. He almost tells her about last night, how it feels new, a signaling, the beginning of something beyond what he ever imagined. He wants to know why these things are happening. Why they've never stopped happening.

On the walk back to his apartment, they keep talking. About her trip, about Sandy's. She wishes she could've traveled to Europe, she says, even once. *You still can*, Sandy wants to say, but he tucks it away, something to argue about later. Esther says she's glad he's shown the world who he really is, that he can't be bullied, that he's not afraid. *It's about time*, he can almost hear.

"When are you coming home again?"

"As soon as I'm back. We'll do Friday night dinner. Promise."

"Call me from Florida. I don't want to worry."

"I will."

"Wear sunscreen. And lay off the sliders."

"Love you, Mama," he says.

"Be good, my boy," she says.

Once upstairs, the apartment finally emptied and quiet, Sandy lets go of everything inside of him. His face wet and warm, the tension enough to pulverize his bones. He pulls off his shirt, sees the bruise spread out like a stain, ink spilled and soaked into his bare skin. He looks at it in the bedroom mirror as he packs, watches it grow somehow until it fills him then the room and floods out the window and into the air and the river and covers everything he can possibly see.

On the flight down to Florida, Sandy keeps to himself. What happened to him is need-to-know, and so after a brief exchange with Skip, who assures him he'll be on the injured list at least through this series—*concussion pro-tocol*, he says, because there's more discretion that way—he shuffles to the back of the plane, dons his headphones, and tries to disappear. The pressure on his body as they take off is nearly unbearable, like his ribs might suck deeper into him, with no regard for tissue and muscle and organs. He quiets his mind, the way Sabine taught him. He feels Robinson's son watching him. He wanes, hovering at the edge of sleep. When he closes his eyes, he sees his father's map sketched on the backs of his eyelids, runes floating through the miasma like microscopic creatures of mass destruction. He'll be in Florida soon, he reminds himself. Deep breath. He'll see Sabine, and when he tells her what has happened, everything will start to be right. Deep breath. She'll lift him up like she always does. Deep breath. And everything will be right. It has to be. Deep breath. Almost there.

He stands at the front door of the house, but it's not his house. It will be one day, he'll live here with his parents, but for now they exist without him, before they can even imagine him. The paint is fresh. The bay window is new. It's summer, and the sun bathes him. He's a grown man, out of time. Through the window, he sees them reading in the living room—his father sitting legs crossed in his recliner, licking his fingertips before turning the pages of his favorite espionage novel, and his mother, glasses sliding down her nose, folded up in the newspaper. He watches, invisible. His parents laugh together, make faces at one another. This goes on for a lifetime, and they're happy, safe, oblivious. Outside, the sky grays, blocking out the light, and the wind howls. Around him, moving down the streets towards the house, snarls echo, the clicking of animal nails against the pavement. Soon he's surrounded, these creatures tearing at flesh, their mouths dripping; they take pieces of him. They are insatiable. Sandy trips over legs and paws trying to escape, collapses in the middle of the lawn. His body regenerated, new meat for the creatures to devour. They amass before him, a mob of hot breath and teeth. Behind them, a Hakenkreuz, wet and black, painted across the house façade. Sandy sees his parents still inside, unaware, the window glass spidering out but, for now, holding. He closes his eyes; he can smell the blood soaking into the grass, and he waits. He waits for the creatures to descend.

A shaking, a voice—*Feather, wake up*—and he jumps, sucks in the recycled air. Hendrick standing over him, his eyes expectant.

"We're about to land," he says, and Sandy sits up, wipes the half-dried trail from his open mouth, and thanks him. "You're talking in your sleep, too. Sounded intense," the young man says, his smile meant to diffuse his own uneasiness.

"I'm a real chatterbox," Sandy says, tightening his seatbelt. "You remember Nick? He called me Kitty, because he said I was always meowing."

"Yeah, it was like that," Hendrick says, his face wide and innocent, and returns to his seat beside his father.

Sandy feels the humidity the moment they land, pressing against the fuselage. *Welcome to West Palm Beach*, the pilot announces, a faint buzzing from the speakers hanging in the cabin. They walk as a team off the tarmac and onto the team bus. Garcia sits opposite him, and though Sandy knows she wants to talk, sees it in the way she raises her eyebrows when she catches him, he keeps to himself. When they arrive at the hotel, though, before he disappears into his room, she stops him.

"Skip says you're out for the Mantas series." Her duffle bag slides down from her shoulder, revealing her lean muscular arms.

"Yeah. My head's still a bit fucked. Skip thought it best to play it safe."

"Can't risk losing you for the playoffs," she says, the enthusiasm in her tone leading.

"Don't jinx it. We're not there yet."

They share a laugh as they ride the elevator together, each disembarking on the top floor.

"I'm sliding over to short for the series," Garcia says.

"Good. It should be you, no doubt." He shifts closer to Garcia and whispers, "As long as it's not that kid from Norfolk. He was so not ready to be here."

"He's comin' back, I think. Skip's got him slotting in at second."

"L'chaim," Sandy says backing towards his room, his hand raised in the air as if holding a glass. "Get some rest. See you in the morning."

They part ways, and a pang of guilt ripples through Sandy. He should be more of a mentor to Garcia, like Oz and Nick were to him coming up. She deserves it—she's a top-five shortstop, forced to spend her big-league time at second base because of him; her bat's consistent, she's a high-contact hitter; and her speed makes her irreplaceable in the leadoff spot—and yet he kept her at a distance, even without recognizing it. He looks over his shoulder, but she's already gone. Tomorrow, he thinks. He can always be better tomorrow.

*

In the morning, he can barely move. His chest and abdomen—his skin taut, bruises blackening beneath the surface—feel like foreign bodies, like he should cut them away and replace them entirely, these parts of him, these original parts, having outlived their usefulness.

He dresses cautiously and rides to the stadium with the team. The handful of media anxious to speak with him are told he'll be unavailable during his stint on the injured list. A sea of groans, of *you can't do that*s, of reminders about player responsibility to the media do nothing to sway the embargo. They don't ask about the increased police presence who, as Sandy was promised, blend in—a member of the training staff, an equipment hand, an addition to the already-stout stadium security team. Sandy recognizes them only because he has been told. He signs a baseball on his way out of the clubhouse and gives it to one of the officers, a wide hulk of a man shuffling things to the dugout, and thanks him. *For your daughter*, Sandy says. The man grins, then, as if remembering himself, nods his head, and slips the ball into his pocket. He fades into the tunnel, where Sandy remains, staring down the long dark corridor, skeptical of the bright sunlight waiting for him at its end.

After the game, Sandy arranges for a car to take him back to his hotel. He's told an officer will follow behind, and though he argues he doesn't need an escort, he knows it's futile. He waits alone, saying goodnight to teammates as they pass by, some on their way to a club. Sandy declines their invitation, and even as he does, he feels worn out. He rides in silence, every few blocks turning around to see if the officer still follows.

Before Sandy exits the car, the driver says, casual and friendly, "Great game tonight." Sandy doesn't correct him, doesn't say it was Garcia who turned those double plays, who stole two bases, who scored the tying run in the eighth. He says thank you, for the compliment and for watching. He slams the door harder than he means to. He ignores the officer's running car a few feet away, as instructed. *Let them do their thing*, he remembers the detective ordering. *For your own good*.

The lobby is crowded, bustling with people leaking out of the hotel bar. There's a fight on the televisions, something he has seen promoted in Las Vegas, and the crowd watches, spilling their drinks onto one another in rapt excitement. On a couch outside the bar, alone with an untouched glass of wine before her, sits Sabine. The pain in his body, the cloud in his mind, lifts. She sees him, too, and though her eyes widen, her expression remains stoic. She stands without taking a step towards him.

"You look like someone I know," he says, loud enough for her to hear across the room despite the rabble behind her. When she doesn't move, barely acknowledges his presence, Sandy goes to her, he wraps his arms around her torso and squeezes. It hurts him, tendons straining and their bodies held together. She slides her forearms along his shoulders, gripping him by the back of his head, fingers spread through his hair. She presses her face against his neck. She's warm, her breath on his skin. He hears her heart beating. He leans back and cranes his neck until their eyes meet. She seems like she hasn't slept, like she has aged since he last saw her.

"You look terrible," she says.

"Was thinking the same."

"About me, or yourself?"

"I'm gonna go with *yes*."

"Smart boy."

"I'm sorry I didn't message," he says.

She shakes her head. She sits back on the couch, takes the first sip of her wine. "I only ordered this to be polite. They kept asking what I wanted." She doesn't look at Sandy before she drinks again. "I have a match tomorrow. I told them I was fine."

Sandy scoops up the glass. He downs the rest of the wine. He purses his lips, hoping to make Sabine laugh. "So sweet," he says.

"I have missed you," she says, some sense of tenderness finally in her expression.

"Berlin feels like lifetimes ago."

"How is that possible?" she asks.

"I saw you on TV, at the memorial. That must've been hard. I can't believe you played Gstaad after that."

"You are doing it too," she says, as if Sandy has accused her of something. "We grieve by playing until we can barely stand, right?"

Sandy joins her on the couch, feeling blockish standing over her. "I don't know anymore." He leans back, hand on his abdomen. He wishes secretly for that replacement body. To again feel what it's like to run without pain, dive into the infield dirt to dig out a grounder. To hold the weight of a bat, of a team, on his shoulders. To move, float, like a feather.

"Is it not still important to you?"

Sandy can't help but absorb her concern, her questioning. "The game?"

"Being the best," she says. "It used to be everything."

"I'm not sure I can ever get that back," he says.

"You talk as if it is already gone. I have seen that fire."

"I'm exhausted, Sabby. I'm so fucking tired."

"Then rest." She takes his hand in hers, like she needs it to keep from falling. "But you cannot be done."

He shakes from her grip, leans forward on the couch. "What's gotten into you?"

"Nothing," she says as she stands, her legs banging the frame of the couch. "You give up too easily."

"Am I giving up? Is that what you think?"

In the silence that follows, he hates the way she looks at him, full of pity. While he's leaned on her, maybe too much, he thinks, he knows she prefers to face things alone. She has disappeared before, pushed Sandy far enough away to nearly sever what connects them. As she towers over him, he wonders if she's doing the same, though why he can't say. She shakes. He watches her fingers tremble.

"I'm fine," he says. He holds back, tries to tamp down what feels close to exploding out of him. "Don't worry. I promise."

Alone in his hotel room and no longer able to keep it at bay, Sandy brims over. For hours he lays in bed, staring at the ceiling or television or out the window, helpless to find sleep. He'd left Sabine in Berlin, and though she said it was all right, he's not sure now. They'd spoken since, though, hadn't they, and everything was fine. He checks his phone, scrolls through messages and Prattlr posts. She was quiet, a little distant, but otherwise okay. He slides his finger back and forth across the keyboard, lines becoming words. *I love you, Sabby. See you at your match tomorrow. Guten nacht.*

He silences his phone, tosses it to the other side of the bed. A boat on the Intracoastal blows its horn and the echo lingers in the room like a ghost. He feels out of place here. He should've stayed in New York, let the team travel without him. The aching in his chest a constant reminder he's not playing, and now he's alone and watching cooking shows in the middle of the night, the few remaining lights along the water dotting the dark sky, trying, failing, to shine bright enough to guide the way.

*

He has the dream again. It's nearly the same, the house and the smells and the wolf-like creatures. This time, as they take him apart, he doesn't regenerate. There's simply less of him after each bite until, just before he wakes, they take everything.

The tennis stadium foregrounds against the beach, discrete but beautiful in its detail. It's a Florida venue, Sandy thinks, noting the murals of underwater life decorating the walls around the grounds. Palm trees flicking their fronds in the early afternoon breeze. People sipping margaritas as they wander from court to court. Sabine's match is first up and Sandy is early, unable to tolerate another minute alone in the hotel. After the match he'll head to his game, dress but never leave the dugout, cheering for his team, his baseball family, with what little fire he has left. But for now, he's on his own, free to roam, play tourist, and watch Sabine play.

When he eventually enters the main court, finds his seat in Sabine's corner, Sandy is surprised to see Jürgen Hellewege. The expression on his face reminds Sandy of a toad.

"Mr. Hellewege!" he says, a reflex. He hasn't seen Sabine's father in years, since before Sandy was called up to the majors. He extends his hand, certain Jürgen has no idea who he is, and says, "Sandy."

Jürgen grips it firmly without moving other parts of his body. "Mr. Katz," he says, his accent thick. Sandy doesn't bother to correct him.

"I didn't know you'd be here." He leans against the railing rather than sitting, enjoying for a moment having the higher ground. "Does Sabby know you're here?"

Jürgen shifts his weight, sits up straight in his seat. "Sabine is staying at home while she is here." He turns and looks at Sandy. "She asked me to come."

Sandy feels his palms clam, though he doesn't know why. Jürgen has always been intimidating, but no worse than Sandy's used to. Maybe it's everything he knows about him, the fights he and Sabine had over the years, the ugliness of their split. He finds it hard to believe she asked him here.

"That's awesome," he says. "I guess I'll be joining you." He slides down in a seat, leaving two between him and Jürgen, whose attention returns to the court, to his daughter's entrance. He doesn't clap and his expression remains the same. Sandy whistles and hoots when they announce her name, exaggerated to make up for the small crowd still trickling in.

"She's looked good," he says, unable to sit still in the uncomfortable silence between them. "She's moving well."

"She is a slug," Jürgen says, eyes locked on the court.

Sandy does a double take, failing to disguise his horror. "Her footwork's improved. I think she's back in form."

"She does not train enough."

Jürgen's statements, their finality, leave Sandy unable to respond. He focuses instead on the action of the match. Sabine *does* look good. Fast, light. Her strokes heavy like cannon fire. Watching her is almost enough to make him forget last night. He wonders what he'll say to her, if whatever exoskeleton she formed during their time apart will shed. Her opponent, a *lucky loser* according to Prattlr, seems outmatched. It's not a fair fight. Sabine steamrolls through the set at love and, during the changeover, she looks at them for the first time. Jürgen stands, shouts something to her in German, returns to his cross-armed ready position. She doesn't nod, or acknowledge him, simply drinks her water, takes small bites of her banana.

Beside Sandy, a woman appears brandishing a microphone. She startles him. He doesn't want to talk to anyone, certainly not the press. He hoped his presence here would go unnoticed.

"Would you mind?" she asks, pointing the microphone past Sandy at Jürgen.

"No, no," he says, surprised but pleased, "of course not." Sandy shifts back a row, letting her take his place.

An on-court reporter for Tennis Zone, she asks Jürgen what brought on his return to the coaching corner after these years away. Sandy cringes involuntarily in anticipation.

"I am here as Sabine's father," he says without shifting his attention.

"How have you drawn those distinctions in the past, between coach and parent?"

He turns his gaze to her, holds the look. "Supporting my daughter is my only objective."

The reporter nods, and she glances to Sandy, who raises his eyebrows, his eyes wide, and lightly shrugs. He hopes she understands the welp in his crooked mouth. The moment of camaraderie ends, though, when she turns the microphone to him. He shakes his head and his hands. *Okay*, she mouths, and before leaving she says to Jürgen, "Thank you for your time."

"Yes, yes," he says, shooing her away.

The second set—more of a battle though Sabine remains in control, her serve dominant—passes without a word between the two men. Sandy's energized by the match, by watching Sabine return to form. She speaks briefly to the crowd, thanks them for supporting her. The sun blankets everything in sight. The feel of it on Sandy's skin cleanses him.

"It's good you came," he says to Jürgen, and though he doesn't expect a response, he looks at him, this mythic golem in Sabine's life, and tries to curl his lips into a smile.

Jürgen gets up, and as he leaves he says to Sandy, "Yes. You, too."

Sandy waits for him to shuffle up the aisle, disappear down the stairs. On court, Sabine packs her bags. Before she heads into the locker room, she waves to Sandy. He reciprocates, beaming.

He waits outside along with a gathering swarm of fans, phones and giant novelty tennis balls at the ready, for Sabine to emerge. When she appears, a mix of voices shouting her name, she poses for pictures, warm and inviting. He sees why they love her, despite her struggles—she blends perfectly the fire of a champion, a brilliance almost superhuman, with a subtle vulnerability, a humanity, translated by a look or the slight snaggle of her smile. She's what gods would be, if they were chosen.

When she catches sight of Sandy, her expression changes. He tilts his head like a confused puppy. She finishes signing and taking selfies and approaches Sandy. She stands beside him, her posture overly formal.

"Your dad said to tell you you're dropping your shoulder on your serve." He shows his teeth, clasped tight to keep from laughing.

"Hilarious," she says, but it does the trick, her face softens, the crinkle above her brow dissipates.

"Feel good?"

She hesitates a moment before nodding. "Better than Charleston anyway."

"Next match up," he says.

She scrunches her lips together. "About last night," she says, stops.

"*Yeah*," he says.

She shakes her head. "I was tired and frustrated. Things have been— difficult—since Berlin."

Sandy steps closer to her, hand against her cheek.

"We should go," she says, and when she swings her head around, Sandy wonders what, or who, she's looking for.

"Okay? Hotel...beach...your dad's place...you guide me."

"Maybe," she says.

Sandy waits for something more concrete. But she picks up her bags and walks. He hesitates before shuffling to catch up.

"Where're we going?" he asks, a few paces behind her. She doesn't answer, keeps on weaving through the complex, around concession stands and practice courts. Even these simple movements he feels in his chest, his abdomen, his hips. "Hey! I'm not a fucking dog. Slow down and tell me what's going on."

"Please," she says, turning without stopping. "I just want to get out of here."

Sandy follows but the distance between them remains. As they approach the exit, he hears a commotion coming from outside the main visitor gate. He shouts to Sabine, who continues on, and instead of following he curves around the outer boundary of the complex. Voices become distinct as he gets closer, an organized chanting. He hears the words before he sees their source. *Blood and soil*, they cry. *Blood and soil!* Sandy moves faster, his steps and the cries in rhythm. He comes upon them from the side, a mass of white men, some brandishing signs and others with assault rifles draped across their bodies. He keeps his distance, inching closer to the center to see them in their totality. A small crowd has formed to watch, to record, to whisper and to yell back. Sandy joins them and soon, without him realizing at first, Sabine, too. She grips his arm, so tight he knows later there will be marks, an imprint of her fingertips. She's close to him, her hot breath.

"We have to go," she says, nearly inaudible.

He looks away from the men and their eyes lock. His lungs calcify, as if he's turning to stone from the inside out. She fidgets under his gaze. And as the voices grow louder, he sees in Sabine, in her cavernous eyes and demanding expression, something he doesn't expect—she, like him, is afraid, but beyond that, underneath the fear, a reaction far more sinister to him, one of recognition.

"Are these the men you told me about?" He slips his arm away from her.

"I have no idea," she says through clenched teeth.

But he knows they are, sees the emblem on their armbands, the rune Sabine described when they were in Berlin. A black phoenix.

"What *is* all this?"

"Please," she says, still somehow measured, "we have to go."

Sandy hears the severity in her voice, its sincereness, but he won't leave. He returns to the men, to their boundless energy, what minds fueled by hate look like. He moves from the crowd, certain Sabine reaches for him as he does. With purpose, he steps closer to the men. They grow louder, their signs waving madly in the afternoon wind. *You will not replace us!* they scream, at him, at everyone willing to listen, each time more pronounced, the animal within them shaping the sounds into growls. Later, he'll remember Sabine's voice, the way she whispers to him. *It is happening.* He'll wonder what she means, how she seems unmoored and expectant at once. He'll understand only that nothing will again make sense. A beacon has been lit. For now, though, he faces the creatures before him. His sheer presence, his existence, enrages them. Their mouths curved, snarled and spitting. Sandy closes his eyes, absorbs everything. His flesh, this body, ablaze.

THE BRIDGE

During the 1930s, in a hamlet on Long Island called Yaphank, there were Nazis. In New York City, on a February night in 1939, Vanderbilt Square Garden teemed with some twenty thousand men and women for a *Pro-American Rally*, greeted with a thirty-foot tall portrait of George Washington flanked by swastika banners and American flags. Stormtroopers filled the aisles. Rallygoers sang "The Star-Spangled Banner," and, by night's end, the Bundesführer demanded the crowd, the country, *wake up.*

Sandy's mother reminded him of these historical travesties on many occasions, most of which—like his bar mitzvah—were inappropriate for such a conversation. *Tess,* his father would say, *is this really the time?* And his mother stared back, sucking on her teeth, as if to say, *Isn't it always the time?*

When leaflets rained down on the city those years ago, Sandy's first thoughts were of his mother's stories. Yaphank. Vanderbilt Square Garden. And later, with the boy on his stoop. His blood escaping in tiny droplets. All Sandy could think was that his mother was right. *It's always the time.*

As daylight breaks, the magnitude of what happened at the tennis tournament still heavy upon him, Sandy hears his mother's voice, his father's. They've become his own, and finally he understands: now, in this world, in this country, on the islands of his city, there are Nazis.

There is nothing on the news about the men. She flicks through channels on the living room television. Tennis Zone ignores the disturbance entirely, focused instead on the tournament. Sabine watches Lolo run through highlights, jealous of her lightness. She knows what her friend has been through, the difficulties in finding a new place in tennis off the court, yet Sabine cannot spell her envy, her desire to retire her body, her concentration, from this sport.

She flips to a news station she would normally avoid, and the crawl announces an executive order, one meant, in the words of the reporter, to extend civil rights protections: *Administration to Interpret Judaism as Nationality*. Sabine turns up the volume until the reporter's voice is all that can be heard echoing through her father's house.

"Coming on the heels of the recent Immigrant Registration Act—which requires anyone living in the United States of Muslim or Middle Eastern descent, as well as those hailing from Mexico and South American countries, to register as part of a larger database aimed at bolstering national security—reaction to this change in status for Jewish Americans has left many confused, some angry. To quiet these concerns, the administration released a statement reiterating this change will only be used to combat discrimination, that quote *the vile poison of antisemitism must be condemned and eradicated anywhere it appears.*"

His voice trails off, taking Sabine's mind with it. It terrifies her, how deep this nadir, how powerful the participants. She wants it to be a coincidence, or, better yet, exactly what they say it is, a protection. But she cannot delude herself enough to believe it. The headlines read like a call to action—a group of men in China, caught on video breaking a Muslim child's hands before beating him to death; a gathering of Orthodox Jews in upstate New York stabbed during a celebration in a rabbi's home; a refugee family trampled during a march in Warsaw—and its totality overwhelms her. Everything is as Petra said it would be. The signal given, the torch lit.

She yells to her father, over and over until she hears his heavy steps coming down the stairs, until he stands in front of her, face of stone but eyes bloodshot, and she says, "What do we do now?"

"Play," he says. "You have a tournament to win."

That cannot be all. He knows it, too, but she nods, to placate them both. "And then?"

"You go to New York for the ceremony."

She shakes her head. She cannot bear the thought of it now, of being back there, knowing what truly happened.

"And after you will play. You will keep playing. That is who you are."

She wants to call Sandy and explain about the men, about Berlin, tell him everything. The longer she puts it off, the stronger its roots. The more difficult to unearth. But what she keeps from him protects him. She knows this, yet she wants to unburden. She wants them to share this secret, this panic, side by side with him against what is to come. Maybe then this pit inside of her would find its end.

———

Sandy leaves the team early and returns to New York. *Medical tests* are the official reason, but after the encounter with the men, he knew he couldn't stay in Florida. He wasn't playing—Garcia's performance helping make Sandy's absence almost unnoticeable—and now he's no good to his team-mates either, his nerves rattled beyond his ability to take the field. Skip demands he rest, take time to *clear his head*, and his agent asks him to lay low, at least until the media loses interest. *In what*, Sandy wants to press but doesn't. The team charters a private flight for him into Newark, and he sleeps on the car ride to Manhattan. From the outside of his building, nothing appears amiss. No caution tape or police warnings, no flyers in the mail room. The doorman greets him. Inside his apartment, the window glass has been replaced, the floor cleaned. No evidence or indication that anything happened here. If not for his father's map rolled up against the breakfast bar, Sandy could believe the past few days have been a dream, a waking nightmare.

In the shower, under a near scalding waterfall, he massages his temples, waits for the pressure to alleviate. He hopes it's from the flight, that the headaches haven't returned. The steam fills him. He scrubs at his skin, at a dirt he can't see. The heat lightens his head. When he steps out, before he can dry himself, he leans over the toilet bowl, sick. The sound of his own retching, the sour water emerging, keeps him gripped to the porcelain.

Later, stretched out on the couch watching his team, able to move but unwilling, he receives a message from his mother. Its ping interrupts Robinson's at-bat. *You're not playing*, she writes. *Where are you?* He weighs the cost-benefit of saying he's there but out of sight, nursing an injury. An easy lie. But when Robinson bounces into a double play, the color commentator interjects, "That's six left on base so far for the Atlantics, and we're only through three. They're desperately missing Katzmann's bat at the top of this lineup, down two early in this one." The game goes to commercial, and Sandy waits for his mother's next message. In the delay, his heart pounds, knocking against his rib cage, an alien entity desperate to burst free.

Resting, he writes, innings later. *Just resting.*

Long before the game ends, he falls asleep. It's ample and full, for the first time in ages. When he wakes, he forgets where he is. The sight of Brooklyn across the river centers him. The Wallabout Bridge lit up, subway trains crisscrossing. He could stay here watching this, he thinks, and everything would be good again. Simple, uncomplicated. This city still his.

He's had enough, though. He feels it in the tips of his fingers, the edges of his shoulder blades. This wallowing, this hiding, how it must stop. He puts his hand to the gauze on his chest, the wound beneath. Though it'll heal, it can't be disappeared. No new coat of paint, no new pane of glass. His skin will bear the marks, and all that's below. The scars, like this city, are his.

———

For days, Sabine tries to reach Sandy. She discovers via Prattlr he has traveled back to New York for medical testing, though no details beyond that. She wishes he was still here and is glad he is gone. It is better if he is home, she tells herself.

From the backyard, her father beckons her. She writes Sandy a final time, to quiet her own nerves—*Hope you are tucked and feeling better. I am sick about what happened. We should talk when I am there for the ceremony. Love you.*—and leaves her phone behind as she meets Jürgen on court. He holds his old racket, frame worn around the edges, overgrip dark with sweat and clay, and bounces a ball on top, like someone tapping their foot in anticipation. Tonight's quarterfinal against Monica Nieves cannot arrive soon enough. Sabine is restless, fighting sleep night after night, the cries of nature and violence surrounding them, leaving her unable to find a center, to focus, to allow her adrenals a moment to disengage.

"You took your time."

"Apologies, Papa."

"Did you sleep?" he says, though she knows what he is really asking is if she is ready, if her body will stand the test of this match and beyond.

She ignores the question and trots onto court. She stretches, helicopters her racket above her head. Her shoulder is sore, a product of her father's overworking her serve. Their last session ended with her threatening to strangle him if he said once more she was dropping her shoulder. When he raised an eyebrow, pointed it at her, she said, *try me*. This morning, she knows he wants to help, wants to distract her from the swirling noise around them, wants to ensure she is champion in Boca Raton once again. They have not spoken about Sandy, or the men, and they will not if Jürgen has his way. Neither has mentioned Petra, even though Sabine sees her name written on her father's face, on both of their faces. A living ghost, haunting them in resurrection.

They practice volleying, serving, overheads until Sabine says it is enough. Her father abides, and she wonders if a new dynamic is emerging, one finally born—instead of paternal tyranny—of respect. She will not hope for too much.

Before her match, she spends extra time getting her shoulder massaged, her ankle soothed. She sees Lolo, and they promise to talk, on and off camera. The exchange is cordial, but nothing like what it should be between them. Sabine puts it out of her mind when she steps on court. During warm-ups, unexpectedly, a tribute video plays on the screens around them, celebrating the tenth anniversary of Sabine's first title here. She looks so young, her hair short, hugging her jawline. She barely remembers that girl.

She smiles at her opponent, Monica, across the net, perhaps to quell her own discomfort. Theirs is the final match of the day, bleeding into night, and the court's bright lights, contrasted against the expansive darkness of the ocean beyond, bring a gladiatorial energy, one matched by the crowd. Ninety minutes later, when Sabine closes out the third set six-two, she knows they are hers, these fans and this court and this place. The collective rush of their voices, their weight, is enough to carry Sabine off, to let her forget, even for the briefest moment.

Jürgen is nowhere to be found after, and Sabine instead seeks out Lolo. The agreed-upon interview will be quick, Lolo promises, and as they sit together, Lolo reaches over and pats Sabine's cheek. "You look good, baby," she says, and the sheer lift of her voice fills Sabine.

"Liar." She smiles for what feels like the first time in days, weeks.

"Out there, at least," Lolo says, smirking, her sarcasm a testament to their friendship, to the way they have long understood each other.

"I could sleep for a week."

"You probably should." Beneath the words, Sabine hears Lolo's bite, a slight jab at her mood of late.

On the other side of Lolo, María Hernández joins them. They exchange hellos, and María compliments her on the match. Sabine, though she sat in this proverbial seat many times before, feels nervous. She thanks María, and before the cameras roll, she turns back to Lolo.

"About Charleston," she begins, and though Lolo shakes her off, those eyes a warm blanket, she goes on, her voice low. "There was so much happening. I was an ass."

"And now?"

"Still an ass," she says.

"Well don't fucking do that again," Lolo says, her hand on Sabine's. "I'm your girl. Don't you dare."

The cameraman starts the countdown to air, and Lolo adjusts, releasing Sabine and sitting up straight. Soon they are rolling, and when Lolo comments on her play, that it looks more aggressive, focused, and asks what has changed since Charleston, Sabine shrugs and says, "Nothing, really. But now I am home. I think that makes all the difference."

Sleep once again evades her. When she does dream, she is trapped, locked up in Petra's restaurant, in darkness, her body inflamed, an invisible weight against her, surrounding her. Like she is still beneath the rubble.

It wakes her, the gasping for air. Her muscles remain sore. She leaves Roger curled in bed and tiptoes to the kitchen, careful not to wake Jürgen. She sucks down a glass of water, her throat dry, as if her thirst cannot be quenched. Outside, the world is black. She slides on her sneakers and steps into the backyard, the crunch of grass underfoot echoing for eternity. She moves slowly, purposefully. As she reaches the court, she uses the fence to lead her further into the yard. She touches the phone in her pocket, considers its flashlight to illuminate the way. She is close, though, she can tell, branches snapping and grass taller and unmanaged. She is in the place between, crossing over into the neighboring property. Things are quiet. She feels as if she is walking through a cemetery. She bumps into a hay bale and nearly loses her footing. She does not know what she is doing there, what she is looking for. A sign of their plan, maybe, their purpose. Anything to understand why. And the hope—buried deep and foolish but no less real—that Petra, even after all Sabine knows, will not be the monster behind this mask.

The house, still a few hundred yards away, is larger than she expected. It dwarfs her family home next door, and she wonders how many people live there, if the bedrooms are teeming with fascists. Flood lights at the back of the house make maneuvering this part of the yard easier. On the last bale, she sees a picture, drawn like an old-timey wanted poster, of a female politician, one she recognizes but cannot place, riddled with bullet holes. How could Petra be part of such an organization, one that hates women so transparently. Sabine remembers her father's words after her mother was gone, after it was just the two of them: *There is no sense in it.* She steps clear of the bale, out in the open as she crosses the field. Flying above the porch, a flag rises and falls in the light breeze. Sabine knows the emblem, the same as she had seen before. Petra's phoenix. The sight of it shakes her, as it has since she first discovered it in her mother's notebook all those years ago. Something about the red on black always unsettled her. Now, seeing it move in rhythm with the wind gives it new life, a new kind of terror.

Time slows, space stretching out as she watches it dance. A snapped branch pulls her back. Flashlights, the hints of faces, guns. Voices chattering. Her everything tenses, heightened, like the few seconds before the start of a match. She resists the urge, the instinct, to rip away the weapons and pummel these men. *What'reyoudoinghere*, someone yells. *Thefuck'reyounuts*, another shouts. These are not questions, and Sabine does not respond. Her hands are in the air though she does not recall putting them up.

"Wait!" she cries out. "Please."

They cannot see her, not directly. A faceless voice in the back shouts orders. *Move. Hold. Torch.* They inch closer. Commotion in the darkness. She tries not to think about how many there are, how much trouble she is in. The voice asks questions—*Who'reyou* and *Why'reyouhere*—and she says nothing. She is certain anything she says will hurt her. She turns slightly, hoping her house is within sight, but the glare of the lights aimed on her only deepens the absence. She imagines running, fast and far, plummeting down into the nothing. Down, down, down.

Holyshit, someone says, and something feels cracked open, Sabine herself leaking out. *D'youfuckingknowwhothisis.* The flashlight directly in her face switches off and others along the perimeter ignite. In the silence that follows, Sabine thinks they are waiting for her. A new order is given then, firm. *Disengage.* From the blackness, a man steps closer. She does not know him, though she feels unmistakably recognized. He salutes her, his back straight, heels and legs together, arm raised high.

"I should not be here," Sabine says.

The man, this tall, unremarkable fascist, relaxes, and he moves near her. She smells his breath. "If we'd known it was you, Ms. Hellewege," he says, and the taste of her family's name on his tongue is enough to wrench Sabine's stomach. "But you shouldn't be here. It's the middle of the night. We could've killed you."

If we'd known it was you.

As if she is somehow safe among them.

"I was out walking. I must have gotten turned around."

The man, his mouth ugly. "We don't see your dad much. But we've wanted to meet you. It's an honor, really. Some of the men said they saw you at the tournament. That you looked upset."

"You are all pretty fucking upsetting, aren't you. You and your guns."

He holds up his hand, chuckling under his breath. "Apologies, again. You startled us. We've gotta be careful. Stand our ground. Day X is almost here."

Questions tear through her. *What does that mean? What is Day X?* The existence of these men continues to confound her. "Who are you people?" she shouts.

The man cranes his neck, signals to someone behind them, and from the porch the field illuminates. There are not as many as she thought. Some are men, gnarled like ancient trees, but also boys, too young to be a part of something so hateful. She cannot imagine an explanation that will suffice, an answer that could bring any understanding.

"Loyal friends, Ms. Hellewege." Behind him, his body silhouetted by red and black, the phoenix waves.

Loyal to what, she wants to ask. *Petra*, she wants him to say. Instead, she nods as if she understands, as if they are speaking remotely the same language, and she turns and runs. She half-expects someone to give chase, to feel the hot sting of a bullet melt through her skin. She does not look back. She lets the years of training etched into every fiber of her legs carry her through the trees, across into her own yard, past the tennis court and into the house. She slams the back door, no longer worried about waking her father. Her whole body is on fire. She collapses at the kitchen table.

She remains there in the dark, until the sun begins to rise and, slowly, there is light.

—

I'll die before I register, the message reads. Even in its severity, his mother's flair for the dramatic makes Sandy feel better. He agrees with her—he would leave the country, play ball in Japan or somewhere else, rather than add his name to a national list of Jewish citizens—but he doesn't want to incite her, so he responds simply, *Don't worry so much.*

Your father's son, she sends back, and after he tucks away his phone. He changes clothes, takes the elevator to the building gym on the fortieth floor. The view is similar to his own apartment, only closer to the steel and Warren truss of the bridge. He starts the treadmill, looking past the televisions and out over the river. The news alerts, though, their seizure-inducing flashes across the screen, are impossible to ignore—*Communities on High Alert after Record Numbers of Targeted Attacks*, accompanied by video from Philadelphia, Los Angeles, Brooklyn, footage of Orthodox Jews walking along Eastern Parkway or congregated at temple, even images of the boy, and swastikas scorched into Midwest cornfields. He closes his eyes, pretends when he opens them again all of it, this reality, is gone. He runs. His abdomen screams but he runs. He wishes his parents were here, both of them together in this room, Nick and Sabby, too, all the people he loves; they would make this okay. They would let him know that everything would be fine. He wishes he saw a different world. His eyes wide open. He wishes and he wishes and he runs.

With the ceremony three days away, Sandy can't imagine being back at New Ebbets. He has lost track of the progress, how close the stadium is to being repaired. The idea of playing there again, soon or ever, feels absurd. In a strange way, the team has embraced their new identity, the nomadic Atlantics. Who they'll be upon their return to Brooklyn, though, Sandy wonders if he'll be there to see. His bubbe—the true baseball fan in the Katzmann family—used to say he was destined to play in the city, to bring home a World Series title, that he would be wasted, unappreciated, anywhere else. He knows she meant it warmly. But now, they're living in strange times, a golem of paranoia and fears brought to life. And she was right about him, he feels that now more than ever. His place is here. New Ebbets, its infield dirt and outfield grass, the curve of the mezzanine seats, his DNA. So when they call his name he'll stand up, for himself and for his team and for this city; he'll accept the honor bestowed, that of simply surviving, of living when others did not.

On the elevator, he throbs in time with the ticks of each passing floor. He takes out his phone, scrolls through Sabine's messages. He isn't angry with her—how could he be—but when he saw those men, Sabine gripping his arm, he was overwhelmed with embarrassment. Shame. He steps into his apartment, shaking his head and laughing to himself. *It's Sabby*, he says out loud. She has seen him at his worst and his best, knows his insecurities and his joys, his loves and his heartbreaks. He shouldn't have run away in Berlin, and he won't push her away now, not after everything they've been through. He remembers when they weren't speaking, when she chose to hide herself away, and though he understood why she did he never forgave her for that, not completely, he realizes.

Can't wait till you're here, he writes her. *Miss you, too.*

After breakfast, he rides the train uptown to the team's makeshift facilities. He needs to feel a bat in his hands, his body moving like it's meant to. The muscles in his chest and ribs still pulled tight but desperate for release. He greets the few people he sees, mostly Highlanders staff, and slips into the virtual batting cages on the far side of the complex. He stretches and, at first, swings lightly. The vibration of invisible ball against tangible bat travels through his fingers and up his arms and down his spine. It kicks his heart like an electric shock. He cuts, pitch after pitch, until his rhythm sends them over the tall right field wall. If Nick were here, he would tell Sandy to level his swing, go opposite field, take advantage of the short porch in left. But Sandy lacks the patience; he jumps on each fastball and slider and closes his shoulders and pulls them down the line, a current relentless and absolute. He knows he'll be in pain tomorrow, but he doesn't stop. After, in the bathroom, he checks that he's alone before getting sick. Adrenaline and bile indistinguishable. The seizing at his core makes his eyes water. When it's over, the air thick, he washes his face and goes. He sneaks away as if he was never there.

The subway teems with the evening rush hour. He stands in the corner at the end of a car, hat pulled down enough to hide his face. His beard, days of apathy, helps conceal him further. His stomach rumbles as they go. A family of tourists collect in front of a map, begging in broken English for someone to help them find their way. The woman seated before them points, moves her finger along a colored line on the map, and after several nods and thanks, the family is gone, shuffled down the car. But Sandy's attention remains on the frame of the map, its upper corner. He moves from his spot, feels in his knees the shaking of the tracks below. He sees the words clearly now, black permanent marker, childlike handwriting. *Jews beLOng n the oVEn.* Below it, a Hakenkreuz, equally cartoonish, as if the person who'd drawn it did so without really knowing what it was supposed to look like, the devastating power it held. He'd gone most of his life without seeing one, and now it has become commonplace. He looks around—could any of these people have done this? He searches the car for some other human being with which to commiserate. To ask for help. With his bare hand, he wipes at it. He spits on his palm and tries again. He pushes until he feels the frame about to give, swipes back and forth, his shoulder cramping. He feels ready to split open, like there's a seam running headlong down his body, a fault line on the verge of rupture.

"It ain't gonna come off like that," someone says, and Sandy stops, noticing everyone on his end of the car watching him.

"What then?" he asks no one in particular. "It can't stay there."

A few people type on their phones, others step closer to get a better view, squinting their eyes as if solving a great mystery. The woman seated in front of him rifles through her bag, hands Sandy a small bottle of hand sanitizer. In his confusion, she says, "The alcohol, honey. It'll take it right off."

Sandy removes his hat, a beat up vintage Atlantics cap he has had since before he was a professional, and coats the top of it with the sanitizer. He uses it like a rag, and the words disappear. The symbol disappears. His hat stained black.

"There's more here," a boy shouts from down the car, and Sandy tosses him the bottle. He puts it to the frame, uses his hand to spread it.

"Here, too," a tall young woman says, pointing to the subway door. She shifts her backpack so Sandy can see the large fractured phoenix, *Ein Volk* written in a circle around it. She unclips her own bottle of sanitizer from her bag and uses a tissue to wipe the door clean. In its place, where the dirt and ugliness have been removed, a clear spot remains.

Through the blackness between stations, Sandy catches his reflection. His hair tousled, forehead glowing with sweat. Eyes tired and heavy. But something else, too. A person he doesn't recognize. A person ready. A person hopeful. Finally, a spark.

Before he leaves the train, Sandy says thank you. In his mind, the car fills with applause for those who stepped up, those who did the right thing.

But in reality, he says his thanks and he's gone. Behind him, the subway doors chime and close, and the train, the lives it carries, barrel on.

—

In the finals at Boca Raton, Sabine easily handles a Hungarian qualifier in straight sets to win the title. She sits with Lolo and María after, a brief interview full of platitudes and wide smiles. *I want to stand before my fans as their champion*, Sabine says. *One step at a time.* They ask her about the World Day ceremony in New York. She looks at the camera when she says she is honored to go, to represent the tour and stand for all those they have lost. Once the cameras have switched off, she kisses Lolo on her palm before she leaves.

Jürgen waits and they drive home together. Sabine remembers seeing the house for the first time, how unimpressive she found it, this entire swampland. And yet, she cannot help but see it now for what it is, what they—she and Jürgen—have made it. Something close to a home.

She fights her impulse to look beyond the woods next door. She wonders if the men contacted Petra, if she knows Sabine was there. She does not tell her father, will not. Over dinner, they talk about New York. He will remain here, he tells her. This ceremony is for her, and he has no place there. She will leave Roger here with him, for the time being. He gets lonely by himself. Each declaration is an impenetrable fortress. She does not argue. They make plans for the morning, one final go-around before she leaves.

"Still dropping that shoulder," he says before she heads to bed.

Later, after hours of sleeplessness, flicking through Prattlr and the news, she comes across a story—a deli vandalized, glass broken and set on fire—and a photo that makes her sit up. She recognizes the place, around the corner from Sandy's apartment. They have been there together, Sandy swearing it would be the greatest sandwich she had ever eaten. It was a near perfect day, as she remembers it. But now, unable to keep from breaking down, she cannot shake the sadness of how quickly something so crystal, so vivid, can be destroyed.

She messages Sandy from the plane to let him know she is on her way. He responds with a heart, nothing more, but it is enough. She will see him at the ceremony. She is desperate to be close to him again.

On the car ride from the airport, Sabine is struck by the reality of being back in the city. Butterflies while crossing the bridge. Watching the boats churn on the river. She stares up at Sandy's building as they inch towards Manhattan, pretending she will see him in his window, wave to him, share a moment unnoticed by the millions of other people hurtling around this island. The city unsettles her as it always has, but having experienced something uniquely terrible here has made it more tangible somehow, more human. She no longer sees it as a place capable of swallowing her up, disappearing her, because when it had the chance to do so, it failed. She emerged, and lived, and now, she returns.

She wonders, though, how Sandy, how anybody, has remained here after World Day. How do lives carry on in the wake of such a massive loss. They ask her how she continues to play tennis, to win championships; they ask Sandy where he finds the courage to give it his all game after game, to dive for a ground ball or send a pitch into the upper deck; but as they slide along downtown streets filled with tourists and neighbors and passersby, what Sabine wants to know is how the taxi drivers keep on, the train conductors and the students and the sanitation workers and the teachers—how do they get up every day, go to work or school, knowing what happened, what could happen again at any moment. How are they capable of such strength.

I am here, she messages Sandy from the elevator up to her hotel room. *See you soon xo*. She changes out of her plane clothes into a jumpsuit, something Alina bought for her as a birthday present years ago. She does her makeup and waits in the lobby as the concierge flags her car. "We're honored to have you here, Ms. Hellewege," he says, opening the rear door for her. She slides in, hands pressing into the black leather seat. "We'll all be watching the ceremony on TV. I mean, not just us," he says, his face flush and sweaty, "the whole world, right?" She thanks him, and when they drive off, she closes her eyes. She wonders not if the world will watch, not those billions, but rather *her*. Will *she* be watching. Will she see Sabine standing alongside those she hates, those she tried to kill. Will she see Sabine honoring those she did. Will she watch as Sabine does her best to fill this city, this nation, this earth with a hope they thought lost. Will she turn away. Will she.

The whole affair, this World Day reunion, isn't what he expected. Or, somehow, it's less and more simultaneously. The place swarming with security, bulletproof vests and assault rifles. Not the New Ebbets he remembers. Skip joins him, along with the owner of the Atlantics, Mel Burbank. Family members of those players that died. Representatives from the league. Sandy poses for photographs, stands where they tell him. His eyes fill but don't burst when they hand him Nick's old jersey, when he lays it over home plate.

At the pond between the two complexes, speeches are given. Sandy hasn't prepared anything. He thanks everyone for being here, for showing the world once more the importance of coming together, of peace. He promises this is not the end, rather the beginning of change, of something radical. *We will not be afraid*, he says, repeats it before leaving the podium. The crowd, the hundreds of media collected, erupt in applause. Sabine takes his hand as he sits beside her. She keeps hold of him, tight and protective, until it's over.

When the reporters have left them, Sandy returns to the stadium. Sabine joins him, and as they walk together, he realizes they've barely spoken. Their tears, their careful touches, have been their words. They're side by side, stride for stride the length of the field, and when they reach home plate, Sandy falls to his knees. He crumples Nick's jersey, holds it to his face, and he screams. It's an animal sound, guttural and familiar. He goes until he's emptied, until Sabine helps him to his feet, jersey still gripped in his right hand, his left held by Sabine, who somehow hasn't cried, hasn't broken down, not even for a moment. She lost friends, too, lifelong intimacies, but she wears none of it. Her expression solemn, her eyes wet but careful. They take a car together, out of Brooklyn and over the bridge, to Sandy's apartment. Sabine jokes that the place looks like a model, nothing out of place. He says he'll tell her tomorrow how wrong she is.

Into the night, Sandy lays awake in bed, Sabine asleep curled against him, her head pressed below his collarbone. He watches television, a replay of the ceremony. It looks different, events and speeches interspersed with video montages, tributes, footage from World Day. On screen, the whole thing appears grander, perhaps the event Sandy had pictured in his mind, as if somehow real life paled in comparison to this retelling. When it's over it begins again, and Sandy keeps watching. He listens to Sabine, her heartbeat and her heavy breaths, how they calm him. He closes his eyes, though he knows he won't sleep. Waves cresting and crashing, pulling him into the current and out until, when the sun rises, the world begins again.

——

She wakes alone, her body diagonal across Sandy's bed. Outside, ever so faintly, she hears sirens, a chorus of robotic shrieks. "What is it?" she asks. She waits for a response that does not come. She slides out of bed and finds the apartment empty. A used mug atop the breakfast bar, a handprint on the window. She forms a picture of him standing in his boxer briefs, hand to glass, steam rising as he watches the movements of the city. She wonders where he has gone. She uses the bathroom, and though she feels rested, her eyes betray that. She pours a cup of coffee and collapses on the couch. In the skies above the river and over Brooklyn, drones climb and fall, helicopters chop through the air. The sirens still calling out.

When Sandy opens the door, his footsteps into the apartment are light and considerate.

"You're up," he says, his soft smile warming. She sees in the lines on his face he has not slept.

"You should have woken me."

He slips a tote off his shoulder, empties its contents onto the bar. Bagels and cream cheese, vegetables and lox. He pulls out a plate, begins arranging things. She gets up and hops into the kitchen. "I can help," she says as he slices a tomato, its bright red flesh serrated and bleeding.

"You remember the deli around the corner," he says, and she nods, the grin on her face an *of course*, replaced almost immediately by the realization of what he is about to say. "It got fucking burned down. I just went to get us breakfast. There's police tape and glass all over the sidewalk. The whole front's torched."

"Do they know what happened?" she asks, cutting open a bagel.

"Amir downstairs said they caught a couple of assholes on the ATM camera across the street. Smashed their way in, tore up the place." He shakes his head. "It's been on the news, he said, so hopefully they find them."

Sabine remembers the report, the grainy video of the young men, one wearing a t-shirt with *Endlösung* printed across the chest as if it were a vintage band shirt, something to parade around ironically. She wonders if they even know what the word means, if they could possibly comprehend.

She hears his teeth clicking together as they prepare their plates. The spread looks enough for a party. They settle on the couch, stretched out facing each other. Sandy turns on the television, flipping through to the local news.

"Thank you for this," Sabine says, and she means more than the breakfast, more than the comfort of being here, of falling asleep with his arm around her, the warmth of his friendship.

"I'm glad you're here," he says. Over the voices on the television, the din of emergency again seeps into the apartment. They both take notice. Sandy leans forward, wipes a stray piece of lox from Sabine's cheek. "It's weird out there right now."

"What do you mean?"

"Everything just feels…off. Since before Florida even. I felt it at the ceremony yesterday, too. Didn't you?"

"It was a memorial. Everyone was sad."

"No, it's more than that. Like everything has turned gray." Something on the television catches his attention, the swirl of police lights. "I don't know how else to describe it."

Sabine waits before responding. She wants to tell Sandy, she knows she should. She cannot know if he will be safer, though, or if his ignorance is the strongest protection. She worries this battle inside her will continue until it is too late.

"I saw the men again."

Sandy sits up, his full attention on her. "At the tournament?"

"No," she says. "I went over there, next door. I wanted to see."

"Are you insane?" He slams his empty plate down on the coffee table. "What the hell?"

"I could not leave it. I am not afraid of their guns."

"They could've killed you, Sabby. People like that don't think twice about it."

"They are just small men. Cowards."

"Did you talk to them?"

She considers what to tell him, how much truth she is ready to share. "Only a little. I told them to stay away from the tournament, and to never come near my family."

Sandy rolls his body off the couch, winces as he stretches upright. "Jesus Christ, you're insane. Can't they just shoot you for being there or looking at them? Isn't that the definition of Florida?"

"I do not like my father being so close to them," she says, trying not to let Sandy's sarcasm stumble her. "They would not bother him, but I wanted to be sure. Jürgen can be a bull sometimes."

"No, I get it. You're just crazy, Sabby. I can't believe you. You're brave as fuck, my god."

She squirms at the thought. Sandy scoops up his empty plate and hers, takes them into the kitchen. They clang as he places them in the sink.

"Maybe a little stupid, too," she says.

When he turns, laughing and gripping his ribs, she joins in, and it feels good. She leaves it there. She tells him nothing more about the men, about Petra. She will figure another way. She will convince herself—now and after and after still—she has done the right thing.

—

Sandy lets her leave without explaining. He says he's tired, still not recovered from his *soreness*, as he calls it, and he's meeting his mother later for dinner. Sabine seems hesitant to go. She's only in the city for another night, then off to California, and she wants to spend as much time with him as she can. Drinks after dinner, Sandy suggests, and maybe breakfast in the morning. *Just need a slow day*, he says.

What he doesn't explain is the map, his father's map, half unrolled on its own in the corner, or the bruising on his chest, now turned a yellowish brown. She's hiding things from him, too. He won't push, and neither will she. Not yet.

Outside, the world is shifting. Police cars zipping by every few blocks. Fire trucks he can see and hear avenues away. If he didn't look too hard, though, nothing would seem too far from ordinary. This could be just another day, a full moon rising or Mercury in retrograde. Some days in the city are like this.

But even as he thinks it, Sandy knows this is something else. He walks to the grocery, pharmacy, dry cleaners. He tries to relish the mundanities of the day. He calls his mother. She's busy with her friends at book club, but she would love to have dinner, she writes. She'll even come into Manhattan. He pretends not to be suspicious of her generosity. *Are things nuts out there?* he asks, and later she writes back, *Things were quiet this morning. Parade or something happening now. See you tonight.* He gets the distinct impression he's bothering her, interrupting her monthly wine and cheese and book time, so he leaves it at that. They'll eat at the diner she loves on Second Avenue. They'll catch up finally, beyond the pleasantries afforded by messaging and intermittent calls. Things will, somehow, get back to normal.

—

She has a guest, the lanky person at the front desk tells her.

"What does that mean?" she asks. She realizes she is wearing one of Sandy's t-shirts, her hair a bit disheveled, no makeup. She would prefer a little time.

"She's waiting in the bar for you," they say. "Let us know if you need anything." They smile, and Sabine reciprocates.

Lolo, it must be. No one else would show up unannounced, and no one else save for Sandy knows where she is staying. She runs a hand through her hair. She feels a mess, but her mess. Lolo will not mind.

A few small groups sit among the couches, sipping oversized cocktails. She scans the room and does not recognize anyone, Lolo nowhere to be found. At the far end of the bar, though, Sabine sees her. Glass of red wine, tinted black by the soft lighting. She looks up, as if knowing exactly when Sabine would enter. And despite all that has happened, all she knows, Sabine still feels as if she sees a ghost.

What if she runs. What if she leaves and does not come back. What if she goes to the police. What if she simply screams right here in this room.

In Petra's eyes, Sabine watches her anticipation. She reads Sabine, who tenses at the recognition. She has no choice. Sabine walks to her, hesitates before sitting. "How dare you," she says.

"Hello, my dear."

"Leave. Go and stay away."

"If that's what you want."

"I *will* call the police."

Petra shines, and it angers Sabine to know Petra is getting the reaction she desires. She takes a long pull from her wine. "We are passed all that, aren't we?"

"What do you want?" Sabine hears it in her own voice and hates it, that mix of rage and curiosity.

"I hope you've thought on what we talked about."

Sabine keeps her voice low. She can smell the tang of wine on her breath. "I have not thought of you once since leaving Berlin. You are still dead."

"I've been honest with you. I ask only the same."

"You are a monster. You get no kindness from me." She grips the edge of the bar, her fingers digging into the rough wood underneath.

"You looked lovely at the ceremony. So noble. Such a credit to your race." Petra reaches up, her fingers delicate, to move Sabine's bangs off her eyes. Sabine flinches and swipes her away, catching the glass and sending it crashing to the floor. The shatter grabs the attention of the other guests, who turn to Sabine, their judgement and their daytime drunkenness on display. She freezes, nervous they will recognize her or, worse yet, Petra. But almost in unison they shift back to their conversations, their laughters, and though she is glad, Sabine finds herself jealous of everyone else in the room, their frivolities.

"I want you to leave. I am not interested in anything you have to say. You cannot stay here."

"I'll be gone tonight. No need to worry."

"Then let this be it. Go back to your invisible castle and fucking disappear. Let this be the end."

Something happens then that Sabine does not expect. Petra's expression changes, not smiling but not unhappy. She takes in Sabine. She seems to enjoy it, the simple act of looking at her. A softness in her eyes, a calming in her cheeks. The way she leans her head against her closed hand. Sabine sees it though she does not want to. Her mother alive, there in this vessel, if only for a moment.

"Please go," she says, begs, gooseflesh rising along her skin.

With that, Petra breaks her gaze. She collects her purse, uses a napkin to dab at spots of wine on her skirt. She stands, careful not to touch Sabine. She leans in close to her, though, and in the second before she speaks, Sabine hears her lips part. "Avoid the bridge, my sweet." And as she walks away, Sabine on the verge of ignition, desperate to know, Petra turns and says, "We will speak again soon."

Sabine absorbs the click of Petra's heels on the hardwood floor. The way they echo, trapped in this place with her, the way they burrow inside of her, take hold, the way they tear her apart.

―――

As day crawls to night, Sandy feels a shift in the air, like the pressure before a storm. He keeps his distance from the windows. He turns off the television, the news further rattling his nerves. On the counter, his father's map spreads out. Sandy hovers over it with his phone, snapping pictures. He'll show them to his mother at dinner. He's sure she knows, has long ago seen the map, what it represents, but he wants to share this with her. It's time.

Outside, the streets are curious. People chatter on the sidewalks in front of shops and restaurants. Sandy cuts through Sara Roosevelt Park. The basketball courts are nearly empty, the music normally filling the open space muted. Even right after World Day, when people were afraid to leave their homes, a camaraderie and compassion took over, a sense they would need one another to survive. But not now. Sandy feels unsettled, the city uncertain.

Further in, he comes upon a community garden that has been vandalized, pots shattered and overturned, terra cotta spread over the concrete like a tornado has passed through only this square of parkland. He slides pieces of clay off to the side, collects dirt into discreet mounds, as if this small act could possibly mean anything. He continues on, the soccer field empty, too, the space where voices used to be occupied only by the white noise of the neighborhood.

Along Second Avenue, police and emergency vehicles weave across the thin streets. Storefronts with their windows broken. *America for Americans!* spray painted on the sidewalk. The smell of smoke permeating the air. He hurries, anxious to get to the diner, to settle into its familiarity alongside his mother. He messages her, asking if she's on her way, if she's all right. He arrives and sits at the counter. He orders a coffee and waits for her to respond. He reads news updates on Prattlr. His timeline is anxiety incarnate.

A man comes in and, despite open seats otherwise, sits next to Sandy. His missing teeth create a whistling sound when he speaks, the volume of which is too loud for such close quarters. "Got the right idea," he says, and when Sandy doesn't respond, distracting himself with the tall menu, the man nudges him, shoulder to shoulder.

Sandy looks up, feigning surprise, and smiles at the man. "What's that," he says.

The man laughs, and Sandy knows it's because he recognizes him. "Hiding in here! A boy like you! Good. The damn world's ending out there."

"Is it?" Sandy says.

When the server comes over, the man orders pierogi and a cup of borscht. "I seen bodegas burning, folks beat up on the street. Damn cops everywhere gettin' pushy. Shit is crazy, man."

His borscht arrives, and Sandy slides over, giving them each some room. "I'll leave you to it," he says. The man raises his soup spoon in place of a drink. "You watch yourself."

Sandy checks his phone. Nothing from his mother. He calls, lets it ring through twice. If she's on the subway, he thinks, it'll go straight to voicemail. But she's not answering. He sends another message, calls again. The server comes by, asks if he's still okay. Sandy says yes without looking up from his phone. The longer he waits, the harder he feels his pulse pounding in the back of his head. When he can't stand it any longer, he throws money down on the countertop and runs outside. He heads south towards the subway, looking for cabs along the way. He calls again and again. The ringing too much. He descends the subway stairs two at a time. In the station, the turnstiles are blocked by caution tape. Two cops stand off to the side, uninvested in the activity around them.

"What's going on?" Sandy asks, pointing his open palm at the barricade.

"No trains right now," the smaller of the two says, shaved head and stocky, thick Queens accent. "System-wide shutdown until everything calms down."

"What do you mean?"

"What do you mean what do I mean? Ya been out there?"

"You should be getting alerts or something," the other says, her tone helpful and tinged with actual concern. "My phone's been lightin' up."

Sandy remembers turning off the emergency alerts after the Roebling bombing, overwhelmed by the constant reminders.

"We gotta ask ya to leave the station. We don't want people collecting down here or anything."

He's back out on the street without another word to them, frantically typing to his mother. The phone ignites, interrupting him, announcing a call.

"Ma?" he yells, his panic carrying down the avenue. "Fuck, are you okay?"

A pause, rumbling on the other end.

"Can you hear me?" The sound of her voice stops him. He could burst apart if he let himself. "Sandy?"

"I'm here I'm here yes I hear you where are you?" He's out of breath, in a way his body usually won't allow.

"I'm walking home," she says, shouting though she doesn't need to be. "The subway's a dud."

"What?" he says, matching her volume.

"A *dud*," she says. "Something's going on, nothing running into Manhattan."

He stops walking, nearly doubled over. He realizes he's shaking. "But you're home. That's fine, that's good. Just stay there." He hears her rustling for keys, unlocking her front door.

"Are you all right?" Her voice echoes in the living room. "What's going on?"

"I don't know," he says. "Things are a little wild here. I'm just glad you're okay."

"Of course I am," she says.

He laughs, his mother's uncanny ability to read him, lighten him. He wishes he lived closer—it's what she always wanted—this river between them an ocean, suddenly uncrossable. But Esther Katzmann's little patch of Brooklyn is a safe harbor now, and for that he's grateful. He steadies himself. He knows he should tell her more.

"Dinner tomorrow," he says, "in Brighton."

"If we're still here," she says, the kind of sarcasm his father couldn't get enough of.

"Lock up and stay inside, please. Until things are back to normal."

"Listen to you," she says. She clangs the tea pot against the kitchen faucet. The water running. He knows she'll turn on the news later, start to see what's going on, and she'll worry about him. She'll message and apologize for it being so late, and he'll tell her it's not late at all, that he's fine, he's tucked high above the Manhattan streets in his apartment, that up here all's quiet, all's well. *I can see the house from here*, he'll say, and it'll make her laugh. She'll say she's waving, and him too, and it'll be enough to put her mind at ease.

"Are you home yet?" she asks.

"Almost," he lies.

"Good," she says, and soon after they say their goodnights. He's going to send her some pictures, he says, something he found of Dad's. He'll see her tomorrow and they'll talk about it. He slides his phone into his pocket, and he walks towards the river. Around him, the world has gone mad. Broken glass scattered like crumbs over the sidewalks, streets blocked and crowds mounting. The city is restless. Sandy keeps on, unsure where he's going. Through all the noise in his mind, all this chaos, there's one clear sound. A bell has rung, invisible and incessant. A beginning, or an end, but nothing ever the same.

———

Sandy is not at his apartment. The doorman tells her he left a while ago, to meet his mother for dinner, he thinks. She asks where, and he shrugs. They were supposed to meet for drinks after dinner, Sabine says. She paces the lobby. She checks her phone—no response to her messages. Where could he be. She wishes she had stayed with him. Petra's words pound at her temples. *Avoid the bridge*. What are they planning. Another bombing, another World Day. Is Sandy in danger. Is the city. She should have asked more questions. She should have shaken Petra, gripped her arms until her skin bruised, until Sabine cracked her thin bones. Petra would have told her. She wanted to tell Sabine everything. But she was not ready to listen, she could not. Now she does not know, and she wants to. She has to.

Sabine is gone without another word. Her steps are heavy, as if she played two long sets and must summon the energy for a third. She moves south along the river. She peers up at the Wallabout. Cars have stopped driving, and no trains pass overhead. The quiet of it unsettles her. She turns, faces north, then back south. She wonders what she is even looking for. So many bridges throughout the city—how can she know which one Petra meant?

She continues on until she sees what's left of the Roebling, spanning and unlit. And there, faint but visible, smoke curling from its dark center. Flickers of flame, flashes of light. She picks up speed. She runs without thought. Sirens in every direction. Glass broken, messages scrawled on buildings and doors. Crowds blocking sidewalks. She runs until City Hall. The park is nearly empty. Trash cans overturned or burning. A police car driven up onto the square, abandoned, quarantining the entrance to the subway. She smells ash all around. Streetlamps show the entrance to the bridge. Food carts and souvenir tables deserted. She sprints along the walkway, heading towards Brooklyn. As she advances, three men armed with large guns charge, cursing for her to turn back. When they are close, she sees the familiar armband they wear.

"What is happening," she yells, pointing out towards the smoke, the unseen commotion beyond them.

"Go away," one of them says—the three could be triplets, pasty and unshaven, save for their skinned heads—and another points his gun-toting arm at her. "This ain't got nothin' to do with you."

She looks behind her, to the road on either side, searching for police, someone to come to her aid, someone to warn. There is no one, and in a moment the men are upon her, the tips of their guns inches from her flesh.

She sucks in the ashen air. "Let me pass," she says.

And they cock their guns, and they raise them. "Last chance, lady," one of them says, half-hearted, like he would relish the chance to shoot her dead.

She can pass; she knows how. She fights her own nerves but suddenly it is out, her mouth is open and she has said, "Do you know who I am?"

"Fuckin' dead if you don't get the hell outta here."

The guns, the cowards attached to them, slide closer.

"I am Sabine Hellewege."

They look at one another, these men of terror. "The fuck you are," they say.

She steps into them, and they each retreat, barely noticeable, in response. "If I am not, how would I know?" It is ugly and it is liberating. "How would I know what that name means to you."

The way the one in the middle looks at Sabine, she knows he recognizes her. "Why're you here," he says.

She bites the inside of her cheek to keep from screaming. "Petra sent me," she says.

Behind them in Manhattan, Sabine hears sirens, loud but far away still. The men lower their guns one at a time. They open a space between them for Sabine to walk. She takes a step, another, before she runs. They holler as she goes, and it echoes through the railings. The wood underfoot rattles, pieces broken and charred.

As she gets closer to the source, she slows. She can hardly see. Men with torches are the only light here. There are voices, too, and she moves through the smoke until she finds them. People on their knees, rows of them lined up, hands bound. Battered and bruised. Bleeding and crying out. There are children. They look at her, these men and their captured. What is about to happen written on their faces.

The air fills with it then, a sound she cannot imagine is real, one she will replay in her mind, unable to make sense of its madness.

"Sabby," he asks. His voice like scratched flesh.

She sees him through the veil, hovering above the others somehow.

He looks at her, his eyes screaming. "Save them," he says.

She hears him in a way that feels unending. Like the words will live inside her and when she dies they will enter the soil with her, they will live and they will grow anew and for generations the words will be real, tattooed on this very earth.

Save them.

—

"They took them!" the woman says, fallen to her knees and wailing.

Sandy crosses diagonal through the intersection, forgetting to check for traffic. A taxi and a black sedan both barrel through, barely missing him. A small group has come to the woman's aid. Her nose bleeds, her eye and forehead swollen.

"Who," someone asks, "where?"

She shakes her head, drooped and sobbing. "I don't know where they went." She looks up at Sandy, who kneels before her. "I tried to hide them. They came in with guns. I thought they would shoot us all."

"Who," Sandy says. "Take a breath. We can't help if we don't know."

"I tried to keep them safe. I locked them in the supply closet."

Sandy turns to others in the group, motions for them to go into the building and search. It's then he sees the small white sign beside the entrance, written in Hebrew, announcing the name of this primary school.

He remembers her first words. "Who did they take?" he asks. He grips her shoulders, leaning on her, too, trying to hold them both up.

"I didn't see them hiding in the classroom. They didn't come with the rest. And the men stormed in, and they took them, three of them."

Sandy feels her body might unravel in his hands.

"They have them?" He tries not to raise his voice but he can't help it. "Why?"

She looks at him, for the first time with clarity.

"Where? Where did they go?"

She points east, towards the river, the Roebling. She says they could see through the tiny window in the closet. They watched as they took them away.

One by one, people emerge from the building with children. The street fills with the sounds of their crying and the adults carrying them, a collected orchestra of grief and relief at once. Sandy tells the woman he's going; he's going to find the ones they took. He'll bring them back.

"Toda raba," she says. "Keep them safe."

Then, Sandy runs. He forgets the pain in his chest, and he runs. He has always been fast but never like this. He's carried, he feels it, his feet barely touching the ground. As he gets closer, he smells the river. And something else, something burning. A banner, filthy and soiled, hangs from the bridge—*Life Liberty Victory*, it reads, swaying in the evening wind. He flies towards City Hall. Everything looks abandoned, but from all around he hears shouting. Together they are confusion and fear.

He runs onto the wooden walkway towards Brooklyn, towards the rising smoke. *The whole world is a narrow bridge*, he thinks. Atop one of its still-crumbling arches, an American flag waves. Its flapping sounds like gunfire. But he doesn't stop, even when he realizes it's not the flag, the *pop pop pop* filling the air. He's upon them before he can react, a crowd of men with machine guns and rifles. They remind him of the men in Florida, with their armbands emblazoned red and black. Their snarling barks. In front of them, hands bound behind their backs, are rows of men and women. Children. They've been beaten, tossed about, all of them. One of the children still wears his kippah. The men, the things they scream. Sandy struggles to take it in, to process what he's seeing.

"On your knees!"

In the chaos, no one knows what to do, where to look or how to listen. A man, tall and slender, doesn't kneel quick enough for their liking, and the butt of a rifle shatters his jaw. The children take direction; they go to their knees and face forward. They cry but do as they're told. A woman beside them tries to provide comfort. Bullets fired into the air as a warning stop her. Her eyes catch Sandy, and though she doesn't linger, it's enough, and the men turn to him. They descend, and Sandy, afraid for these people, for himself, doesn't fight. Their fists and their guns pound into him. He feels his nose break, his ribs. Blood inside him no longer contained by vessels. Eventually the men stop, their muzzles trained on him. Someone fires another shot into the night. They drag Sandy to his feet, tell him to join the others. He stands out in front of them—these *others*—and keeps his hands raised. He feels the heat coming off the fire nearby, a pile of cracked wood and paper and all manner of detritus. He stares at the men as they wait for him to acquiesce, to take his place at the end of the line.

"Sit the fuck down," one of them says, accompanied by a click of preparation in their guns. Sandy remains, though. He barely moves, only the sharp heaving behind his rib cage. His face swollen and wet.

Laughter then, an evil sort of cackle. "Ho-ly shit," the one closest to him says.

"You know me," Sandy says, a confidence in his voice he was certain he would never find.

The laughing man nods, and another joins in the sniggering. "Of course we do," he says, his gun an extension of his hand, pointing in all directions. They stare, their eyes blank even with their mouths curved.

"I'm Sandy Fucking Katzmann."

"Brooklyn's very own cake boy," the laughing man says. From behind him, someone says, "Remind me to get your autograph later," and the lot of them share in it, this sick, perverse entertainment.

"And I know you," Sandy yells over them. "I know what you want."

A shot fires, from the side perhaps but Sandy doesn't see, only hears. He flinches, as do those kneeling, but no one has been hit. A warning echoing between boroughs.

"And what do we want," the laughing man says, readjusting his weapon against his shoulder.

These aren't soldiers, Sandy thinks. They're bullies, full of hate and narcissism, their weapons a compensation for what they lack.

"These people," Sandy turns, searches the faces of the captured, sees in their eyes a kind of strength he never imagined existing in a person, "they're nothing. For fuck's sake, there are children."

"Cockroaches," the laughing man says.

Sandy wishes he could release his rage onto this bridge like a magic spell, disappear these bogeymen.

"These people aren't worth your bullets." He feels the discomfort in his body begin to melt away, and he stands up straight, his shoulders broad, his chest a shield. "But I am." The men look at one another and back to Sandy. They slide closer, their guns still locked on him. "You let them go, and you have me."

The laughing man steps forward, orders Sandy onto the railing. Smoke fills the space around them, a translucence to further unnerve him. He climbs up, hands gripped tight to the cables. Behind him there's nothing, the barriers that once were exploded years before, left in disrepair. The wind whipping off the bay shakes him. His weight pushes back against it, hoping to steady, to not fall.

"Or we kill all ya right here, right now." The laughing man half-turns his head, raises his mouth to the sky. "How's *that* sound boys?" They respond as one, a collective sort of howl.

"Please don't do this. Their deaths would mean nothing. And the children—you'd be monsters, not liberators. I know that's what you really want. But I'm someone. You could mount my head on your fucking wall."

The smoke, thicker now, singes his eyes and his throat. He chokes but tries not to look away even for an instant. One of the kneeling men cries out. A knife exposed, held to the man's throat. Blood trickling down his neck. The women beside him shrieks. Sandy sees in the laughing man's expression how excited he would be to cut this man open. Sandy's legs, his whole body, engage. He's ready for this to end.

"I've got money. I'm what you people are after. Goddammit leave them alone. Let them live their sad little lives in fear of you. Isn't that what you want anyway. I'm right fucking here." He pounds his chest, he feels the cracks underneath spreading. "Take me."

The laughing man considers what's been offered without retreating his knife. He smiles at Sandy, who can imagine a reaction no more frightening. Through the haze then, there's movement. A body rushing forward. Sandy braces himself, hands tightening around the cables. And when she steps out from the darkness, somehow he knows it's her.

"Sabby," he says. He wants to ask how she's here. Why. He wants to jump down and be wrapped in her arms. He wants her to know. But she already knows. "Save them," he says. "Please. Save them."

"What the fuck's this?" the laughing man says, sheathing his knife, his attention turning.

From behind Sabine three men appear. They're out of breath, running with their guns and their bellies. "She says Petra sent her."

Sandy recognizes the name, that of Sabine's long-dead mother. He watches Sabine, trying to make sense of her presence here, any of this.

"Bullshit," the laughing man says and, after what has been an eternity, disengages from Sandy. "Why the fuck would you assholes let her down here." He steps towards her, and Sandy can't believe how she doesn't waver. "Who the hell are you."

She says her name like a proclamation. Her voice alone enough to wreck Sandy.

The laughing man, the others, they go to her. She says things to them he can't hear. She doesn't look scared. They listen to her. How. Why.

"Tell them, Sabby," he says suddenly. "Tell them to let these people go. They have me. Tell them."

A breeze opens a space in the smoke, the blackness of the night thicker now. She meets his gaze, and between them there's understanding, a trading of something beyond words.

"His life for theirs," she says. "I think Petra would like this exchange." Her confidence, her stature, they overwhelm Sandy. He doesn't know what's happening, but he waits, hoping.

"Are you sure?" the laughing man asks. "We've done exactly as instructed."

"We do not need children. No one knows these people. But him," she points to Sandy, and he can almost feel it, the extension of her touch, "him they will know."

The laughing man steps away from Sabine, back to the people he's kept on their knees. "It won't matter, you know. We'll find them again. We'll hunt them down."

The children shake, shock settling in. The women and men still weeping, their eyes to the wood and water below, some praying and others silent, their breaths almost unnoticeable. The laughing man walks along the row, and from his belt he removes a handgun, points it down at each person he passes. He whispers to them. He stops in front of the little boy, rips the kippah from his head. He aims, pulls back the hammer.

He looks to Sabine. "Sieg Heil," he says.

When he fires, Sandy can't bear to watch. He feels a pinch in his gut, a hollow sting. Sirens ringing like a distant clock. He hears Sabine crying out. He opens his eyes, and the people on their knees are looking at him. The boy, he's there; he's okay. He's okay.

And Sandy's warm then, his head light. He sees her—*my Sabby*—and he doesn't understand her tears, her pain. They did it. They won. Everyone will be safe. When he looks down at himself, his body opened up, his hands, they slip from the cables. The entire city moves along with him. The seconds and milliseconds, they slow almost to a stop. He floats, his arms outstretched, his palms spread wide. The laws of time and space abandoned, he's bound no longer to this earth. A rush, the brilliant lights of Brooklyn. The cool, cool water around him. The everythingness, finally, his.

WE THE BEGINNING

He saved them. That's what they tell us when we find them, what plays on the news reports for days after. We ask how they escaped, why they were let go. Because of him, they say. He saved us all.

What happened in New York and Prague and Paris and in cities large and small around the world cannot be undone, cannot be ignored or swept aside. No one was safe. We hid in our homes and we came together on the streets. We embraced one another. We comforted our children.

We are the beginning. We are no longer the remainders; we are the living. We are afraid. We are sad. We are vigilant. We are happy to finally speak our minds. We are lucky and we are devastated. We fall apart. We are held together by one another. We rebuild. What had burned turned to ash. The day new, and we a part of it. The sun rising.

We want to be happy. We make our dinners, and we keep our families close. We will remember those who have lived, those we have lost. Nothing will ever be the same.

Because of him. He saved us all. We will never forget.

SANDY

She never imagined. Even as he fell, she never imagined. It could not be real. She could stop it still, she is sure. But then she wakes, the night having cradled her like a thornbush, and everything is. All that is has happened. All that will, she cannot stop. What comes after is life, the burden of the next day. There are no nightmares for the living dead. There is only now, and she is awake.

She has a message waiting for her at the front desk. She takes it in hand, leaves it sealed. She knows without looking it is from Petra.

She feels she has been hiding in her hotel room for weeks, though only a few days have passed. She settles on a couch in the bar and asks for coffee. She considers calling Jürgen, checking in on him. Petra would never, of that Sabine is certain. Still, those men so near him, and his stubbornness. She will call later, she tells herself.

Televisions scattered around the room play the news on a loop, a continuous, ever-shifting narrative. The images, videos, interviews knit a tapestry of bedlam and terror. *So much left to figure out*, they say. *Understand*. Sabine wonders how anyone could ever make sense of this. They know so little, only what is reported, what they choose to believe. But she knows what happened. She knows why; she wishes she was alone in this.

When Sandy's face appears on-screen, the words *Katzmann Presumed Dead* scrawled underneath, she is pulled back there. Eyes stinging from the smoke. The wind picking up. The voices, the way they mix now in her mind. How quickly things move. How suddenly the shot rings out, his hands slip away. She is at the railing in time to see him hit the water, disappear. The river black like oil. The shock of it, the clawing realization he is gone, her Sandy; she failed to protect him. His words—*Save them*—like a music in her head. If she screams, it is only inside her. She turns back to the hostages, to their captors. She demands their release. The certainty in her tone, the authority, surprises her. They do as she says. The man who shot Sandy questions why, but he does not stop it. She instructs the hostages: *tell the world about Sandy Katzmann.* They do not answer her and shuffle away along the bridge. Each of the children scooped up in the arms of an adult. They are all alive somehow. She has done what he asked. She tells the men—*her* men, she thinks and nearly gasps at the thought—Sandy Katzmann will be a martyr. These people will erect statues and tell stories. He will become a symbol. And his death will do more for the cause than a thousand others, a million. *Petra will be pleased*, she says. She gnaws on her own tongue, tastes its iron.

The coffee brims over the mug as she drops it to the table, rushes to the bathroom. She retches into the sink, her stomach and chest burning. She spits water and stale coffee. She cannot bear herself in the mirror. Her rage, it boils. She smashes her hands down against the porcelain. Again. Again. She feels it give. She stops, water leaking from the faucet and the wall. Small drips. She hears them land on the tile below. She tells them at the front desk. They thank her for letting them know. The politeness of it all sickens her. She wants to run through this lobby onto the street; she wants to cry out until her throat bleeds; she wants to destroy everything she touches.

On the news, they show people mending their broken storefronts, men in yarmulkes leading cameras through burned-out buildings. Each story's ending is the same: *we will rebuild*, they say. How can there be hope in such hopeless times. She feels the question eating through her flesh. Sandy saved those people, she thinks, but they are only a few. What of the others. What of the rest to come. What they do not know. What will become of them. What could she possibly do to stop it.

She asks the bartender for a glass of water. Its iciness calms her inflammation. She sucks it down and the bartender refills.

"Are you all right, Ms. Hellewege?" they ask. The sound of her own name, of a stranger speaking it, feels suddenly the most alien of sensations. "You look—" and they stop. With a warm wet towel, the bartender wipes down the countertop, where Sabine's water has spilled slightly.

"What," she says. She stares at them. "Say it."

They hesitate, intimidated, something Sabine is long used to, though perhaps she has forgotten the sensation. "Unwell," they say. "Apologies if that's too much."

"It is," she says. She moves back to the couch, the condensation on her glass dripping down her fingers. "But who the hell is well these days."

The envelope sits on the table, untouched. When she can resist no longer, Sabine tears at it, the edge of the paper slicing through her skin. The message is not from Petra. Instead, it is a phone number, an address. *Esther Katzmann*, the name reads. She begs Sabine to contact her. She has questions. She hopes Sabine can help. She thanks her. Sabine goes over the message, her eyes darting through each line. Her insides again upending, but she remains. If she were still on that bridge. What has she done. She settles into the feeling. Demands it. It is a necessary one. A roasting, a cleansing. She hopes, when it is done, there will be nothing left of her.

ESTHER

Sabine takes the train to Brighton. The trip over the river and curving under and above these Brooklyn streets brings her closer to Sandy. She imagines him with her, narrating the journey. It seems impossible she will never see him again. His voice in her head, clear as this day. She remembers walking in Berlin, Sandy telling her the same about Nick. The conversations they still had. She is not ready for that, though. If she tried talking to him now, this soon, she is terrified of what he would say in return.

Why am I doing this, she wonders out loud. An older woman across from her looks up, shrugs, and continues reading. Sabine adjusts herself, stretched diagonal along the seats to face out the window. Despite all that has happened, she understands why Sandy loved this city so much. Something at once new and familiar, comfortable and exciting. She could never live here—she craves somewhere with less contradictions, if such a place exists—but the draw of its energy, even now, is undeniable. And Sandy carried it with him every day, the intangible essence of this city.

She checks the directions on her phone. She is close, and her palms sweat. She has avoided the nervousness of facing Esther, of what she could possibly say to her. What she expects of Sabine. It is enough to make her sick right here in this train car, her own audacity, to somehow represent Sandy to his own mother.

Esther meets her outside the house, waving as Sabine approaches. She is barefoot and a foot shorter than Sabine. Her hair almost black, peppered with silver. They say nothing to each other before embracing, there on the front lawn. Bound by grief, they hold one another. Sabine feels, almost immediately, like a fraud.

Inside, the walls are decorated with charts and maps, artwork and photographs. Sandy through the years. Missing his front teeth. Giving his high school valedictorian speech. A minor league action shot, Sandy's uniform almost too big for him. Sabine recognizes that young man, the Florida sun. The first version of Sandy she loved, she thinks but does not say. Newspaper articles framed chronicling his career. He lives here still. He is happy here.

Esther makes them tea. Sabine sits at the kitchen island waiting for her to speak. Though Esther is small, she carries herself like a titan.

"I saw you win your first title in Boca—I mean I was there. Did Sandy ever tell you that?"

She says his name as if nothing has happened, as if he might be in the other room. Sabine shakes her head, flattered but overwhelmed by being here. The kettle whistles.

"We were visiting my sister while Sandy was playing for Palm Beach. He got us tickets as a surprise. He knows how much I enjoy tennis. Lenny, my late husband, and I were regulars at the City Open for years." She readies the tea and hands Sabine hers. "Anyway, and you were there. One of the best I've ever seen, if I do say so." She holds up her cup and reaches across the island. "L'chaim," she says.

Esther leads Sabine out to the deck. She tenses waiting for Esther to ask about Sandy. The longer they sit, each sipping politely and taking in the view, the more uncomfortable she becomes. There is so much she cannot say.

"It's curious, don't you think?" Esther's voice fills the space perfectly, as if carved out by its vibrations. "Two people knowing so much about one another, caring about one another, even though they've never met?" She picks up her tea, puts the cup to her mouth, holds it there but does not drink.

"I wish I was finally here for a different reason."

"He's always wanted us to meet."

The clank of her cup against its saucer echoes off the deck, disappears somewhere beyond where Sabine can see.

"I loved him very much," Sabine says, holding herself steady. "He was very important to me."

"All he ever talks about is you and Nicky. You two are his world."

"Ours, too."

She watches Esther, whose gaze is locked on something near the horizon. She is strong in a way Sabine is not. She talks about her son without a hint of sadness. As if this is simply something else, after a lifetime of somethings, to bear. She seems to Sabine etched from stone.

"I was supposed to meet him, you know, that day." She shifts her attention to Sabine. Her eyes are big and brown and full. "We were going to have dinner. But the subways were down, I ended up stuck out here. We spoke on the phone. He sounded upset—maybe not upset, concerned really. But still him."

Sabine thinks about one of the last real things Sandy said to her. He called her brave. The mere thought of it now is enough to rip her open.

"We were together at the ceremony," she says. "A little bit after, too. It was good to see him. It was always good."

"He sent me pictures, too. After we spoke. I didn't understand what they were at first." Esther takes out her phone, flicks at the screen until she finds what she is looking for. She turns it to Sabine, so she can see. "Have you seen this before?"

She barely has time to absorb what she sees before Esther withdraws her phone.

"It's his father's map. Lenny worked on it for years. It was a bit of an obsession."

Sabine remembers it from Sandy's apartment, spread half-open against the breakfast bar, though she had not really looked at it. "Sandy had this," she says, making it sound like a question.

"He must've found it here, in the attic," Esther says. "I'm glad he did. Lenny would've wanted Sandy to see it. To understand it."

"May I see?" Sabine asks, pointing at the phone. The intersection of her curiosity and her fear cracks her voice.

"Hold on," Esther says. She stands, tucks her phone away, and goes back inside the house. When she returns, she's holding the map. "Come," she says.

Sabine follows, and in the dining room, Esther spreads the map open on the tabletop. "I found it at Sandy's apartment. After. I didn't want it lost."

Sabine tries to comprehend. Cities and swastikas covering the country. She feels Esther watching her. "What is this," she asks, though it does not take long for her to understand, to recognize what Petra had told her. She sees the curling penciled letters in the corner. *Lebensraum.* A new space. A new way of life in this country. A new vision for this land.

"Before my husband died, he spent much of his time—" and she stops, taking in a deep breath and Sabine at once, "let's say researching. He was long convinced that something was coming, and if we looked in the right places, we'd find a pattern."

"And this map," Sabine says, soft, trying so hard not to betray what she knows, what she is certain she must keep hidden, "this is what Sandy discovered? This pattern?"

Esther shakes her head, presses her hands against the table. "I don't know. He wanted to talk about it. At dinner. And then."

Esther adjusts her body, and Sabine knows what is coming. She braces for it.

"Why the hell was he on that bridge?" Esther says.

Sabine lowers her eyes. "I wish I knew." She fidgets in her skin. "He must have seen the fire on the bridge. And he went there to help. Because he is Sandy. He could never have known what he would find there."

"He knew," Esther says, her voice strong, tapping her finger against the map. "His father knew, and Sandy knew."

Sabine wants to understand this, the possibility, the extent, of what Sandy knew. She sees in Esther, though, that nothing more can be said.

"He's stupid and brave in equal measure, my boy."

Sabine takes a drink from her tea, still warm. Her fingers tremble. She is an imposter. A traitor, she thinks.

Esther clears her throat, as if sensing Sabine's spiral, shaking her from her own thoughts. "Whose blood is redder," she says. Sabine does not understand. "If Lenny were here, he'd never stop asking that question."

"What they say he did," Sabine begins, and she presses her palm to her thigh, digs in her fingernails. "They would be dead if not for him."

Esther nods. "Like father like son," she says. She opens her hand on the table between them.

Sabine rests her hand atop Esther's, who squeezes her tight. She feels on the verge. Supernova, Sandy would say. *Like father like son.* How true those words—the Katzmann men, Esther's loves, both lost on the same bridge. Taken by the same hate. Sabine wants to go on. She chokes on the words she does not say. *I watched him die.*

"He was the best," Sabine says finally. "The absolute best. Our beautiful rebel."

"He's a pain in the ass," Esther says, her wry laughter a salve. "But he's my Sandy Beach. And I'm so grateful to you for loving him."

"You are an incredible woman. And you raised an amazing son. He changed my life." *My Sandy*, too, she leaves unspoken.

When Esther looks at Sabine, it is for the first time on the edge of breaking. "He deserves better than this. He deserves better than the bottom of the East River."

Sabine knows it is time to go. There is only so much.

They bring their cups to the kitchen. Sabine offers to wash them, and Esther waves her away.

"Do you…" Esther starts, ceramic clinging against the sink. She stops, her hands covered in soap, and collects herself. "Would you want the map?"

The question catches Sabine, and for a moment she is speechless. "No," she says, "I could never. You should have it."

Esther turns back to the running water. She holds her hands under the faucet until they are clean. "Yes," she says. "I'll send you the pictures."

In the living room, they say their goodbyes.

"I am so grateful," Sabine says. "Being here means the world."

Esther thanks her for coming. "It's a long trip, I know," she says. "Promise you'll visit next time you're here."

"Of course," Sabine says. "For the Open. I will leave tickets for you. You can come and watch once again."

Esther smiles, genuine and warm. "Maybe," she says.

Before Sabine leaves, they embrace. They say no more about Sandy, though she knows they both want to. They want to stay here together and talk about him. They want to share this grief. But neither can stand it a moment longer. To be so close but without him. Each of them destroyed. Through the bay window, they watch the sky changing, nearing sunset, a purple and blue fire. In this house, Sandy will remain. Here, he will be safe.

SABINE

In her dreams, Sabine is falling. The locations change—a court on the edge of a mountain, a plane over water, a sinkhole behind Jürgen's house, the very earth swallowing her up—but the sensation remains consistent. An endless descent. No possibility of release, of stopping, of her feet feeling the ground ever again. And when she wakes, her face cold with sweat, the muscles in her thighs and her calves pulled to their extremes, she finds herself incapable of movement.

For days after, Sabine ignores the world. She withdraws from the tournament in Cleveland. She has not trained. Her body in atrophy. Yet she knows she cannot remain here. She showers before ordering breakfast, and when it arrives, she tells the server she requires a luggage cart. She will be going soon, she says.

Another day passes, though, before she is ready. She keeps the news on in the background, a passive debilitating self-harm. Protests in major cities here and abroad are met with counter rallies; violence erupts; the administration releases a statement, asking *good people* on both sides to find a middle ground; many question where such a place exists on a battleground of hate; others demand only silence, obedience, a recognition of what will make this world *right*; everyone, it seems, full of rage.

*

When the time comes, her muscles and her motivation finally in sync, Sabine leaves the city. Security at the airport is chaos, but not for her. She is escorted to her private plane. She feels invisible, in a way only privilege and money can bring. She sleeps, a heaviness in her brow caused by the pressure, and as she wakes, she takes in the ocean, from this distance moving without effort, the way it changes colors, the way it turns almost black in its deepest parts.

The drive from the airport is quick. She remains in the back seat for a moment once they arrive. As she steps out, the earth reminds her where she is, a feeling she would know blind. The driver helps unload the car, stacking Sabine's bags by the front door. When he is gone and she is alone, she waits, unsure when she will be ready to step inside. She hears Roger then, his whimper through the door, his scratching, and she bursts. She lets Roger out and his thick tiny legs climb her and she lifts him into her arms. His tongue attacks her face without mercy. He makes a sound, a joyous overwhelming cry, as he licks her, and she struggles to hold his wriggling body. "Okay, okay," she says and puts him down. He darts into the yard, running in circles, tearing up the grass.

The house is quiet, save for Roger's nails like tap shoes across the tile floor. Sabine piles her bags in her bedroom, waiting for some sign of Jürgen. She brings Roger out back, and she sees her father a few hundred yards away, walking back towards the house. Head down, his matching hoodie and sweatpants a familiar uniform. She waits until he looks up, and waves. He returns the gesture and, to her surprise, smiles. His arms extended, reaching out, as he approaches.

"I should have called first," Sabine says. She picks up a stray tennis ball, hurls it for Roger to give chase.

"Never," he says. "This is your home."

Roger returns, drops the ball at her feet, and they repeat. "I am not playing Cleveland."

He slides past her and into the house. "Shame," he says. He leaves the door open, as he often does on cool afternoons.

Though she is unsure what he knows, she cannot keep silent. She has pretended, lied, but Jürgen must hear the truth. She follows him inside, pours herself an iced tea. They sit at the table, watching Roger roll in the grass.

"Everything that happened," she says.

"I am glad you are safe. It feels like ages since you were here last."

It does, she thinks. A lifetime somehow. "Yes," she says. "I may never leave again."

He shakes his head. "Silliness. You will stay until you are rested. Then, back to it!" He rattles the table with his energy, nearly spilling their drinks.

"I need to tell you, Papa. What I have seen."

He stands, a tower. "No," he says. "I cannot hear it."

In his tone, Sabine hears an apology, one she is sure will remain unsaid. "My friend, he is dead."

"I know," he says. He moves beside her, hand heavy on her shoulder, then back outside. She does not look but hears him playing with Roger.

"It was her," she says, loud enough she hopes. "I am scared. I am afraid of what will happen now."

He does not respond right away, but when she gets up, finishes the last of her iced tea and walks towards her bedroom, he says through the open door, "She will not hurt you. I am sure of that. She would never."

"She already has, Papa."

"This is too much," he says, waving his massive palm through the air. "You came to heal. So, heal."

Her mind races and she cannot switch it off. She wants to scream. She wants her father to listen. To be afraid with her. To somehow give her the answers, the certainty, she desperately needs. But she will do as he says tonight. She needs sleep. Sleep until the thought of it makes her restless. Until her body feels ready to ignite once more.

During the night, her phone comes alive. She ignores it and rolls over, half dreaming. In the morning, her muscles feel soft as sand. The pressure in her head subsiding. She checks her messages, still bleary-eyed. There is one, and she nearly leaps from the bed. She reads twice to make sure she is not imagining. *Sabby! Please tell me you're in FL right now*, it says. *I'm there tomorrow and I miss my sis.* Sabine writes back furiously, barely able to form the words. *My precious Alina! Come soon! Come now!*

Sabine offers to pick her up at the airport, but Alina says she will meet her at the house. To pass the time, Sabine runs. She avoids the path north—though they have not heard a sound from the men—and instead goes south along the wetlands. As close to a happy place as she can imagine now. The water is high against the bank, peppered with egrets standing stoic and still, turtles perched on tree roots. If she could, she would disappear into this place. She goes until her gut and her hips and her legs can take no more. She feels sturdy, though, and she bounces in place at the thought—the possibility, the hope, that what is broken within her will one day heal.

After her run, Sabine sets up the ball machine on their court. She takes backhands then forehands; she drops a basket of balls beside her and serves until it is empty and her shoulder is sore. She goes upstairs, rides the stationary bike. She keeps moving, her body kinetic.

When Alina arrives, her knock met first by Roger's high bark, Sabine swings open the door and throws her arms around her. The two hold each other, and all that has been stored away pours out. Roger trots circles around them, bumps their calves, whines until Alina looks down at him, her eyes as wide as his, and she shrills with joy.

The day gets away from them. Sabine asks about Alina's family, her life in Basel. She tries to keep the conversation away from herself. Alina obliges, goes on about her new girlfriend—*she hates tennis*, she says, which gives them both fits— and her new job working within parliament, and how she misses Sabine, their daily closeness. Sabine is happy for her, for this life she has built for herself, pulled literally from the ashes.

When Jürgen returns from his errands, he finds them on the couch talking, half-empty glasses of wine on the table.

"Have you moved since I left," he says, and from the kitchen shouts to them, asking what they want for dinner.

"It's that late?" Alina says.

Sabine shrugs, sipping her wine. "You cannot leave, so what does it matter," she says.

"I should. I'm flying out tomorrow night, and I've got a few things to do before I go."

Sabine watches Alina, and though she has not seen her for what feels like years, she can still read her, and vice versa. She sees in her expression that she wants Sabine to make her stay.

"Settled then," Sabine says. "Dinner, and after we will take a walk. Then I release you!" She raises her glass, and eventually Alina meets it, the soft clink like a tiny celebration.

To their surprise, Jürgen cooks, a spicy paella fit to feed a small army, and at the table he is surprisingly chatty. He always liked Alina,

Sabine knows, one of the few people he allowed himself to feel comfortable around. They talk tennis, a subject Sabine and Alina had otherwise avoided.

"She is not playing Cleveland," he says.

Alina looks at her, curious.

"After everything," Sabine says, stopping herself short. "I need a breather."

"I still don't really know what happened," Alina says. "There was some shit in Warsaw and Paris, but here seemed so much worse."

"She was there, you know," Jürgen says, pointing his wine glass at his daughter. "She was in the middle of that mess in New York." He reaches over, pats her arm. "Roger and I are glad to have her home."

Alina looks to Sabine, her eyebrows raised. Sabine is glad she notices, too, the oddness of her father's sudden affection.

"I saw the ceremony," Alina says. "I can't imagine how hard that was."

Like a flash, Sabine thinks of Sandy. She tries to hide away that sadness. "It was nice," she says, "to see people. Remember we are still here."

"Prost to that," Alina says, and they touch glasses, drink to something Sabine does not truly believe.

Tipsy and full, they take Roger for a walk. "Not too far," Jürgen says without looking up from the sink. It strikes Sabine, that her father is worried about her. She is not sure she has ever felt this from him, this kind of protectiveness.

"We do not have to talk about it," Sabine says, Roger tugging, trying to outpace her. "But I would love to know why you are really here."

Alina gives her a look. "Work, I told you. Isn't that enough?"

"I have become suspicious in my old age," Sabine says, smiles from the side of her mouth.

"I couldn't be here and not see you."

They curve along a trail, let it take them away from the house. The sky is still bright but sheltered by the trees around them.

"How about you? What really happened in New York?"

Sabine scrunches her brow. "You have seen the news, I imagine."

Alina stops, reaches her hand against Sabine. "And Sandy?" She opens her palm, releases Sabine's arm. "We don't have to talk about it if you don't want to."

"They say he is dead."

"How can they not know?"

Sabine walks, Roger no longer willing to wait.

"There were people on the bridge. They say he sacrificed himself to save them."

"And they…they haven't found him?"

Sabine shakes her head.

"Jesus, Sabby, I'm so sorry."

"I am not ready to accept it, I think. I am still not sure it all really happened."

"What didn't?" Her tone shifts, Sabine notices, soft but something inquisitive.

"Never mind," she says. She lets Roger lead her, faster then slower, until they have come to the other side of the swamp. Sabine smells the water, its familiarity a comfort. "How—" she says, but when she looks beside her, Alina is not there. She turns around to find her several yards behind, watching Sabine but not advancing. "Are you okay, what are you doing?"

Sabine swears she can see Alina's breath, despite the heat and humidity around them.

"I know," she says, nearly shouting to bridge their distance. "I know you were there."

"Where," Sabine says, going back to her, fighting Roger's insistence.

"I came here—" she takes a moment, her chest heaving, as if she is about to dive into the surf, "I needed to see you. To tell you."

"I do not understand," Sabine says.

Between them, Roger cries, anxious to keep moving. They turn back along the trail again, headed to the house. When they can see the backyard, Sabine lets Roger off his leash, and he sprints ahead, a fat little missile, and rolls in the grass until he is exhausted. Alina walks onto the court, runs her hand along the Har-Tru, her fingers greening.

"Please," Sabine says, hoping her confusion, her interest, is heard. "Why are you here?"

Alina leans on the net, and it reminds Sabine how tall she is, how beautiful, like an old movie starlet. She is thicker now, though, Sabine notices, arms muscular, shoulders sharp.

"I'm curious," Alina says finally. "How did you know to go to the bridge?"

Sabine looks back at her but says nothing.

"Was it the fire, the smoke? Just a horrible coincidence?"

"What do you mean," she says, but she knows, and Alina, too, it is her last lie. She has run out, the energy to sustain them too great.

"I don't want to be the one to tell you if you don't already know, Sabby. So please be honest. Why were you on the bridge?"

"You tell me," Sabine says, the stress in her voice shaking, the questions overwhelming. "Tell me what I should already know."

Alina releases the net and paces between the service boxes. "Your mother. I think she told you." She stops and faces Sabine, who cannot believe what she has heard.

"How dare you," she says. She has questions, so many her mind cannot keep them straight.

"When did you first know?" Alina asks. "Did she reveal herself, or did you find her?"

"I could kill you." The words surprise Sabine, that they have come from her mouth. "Do you hear yourself?"

"Please," Alina says, her voice gentle. "I don't want to upset you. But I have to know. I love you, you're my family. I have to know."

"You have to know?" She steps to the net, nearly lunging. "*I* have to know."

"I came here to tell you. I'll tell you everything I can."

Sabine grips the tape at the top of the net. She squeezes, her nails scraping. She could tear it apart if she wanted to. "That is what *she* said. That she would tell me everything. And now—"

"If you start, if you tell me about Petra, we'll be in this together."

Sabine composes herself, overcome by the name on Alina's tongue. First Jürgen, now this. Who else could know. Who else could keep such a thing from her.

"Have you always known she is alive?"

Alina shakes her head, holds the sides of her neck. From the clay on her fingers, she leaves a streak on her skin.

"How long then?"

"Long enough," she says. "But I need to hear you first. I'll answer every question, I promise. I know you're angry. This is hard for me, too. I need you to trust me."

Sabine shields herself, her outrage, from Alina. "Do you work for Petra?"

Alina places her palms together, folds her fingers between their opposites. "Of course not," she says.

Sabine wants to believe her. "I do not understand any of this. How do you expect me to simply talk, when I know this could get me killed. My father. How can we be safe."

"We'll make sure," Alina says.

It shakes Sabine, to hear her say *we*. The most awful sort of déjà vu.

"I cannot trust you," she says, trying to keep steady, "as I cannot trust her. You are both liars, playing some sick game, and I do not want to be in the middle."

"You asked me, but you haven't answered—how long have you known?"

Sabine kicks at the clay, creating tiny, diffusive clouds. "After Stuttgart, I met Sandy in Berlin. Once he was gone, she took me."

Alina stands up straight, her eyebrows raised in a dance. "Did she hurt you?"

"No," Sabine says. "But the shock of it has not worn off."

"And she told you *everything*?"

"As much as I was capable of hearing."

"I can't imagine."

"No."

"Did you see her in New York?"

Sabine nods. She finds even the mention of Petra exhausting.

"And?"

She notices Alina moving closer to her, as if approaching the edge of a cliff.

"You obviously already know. She came to my hotel. She wanted me to, I do not know, go with her or something. She wanted me to understand. I told her to leave the city and she agreed." She replays the conversation, the click of Petra's heels. How that woman haunts her. "*Avoid the bridge—* that is what she said. That was the last I heard of her."

"If she warned you…why did you go?"

She worried for Sandy; in her worst fears, he was there. The burning, the smoke rising. She worried what Petra was capable of. She had to go, and she knows that now. There was no choice. "How could I not?" she says.

They become silhouettes in the dusk as evening takes over. They both stand at net, facing each other as if at the end of a long match.

"We should go in."

"Will your father mind?"

Sabine lets Roger in first, and they follow. "He will go to bed soon."

Sabine pours them both a plum brandy, and they settle in their places on the couch. There is comfort in the late nights they have spent here over the years.

Sabine sips, feels the sweet burn coat her throat. "Is it my turn yet?"

"I'm all yours," Alina says, raises her glass before taking a drink.

"Who the fuck are you?"

Alina covers her mouth to keep from spitting her brandy. She laughs, but Sabine can see she is nervous. "Let's jump right in then."

"Seriously, Al." She trips over the divergent things she wants to say. "How could you not tell me about Petra?"

"How could I?"

"All this time. How could you keep that from me?"

"It wasn't my place."

These people and their secrets, Sabine wonders, do they ever take responsibility for their choices.

"Did you know she would tell me?"

Alina bites the inside of her lip, a nervous habit Sabine thought she had long ago laid to rest. "We weren't sure. We heard she was trying to contact you just before World Day. I was torn, please believe that."

"Belief and forgiveness are enemies here."

"I know," Alina says

Sabine crosses her legs on the couch, faces Alina completely. "I am so confused," she says.

She is patient while her friend collects herself and begins. The information comes at Sabine in waves. Alina does not say *spy* but it is what Sabine hears. *Us. We.* The longer she goes on, the less Sabine fathoms.

"Have you always been—I mean, for as long as I have known you?"

Alina shakes her head, exaggerated. "Of course not," she says in a way meant to comfort Sabine.

"Silly me," she says, sarcastic, and empties her glass. She refills it, knowing the bottle will be done by night's end.

"I'm still relatively new at this." *Years*, she does not say but is understood nonetheless. "And, frankly, you're the first person I've told."

She will have to come to terms with it at some point, these lies and their liars. "Wait," she says, shuffling closer to Alina, "how? What do your parents, your friends, think you do?"

"Same as I told you. And it's a half-truth, really. It allows me the kind of access and freedom I need to travel. From the outside, no one would question."

"And on the inside?"

"We're a small, private operation. We're not many, but we're well represented."

"Like MI6 or something?"

"Not quite. Let's say this—there are members of MI6 within our ranks. CIA, politicians, ordinary people. We're not part of any government. We remain secret even to those who are themselves secret." She reaches over and wraps her hand around Sabine's foot, squeezes in and out, a familiarity, a remnant of their past together. "Does that make sense?"

"Of course not," Sabine says.

Alina laughs and it wakes Roger, stretched out on the floor beside them. "It barely does to me," she says.

"What then? Why this secrecy?"

Alina leans in, puts her glass down on the table. Sabine smells the fruit on her breath. She speaks low, practiced and careful. "We can stop now and pretend like this never happened. But from here on out, you're a part of this."

She feels that same pull, the untenable curiosity she felt in Petra's dark restaurant, and she hates herself for it. "Please," she says, and, like in Berlin, she lets the revelations wash over her, her mind quickly underwater. They—Alina's *We*—are working to stop what has become a pandemic, this growing shadow; that is what she calls it, a *shadow*. Sabine wants to stop her, but she listens as Alina keeps going. She tells Sabine about Petra, how she has known—for too long a time—and what she has known. How after World Day they escalated their efforts. How the bridge and the violence were never supposed to happen.

"The timeline changed," she says, "and we still don't know why. We were scrambling."

"You knew this would happen?"

"No," she says over and over; Sabine hears her trying to convince herself as well. "But we're getting close. Petra, some of the other leaders, they met in New York. It was brief, but we understood something was shifting. Something unexpected."

"And so you are here," Sabine says, meaning it as both a question and demand.

"I miss you," Alina says, and in her tone Sabine feels handled, her emotions managed. "I should've been here sooner."

"I miss you, too. I fear I will be stuck missing people forever." She watches Alina collect her thoughts. She has been careful, Sabine thinks, with what she has said, with what she has shared. "But that is not why you are here now."

"I hate the way you read me," Alina says, fighting her own smile.

"No more bullshit," she says.

Alina straightens her back, steadies her chin. "I was asked to come to you—I *wanted* to come." Sabine fights the urge to explode with questions, letting Alina go on. "It wouldn't look strange me being here, given our history."

"Why take the risk, even a little?" Her mouth is hot and dry.

"They don't know about me. There's nothing to suspect."

"Why come just to tell me all this?" She cannot move, her body locked in anticipation.

"After World Day, one of the last things you said to me…you asked if I needed anything. If there was anything you could do."

"I remember."

"I almost said something then, but I was too afraid. I was still in shock."

"I meant it," Sabine says. "Anything." She needs more brandy, but she does not budge from the couch. "Everything Petra said, everything I have seen—it is yours." She turns, points behind her into the yard. "There are these men, right next door. Part of her deranged militia." The look on Alina's face, though, tells her she already knows. "I have pictures, too, of a map. It belonged to Sandy's father. A map of America. Maybe it is nothing."

"No, send them to me. I want to see. It's all important, it is." She takes Sabine's hands in her own. They could stay this way, but Sabine knows whatever is coming will, whether she wants it to or not, change them both. "But it's you, Sabby. We need *you*."

"What could I possibly do."

"I think you know.

"You give me too much credit."

"Do you know how important you are? Why your mother—"

"Petra," Sabine says, flat but stern.

"She has plans for you. Hopes. It's why she finally approached you."

"I want nothing to do with her. I made that very clear."

Alina nods, such that the couch trembles with her movements. Roger takes note, raising his ears.

"I know. Of course I know. But Petra, she's not someone who accepts defeat. She'll keep trying. She'll keep coming. She wants you by her side."

"What would you have me do then?" She is unsettled, her head light from the brandy.

"Take your place."

Sabine springs from the couch, scaring Roger into the other room.

"You cannot be serious."

"It's a unique situation, Sabby. No one could get as close as you. Think about it. You could see, know, everything that goes on."

"She would never trust me."

"In time. This is what *she* wants."

"How can you be sure? What would stop her from killing me, or my father, or you?"

"She came to you. She risked a lot in Berlin, revealing herself. She must've hated you being there with Sandy. And after World Day, how close you came, I don't think she's willing to leave it to chance any longer."

"This is all so much, Al."

"You could do this. We could. Ensure nothing like World Day, like what happened to Sandy, ever happens again. For god's sake, we can't just sit back and hope things get better."

"I am not a spy."

"No, you're a tennis player. A champion. And the daughter of one of the most powerful Nazis in the world. You would just need to be there, to see and hear."

"That does not sound crazy to you?"

"No it does. But we need to do something. We have to figure a way to turn the tide."

"And you think I am it?" She fights the incredulousness in her voice.

"I know you are. There's not a doubt in my mind."

"You will have to talk me through this. And start over and go again. And again."

"I know you. I have no doubts."

She wonders how long, how often, Alina practiced this speech. If she has given it to anyone else.

"I promise nothing," she says, but Alina is somewhere else, her eyes ticking, her forehead dancing with thought. Sabine knows, too, because they have made it this far, only this short distance, she has already promised.

"Details will come," Alina tells her later. And the way she says it, the way she touches her hand to Sabine's cheek after, it is impossible for Sabine not to trust her, believe in her, in this, this wild unimaginable future.

*

The hangover in the morning keeps Sabine attached to her pillow well past when she hoped to wake. Alina is gone, and although she expected as much, Sabine feels it as a punch, the wind knocked clean out. *What do I do now*, ticking through her mind. But her phone, lit up with messages, provides a solace. *Miss u already*, Alina writes. *We'll be in touch. Get back on court. Win.* Nothing else, nothing about Petra or what comes next. "Only in person," Alina said last night, before Sabine went to bed and stared at the ceiling, sugar and alcohol racing through her veins. "Petra will reach out again," Alina went on, her tone a promise, and when Sabine asked how she could know such a thing, she said, ignoring the question, "It'll happen soon."

Sabine thinks about it now, how far-fetched it seems. How, after the bridge, could she speak to Petra? How, when Sandy is dead, when so much has been lost. How could she do what Alina has asked of her. How could she ever be so brave.

To steady her mind and her nerves, Sabine returns to a regiment reminiscent of those days before her ankle injury, before Budapest. She settles into this rhythm, one that not long ago felt unfamiliar. She goes to the grocery with Jürgen; they cook meals together, take Roger on long walks along the marshes, argue whether the throaty croaks they hear are alligators or merely frogs. For Sabine, it is a journey home.

With her next tournament looming, she understands what must come next. She tells her father as he cooks breakfast, and he nods. "Of course," he says, as if it is the only answer. And, to her surprise, "Perhaps I will join you."

Steam rises from a bowl of eggs between them at the center of the table. They eat in a warm silence. More days like these, she hopes.

During Jürgen's late afternoon walk, there is a knock at the door. Sabine, upstairs on the bike, races down to answer. She is met by a young man, short and unkempt. The tattoos on either side of his neck—the numbers fourteen and eighty-eight—pop from his pale flesh. She greets him; he does not look her in the eyes.

"Miss Hellewege?" he says, his voice thin and cracked.

"Who is asking?" She stands with her body across the doorway, blocking the way in. He looks familiar, this not-yet-a-man, but she cannot place him.

"I have a message." He reaches into the pocket of his hoodie, and her body tenses. When he removes his hand, she flinches. But all he holds is a letter, the edges of the envelope folded and crinkled.

"Who is this from?" No name or writing on the outside, no handwriting to recognize.

The young man turns and leaves without another word, his gait awkward. She notices it then, the gun concealed beneath his hoodie, and knows where he has come from, watches him disappear along the long driveway.

It is just as Alina said. Petra's letter is short and direct. An address in Washington, DC. A date and time. No capacity for refusal. A demand without demanding, the very essence of Petra Hellewege.

She tells her father she must go but does not tell him where. He does not ask why. She packs up Roger, too. Jürgen will meet her in California for the tournament. Without much discussion, they agree. Even amongst her own scattered thoughts, Sabine is amazed by how easily they have rediscovered their routine, how effortless the transition back to father and daughter, coach and student. He drives her to the airport, Roger standing on her lap in the passenger seat, his nose smushed against the window glass.

In the air, Sabine taps her foot against the seat in front of her, nervous energy in need of expulsion. She wishes Alina were here to guide her, help her sort out this panic. She hears Roger's snoring through the static of the airplane, and she is jealous. She passes the time watching an old black and white movie, removed from the rest of the world.

This is merely a stopover on the way to California, she tells herself. She rides downtown in an SUV filled with her tennis bags and suitcases. She walks Roger by the river once they arrive at the hotel. She showers, takes her time getting ready—a purposeful delay—and dresses formal per Petra's direction. They meet at a restaurant not far away, noisy and dim. Petra is already there, seated near the back; she has ordered them a bottle of wine, and begun.

"Thank you for coming," she says, as if the entire affair is business as usual.

"Did I have a choice?" Sabine sits, and immediately a server appears, fills her glass.

"Always."

Every time they speak, Sabine thinks, she is just the same. Robotic and elegant at once, almost hypnotic.

"Please tell me why we are here so I can go."

Petra leans back and crosses her legs, lifts her glass all without breaking her gaze. "We must eat," she says.

"No thank you. Just tell me why you summoned me."

In the space before they speak again, bread and oil and salads arrive.

"You've come all this way. No need to rush."

You are a snake, Sabine wants to yell. Draw attention, make a scene. Expose this woman. She cannot do this. How can she be what Alina wants. She clangs her fork, poking at the lettuce.

"We've been here before, you know," Petra says between bites. "This very restaurant, years ago. Your father knew the chef. We came for one of your tournaments. You were young but already so promising."

"I do not remember," Sabine says, but she sees it clearly in her mind—a table by the front window; a giant man came out from the kitchen and greeted her parents, even sat with them, his beard stinking of what smelled to her then like pizza; others joined them eventually and bottles of wine went from full to empty and full again; when it got too late her father took her back to the hotel, leaving her mother behind, as they so often did, to carry on with her new friends.

"How is Jürgen doing?"

"No," Sabine says. "You do not get to ask about him."

"I kept my distance, as you asked." The consolation in her tone catches Sabine off guard.

"Clearly not from me."

"I told you we would see each other again."

"I wanted you to disappear. I begged you."

"I've been more than accommodating." Petra flicks her tongue and finishes her glass.

"My presence here begs to differ."

"It tells me you're willing to have a conversation, despite your protests."

"I fear for my father, for my friends. I fear what you will do if I do not acquiesce."

"Is that why you went to the bridge, even after I told you to avoid it—to protect your friend?"

She cannot suffer this. To hell with Alina and her plan, this careful subterfuge. How dare this woman mention Sandy. How dare she so flippantly reprise the very moment Sabine's heart was pulverized. If Petra dared speak his name, Sabine would certainly take this fork and pull her close and sink it into her neck.

"You are mad," she says, trying to keep from trembling. "You are a murderer. I wish you were dead. I would trade you for the lives you have taken a thousand times over."

Petra leans forward, and Sabine hopes she has rattled her, if only for a moment.

"And yet you invoked my name," she says, barely above a whisper. "Your friend saved those people. They escaped to tell the stories, to tell the world what he did for them. But it was my doing, I hear. I would be pleased, they said."

The memory, the rewinding and twisting of words, sucks the air from her lungs. "I needed them to listen," she says, stumbling.

"On my authority," Petra says, her voice no longer kept low.

"I would have done anything to keep them from killing those people."

"I know," she says and signals for the server to refill her wine glass. "So you did."

Their entrees arrive, though Sabine has not ordered anything. A filet of steak, seared crispy. "Medium rare, as requested," the server says. Sabine looks to Petra, who smiles and thanks them. She does not wait for Sabine to begin.

"I do not want this," Sabine says, though the smell spiders down into her stomach, and she feels it tense.

"It'll look strange if you leave it," Petra says. "Pretend, at least."

A quiet falls between them. Sabine imagines that anyone else in this restaurant would have no concept of the anger and fear and bottomless hate making up the participants of this quotidian meal. When Sabine slices her steak, juices pouring from red flesh, the knife slides along the plate, tiny effortless screams.

"Do you remember the letter I wrote you?" Petra asks, her tone practiced.

She does; she could never forget. "No," she says. She lets the first bite linger in her mouth, tastes its rareness on her tongue.

"*Mighty. Irreplaceable.* You've become—you are—those things. Everything I hoped for you. The day you were born," she stops, trails off, seemingly lost in thought. "Only if you're *looking. Seeing.* And so here we are. I know you're looking. You're close. But are you seeing, my dear?"

Sabine places her silverware down. "Tell me what you want, Petra. I am tired of this, of you. Please, so I may go."

"Let them take this," she says, motioning to their plates and bread scraps, "and we will finish over dessert."

Sabine shakes her head. She has had enough, and she knows Petra senses it, that she is stretching this out simply to see how long Sabine will remain. Sabine folds her napkin and rests it on the tabletop, slides her seat back and stands.

"Sit," she says, and when Sabine refuses, Petra straightens herself in the chair, points her full glass at the empty seat opposite. "I won't ask again."

The server interrupts once more, dropping off dessert for each of them. "Is everything to your satisfaction?"

"Everything's perfect," Petra says. She takes a spoonful of her pot de crème, savoring. "I ordered you a lemon tart. Your favorite. It's not even on the menu." Sabine stays standing, watching Petra. "You're embarrassing yourself."

Sabine looks around. Somehow everyone, yet no one, stares at her. She sits, slides the tart away from her.

"Good girl," Petra says, which only enrages Sabine more.

"What the hell do you want? Why do you keep this up?"

Petra grips her fork between her thumb and forefinger. "There were cameras, you know." She reaches across the table, cuts a piece of tart, and eats it. "On the bridge. My men." She waits; Sabine knows she is drinking in her reaction, studying the widening of her eyes, the slight gape of her lips. "You looked very much the part, my dear."

"What does that mean? I was terrified. What they did—"

"I've seen myself. All quite confusing. Frankly, it's almost impossible to tell whose side you're on."

The fight drains out of her, as if someone has opened an artery and emptied her. Did Alina know, she cannot help but wonder. Is this where new secrets begin, the next wave of manipulations.

"I hate you," she says. She hears the defeat in her voice, the acknowledgement that this is not the end of something but rather a foul beginning.

"We're close. You can't ignore it any more than I can pretend otherwise."

It is all Sabine can stomach. She is out of her chair and out of the restaurant without a thought. She is halfway down the street, wind whipping off the river, before she hears those familiar clicks approaching.

"So dramatic."

"Leave me alone, I am begging you. I do not want you in my life."

"You don't understand what's happened," Petra says. She steps close, the wine still hanging on her breath. "The men, what they saw and the stories they told. You're a part of this now. They believed you. You convinced them."

She wants to turn and run, lock herself in her hotel and leave for California and never look back. She wants this to end. Yet she hears Alina, urging her on. Sandy. *Save them.* She wants to cry out and let the river sweep her words across the ocean and beyond, to anyone who might listen.

"What would you have me do?" she asks, though she knows the answer.

The look in Petra's eyes is unmistakable. Victory.

"Tomorrow," she says, "we'll come together. It'll be the first such gathering in almost a century. Representatives from around the world. I wish you to be there, to bear witness. To begin to understand."

"And you? What is your role?"

"Come, please. To have you by my side after all these years—it fills me with hope, as it will others. The Hellewege women. They'll see us." She wraps her long fingers like ropes around Sabine's arm, squeezes.

Though she does not agree, not out loud, Sabine knows the decision has been made. Petra releases her, and she turns, ready to walk away. Sabine does not waver. She wants Petra to hear her. "I loved him. I will never forgive you."

"Tomorrow," Petra says. "The details will be at your hotel. When you arrive, you'll ask for a man named MacDonald. He'll bring you to me."

She remains on the street, watching until Petra disappears. Soon, Sabine will be on a plane to California; in a few days, she will be on a tennis court again. She focuses on this. Her body in its natural state.

Back at the hotel, Roger punishes her for her absence. They take a walk, but after he wants to play, a compact bundle of energy. Sabine has nothing left, though. She washes her face until she is bare, curls into bed. She calls for Roger. He barrels up, pushes beneath the covers. He stretches his body, keeping himself pressed against her. Sabine knows she will not sleep, exhausted as she is. She will get back up in a while, restless, and return to the same spot. She will position herself such that Roger will never know she was gone. She will listen to his little snores, watch his belly expand and contract. She will not close her eyes. She cannot tolerate what she sees when her mind takes her. The bridge burning. The world in darkness. How she cannot save what has been lost.

*

The directive arrives with her breakfast. She takes out her phone, types a message to Alina. *Morning, love*, she writes. *Good dinner last night. Taking a walk later by the river. Hoping to see some old friends before heading to California.* The language Alina gave her—old friends, locations as innocuous touristing—feels natural, nothing out of the ordinary. The sheer act of it, though, makes it feel as if Alina is more her handler than a friend. Still, Sabine is grateful for the tether. She cannot do this alone.

Roger whines, begs to go outside. She feels lucky to have him, her familiar, the comfort and responsibility of loving this little creature. He brings her joy, calm in her worst moments. She remembers the contention of whether she needed him on tour with her, if he was a distraction. She does not care now what anyone thinks. She needs him and she is happy for the needing.

They walk to a dog park near the water, and beside them stands a stadium, home to the Senators, the city's storied baseball team. As Roger circles and barks, releasing the energy of a star, Sabine tries to relax, enjoy him and the surroundings. Knowing Sandy played here brings her solace. She wants to seek out these reminders. Find him wherever she goes. Always with her, always safe.

When Roger exhausts himself, she carries him in her arms back to the hotel. The car will be there soon to pick her up. She does not yet know the destination, only that it is close. She wears her black jumpsuit, at Petra's suggestion. She keeps her hair down, long and bright. The front desk calls her when it is time. In the mirror before she leaves, Sabine catches a glimpse of how others might see her: athletic and tall, white and blonde. Somebody's ideal. Downstairs, the driver opens the car door for her. It is dark, the windows tinted. She keeps her sunglasses on. She puts down the window enough to see a sliver of the world outside. They are close to the Potomac. The president resides nearby. Museums and memorials all around. Eventually they approach an arena, one Sabine recognizes—she recalls playing team tennis here—and the driver curves to the rear of the building. He gets out and opens her door again. She realizes he has not spoken a word to her. She thanks him, and quickly he is gone.

She follows Petra's orders, asks the armed men guarding the entrance for someone named MacDonald. They tell her to wait, each mumbling into their earpieces. A minute or two passes before a man, short and round, bald except for a patch in the front and back, appears.

He adjusts his glasses, looks up at Sabine. "Miss Hellewege," he says. "Such an honor."

He opens his chest, pointing the way in with his arm. She steps through the entranceway, and the sound of the heavy door slamming behind echoes through her. She is inside; she is here. MacDonald guides her, explaining what is about to happen. Twenty thousand will fill the arena. From the back she sees the banners hanging above the stage, one adorned with their symbol—Petra's black phoenix—and the other with the words NEW AMERICA written in red. It is enough to make her sick. The sickness in her welling up, brimming out, burning her, ready to burn.

As Alina instructed, Sabine takes pictures when possible, sliding her phone slightly from her pocket, inconspicuous, enough to record what she can. MacDonald settles her in a private room, tells her to wait until someone gets her. She asks after Petra, wonders when she will see her. MacDonald responds curtly—"Your mother is preparing. You'll see her when we begin."—before shutting the door, locking her in. She messages Alina once more, simple and nondescript. *About to see old friends. Cannot wait.*

And then, she waits. She hears people gathering, the conversations and commotions growing louder. She has never been before such an audience without a racket in hand. She wishes Roger were here to calm her. She focuses, the sheer act of breathing and its miracle. She can do this. She is ready.

When MacDonald comes for her again, he leads her onto the stage, the lights overwhelming in her eyes. The arena full, a turbulent sea of what humanity has become. Petra stands beside the podium, her arms spread wide. A moment passes before Sabine realizes this is meant for her. She steps with purpose, lets Petra embrace her. She smiles, something polite and civilized. Petra and MacDonald each raise an arm in salute, reciprocated by the masses. MacDonald lowers the microphone and introduces Petra—*our Reichsleiter!*—met with great applause, before he leaves the stage. They remain there, the Hellewege women, side by side. The cheers feel unending.

Petra lowers her arms to quiet the arena.

"Before we begin," she says, her voice like a meteor, "I want to introduce you to my daughter. Many of you know her; she's a great champion, after all! She comes here today to celebrate as we do, to usher in this new world. We're honored to have her with us."

She turns to Sabine, directing her to the microphone. She is caught off guard, unsure of what to do. Petra whispers in her ear. "Tell them who you are, my dear. Make them yours." Her hand on Sabine's cheek, her expression ablaze, like she is someone Sabine has never seen before, someone she has never known.

Sabine steps to the podium, her fingers tight, as if they are not her own. She cannot be uncertain. A silence fills the arena. She must.

For Alina. Jürgen. Lolo.

Drago and Florian. The faces she will never again see.

For Sandy. Her Sandy.

She will remember this, the moment her life becomes something new. Reborn. A double life. A champion and a spy. A fighter. Victory.

She opens her mouth to speak, her breath electrified through the microphone. She is strong and full. She is precise; she is steady.

"I am Sabine Hellewege," she says.

And after, the crowd, the crowd rises, and roars.

WE THE REBORN

In the Brooklyn borough of New York City, a new baseball stadium is born. Across the way, its counterpart, the grand rebuilt City Open Tennis Center, rises. The world will watch as the country comes together to celebrate this dawn. We have shaped the present; we can remake the future.

We are united.

We are one voice, loud and true.

We are the faces of this new day.

We are brightness escaping from the darkness.

We are those who remain.

We are the forgotten.

We who have been quieted.

We are those lost.

We are remembered.

We are one people.

We are them.

We are you.

We are a body at the bottom of the river.

We are no longer ash.

We watch our champions. We stand, and we cheer.

And some of us, so very few, we see what lies beneath. We see the light in the shadow. We see our hero, the work she does, the battles she fights, even when the world is no longer watching.

ACKNOWLEDGMENTS

This novel wouldn't exist, its writing not remotely possible, without a great many wonderful people. I feel spoiled in this life.

First and foremost, to my publisher, LEFTOVER Books, and my editor, Patrick Trotti—for your vision and enthusiasm, your endless well of creative energy, I am forever thankful. I'm lucky to have my debut novel in such generous hands.

To Joanne O'Neill, for your brilliant and moving cover. I couldn't imagine anyone else designing this cover, and I feel so damn fortunate. I can never thank you enough.

To my early readers and cheerleaders, for your time and kindness in championing this book: Leah Angstman; Jami Attenberg; Stephanie Austin; Jillian Cantor; Jiordan Castle; Heather De La Garza; Myles Ehrlich; Andrew Ervin; Miciah Bay Gault; Claire Hopple; Chantal James; Sara Lippmann; Nicholas Mainieri; Ilana Masad; Devin Murphy; Emily Nemens; Rebecca Renner; Sarah Seltzer; Courtney Sender; Daniel Torday; Carmen Toussaint; Simon Van Booy; Catherine Adel West; Kevin Wilson; and David Wojciechowski, for your gorgeous design work.

To SB, for your edits and your beautiful stubbornness, for your warmth and honesty over the years. For our days and nights spent at the ballpark, for giving me the space to be vulnerable and real. That's good scrimshaw.

To NM, for being the greatest writer I know, for inspiring me with every written word, every conversation, every smile. If you're out on the street, and it starts to go down, I know you won't back off until it's finished.

To CJ, for never giving up on me, even when I'd lost my way. For making me laugh, for always being there. You are the true Mayor of Rightville.

To DS, for your decades of friendship, for pushing me when I needed it, for lifting me up when I was certain I would fall. For embracing my whole self, since the day we met. I love you. Boosh.

To Jeanne Leiby, who started me on this path. Your words are forever with me.

To Mom, David, and Kelly—for putting up with me, for helping me grow, for letting me cry, for the fun and laughter. You're my world.

To Estelle and Sidney, Steve, Jimmy, and Dad—I miss you every day. Your voices have become my own.

To anyone who provided me with coffee—bless you.

To baseball and tennis, to women's sports, to the athletes making this world a better place.

To all those standing up to hate, to fighting for good.

Thank you so much to all my family and friends, for your support and boundless encouragement, for suffering me and making me feel loved. Truly, I couldn't do this without you.

To Zadie and Charlotte, my editorial cats, for keeping me sane, for your early morning wake-up calls, for your snuggles and your sweetness. Belly rubs incoming, my girls!

To Laura, my absolute everything. My first editor, my North Star. My witch. I can't imagine how exhausting I am, but you never make me feel so. You are the love of my life, but so much more than that. You've made me a better person, a better writer, a hundred times over. This novel is so much stronger because of you. Thank you for giving me a mess to clean when I need a break, for our crosswords and our adventures. May they never end. My one.

Danny Goodman's writing has appeared in various publications, and he was the recipient of a writer-in-residence fellowship from Rivendell. He earned his MFA in Fiction from the University of New Orleans, where he was a two-time winner of the Samuel Mockbee Award. He lives in the Hudson Valley with his wife, a book editor, and their editorial cats. *Amerikaland* is his debut novel.